The question of the relationship between science-fantasy and general or "mainstream" fiction is one which is sure to provoke a lively response among SF enthusiasts. In any specialty field of literature there are always the total integrationists, who object to any categorization as invalid. Others prefer a separate-but-equal doctrine, fearing that any blending with the mainstream would result in a dilution of the specialty field's vigor.

In practice the gap between science-fantasy and fiction of the mainstream is becoming less discernible, and for the time being, this seems to me a good thing. As SF has grown more sophisticated, the general reader has become aware that the field has more to offer than stories of space travel and computers-taking-over-the-world. And probably the SF addict is less likely to picture most contemporary mainstream fiction as a jejune and muddy canvas of neurotic housewives and teenage drug addicts.

The rubbing-off process has been good, but the separateness remains, and that is good also. For from it comes the freshness and vigor and freewheeling inventiveness which is the identity of science-fantasy. There is a difference between SF and mainstream fiction. The unfortunate thing is that the gap is widest at the point of the label. The trouble with categorization is that, while it is a handy device for critics and a useful one for publishers, it sets up blocks for the reader who is unfamiliar with the "category."

Most people who have an affection for science-fantasy (I include the regular reader as well as the professional writer or editor) attempt at one time or another to arouse the interest of a non-devotee. The method of least resistance is to force in a few matchless classics and hope the injection will take. This usually works at the start, but is often followed by a period of partial, then total immunization. Much better, really, to save the big guns for later and open with a more representative sample—such as this volume. There may be a "classic" in these pages; the stories are too fresh to make such a determination. I can say with certainty that there is enough variety and good writing to please the regular and casual reader and, I think, enough to interest those new to the field. It's one well worth getting to know.

EDWARD L. FERMAN

The Best from Fantasy and Science Fiction

16th Series / Edited by Edward L. Ferman

ACE BOOKS

A Division of Charter Communications Inc.
1120 Avenue of the Americas
New York, N. Y. 10036

TO MY MOTHER AND FATHER

ACKNOWLEDGMENTS:

The editor hereby makes grateful acknowledgment to the following authors and authors' representatives for giving permission to reprint the material in this volume:

Gilbert Thomas for *Luana*

Lloyd Biggle, Jr. for *And Madly Teach*

Joan Patricia Basch for *Matog*

Isaac Asimov for *The Key*

Mose Mallette for *The Seven Wonders of the Universe*

Scott Meredith Literary Agency, Inc. for *A Few Kindred Spirits* by John Christopher, *We Can Remember It for You Wholesale* by Philip K. Dick and *The Age of Invention* by Norman Spinrad

John Shepley for *Three For Carnival*

Collins-Knowlton-Wing, Inc. for *Experiment in Autobiography* by Ron Goulart

Kenneth Bulmer for *The Adjusted*

Robert M. Green, Jr. for *Apology to Inky*

Roger Zelazny for *This Moment of the Storm*

CONTENTS

"I think you'll agree with me, Chief, that this time we've really put our finger on the bottleneck."

When science fiction is at its best, it conceives a perfect story out of the inconceivable; a story which has interior logic, which says something about the human situation and which contains a minimum of contrivance no matter how startling the concept. Here's a perfect example, a wryly humorous closeup of a remarkable by-product of a Gemini flight—and its odd but appropriate effects upon the two men who share in its discovery.

LUANA
by Gilbert Thomas

After a day of mycology—my specialty—I would turn to painting, to sculpture. Cutting women out of my life—I had been hurt enough. Art, life's shadow, is not a good substitute, but it would have to do. I'd begun by painting water colors of fungi. Nothing is so lovely as spring lichen spreading across the face of crisp rock, cracking it into sand. Fungi shattering the Parthenon into chips of marble has never failed to amaze me with its power. Thus does beauty become soil.

It was after losing my first wife that I turned to sculpture. Although I had captured the loveliness of Monascus purpureas on canvas, and my shaggymanes in tempura—guarded against decay by infusions of deoxyribonucleic acid, DNA, without which life cannot exist—had been purchased by the Museum of Modern Art in New York for their files.

I wanted to get my hands on something big. Although my first wife had not been large, nor my second. Little women in fact, docile as the gentle morel, delicious fried in butter or added to soups. Evidently they found me more docile still, interested only in my work. That the lowly ubiquitous Penicillium had saved millions and blue cheese gave them

9

no cause to rejoice. They didn't care that man's journey into the expanding universe of the mind is powered by diethylamide tartrate of D-lysergic acid—LSD-25—rooted in ergot, fungus.

My first wife screwed up her courage to the point of calling me moldy. "You moldy bastard," she said one morning over coffee and figs. I had taken to eating fruit for breakfast after my latest trip to Europe and found it suited my system. "Moldy fig!" our daughter Priscilla shot from the next room—she'd been put up to it, a fat little girl, clinically speaking. Then Elva had gone to the cookie jar and pulled out a sack of glazed doughnuts; and defiantly dumping them on the table was about to eat one when she noticed —may God strike me dead—they were moldy. Bursting into tears she ran from the room screaming: *You did it—you did it!* I hadn't, of course. The fact is: spore is all around us, ready to feed on anything. Basidiomycetes will feed on solid plastic, changing it into sugar. Elva had waited too long to make her move and the hyphae had taken over.

Picasso is a good sculptor. (A man must have his heroes—particularly when depressed.) I've always enjoyed his goat, created at Vallouris in the 50s, using a multiplicity of materials. Whatever came to hand. Wire, plaster, fruit crates. Finished, he discovered something was missing: the genitalia. His remedy—take an old tin can, flatten it and double it back on itself, then insert it in the moist plaster just below the stiff upturned tail and protruding gaspipe. Daring. I like to think I model myself on that Picasso.

My second wife, the Greek, was dark and dainty but she turned up one morning black and blue. She had taken to staying out overnight without my permission and I had noticed bruises and what appeared to be the marks of teeth on her from time to time. These occurred most usually about the throat with some finding their way down to the breast. Pressed for an explanation she would say she refused to wear glasses and had run into something. When I said it was more likely something had run into her, she asked for a divorce. I didn't remember her as being nearsighted. At the little quayside cafe at Piraeus she had seen well enough. Well enough to come over and ask: "Aren't you Doctor Raymond Kelpe, the famous mycologist from the United States?" When I said I was, she blushed, saying she was interested in molds herself, was in fact an advanced student specializing in torula as it pertains to cracking oil into food —petro-proteins—at the University of Athens; had actually seen me in lecture and knew I was in town to help save the Parthenon. Which still may be possible; often of a morning I've joined the little workman there on the Acropolis, his cup of cement helping us restore the chips to their historic position.

Pallas became my assistant, warning me to beware of the "I love you, *kiss*—ing" girls of Athens; and to make sure that I did, seduced me. It was simple in the laboratory, for I often work late. We were among the trays of saprophytes, which had just hatched—you could actually see the little *champignons* rise from their beds of crushed acorn, dead leaves, and coffee grounds lightly laced with *merde*. There in the moist scented air—for the little tan fruit has a delicious odor—she reached for a retort and fainted. Falling on a soft bed of mushrooms six feet long. Her laboratory dress, buttoned down the front, was somewhat askew, and as I bent to lend mouth-to-mouth resuscitation, she moaned.

We were married; and it was soon after arriving back in the United States that I noticed she was spending more and more time away from me—in the company of Dr. Gilroy Mannfried, doing research in parasurgery in Building 29. I am in Building 28. Although still my assistant, Pallas said she was sick of it and wanted to go back to Greece where the light was right, that she was only 18 and fungi had been a passing thing of youth. That she was now more interested in parasurgery, and stuck her tongue out at me. Until now she had been docile, kind—I didn't like to see my wife chewed up. I couldn't help thinking Dr. Mannfried had given her something—dexamyl or the like. And I found myself getting sleepy too early in the evening—8 or 9—sleeping like the dead at 10 or 11. I wouldn't have put it past them to be slipping me a little chloral hydrate. Love will find a way. No one knows better than a doctor that the Oath of Hippocrates is as outdated as the general practitioner. Once I thought I heard her scream but couldn't rouse myself from my stupor; it was possible they had invaded my bedroom for added thrills.

I returned to sculpture, experimenting after the manner of Picasso, using bread as the basic material; malleable,

11

sprayed with plastic, a variety of textures and colors was possible, whole wheat to white to rye and pumpernickel, the whole allowed to overrun with algae to give a patina of age. I was invited to display in the patio of the Los Angeles County Art Museum, drawing much good comment among the works of Giacometti, Rueben Nakian and Peter Volkos. My work was impervious to the weather and this being a modern era no one found fault with my using bread as the basis for a work of art. Tempura, after all, being egg.

And I still had to do my job. Gemini 1, 2, 3, 4, etc. Trickier and more complex every year. One of these bitches was going to cause me to blow a gasket.

Pallas showed up one Wednesday morning bleeding about the cheek. She now had enough of all Americans and was returning to Greece immediately via—so help me—the Far East where she hoped to gain some peace of mind through an examination of their religions. I was to give her passage. And, oddly, she now used Elva's nasty remark, exactly. If fungi is my jugular, Greece was hers. I called her a name and was immediately sorry; I believe in integration. That's Italian, she said, and stuck out her tongue. What a beauty, crying, bleeding, her clothes torn and her tongue sticking out. My last young girl. I had to give her her freedom, but not before talking to Dr. Mannfried. "I don't know what you're talking about," he said, licking his lips. He was a big bastard, like lots of them are with the knife. They look like butchers but can thread a needle with their thumbs. "I hardly know your wife," he said, "but I'll say this for her —I admire your taste, she's delicious."

I wanted to hit the big son-of-a-bitch, but what would that prove. I needed my hands for my work as much as he needed his.

"Yes, isn't she," I said, and went to the market to buy all their second-day bread. I'd have to keep busy, now that I would be alone.

Oddly, Dr. Mannfried seemed drawn to me after Pallas left for Hong Kong. He enjoyed talking about her, the bastard; even mentioning my first wife made his mouth water, although he hadn't made a pass at her because that was before his son had graduated from college and he said he'd taken a solemn oath in his youth not to screw up his life until his boy was 21. I'm not much of a talker, but I'm a good listener—and I listened as I patted sandwich loaf into patterns of desire. I kept sculpting women; it was a compulsion.

What happened next was magnificent, and almost cleared my mind. Man's first walk in space. (Actually the second, after the USSR.) As usual, I had been called to the Cape to head the decontamination and sterilization crew, getting Gemini 4 ready for space. The planets must not be a dumping ground for human waste. This was drill—preparation for our coming flight to the moon. After Gemini 4 all my space flights would be *etc.*—all my systems were *go*. But I didn't know it then.

The microorganisms carried by a single astronaut—any man—total approximately 10^{12}, 10 followed by 12 zeros. I cleaned up our boys, using ethylene oxide gas on the capsule to spare the components. Everything shipshape and clean as a whistle. But when they opened the hatch in stellar space . . . something was coming the other way.

I found spore. There was no doubt about it, and only one. It was impossible at that height—it couldn't be one of ours. It had been sucked into the capsule vacuum-cleaner in space, after the hatch had been resecured. That space is filled with more than nothing—anti-matter matter and the like—this we know: but *spore.*

I took it to my laboratory—home—by jet toward an optimum environment; and perhaps selfishly told no one about it.

I had no idea what food it would take. I gave it a loaf of bread and stood back to wait. Was it alive?

It had withstood the all but absolute temperature of space; it had withstood the devastating effects of radiation—it might prove a mutation of its original form on another planet.

I confess, I fell asleep watching the load of rye bread on its emulsion of fungi-free earth. I'd been up since the discovery—and sleep is a protective device against sustained excitement. Perhaps it hadn't been chloral hydrate. It was quiet in the laboratory, a single overhead light on the experiment. I had even cut off the Muzak the President feels will ease our progress. It must have been ten o'clock; it was dawn when I awoke.

My God, it was huge! I'd never seen anything like it. At first I thought it was a tree, the trunk was three feet through. It was six feet tall, of a perfect symmetry, a ruff under its chin and the most beautiful mushroom I had ever seen. A creamy off-white, its cap a brilliant orange flecked with chaste white dots. The bread was gone and it was feeding on earth and the wood surrounding it. I ran to my quarters off the laboratory, where I do my sculpture, returning to bank loaves of bread around the trunk. It rejected them, having taken its full growth. Such texture! What *tournedos aux champignons* it would make! This mushroom would make me famous! But now I couldn't reveal my secret; we're supposed to tell NASA everything; to hell with NASA. This was one triumph I could enjoy privately. I didn't need the roll of drums and a wire from Stockholm. I touched its flesh. That it might eat me crossed my mind, but where work is concerned I am not passive. I squeezed it. It was warm, soft and giving, like a girl's trunk. I put my arms around it—what a baby! I kissed it and the odor was sweet and sophisticated as some mushrooms. Even here on earth. Now this one was on earth and it was mine. But would it spore? Go inky or blow away as so much of our dew-raised fungi spores do blow away, sight unseen in some forgotten pasture? No. The second and even the third day found it standing firm but undulating slightly in the morning air. I had taken the mushroom across campus to my home, for the sake of privacy and experiment. It was surprisingly light, no heavier than a girl. But then the world's record yield of mushrooms per square foot is only 7.35 pounds.

Its flesh seemed alive, palpitant—I'm no pantheist, yet I've often felt that plants, trees, flowers, have a life we know nothing of. I left the window open to let it breathe. The curtains moved gently with the breeze and my mushroom would softly sway.

Where in hell had it come from? That there was some form of life on other planets, now we knew. I knew. Well, others would find out in time. Now the experiments could begin. Had to begin. I was a scientist, after all, and had to do it. I had to cut. I didn't know what to expect, so gingerly, gingerly, I approached it, knife in hand, waited, then slipped it in.

It seemed to sigh, but perhaps it was my imagination. It cut nicely. What lovely texture! Like a young girl's thighs. Soft and perfectly grained.

I took a leave of absence from the university; and as the days went by carved more deeply into Lulu. I had now given her a name, after the manner of weather bureaus with hurricanes. Lulu. It seemed a good name for a tanned girl, perhaps a fine mulatto, a girl from the islands, Polynesia —what skin! Luana. Good-bye, Lulu—you are Luana. Aloha —which also means Hello. I couldn't place her in the known world of mushrooms, but that didn't surprise me—and then I left off experimenting, removing my sculpturing tools from Building 28, bringing them home to really go to work. What a figure! It was no trouble at all, she almost carved herself, orange giving way to pale pink-and-gold making flowers in her hair. I swear it was as though she was *there*, although she never spoke—I hadn't gone that far—nor did I speak to her: there were limits. I didn't know whether to leave clothes on her. Or not. But I was never one to go along with that misguided Pope painting diapers on Michelangelo's cupids. I carved her whole and I carved her nude. No abstraction—who wants the portrait of a loved one in abstraction? I'd rather have a photograph. Take my word for it, I'm a good sculptor—the Venus de Milo: that's my sort of thing. Only lighter, more slender, more docile. I knew Luana was docile—perhaps she was Japanese, a sweet Japanese girl lisping syllables I would never understand, little Miss Suke, and that was the day Dr. Mannfried walked in unannounced.

The dirty bastard just stood there, sucking in his breath and staring at Luana. He was stricken. I'd done better than I knew. But then, I was inspired. "My God," he said, "what is it?"

"Just a statue," I said.

"I'd swear it was alive."

"Don't stand too close."

"Why not?"

"She might bite you."

He had the grace to blush; I never thought I'd ever see a surgeon blush. He wanted to touch Luana, but I led him into the patio, rubbing mushroom off my hands. I even had her in my hair. I stopped wiping her off; somehow it seemed a sacrilege. Her flesh was only slightly moist, pleasantly taut, excellent for subtlety with the knife. Dr. Mannfried picked a piece from my hair and stupidly said, ". . . it's springy."

"Yes," I said, "isn't it."

"What is it?"

"What's what?"

"What material are you using?"

"A new plastic."

"Oh."

But I could see he didn't believe me. And then I made of the mistake of saying:

"I'd prefer you didn't tell anyone about this."

He smiled that rapacious smile; he had something on his mind. I knew I shouldn't have trusted the big bastard.

"You can trust me," said Dr. Mannfried.

He came every day to see Luana. And oddly enough, to my knowledge, he did keep his word—no one mentioned Luana or asked what I was doing on holiday.

When there was no breeze I would turn on the fans, two oscillating twelve inchers I had bought for the purpose, placing one on each side of her. I would play "Sweet Leilani" on the hi-fi, "Bali H'ai," and watch her move to the music —a lovely nymph from some lost planet, perhaps now gone from the universe, a billion years ago, for spore is immortal. Almost. Raise the temperature of earth but a few degrees and she would take over the world. My beautiful dancing mushroom, Luana.

I kept her shored with cupcakes in case she wanted to eat; it was impossible to know at what moment she might die. I thought of covering her with moist cloth, but she seemed moist enough and I didn't want to run the risk of fungi forming, fungi on fungi, it would only seem humorous to someone who had never seen Luana. And yet something was missing and I knew what it was. Being shy, I just couldn't do it. But Dr. Mannfried could. Earthy bastard.

"She hasn't got that thing," said Dr. Mannfried. He'd been observing her closely for some minutes. He moved one of the fans and changed the record. We were both sharing her now, there was no way to shut him out, persistent swine.

"No, my friend," said Dr. Mannfried, "you are a great sculptor, but she hasn't got that thing."

I still hadn't allowed him to touch her.

"That's my department," said Dr. Mannfried.

Remembering Picasso and the goat, I felt an inadequacy that goes beyond belief. That full-blooded Spaniard could do it, but not me. I had even considered draping her with a pareau, a little one, about the hips. Dr. Mannfried was right. I had to let him have his way.

"I've taken a lot of them out," he said, "but this is the first time I've ever put one in," and he was sweating, even with the fans on, his eyes beady.

"Now?" I asked.

"Now," he said.

"Can . . . I watch?"

"No, it'll be better if you wait outside."

"You'll be careful . . ."

"Please, I know my business."

"How long will it be, Doctor?"

"I'll let you know when it's over. There's nothing to worry about." And taking my smallest, sharpest knife, he started for Luana. His eyes never left her and his hand was shaking.

I must have walked the floor for 10-15 minutes, smoking cigarette after cigarette, which isn't like me—up and down outside that door—letting Dr. Mannfried do what I should have done. It was his sudden scream that sent me hurtling into the room of my beloved. Dr. Mannfried was hanging on her, torn by ecstasy, his teeth buried deep in her neck.

I'll never know how I got through the next few hours. I tried patching her throat with brown bread, but it wasn't the same. I didn't turn on the fans or play the music that night.

It was sometime after midnight when I received the call from my colleague Dr. Shih. He told me to come over to Dr. Mannfried's house at once, that this was an emergency. Oddly, I still believe in Hippocrates, and so I went, to be met at the door by a wide-eyed Dr. Shih with the contents of a stomach in his hands.

"Raymond, Raymond," he said, "Mannfried is dying . . ."

"Is that so," I said.

A ripping yell filled the house, as if all the voices of the damned were being forced through the throat of one man. I ran to the bedroom—what had been Dr. Mannfried lay stretched on the mattress. One look at his face and I knew what was wrong. I had seen that look on the faces of a family of seven who had died in the 15th century—mummified in the catacombs of France—the look of unendurable pain persisting through the centuries. Only one thing could put that look on a man's face—a look he would carry to his grave under his cosmetics—poisoning by the Amanita.

Luana was a toadstool.

I was afraid of that.

A college sophomore, applying for a summer job, was asked
to give the names of two professors as references. She
couldn't think of anybody whose names she could put down.
Nobody knew her! This comes to us second hand, but in a
day when an educational tool is likely to be pictured as a
hunk of machinery, we find it both credible and disturbing.
Whether or not you agree with the point of view expressed
in this story by Lloyd Biggle, Jr., you are certain to find
it an absorbing and, more than likely, frightening extrap-
olation of the impact of technology on education.

AND MADLY TEACH

by Lloyd Biggle, Jr.

Miss Mildred Boltz clasped her hands and exclaimed, "What
a lovely school!"

It shimmered delightfully in the bright morning sunlight,
a pale, delicate blue-white oasis of color that lay gem-like
amidst the nondescript towers and domes and spires of the
sprawling metropolitan complex.

But even as she spoke she qualified her opinion. The
building's form was box-like, utilitarian, ugly. Only its color
made it beautiful.

The aircab driver had been muttering to himself because
he'd gotten into the wrong lane and missed his turn. He
turned quickly, and said, "I beg your pardon?"

"The school," Miss Boltz said. "It has a lovely color."

They threaded their way through an interchange, circled,
and maneuvered into the proper lane. Then the driver
turned to her again. "I've heard of schools. They used to
have some out west. But that isn't a school."

Miss Boltz met his serious gaze confusedly, and hoped
she wasn't blushing. It just wasn't proper for a woman of

19

her age to blush. She said, "I must have misunderstood you.
I thought that was—"

"Yes, Ma'am. That's the address you gave me."

"Then—of course it's a school! I'm a teacher. I'm going
to teach there."

He shook his head. "No, Ma'am. We don't have any
schools."

The descent was so unsettlingly abrupt that Miss Boltz
had to swallow her protests and clutch at her safety belt.
Then they were in the ground level parking area, and he
had the door open. She paid him, and stepped out with the
dignity demanded of a middle-aged school teacher. She
would have liked to investigate this queer notion of his
about schools, but she didn't want to be late for her appointment. And anyway—the idea! If it wasn't a school, what was
it?

In the maze of lettered and double-lettered corridors,
each turning she took seemed to be the wrong one, and she
was breathing heavily and fighting off a mild seizure of
panic when she reached her destination. A receptionist took
her name and said severely, "Mr. Wilbings is expecting
you. Go right in."

The office door bore a bristling label. ROGER A. WIL-
BINGS. DEPUTY SUPERINTENDENT OF EDUCATION
(SECONDARY). NORTHEASTERN UNITED STATES
SCHOOL DISTRICT. PRIVATE. Miss Boltz hesitated, and
the receptionist said again, "Go right in."

"Thank you," Miss Boltz said and opened the door.

The gentleman behind the desk at the distant center of
the room was awaiting her with a fiercely blank expression which resolved into the hair-framed oval of a bald
head as she moved forward. She blinked her eyes nervously and wished she'd worn her contact lenses. Mr. Wilbings's
attention was fixed upon the papers that littered the top of
his desk, and he indicated a chair for her without bothering
to look up. She walked tightrope-fashion across the room
and seated herself.

"One moment, please," he said.

She ordered herself to relax. She was not a young lass just
out of college, hoping desperately for a first job. She had

a contract and twenty-five years of tenure, and she was merely reporting for reassignment.

Her nerves disregarded the order.

Mr. Wilbings gathered up his papers, tapped them together, and returned them to a folder. "Miss—ah—Boltz," he said. His curiously affected appearance fascinated her. He was wearing spectacles, a contrivance which she hadn't seen for years; and he had a trim little patch of hair on his upper lip, the like of which she had never seen outside of films and theatricals. He held his head thrust forward and tilted back, and he sighed at her distastefully along the high arc of his nose.

He nodded suddenly, and turned back to his desk. "I've gone through your file, Miss—ah—Boltz." He pushed the folder aside impatiently. "My recommendation is that you retire. My secretary will give you the necessary papers to fill out. Good morning."

The suddenness of the attack startled her out of her nervousness. She said calmly, "I appreciate your interest, Mr. Wilbings, but I have no intention of retiring. Now—about my new assignment."

"My dear Miss Boltz!" He had decided to be nice to her. His expression altered perceptibly, and hovered midway between a smile and a sneer. "It is your own welfare that concerns me. I understand that your retirement might occasion some financial sacrifice, and under the circumstances I feel that we could obtain an appropriate adjustment in your pension. It would leave you secure and free to do what you like, and I can assure you that you are *not—*" He paused, and tapped his desk with one finger. "—*not* suited for teaching. Painful as the idea may be for you, it is the blunt truth, and the sooner you realize it—"

For one helpless moment she could not control her laughter. He broke off angrily and stared at her.

"I'm sorry," she said, dabbing at her eyes. "I've been a teacher for twenty-five years—a good teacher, as you know if you've checked over my efficiency reports. Teaching is my whole life, and I love it, and it's a little late to be telling me that I'm not suited for it."

"Teaching is a young people's profession, and you are nearly fifty. And then—we must consider your health."

"Which is perfectly good," she said. "Of course I had

cancer of the lung. It isn't uncommon on Mars. It's caused by the dust, you know, and it's easily cured."

"You had it four times, according to your records."

"I had it four times and I was cured four times. I returned to Earth only because the doctors felt that I was unusually susceptible to Martian cancer."

"Teaching on Mars—" He gestured disdainfully. "You've never taught anywhere else, and at the time you were in training your college was specializing in training teachers for Mars. There's been a revolution in education, Miss Boltz, and it has completely passed you by." He tapped his desk again, sternly. "You are not suited for teaching. Certainly not in this district."

She said stubbornly, "Will you honor my contract, or do I have to resort to legal action?"

He shrugged, and picked up her file. "Written and spoken English. Tenth grade. I assume you think you can handle that."

"I can handle it."

"Your class meets from ten-fifteen to eleven-fifteen, Monday through Friday."

"I am not interested in part-time teaching."

"This is a full-time assignment."

"Five hours a week?"

"The position assumes forty hours of class preparation. You'll probably need much more than that."

"I see," she said. She had never felt more bewildered.

"Classes begin next Monday. I'll assign you to a studio and arrange an engineering conference for you immediately."

"A—*studio?*"

"Studio." There was a note of malicious satisfaction in his voice. "You will have approximately forty thousand students."

From a drawer he took two books, one a ponderous volume entitled, *TECHNIQUES AND PROCEDURES IN TV TEACHING,* and the other, mecha-typed and bound with a plastic spiral, a course outline of tenth-grade English, Northeastern United States School District. "These should contain all the information you'll need," he said.

Miss Boltz said falteringly, "TV teaching? Then—my students will attend class by television?"

"Certainly."

"Then I'll never see them."

"They will see you, Miss Boltz. That is quite sufficient."

"I suppose the examination will be machine-graded, but what about papers? I couldn't get through one assignment in an entire semester."

He scowled at her. "There are no assignments. There are no examinations, either. I suppose the educational system on Mars still uses examinations and assignments to coerce its students into learning, but we have progressed beyond those dark ages of education. If you have some idea of bludgeoning your material into your students with examinations and papers and the like, just forget it. Those things are symptomatic of bad teaching, and we would not permit it if it were possible, which it isn't."

"If there are no examinations or papers, and if I never see my students, how can I evaluate the results of my teaching?"

"We have our own method for that. You receive a Trendex rating every two weeks. Is there anything else?"

"Just one thing." She smiled faintly. "Would you mind telling me why you so obviously resent my presence here?"

"I wouldn't mind," he answered indifferently. "You have an obsolete contract that we have to honor, but we know that you will not last the term out. When you do leave we will have the problem of finding a midyear replacement for you, and forty thousand students will have been subjected to several weeks of bad instruction. You can hardly blame us for taking the position that it would be better for you to retire now. If you change your mind before Monday I will guarantee full retirement benefits for you. If not, remember this; the courts have upheld our right to retire a teacher for incompetence, regardless of tenure."

Mr. Wilbings's secretary gave her a room number. "This will be your office," she said. "Wait there, and I'll send someone."

It was a small room with a desk, book shelves, a filing cabinet, a book-film cabinet, and a film reader. A narrow window looked out onto long rows of narrow windows. On the wall opposite the desk was a four-foot TV screen. It was the first office Miss Boltz had ever had, and she sat at her desk with the drab brown walls frowning down at her and felt lonely, and humble, and not a little frightened.

The telephone rang. After a frantic search she located it under a panel in the desk top, but by then it had stopped ringing. She examined the desk further, and found another panel that concealed the TV controls. There were four dials, each with numbers zero through nine. With almost no calculation she deduced the possible number of channels as 9,999. She tried various numbers and got a blank screen except for channel 0001, which carried an announcement: CLASSES BEGIN MONDAY, SEPTEMBER 9. REGISTRATION IS NOW IN PROGRESS. YOU MUST BE REGISTERED TO RECEIVE GRADUATION CREDITS.

A knock sounded on her door. It was a kindly-looking, graying man of fifty plus, who introduced himself as Jim Pargrin, chief engineer. He seated himself on the edge of her desk and grinned at her. "I was afraid you'd gotten lost. I telephoned and no one answered."

"By the time I found the telephone, you'd hung up," Miss Boltz said.

He chuckled and then said seriously, "So you're the Martian. Do you know what you're getting into?"

"Did they send you up here to frighten me?"

"I don't frighten anyone but the new engineers. I just wondered—but never mind. Come over to your studio, and I'll explain the setup."

They quickly left the rows of offices behind them, and each room that they passed featured an enormous glass window facing on the corridor. Miss Boltz was reminded of the aquarium on Mars, where she sometimes took her students to show them the strange marine life on Earth.

Pargrin unlocked a door, and handed her the key. "Six-four-three-nine. A long way from your office, but at least it's on the same floor."

A hideous black desk with stubby metal legs squatted in front of a narrow blackboard. The camera stared down from the opposite wall, and beside it was a pilot screen. Pargrin unlocked a control box, and suddenly lights blinded her. "Because you're an English teacher, they figure you don't need any special equipment," he said. "See these buttons? Number one gives you a shot of the desk and the blackboard and just about the space enclosed by that

24

floor line. Number two is a closeup of the desk. Number three is a closeup of the blackboard. Ready to try it out?"

"I don't understand."

He touched another switch. "There."

The pilot screen flickered to life. Miss Boltz faced it—faced the dumpy-looking, middle-aged woman who stared back at her—and thought she looked cruelly old. The dress she had purchased with such care and for too much money the day before was a blur of repulsive colors. Her face was shockingly pale. She told herself sadly that she really should have spent more time on the sun deck, coming back from Mars.

"Try number two," Pargrin suggested.

She seated herself at the desk and pressed button number two. The camera twitched, and she contemplated the closeup of herself and shuddered. Number three, with herself at the blackboard, was equally bad.

Pargrin switched off the camera and closed the control box. "Here by the door is where you check in," he said. "If you haven't pressed this button by ten-fifteen, your class is automatically cancelled. And then—you must leave immediately when your class is over at eleven-fifteen, so the next teacher can get ready for the eleven-thirty class. Except that it's considered good manners to clean the blackboard and tidy things up. The stuff is in the desk. Everything clear?"

"I suppose," she said. "Unless you can tell me how I'm to teach written and spoken English without ever hearing my students speak or reading anything that they write."

He was silent as they left the studio. "I know what you mean," he said, when they reached her office. "Things were different when I was a kid. TV was something you watched when your folks let you, and you went to school with all the other kids. But it's changed, now, and it seems to work out this way. At least, the big shots say it does. Anyway—the best of luck to you."

She returned to her desk, and thoughtfully opened *TECHNIQUES AND PROCEDURES IN TV TEACHING.*

At five minutes after ten o'clock on the following Monday morning, Miss Boltz checked in at her studio. She was rewarded with a white light over the pilot screen. She seated herself at the desk, and after pressing button number two she folded her hands and waited.

At precisely ten-fifteen the white light changed to red, and from the pilot screen her own image looked down disapprovingly. "Good morning," she said. "This is tenth-grade English. I am Miss Boltz."

She had decided to devote that first class period to introducing herself. Although she could never become acquainted with her thousands of students, she felt that they should know something about her. She owed them that much.

She talked about her years of teaching on Mars—how the students attended school together, how there were only twenty or twenty-five students in one room, instead of forty thousand attending class by way of as many TV sets. She described the recess period, when the students who went outside the dome to play had to wear air masks in order to breathe. She told about the field trips, when the class, or perhaps the entire school, would go out to study Martian plant life, or rocks and soil formations. She told them some of the questions her Martian students liked to ask about Earth.

The minutes dragged tediously. She felt imprisoned under the unblinking eye of the camera, and her image on the pilot screen began to look haggard and frightened. She had not realized that teaching could be such a strain.

The end of the hour came as a death throe. She smiled weakly, and from the pilot screen a hideous caricature of a smile grimaced back at her. "I'll be seeing you tomorrow," she said. "Good morning."

The red light faded to white. Miss Boltz took a last, shuddering look at the camera and fled.

She was seated at her desk, forlornly fighting to hold back her tears, when Jim Pargrin looked in on her.

"What's the matter?" he asked.

"Just wishing I'd stayed on Mars."

"Why would you be wishing that? You got off to a very good start."

"I didn't think so."

"I did." He smiled at her. "We took a sample Trendex on you this morning, during the last ten minutes. We sometimes do that with a new teacher. Most students will start off with their assigned classes, but if the teacher isn't good they switch to something else in a hurry. So we check at the end of the first hour to see how a new teacher is doing. Wilbings asked for a Trendex on you, and he came down to watch us take it. I think he was disappointed." He chuckled slyly. "It was just a fraction under one hundred, which is practically perfect."

He departed before she could thank him, and when she turned to her desk again her gloom had been dispelled as if by magic. Cheerfully she plunged into the task of rewriting the outline of tenth-grade English.

She had no objection to the basic plan, which was comprehensive and well-constructed and at times almost logical. But the examples, the meager list of stories and novels and dramas supplied for study and supplemental reading—these were unbelievable. Just unbelievable.

"Recommended drama," the outline said. *"You Can't Marry an Elephant,* by H. N. Varga. This delightful farce—"

She crossed it out with firm strokes of her pen and wrote in the margin, "W. Shakespeare: *The Merchant of Venice.*" She substituted Dickens's *A Tale of Two Cities* for *Saddle Blankets and Six Guns,* a thrilling novel of the Old West, by Percivale Oliver. She found no unit at all which concerned itself with poetry, so she created one. Her pen slashed its way relentlessly through the outline, and her conscience troubled her not at all. Didn't the manual say that originality was encouraged in teachers?

The next morning, when she started down the corridor toward her studio, she was no longer nervous.

The vast unfriendliness of the building and the drab solitude of her office so depressed her that she decided to prepare her classes in her apartment. It was the middle of the third week before she found her way to the tenth floor, where, according to her manual, there was a cafeteria. As she awaited her turn at the vending machines the young teachers who silently surrounded her made her feel positively prehistoric.

A hand waved at her when she turned toward the tables. Jim Pargrin bounded to his feet and took her tray. A younger man helped her with her chair. After so many hours of solitude, the sudden attention left her breathless.

"My nephew," Pargrin said. "Lyle Stewart. He teaches physics. Miss Boltz is the teacher from Mars."

He was a dark-complexioned, good-looking young man with a ready smile. She said she was pleased to meet him and meant it. "Why, you're the first teacher I've spoken to!" she exclaimed.

"Mostly we ignore each other," Stewart agreed. "It's strictly a survival-of-the-fittest occupation."

"But I'd think that some kind of co-operation—"

He shook his head. "Supposing you come up with something that clicks. You have a high Trendex, and the other teachers notice. So they watch your class, and if they can steal your stuff they will. Then you watch them, to see if they have something you can steal, and you see them using your technique. Naturally you don't like it. We've had teachers involved in assault cases, and law suits, and varying degrees of malicious mischief. At best, we just don't speak to each other."

"How do you like it here?" Pargrin asked her.

"I miss the students," Miss Boltz said. "It worries me, not being able to know them, or check on their progress."

"Don't you go trying to drag in an abstraction like *progress*," Stewart said bitterly. "The New Education looks at it this way: we expose the child to the proper subject matter. The exposure takes place in his home, which is the most natural environment for him. He will absorb whatever his individual capacity permits, and more than that we have no right to expect."

"The child has no sense of accomplishment—no incentive to learn," she protested.

"Under the New Education, both are irrelevant. What we are striving for is the technique that has made advertising such an important factor in our economy. Hold the people's attention, and make them buy in spite of themselves. Or hold the student's attention, and make him learn whether he wants to or not."

"But the student learns no social values."

Stewart shrugged. "On the other hand, the school has no discipline problems. No extra-curricular activities to supervise. No problems of transporting the children to school and home again. You aren't convinced?"

"Certainly not!"

28

"Keep it to yourself. And just between us, I'll tell you the most potent factor in the philosophy of the New Education. It's money. Instead of a fortune invested in buildings and real estate, with thousands of schools to maintain, we have one TV studio. We save another fortune in teachers' salaries by having one teacher for a good many thousands of students instead of one for maybe twenty or thirty. The bright kids will learn no matter how badly they are taught, and that's all our civilization needs—a few bright people to build a lot of bright machines. And the school tax rate is the lowest it's been in the last century and a half." He pushed back his chair. "Nice to meet you, Miss Boltz. Maybe we can be friends. Since you're an English teacher, and I'm a physics teacher, we aren't likely to steal from each other. Now I have to go think up some new tricks. My Trendex is way down."

She watched thoughtfully as he walked away. "He looks as if he's been working too hard," she announced.

"Most teachers don't have contracts like yours," Pargrin said. "They can be dismissed at any time. Lyle wants to go into industry after this year, and he may have a tough time finding a job if he's fired."

"He's leaving teaching? That's a shame!"

"There's no future in it."

"There's always a future for a good teacher."

Pargrin shook his head. "Look around you. The teachers are all young. They hang on as long as they can, because the pay is very good, but there comes a time when security means more than money. Anyway, in the not too distant future there won't be any teachers. Central District is experimenting now with filmed classes. Take a good teacher, film a year of his work, and you don't need the teacher any longer. You just run the films. No, there's very little future in teaching. Did you get your copy of the Trendex ratings?"

"Why, no. Should I have gotten one?"

"They come out every two weeks. They were distributed yesterday."

"I didn't get one."

He swore under his breath, and then looked at her apologetically. "Wilbings can be downright deceitful when he wants to. He probably thinks he'll take you by surprise."

"I'm afraid I don't understand these ratings."

"There's nothing complicated about them. Over a two-week period we'll take a thousand samples of a teacher's students. If all of them are watching their assigned class, as they should be, the teacher's Trendex is 100. If only half are watching, then the Trendex is 50. A good teacher will have about a 50 Trendex. If a teacher's Trendex falls below 20, he's dismissed. Incompetence."

"Then the children don't have to watch their classes unless they want to?"

"The parents have to provide the TV sets," Pargrin said. "They have to see that their children are present during their assigned class hours—'in attendance,' it's called—but they aren't responsible for making them watch any particular class. They'd have to supervise them every minute if that were so, and the courts have held that this would be unreasonable. It would also be unreasonable to require sets that worked only on assigned channels, and even if that were done the students could still watch classes on channels they're supposed to use at another time. So the students are there, and their sets are on, but if they don't like your class they can watch something else. You can see how important it is for the teacher to make the classes interesting."

"I understand. What was my Trendex?"

He looked away. "Zero."

"You mean—*no one* is watching me? I thought I was doing things correctly."

"You must have done something that interested them that first day. Perhaps they just got tired of it. That happens. Have you watched any of the other teachers?"

"Goodness, no! I've been so busy I just never thought of it."

"Lyle may have some ideas for you. I'll ask him to meet us at your office for the two o'clock class. And then—well, we'll see."

Lyle Stewart spread some papers on the desk in front of her, and bent over them. "These are the Trendex ratings," he said. "You were supposed to get a copy."

She glanced down the list of names, and picked out hers.

30

Boltz, Mildred. English, tenth grade. Time, 10:15. Channel 6439. Zero. Year's average, zero.

"The subject has something to do with the tricks you can use," Stewart said. "Here's a Marjorie McMillan at two o'clock. She teaches eleventh-grade English, and her Trendex is sixty-four. That's very high. Let's see how she does it." He set the dials.

At precisely two o'clock Marjorie McMillan appeared, and Miss Boltz's first horrified impression was that she was disrobing. Her shoes and stockings were piled neatly on the floor. She was in the act of unzipping her blouse. She glanced up at the camera.

"What are you cats and toms doing in here?" she cooed. "I thought I was alone."

She was a trim blonde, with a flashy, brazen kind of prettiness. Her profile displayed sensational curves. She smiled, tossed her head, and started to tiptoe away.

"Oh, well, as long as I'm among friends—"

The blouse came off. So did the skirt. She stood before them in an alluringly brief costume, consisting exclusively of shorts and halter. The camera recorded its scarlet and gold colors brilliantly. She pranced about in a shuffling dance step, flicking the switch for a closeup of the blackboard as she danced past her desk.

"Time to go to work, all you cats and toms," she said. "This is called a sentence." She read aloud as she wrote on the blackboard. "The—man—ran—down—the—street. 'Ran down the street' is what the man did. We call that the predicate. Funny word, isn't it? Are you with me?"

Miss Boltz uttered a bewildered protest. "*Eleventh*-grade English?"

"Yesterday we talked about verbs," Marjorie McMillan said. "Do you remember? I'll bet you weren't paying attention. I'll bet you aren't even paying attention now."

Miss Boltz gasped. The halter suddenly came unfastened. Its ends flapped loosely, and Miss McMillan snatched at it just as it started to fall. "Nearly lost it that time," she said. "Maybe I will lose it, one of these days. And you wouldn't want to miss that, would you? Better pay attention. Now let's take another look at that nasty old predicate."

Miss Boltz said quietly, "A little out of the question for me, isn't it?"

Stewart darkened the screen. "Her high ratings won't last," he said. "As soon as her students decide she's really not going to lose that thing—but let's look at this one. Tenth-grade English. A male teacher. Trendex forty-five."

He was young, reasonably good-looking, and clever. He balanced chalk on his nose. He juggled erasers. He did imitations. He took up the reading of that modern classic, *Saddle Blankets and Six Guns,* and he read very well, acting out parts of it, creeping behind his desk to point an imaginary six-gun at the camera. It was quite realistic.

"The kids will like him," Stewart said. "He'll probably last pretty well. Now let's see if there's anyone else."

There was a history teacher, a sedate-looking young woman with a brilliant artistic talent. She drew sketches and caricatures with amazing ease and pieced them together with sprightly conversation. There was an economics teacher who performed startling magic tricks with cards and money. There were two young women whose routines approximated that of Marjorie McMillan, though in a more subdued manner. Their ratings were also much lower.

"That's enough to give you an idea of what you're up against," Stewart said.

"A teacher who can't do anything but teach is frightfully handicapped," Miss Boltz said thoughtfully. "These teachers are just performers. They aren't teaching their students—they're entertaining them."

"They have to cover the subject matter of their courses. If the students watch, they can't help learning *something.*"

Jim Pargrin had remained silent while they switched from channel to channel. Now he stood up and shook his graying head solemnly. "I'll check engineering. Perhaps we could show some films for you. Normally that's frowned upon, because we haven't the staff or the facilities to do it for everyone, but I think I could manage it."

"Thank you," she said. "That's very kind of you. And thank you, Lyle, for helping out with a lost cause."

"The cause is never lost while you're still working," he said.

They left together, and long after the door closed after them Miss Boltz sat looking at the blank TV screen and wondering how long she would be working.

For twenty-five years on barren, inhospitable Mars she had dreamed of Earth. She had dreamed of walking barefoot on the green grass, with green trees and shrubs around her; and over her head, instead of the blurring transparency of an atmosphere dome, the endless expanse of blue sky. She had stood in the bleak Martian desert and dreamed of high-tossing ocean waves racing toward a watery horizon.

Now she was back on Earth, living in the unending city complex of Eastern United States. Streets and buildings impinged upon its tiny parks. The blue sky was almost obscured by air traffic. She had glimpsed the ocean once or twice, from an aircab.

But they were there for the taking, the green fields and the lakes and rivers and ocean. She had only to go to them. Instead she had worked. She had slaved over her class materials. She had spent hours writing and revising and gathering her examples, and more hours rehearsing herself meticulously, practicing over and over her single hour of teaching before she exposed it to the devouring eye of the camera.

And no one had been watching. During those first two weeks her students had turned away from her by the tens and hundreds and thousands, until she had lost them all.

She shrugged off her humiliation and took up the teaching of *The Merchant of Venice*. Jim Pargrin helped out personally, and she was able to run excellent films of background material and scenes from the play.

She said sadly, "Isn't it a shame to show these wonderful things when no one is watching?"

"*I'm* watching," Pargrin said. "I enjoy them."

His kindly eyes made her wistful for something she remembered from long ago—the handsome young man who had seen her off for Mars and looked at her in very much the same way as he promised to join her when he completed his engineering studies. He'd kissed her good-bye, and the next thing she heard he'd been killed in a freak accident. There were long years between affectionate glances for Miss Mildred Boltz, but she'd never thought of them as empty years. She had never thought of teaching as an unrewarding occupation until she found herself in a small room with only a camera looking on.

LLOYD BIGGLE, JR.

Pargrin called her when the next Trendex ratings came out. "Did you get a copy?"

"No," she said.

"I'll find an extra one, and send it up."

He did, but she knew without looking that the rating of Boltz, Mildred, English, tenth grade, and so on, was still zero.

She searched the libraries for books on the technique of TV teaching. They were replete with examples concerning those subjects that lent themselves naturally to visual presentation, but they offered very little assistance in the teaching of tenth-grade English.

She turned to the education journals and probed the mysteries of the New Education. She read about the sanctity of the individual and the right of the student to an education in his own home, undisturbed by social distractions. She read about the psychological dangers of competition in learning and the evils of artificial standards; about the dangers of old-fashioned group teaching and its sinister contribution to delinquency.

Pargrin brought in another Trendex rating. She forced herself to smile. "Zero again?"

"Well—not exactly."

She stared at the paper, blinked, and stared again. Her rating was .1—one tenth of one percent. Breathlessly she did some mental arithmetic. She had one student! At that moment she would have waived all of her retirement benefits for the privilege of meeting that one loyal youngster.

"What do you suppose they'll do?" she asked.

"That contract of yours isn't anything to trifle with. Wilbings won't take any action until he's certain he has a good case."

"Anyway, it's nice to know that I have a student. Do you suppose there are any more?"

"Why don't you ask them to write to you? If you got a lot of letters, you could use them for evidence."

"I'm not concerned about the evidence," she said, "but I will ask them to write. Thank you."

"Miss—ah—Mildred—"

"Yes?"

"Nothing. I mean, would you like to have dinner with me tonight?"

34

"I'd love to."

A week went by before she finally asked her students to write. She knew only too well why she hesitated. She was afraid there would be no response.

But the morning came when she finished her class material with a minute to spare, and she folded her hands and forced a smile at the camera. "I'd like to ask you a favor. I want each of you to write me a letter. Tell me about yourself. Tell me how you like the things we've been studying. You know all about me, and I don't know anything about you. Please write to me."

She received eleven letters. She handled them reverently, and read them lovingly, and she began her teaching of *A Tale of Two Cities* with renewed confidence.

She took the letters to Jim Pargrin, and when he'd finished reading them she said, "There must be thousands like them—bright, eager children who would love to learn if they weren't drugged into a kind of passive indifference by all this entertainment."

"Have you heard anything from Wilbings?"

"Not a thing."

"He asked me to base your next Trendex on two thousand samples. I told him I'd need a special order from the board. I doubt if he'll bother."

"He must be getting ready to do something about me."

"I'm afraid so," Pargrin said. "We really should start thinking of some line of defense for you. You'll need a lawyer."

"I don't know if I'll offer any defense. I've been wondering if I shouldn't try to set myself up as a private teacher."

"There are private schools, you know. Those that could afford it would send their children there. Those that couldn't wouldn't be able to pay you, either."

"Just the same, when I have some time I'm going to call on the children who wrote to me."

"The next Trendex is due Monday," Pargrin said. "You'll probably hear from Wilbings then."

Wilbings sent for her on Monday morning. She had not seen him since the first day, but his absurd appearance and his testy mannerisms had impressed themselves firmly upon her memory. "Are you familiar with the Trendex ratings?" he asked her.

Because she knew that he had deliberately attempted to keep her in ignorance, she shook her head innocently. Her conscience did not protest.

He patiently explained the technique and its purpose.

"If the Trendex is as valuable as you say it is," she said, "why don't you let the teachers know what their ratings are?"

"But they do know. They receive a copy of every rating."

"I received none."

"Probably an oversight, since this is your first term. However, I have all of them except today's, and that one will be sent down as soon as it's ready. You're welcome to see them."

He went over each report in turn, ceremoniously pointing out her zeros. When he reached the rating of .1, he paused. "You see, Miss Boltz, out of the thousands of samples taken, we have found only one student who was watching you. This is by far the worst record we have ever had. I must ask you to retire voluntarily, and if you refuse, then I have no alternative—"

He broke off as his secretary tiptoed in with the new Trendex. "Yes. Thank you. Here we are. Boltz, Mildred—"

His finger wavered comically. Paralysis seemed to have clogged his power of speech. Miss Boltz found her name, and followed the line across the page to her rating.

It was twenty-seven.

"Evidently I've improved," she heard herself say. "Is there anything else?"

It took him a moment to find his voice, and when he did its pitch had risen perceptibly. "No. Nothing else."

As she went through the outer office she heard his voice again, still high-pitched, squawking angrily in his secretary's communicator. "Pargrin. I want Pargrin down here immediately."

He was waiting for her in the cafeteria. "It went all right, I suppose," he said, with studied casualness.

"It went too well."

He took a large bite of sandwich, and chewed solemnly.

"Jim, why did you do it?" she demanded.

He blushed. "Do what?"

"Arrange my Trendex that way."

"Nobody *arranges* a Trendex. It isn't possible. Even Wilbings will tell you that." He added softly, "How did you know?"

"It's the only possible explanation, and you shouldn't have done it. You might get into trouble, and you're only postponing the inevitable. I'll be at zero again on the next rating."

"That doesn't matter. Wilbings will take action eventually, but now he won't be impulsive about it."

They ate in silence until the cafeteria manager came in with an urgent message for Mr. Pargrin from Mr. Wilbings. Pargrin winked at her. "I think I'm going to enjoy this. Will you be in your office this afternoon?"

She shook her head. "I'm going to visit my students."

"I'll see you tomorrow, then."

She looked after him thoughtfully. She sincerely hoped that he hadn't gotten himself in trouble.

On the rooftop landing area she asked the manager to call an aircab for her. While she waited she took a letter from her purse and reread it.

My name is Darrel Wilson. I'm sixteen years old, and I have to stay in my room most of the time because I had Redger disease and part of me is paralyzed. I like your class, and please, could we have some more Shakespeare?

"Here's your cab, ma'am."

"Thank you," Miss Boltz said. She returned the letter to her purse and stepped briskly up the cab ramp.

Jim Pargrin ruffled his hair and stared at her. "Whoa, now. What was that again? *Class* room?"

"I have nine students who are coming here every day to go to school. I'll need some place to teach them."

Pargrin clucked his tongue softly. "Wilbings would have a hemorrhage!"

"My TV class takes only five hours a week, and I have the entire year's work planned. Why should anyone object to my holding classes for a selected group of students on my own time?" She added softly, "These students *need* it."

They were wonderful children, brilliant children, but they needed to be able to ask questions, to articulate their thoughts and feelings, to have their individual problems dealt with sympathetically. They desperately needed each other. Tens of thousands, hundreds of thousands of gifted children were being intellectually and emotionally stifled in the barren solitude of their TV classes.

"What Wilbings doesn't know won't hurt him," Pargrin said. "At least, I hope it won't. But—a class room? There isn't a thing like that in the building. Could you use a large studio? We could hang a curtain over the glass so you wouldn't be disturbed. What hours would your class meet?"

"All day. Nine to three. They'll bring their lunches."

"Whoa, now. Don't forget your TV class. Even if no one is watching—"

"I'm not forgetting it. My students will use that hour for a study period. Unless you could arrange for me to hold my TV class in this larger studio."

"Yes. I can do that."

"Wonderful! I can't thank you enough."

He shrugged his shoulders, and shyly looked away.

"Did you have any trouble with Mr. Wilbings?" she asked.

"Not much. He thought your Trendex was a mistake. Since I don't take the ratings personally, the best I could do was refer him to the Trendex engineer."

"Then I'm safe for a little while. I'll start my class tomorrow."

Three of the students arrived in power chairs. Ella was a lovely, sensitive girl who had been born without legs, and though science had provided her with a pair, she did not like to use them. Darrel and Charles were victims of Redger disease. Sharon was blind. The TV entertainers failed to reach her with their tricks, but she listened to Miss Boltz's every word with a rapt expression on her face.

Their intelligence level exceeded by far that of any other class in Miss Boltz's experience. She felt humble, and not a little apprehensive; but her apprehension vanished as she looked at their shining faces that first morning and welcomed them to her venture into the Old Education.

She had two fellow conspirators. Jim Pargrin personally took charge of the technical aspects of her hour on TV and gleefully put the whole class on camera. Lyle Stewart, who found the opportunity to work with real students too appealing to resist, came in the afternoon to teach two hours of science and mathematics. Miss Boltz laid out her own study units firmly. History, English, literature, and social studies. Later, if the class continued, she would try to work in a unit on foreign language. That Wednesday was her happiest day since she returned to Earth.

On Thursday morning a special messenger brought in an official-looking envelope. It contained her dismissal notice.

"I already heard about it," Jim Pargrin said, when she telephoned him. "When is the hearing?"

"Next Tuesday."

"It figures. Wilbings got board permission for a special Trendex. He even brought in an outside engineer to look after it, and just to be doubly sure they used two thousand samples. You'll need an attorney. Know any?"

"No. I know hardly anyone on Earth." She sighed. She'd been so uplifted by her first day of actual teaching that this abrupt encounter with reality stunned her. "I'm afraid an attorney would cost a lot of money, and I'm going to need what money I have."

"A little thing like a Board of Education hearing shouldn't cost much. Just you leave it to me—I'll find an attorney for you."

She wanted to object, but there was no time. Her students were waiting for her.

On Saturday she had lunch with Bernard Wallace, the attorney Jim Pargrin recommended. He was a small, elderly man with sharp gray eyes that stabbed at her fleetingly from behind drooping eyelids. He questioned her casually during lunch, and when they had pushed aside their dessert dishes he leaned back and twirled a key ring on one finger and grinned at her.

"Some of the nicest people I ever knew were my teachers," he said. "I thought they didn't make that kind any more. I don't suppose you realize that your breed is almost extinct."

"There are lots of fine teachers on Mars," she said.

"Sure. Colonies look at education differently. They'd be committing suicide if they just went through the motions. I kind of think maybe we're committing suicide here on Earth. This New Education thing has some results you may not know about. The worst one is that the kids aren't getting educated. Businessmen have to train their new employees from primary grade level. It's had an impact on government, too. An election campaign is about what you'd expect with a good part of the electorate trained to receive its information in very weak doses with a sickening amount of sugar coating. So I'm kind of glad to be able to work on this case. You're not to worry about the expense. There won't be any."

"That's very kind of you," she murmured. "But helping one worn-out teacher won't improve conditions very much."

"I'm not promising to win this for you," Wallace said soberly. "Wilbings has all the good cards. He can lay them right out on the table, and you have to keep yours hidden because your best defense would be to show them what a mess of arrant nonsense this New Education is, and you can't do that. We don't dare attack the New Education. That's the board's baby, and they've already defended it successfully in court, a lot of times. If we win, we'll have to win on their terms."

"That makes it rather hopeless, doesn't it?"

"Frankly, it'll be tough." He pulled out an antique gold watch, and squinted at it. "Frankly, I don't see how I'm going to bring it off. Like I said, Wilbings has the cards, and anything I lead is likely to be trumped. But I'll give it some thought, and maybe I can come up with a surprise or two. You just concentrate on your teaching, and leave the worrying to me."

After he left she ordered another cup of coffee, and sipped it slowly, and worried.

On Monday morning she received a surprise of her own, in the form of three boys and four girls who presented themselves at her office and asked permission to join her class. They had seen it on TV, they told her, and it looked like fun. She was pleased, but doubtful. Only one of them was officially a student of hers. She took the names of the others and sent them home. The one who was properly her student she permitted to remain.

He was a gangling boy of fifteen, and though he seemed bright enough, there was a certain withdrawn sullenness about him that made her uneasy. His name was Randy

Stump—"A dumb name, but I'm stuck with it," he mumbled. She quoted him Shakespeare on the subject of names, and he gaped at her bewilderedly.

Her impulse was to send him home with the others. Such a misfit might disrupt her class. What stopped her was the thought that the suave TV teacher, the brilliant exponent of the New Education, would do just that. Send him home. Have him watch the class on TV in the sanctity of his own natural environment, where he couldn't get into trouble, and just incidentally where he would never learn to get along with people.

She told herself, "I'm a poor excuse for a teacher if I can't handle a little problem in discipline."

He shifted his feet uneasily as she studied him. He was a foot taller than she, and he looked past her and seemed to find a blank wall intensely interesting.

He slouched along at her side as she led him down to the class room, where he seated himself at the most remote desk and instantly lapsed into a silent immobility that seemed to verge on hypnosis. The others attempted to draw him into their discussions, but he ignored them. Whenever Miss Boltz looked up she found his eyes fixed upon her intently. Eventually she understood: he was attending class, but he was still watching it on TV.

Her hour on television went well. It was a group discussion on *A Tale of Two Cities,* and the youthful sagacity of her class delighted her. The red light faded at eleven-fifteen. Jim Pargrin waved his farewell, and she waved back at him and turned to her unit on history. She was searching her mind for something that would draw Randy Stump from his TV-inflicted shell.

When she looked up her students were staring at the door, which had opened silently. A dry voice said, "What *is* going on here?"

It was Roger Wilbings.

He removed his spectacles, and replaced them. "Well!" he said. His mustache twitched nervously. "May I ask the meaning of this?"

No one spoke. Miss Boltz had carefully rehearsed her explanation in the event that she should be called to account for this unauthorized teaching, but this unexpected confrontation left her momentarily speechless.

"Miss Boltz!" His mouth opened and closed several times as he groped for words. "I have seen many teachers do many idiotic things, but I have never seen anything quite as idiotic as this. I am happy to have this further confirmation of your hopeless incompetence. Not only are you a disgustingly inept teacher, but obviously you suffer from mental derangement. No rational adult would bring these—these—"

He paused. Randy Stump had emerged from his hypnosis with a snap. He leaped forward, planted himself firmly in front of Wilbings, and snarled down at him. "You take that back!"

Wilbings eyed him coldly. "Go home. Immediately." His gaze swept the room. "All of you. Go home. Immediately."

"You can't make us," Randy said.

Wilbings poised himself on the high pinnacle of his authority. "No young criminal—"

Randy seized his shoulders and shook vigorously. Wilbings's spectacles flew in a long arc and shattered. He wrenched himself free and struck out weakly, and Randy's return blow landed with a splattering thud. The Deputy Superintendent reeled backward into the curtain and then slid gently to the floor as glass crashed in the corridor outside.

Miss Boltz bent over him. Randy hovered nearby, frightened and contrite. "I'm sorry, Miss Boltz," he stammered.

"I'm sure you are," she said. "But for now—I think you had better go home."

Eventually Wilbings was assisted away. To Miss Boltz's intense surprise, he said nothing more; but the look he flashed in her direction as he left the room made further conversation unnecessary.

Jim Pargrin brought a man to replace the glass. "Too bad," he observed. "He can't have it in for you any more than he already had, but now he'll try to make something of this class of yours at the hearing tomorrow."

"Should I send them all home?" she asked anxiously.

"Well, now. That would be quitting, wouldn't it? You just carry on—we can fix this without disturbing you."

She returned to her desk and opened her notebook. "Yesterday we were talking about Alexander the Great—"

The fifteen members of the Board of Education occupied

42

one side of a long, narrow table. They were business and professional men, most of them elderly, all solemn, some obviously impatient.

On the opposite side of the table Miss Boltz sat at one end with Bernard Wallace. Roger Wilbings occupied the other end with a bored technician who was preparing to record the proceedings. A fussy little man Wallace identified as the Superintendent of Education fluttered into the room, conferred briefly with Wilbings, and fluttered out.

"Most of 'em are fair," Wallace whispered. "They're honest and they mean well. That's on our side. Trouble is, they don't know anything about education and it's been a long time since they were kids."

From his position at the center of the table, the president called the meeting to order. He looked narrowly at Bernard Wallace. "This is not a trial," he announced. "This is merely a hearing to secure information essential for the board to reach a proper decision. We do not propose to argue points of law."

"Lawyer himself," Wallace whispered, "and a good one."

"You may begin, Wilbings," the president said.

Wilbings got to his feet. The flesh around one eye was splendidly discolored, and he smiled with difficulty. "The reason for this meeting concerns the fact that Mildred Boltz holds a contract, type 79B, issued to her in the year 2022. You will recall that this school district originally became responsible for these contracts during a shortage of teachers on Mars, when—"

The president rapped on the table. "We understand that, Wilbings. You want Mildred Boltz dismissed because of incompetence. Present your evidence of incompetence, and we'll see what Miss Boltz has to say about it, and wind this up. We don't want to spend the afternoon here."

Wilbings bowed politely. "I now supply to all those present four regular Trendex ratings of Mildred Boltz, as well as one special rating which was recently authorized by the board."

Papers were passed around. Miss Boltz looked only at the special Trendex, which she had not seen. Her rating was .2—two tenths of one per cent.

"Four of these ratings were zero or so low that for all

practical purposes we can call them zero," Wilbings said. "The rating of twenty-seven constitutes a special case."

The president leaned forward. "Isn't it a little unusual for a rating to deviate so sharply from the norm?"

"I have reason to believe that this rating represents one of two things—fraud, or error. I freely admit that this is a personal belief, and that I have no evidence which would be acceptable in court."

The board members whispered noisily among themselves. The president said slowly, "I have been assured at least a thousand times that the Trendex is infallible. Would you kindly give us the basis for this personal belief of yours?"

"I would prefer not to."

"Then we shall disregard this personal belief."

"The matter is really irrelevant. Even if the twenty-seven is included, Miss Boltz has a nine-week average of only five and a fraction."

Bernard Wallace was tilted back in his chair, one hand thrust into a pocket, the other twirling his keys. "We don't consider that twenty-seven irrelevant," he said.

The president frowned. "If you will kindly let Wilbings state his case—"

"Gladly. What's he waiting for?"

Wilbings flushed. "It is inconceivable that a teacher of any competence whatsoever could have ratings of zero, or of fractions of a per cent. As further evidence of Miss Boltz's incompetence, I wish to inform the board that without authorization she brought ten of her students to a studio in this building and attempted to teach them in class periods lasting an entire morning and an entire afternoon."

The shifting of feet, the fussing with cigarettes, the casual whispering stopped. Puzzled glances converged upon Miss Boltz. Wilbings made the most of the silence before he continued.

"I shall not review for you the probably deadly effect of this obsolete approach to education. All of you are familiar with it. In case the known facts require any substantiation, I am prepared to offer in evidence a statement of the physical damage resulting from just one of these class periods, as well as my own person, which was assaulted by one of the young hoodlums in her charge. Fortunately I discovered this sinister plot against the youth of our district before the effects of her unauthorized teaching became irreparable. Her immediate dismissal will of course put an end to it. That, gentlemen, constitutes our case."

The president said, "This is hard to believe, Miss Boltz. Would you mind telling the board why—"

Bernard Wallace interrupted. "Is it our turn?"

The president hesitated, looked along the table for suggestions, and got none. "Go ahead," he said.

"A question, gentlemen. How many of you secured your own elementary and/or secondary education under the deadly circumstances Wilbings has just described? Hands, please, and let's be honest. Eight, ten, eleven. Eleven out of fifteen. Thank you. Do you eleven gentlemen attribute your present state of degradation to that sinister style of education?" The board members smiled.

"You, Wilbings," Wallace went on. "You talk as if everyone is or should be familiar with the deadly effects of group teaching. Are you an authority on it?"

"I am certainly familiar with all of the standard studies and research," Wilbings said stiffly.

"Ever experience that kind of education yourself? Or teach under those conditions?"

"I certainly have not!"

"Then you are not personally an authority. All you really know about these so-called deadly effects is what some other windbag has written."

"Mr. Wallace!"

"Let it pass. Is my general statement correct? All you really know—"

"I am quite prepared to accept the statements of an acknowledged authority in the field."

"Any of these acknowledged authorities ever have any experience of group teaching?"

"If they are reputable authorities—"

Wallace banged on the table. "Not the question," he snapped. "Reputable among whom? Question is whether they really know anything about what they write about. Well?"

"I'm sure I can't say just what basis they use for their studies."

"Probably not the only basis that counts—knowing their subject. If I could produce for you an authority with years of actual experience and study of the group-teaching system, would you take that authority's word as to its effects, harmful or otherwise?"

"I am always happy to give proper consideration to the work of any reliable authority," Wilbings said.

"What about you gentlemen?"

"We aren't experts in education," the president said. "We have to rely on authorities."

"Splendid. I now give you Miss Mildred Boltz, whose twenty-five years of group teaching on Mars makes her probably the most competent authority on this subject in the Western Hemisphere. Miss Boltz, is group teaching in any way harmful to the student?"

"Certainly not," Miss Boltz said. "In twenty-five years I can't recall a single case where group teaching was not beneficial to the student. On the other hand, TV teaching—"

She broke off as Wallace's elbow jabbed at her sharply.

"So much for the latter part of Wilbings's arugment," Wallace said. "Miss Boltz is an expert in the field of group teaching. No one here is qualified to question her judgment in that field. If she brought together ten of her students, she knew what she was doing. Matter of fact, I personally would think it a pretty good thing for a school district to have one expert in group teaching on its staff. Wilbings doesn't seem to think so, but you gentlemen of the board might want to consider that. Now—about this Trendex nonsense."

Wilbings said coldly, "The Trendex ratings are not nonsense."

"Think maybe I could show you they are, but I don't want to take the time. You claim this rating of twenty-seven is due to fraud or error. How do you know those other ratings aren't due to fraud or error? Take this last one—this special rating. How do you know?"

"Since you make an issue of it," Wilbings said, "I will state that Miss Boltz is the personal friend of a person on the engineering staff who is in a position to influence any rating if he so desires. This friend knew that Miss Boltz was about to be dismissed. Suddenly, for one time only, her rating shot up to a satisfactory level. The circumstances speak for themselves."

"Why are you so certain that this last rating is not due to fraud or error?"

"Because I brought in an outside engineer who could be trusted. He took this last Trendex on Miss Boltz personally."

"There you have it," Wallace said scornfully. "Wilbings wants Miss Boltz dismissed. He's not very confident that the regular Trendex, taken by the district's own engineers, will do the job. So he calls in a personal friend from the outside, one he can trust to give him the kind of rating he wants. Now if *that* doesn't open the door to fraud and error—"

The uproar rattled the distant windows. Wilbings was on his feet screaming. The president was pounding for order. The board members were arguing heatedly among themselves.

"Gentlemen," Wallace said, when he could make himself heard, "I'm no Trendex authority, but I can tell you that five ratings, and the circumstances surrounding them, add up to nothing but a mess. I'll take you to court cheerfully, and get you laughed out of court, if that's what you want, but there may be an easier way. At this moment I don't think any of us really know whether Mildred Boltz is competent or not. Let's find out. Let's have another Trendex, and have it without fussing around with samples. Let's have a Trendex of *all* of Miss Boltz's students. I won't make any promises, but if the results of such a rating were in line with this Trendex average, I would be disposed to recommend that Miss Boltz accept her dismissal without a court test."

"That sounds reasonable," the president said. "And sensible. Get Pargrin in here, Wilbings, and we'll see if it can be done."

Miss Boltz sank back in her chair and looked glumly at the polished table top. She felt betrayed. It was perfectly obvious that her only chance for a reprieve depended upon her refuting the validity of those Trendex ratings. The kind of test Wallace was suggesting would confirm them so decisively as to shatter any kind of a defense. Certainly Jim Pargrin would understand that.

When he came in he studiously avoided looking at her. "It's possible," he said, when the president described what was wanted. "It'll upset our schedule, and it might make us late with the next Trendex, but if it's important we can do it. Will tomorrow be all right?"

"Is tomorrow all right, Wilbings?" the president asked.

"Where Miss Boltz is concerned, I have no confidence in any kind of rating taken by your staff."

Pargrin elevated his eyebrows. "I don't know what you're getting at, but if you've got doubts just send in that engineer of yours and let him help out. With this extra load the Trendex men would probably appreciate it."

"Is that satisfactory, Wilbings?" the president asked.

Wilbings nodded. "Perfectly satisfactory."

"Very well. Miss Boltz's class ends at eleven-fifteen. Can we have the results by eleven-thirty? Good. The board will meet tomorrow at eleven-thirty and make final disposition of this case."

The meeting broke up. Bernard Wallace patted Miss Boltz on the arm and whispered into her ear, "Now don't you worry about a thing. You just carry on as usual, and give us the best TV class you can. It's going to be so tough it'll be easy."

She returned to her class, where Lyle Stewart was filling in for her. "How did you make out?" Stewart asked.

"The issue is still in doubt," she said. "But not very much in doubt, I'm afraid. Tomorrow may be our last day, so let's see how much we can accomplish."

Her TV class that Wednesday morning was the best she'd ever had. The students performed brilliantly. As she watched them she thought with an aching heart of her lost thousands of students, who had taken to watching jugglers and magicians and young female teachers in tights.

The red light faded. Lyle Stewart came in. "Very nice," he said.

"You were wonderful!" Miss Boltz told her class.

Sharon, the blind girl, said tearfully, "You'll tell us what happens, won't you? Right away?"

"I'll tell you as soon as I know," Miss Boltz said. She forced a smile and left the studio quickly.

As she hurried along the corridor a lanky figure moved to intercept her—tall, pale of face, frighteningly irrational in appearance. "Randy!" she exclaimed. "What are you doing here?"

"I'm sorry, Miss Boltz. I'm really sorry, and I won't do it again. Can I come back?"

"I'd love to have you back, Randy, but there may not be any class after today."

He seemed stunned. "No class?"

She shook her head. "I'm very much afraid that I'm going to be dismissed. Fired, you might say."

He clenched his fists. Tears streaked his face, and he sobbed brokenly. She tried to comfort him, and some minutes went by before she understood why he was weeping. "Randy!" she exclaimed. "It isn't your fault that I'm being dismissed. What you did had nothing to do with it."

"We won't let them fire you," he sobbed. "All of us—us kids—we won't let them."

"We have to abide by the laws, Randy."

"But they won't fire you." His face brightened, and he nodded his head excitedly. "You're the best teacher I ever saw. I know they won't fire you. Can I come back to class?"

"If there's a class tomorrow, Randy, you may come back. I have to hurry, now. I'm going to be late."

She was already late when she reached the ground floor. She moved breathlessly along the corridor to the board room and stopped in front of the closed door. Her watch said fifteen minutes to twelve.

She knocked timidly. There was no response.

She knocked louder and finally opened the door a crack. The room was empty. There were no board members, no technician, no Wilbings, no attorney Wallace. It was over and done with, and they hadn't even bothered to tell her the result.

They knew that she would know. She brushed her eyes with her sleeve. "Courage," she whispered and turned away.

As she started back up the corridor, hurrying footsteps overtook her. It was Bernard Wallace, and he was grinning. "I wondered what kept you," he said. "I went to check. Have you heard the news?"

She shook her head. "I haven't heard anything."

"Your Trendex was 99.2. Wilbings took one look and nearly went through the ceiling. He wanted to scream 'Fraud!' but he didn't dare, not with his own engineer on the job. The board took one look and dismissed the case. Think maybe they were in a mood to dismiss Wilbings, too, but they were in a hurry."

Miss Boltz caught her breath, and found the friendly support of a wall. "It isn't possible!"

"It's a fact. We kind of planned this. Jim and I pulled the names of all of your students, and we sent letters to them. Special class next Wednesday. Big deal. Don't miss it. Darned few of them missed it. Wilbings played right into our hands, and we clobbered him."

"No," Miss Boltz said. She shook her head, and sighed. "No. There's no use pretending. I'm grateful, of course, but it was a trick, and when the next Trendex comes out Mr. Wilbings will start over again."

"It was a trick," Wallace agreed, "but a kind of permanent trick. It's like this. The younger generation has never experienced anything like this real live class of yours. On the first day you told them all about school on Mars, and you fascinated them. You held their attention. Jim was telling me about that. We figured that putting this class of yours on TV would fascinate them, too. Wilbings took that special Trendex before you got your class going, but Jim has been sneaking one every day since then, and your rating has been moving up. It was above ten yesterday, and now that all of your kids know what you're doing it'll jump way up and stay there. So—no more worries. Happy?"

"Very happy. And very grateful."

"One more thing. The president of the board wants to talk to you about this class of yours. I had dinner with him last night, and I filled him in. He's interested. I've got a suspicion that he maybe has a personal doubt or two about this New Education. Of course we won't tear down TV teaching overnight, but we're making a start. I have work to do, now. I'll be seeing you."

He shuffled away, twirling his keys.

She turned again, and saw Jim Pargrin coming toward her. She gripped his hand and said, "I owe it all to you."

"You owe it to nobody but yourself. I was up telling your class. They're having a wild celebration."

"Goodness—I hope they don't break anything!"

"I'm glad for you. I'm a little sorry, too." He was looking at her again in that way that made her feel younger—almost youthful. "I figured that if you lost your job maybe I could talk you into marrying me." He looked away shyly. "You'd have missed your teaching, of course, but maybe we could have had some children of our own—"

She blushed wildly. "Jim Pargrin! At our ages?"

"Adopt some, I mean."

"Really—I've never given a thought to what I might have missed by not having my own children. I've had a family all my life, ever since I started teaching, and even if the children were different every year I've loved them all. And now I have a family waiting for me, and I was so nervous this morning I left my history notes in my office. I'll have to run." She took a few steps, and turned to look back at him. "What made you think I wouldn't marry you if I kept on teaching?"

His startled exclamation was indistinct, but long after she turned a corner she heard him whistling.

On the sixth floor she moved down the corridor toward her office, hurrying because her students were celebrating and she didn't want to miss that. Looking ahead, she saw the door of her office open slowly. A face glanced in her direction, and suddenly a lanky figure flung the door aside and bolted away. It was Randy Stump.

She came to a sudden halt. "Randy!" she whispered. But what could he want in her office? There was nothing there but her notebooks, and some writing materials, and— her purse! She'd left her purse on her desk.

"Randy!" she whispered again. She opened the office door, and looked in. Suddenly she was laughing—laughing and crying—and she leaned against the door frame to steady herself as she exclaimed, "Now where would he get an idea like that?"

Her purse still lay on her desk, untouched. Beside it, glistening brilliantly in the soft overhead light, was a grotesquely large, polished apple.

Joan Patricia Basch was born some 35 years ago in Brooklyn, was brought up in Brazil, and now is back in Brooklyn. She writes that she "studied for the theatre, appeared in Off-Broadway productions, fragmentary film and T.V., wrote parables and drew cartoons. She soon found, however, that these outside interests conflicted with her primary aim: schizoid withdrawal." We've since received coherent communication from Miss Basch, so we trust that her goal will be put off indefinitely, and that we will have the opportunity to present more good stories like the one below.

MATOG

by Joan Patricia Basch

Times were not easy for Pieter Schnapps, who, in the fashion of other scholars in the sixteenth century, had taken the Latinate name of "Virgilius." He and his fifteen-year-old daughter (appropriately called "Camilla" after the heroic maiden in Virgil's epic), were destitute. Arriving on foot at the village of Dumpf, which consisted of an inn, they were forced to accept the charity of the innkeeper, Johannes.

A short, chubby man with a glowing child-like face, Johannes conferred charity upon them as one accepting favors. Virgilius had some small fame which had at one time reached the innkeeper, who was fond of saying that he had been educated above his station. He suffered from the lack of sublime conversation, and Virgilius seemed a heaven-sent source of supply. According to Johannes, those who usually came to his inn were not truly alive; they merely had insomnia.

Eagerly, Johannes put the traveller's little donkey in his stable, transferred the cartload of books and alchemist's retorts to the wine cellar, and set a fine roast before the dusty pair. His wife, Lotte, a great freckled, carrot-haired woman, made a row. (She treated Johannes as if he were her precocious child, scolding and complaining to his face, and then dotingly confiding to others the inexplicable marvels of his mind and heart.) Upon the advent of Virgilius and his daughter, hungry and penniless, she called Johannes a fool and a dupe, cried out that he would impoverish them both, threw a pan at him, and flung off to their room. There, she knelt before a statuette of the Madonna and murmured, moist-eyed, that she was married to a saint.

Gazing worshipfully upon Virgilius' majestic person as that bearded sage bolted his food, Johannes ventured: "The Lean Years are upon you, Meister?"

"When were the Fat ones?" Virgilius retorted bitterly, attacking his refilled plate with the air of one making provision for winter.

"Meister, I have information which may have a bearing upon the . . . misfortune to which you allude . . . I had meant to refer to it casually, with no coarse hint of its—ah —*lucrative* aspects. . . ."

Privation had thinned Virgilius' patience. He snapped, "Speak out, man! I know you were educated above your station!"

Johannes did not take offense. He said, "You know these are the lands of the Baron von Stellwiper von Vloy von Von?"

"His castle does not fade into the landscape."

"Imposing, is it not? An aerie, one might say, for an eagle like yourself." Virgilius tried to acknowledge the compliment while downing a mug of ale. Johannes planted his elbows on the table, and leaning forward, whispered excitedly: "Chimaerus, Court Astrologer, Alchemist in Waiting, Necromancer in Chief, Protege and Pet Charlatan of His Affluence the Baron, has flown the coop."

"Incredible!" exclaimed Virgilius, who was well informed as to the reputations of his colleagues. "From such a fine situation for one so inept! Confidentially, he had no more ingenuity than the shade of Sisyphus."

Johannes raised his plump hands, fingers spread.

"Ah Meister!" he protested. "Say Chimaerus had no talent. Say he had no learning. Say he had no scruples. But do not say he had no ingenuity!"

"True enough," Virgilius drawled. "One might even say

that he succeeded in discovering the Philosopher's Stone, since he managed to transform the lead of his brain into the gold of the Baron's purse. Why, in the name of un-deserved Fortune, did he leave the Baron's service?"

Johannes again adopted his conspiratorial air. "The question is not 'Why?', but 'How?' " His eyes sparkled. "For two years Chimaerus tried to conjure up a demon, fiend, devil for the Baron to look at. The Baron expects value, and pre-fers spectacle, which he can see, to speculation, which he can't grasp. He would well nigh give his fortune for the sight of genuine devil."

"He has only," Virgilius said significantly, "to wait." Johannes scarcely paused in his narration.

"A week ago, the labors of two years bore fruit. A devil actually *did* appear to Chimaerus . . . and it carried him off."

Virgilius guffawed. Johannes smiled demurely and continued.

"They were both gone so fast the Baron did not see either of them. He missed the treat."

"However, it might be accounted at least a Pyrrhic Victory for poor Chimaerus," Virgilius observed generously. "I suppose the Baron's laboratory is well equipped?"

"Many-tongued Rumor indicates it."

"I have put much study into an attempt to conjure up the fiend Matog," said Virgilius thoughtfully. "He cannot withstand my spells much longer. And now I shall know what to do with him when he does arrive." He glanced at Camilla, who had fallen asleep with her head on her arms, and rose.

The wine cellar was cavernous, with an earthen floor. It boasted little wine, but had a stove, safely apart from the barrels. The stove was lit, and two straw pallets, with blankets, were set on either side of it. Camilla barely woke as her father half carried her down and tucked her in. Virgilius himself did not retire until he and Johannes had put up a trestle table, upon which the alchemist's mystical hardware was lovingly set.

The following morning, Camilla went to the castle with a basket over her arm. Throughout their joint lives, her father had made sporadic attempts to turn to account various remedies he had devised for ailing live-stock. Usually this was only a last resort against starvation, but Camilla felt that Lotte, after all, gained little from Virgilius' conversation and dangerous experiments to compensate for the inroads upon her larder.

The castle, built to be threatening, stood upon a rocky hill. Its towers were wreathed with flights of birds, like calligraphy inked upon the transparent grey sky. The road, winding among fir trees and stunted oaks, was quite steep, but the thin cold air, the early morning chatter and twittering of the birds, the silvery mists evaporating in the rise of the pale sun, all filled her with a mysterious sense of anticipation and anguish. Life might be beginning, at last.

Camilla was a tall, slight girl with a wilderness of curly pale brown hair and enormous grey eyes, an oval face and cleft chin. She seldom thought of her appearance, beyond seeing that her one gown, of faded blue, was kept neatly patched and clean, but on this morning she felt beautiful. It was like a sign of Grace.

Wandering like a gypsy for as long as she could remember, sleeping in palaces and by the roadside, Camilla's religious education (the only kind that mattered among women) was strangely neglected. She did not know that she was on friendly, informal terms with God. Camilla's mother had been a lady, fastidious and no longer young, who had loved the resident scholar-magician and died of it, assisted by the inopportune arrival of her daughter. Virgilius left her family's manor in haste, taking the evidence with him. Sheltered through infancy among the large brood of an accommodating peasant family, Camilla was reunited with her father almost as soon as she could walk, and she had walked a great deal since; barefoot and in wooden shoes, occasionally in pretty slippers.

In this chilly dawn with its mood of awakening, there came cantering up the road a man on a black horse. Coming abreast of Camilla, who flinched from the thudding hooves, he pulled up. He was quite young and well dressed, with a drooping feather in his maroon cap. His olive skinned face was fine and handsome, with gentle dark eyes and lines with commas by his mouth. He raised his eyebrows and smiled at Camilla, and she was proud and happy because she felt beautiful that day, and it would have been a discord if such a man had met a homely girl on such a morning.

He greeted her with grave courtesy, and when she explained her errand, introduced himself as the Baron's steward, Hans, and bought some remedies from her. He politely questioned her, and Camilla, encouraged for the first time in her life to talk about herself, chattered breathlessly. She even divulged that the remedies were the creation of Virgilius, although this was absolutely forbidden. Virgilius regarded these medicines as the product of his baser, peasant nature, and he tacitly disassociated himself from their production, and even from Camilla when she sold them.

As they parted, Hans doffed his cap. Camilla returned to the inn with an empty basket and restocked fancy. Her fancy had always been her true reality, and now it was inhabited by the image of a person of flesh and blood, who had told her she was beautiful (with his eyes as much as in words) and a lady born. Around this fragment her secret reality formed a pearl which enclosed her so completely that meeting a fiend did not flurry her at all.

The fiend arrived that night.

Camilla lay on her pallet pretending to sleep as her father muttered, chanted, and scratched pentagons on the earthen floor, among the vials and retorts whose multicoloured contents glowed in the dark and gave off phosphorescent vapours. In their illumination, cast luridly upwards, Virgilius' craggy face with its fierce brows and flowing white hair and beard, hovered like that of some sinister prophet. (His hair and beard had turned white from shock, alchemy and black magic being a metier full of surprises. This venerable whiteness gave the impression that he was twice his actual age, which, in conjunction with a fifteen-year-old daughter, enhanced his reputation for arcane knowledge.)

Virgilius collected all his forces and cried: "APPEAR!"

There was a disappointing puff of smoke. Virgilius looked around hopefully, but he did not see what Camilla saw—an attenuated black figure decorated with small antlers and a bushy tail, mincing on tiptoe towards the stove.

Drowsy and entranced, Camilla remained still, watching the scene with detachment, from inside her pearl. The creature raised his finger to what might be his lips—his face was concealed by a mop-like orange mane, the same fore and aft—when he saw he was observed. There was something endearing in this unlikely complicity.

When Virgilius, discouraged, left the cellar for a drink and conference with Johannes, the fiend emerged shivering from the stove. "I can't bear it," he said. "Why can't they leave me in peace?"

"I'm sorry," said Camilla.

"Just let me wait it out in the stove. My name is Matog. Until the spell wears off."

"My name is Camilla; how do you do. I can't, Matog. Papa would be so angry."

"Camilla, I implore you."

"All right, Matog. Although I shouldn't."

"Promise? Sacred and Infernal?"

"Promise," said Camilla, touched and impressed.

The same thing happened the following night, and the night after that. Matog would be conjured up, hide, and Virgilius would leave, discouraged. Camilla, who had met Hans twice again on her way to the castle and was wholly absorbed in the aura of these overtly inconsequential meetings, made Matog her first confidant. She crouched close to the stove, whispering and enjoying his unsympathetic comments. They were addressed directly to her, and this was a delightful novelty.

"Dear Fiend," she whispered. "It is hard for me to speak of it . . . It is something . . . so . . . silly but, I thought, since you seem kindly disposed towards me . . ."

"Cut the preface," Matog interrupted, "and get to the narrative."

"I am in love."

"It's all your imagination," said Matog.

"Oh, I know!" Camilla gasped. "It's just that it *feels* so real to me. *Oh*," she sighed, "it's as if I had a fountain in me, a fountain that could cure sickness . . . if I touch something I feel as if I had healing hands . . . you know? And something else. I feel so alive that I think that if a leaf touched me, it would leave a bruise . . . and I feel like a vase which is carrying something so precious I walk carefully so it doesn't spill . . . Oh Matog, if you knew what a *relief* it is to talk about him!"

"You seem to be talking about yourself."

"Was I? I *thought* I was talking about him."

"Who is this nervous seizure?"

"I can't come out and say, Matog. I know you don't mind. I even hate it when other people mention his name, although I listen hard. Oh Matog, I feel as if I had been holding my breath all my life . . ."

The next day, Camilla heard Johannes, in gossiping with Virgilius, say that the Baron's steward, Hans, although of humble birth, had risen to his present eminence through being honest, trustworthy, and laughing at the Baron's jokes.

"A flatterer, then?" inquired Virgilius, while Camilla gazed fixedly at her sewing.

"Oh no," said Johannes. "He really thinks they are funny. It is a quirk," he explained, "such as any might have." He went on to say that Hans had risen so high as to marry an ill-natured niece of the Baron's, of small dowry and less beauty, but still, a step up in the world. Camilla went on sewing, as her fountain dried and her flesh turned to insipid clay and a numbness filled her head.

Walking to the castle the next day with a fresh supply of medicine, she told herself that it had been indeed "a nervous seizure." In any case, she had never believed that life would ever begin in earnest, that anything could really change, or even that this would be at all desirable. She thought of many things as she walked along, until taken aback by the violent beating of her heart. For a moment she thought she might be ill, and then realized that she had passed a spot where she had stopped to talk to Hans, and that had caused the beating. The enchantment had dissolved, leaving heaviness and apathy in its dregs, but desire remained. It was no longer the element in which she lived, but an isolated, aggravating hunger.

Since she no longer wove fantasies around Hans (for that seemed to her to be taking a liberty), she was able for the first time to consider her father and his predicament. Lotte kept threatening to evict her husband's pets, in spite of the money brought in by the medicine . . . they could not stay at the inn forever . . . Johannes was losing some of that adoration in which Virgilius basked and throve, and Virgilius was becoming desperate. How selfish she had been! Further, when she entered the inn she found a scene of consternation. A message had come. The Baron might call that very night, expecting a demonstration.

That night Camilla feigned sleep as before, as Virgilius went through his usual rituals. Again, his eyes glassy with discouragement, Virgilius flung up his arms at the conclusion of the invocation and cried: "APPEAR!" Again Matog materialized behind his back, dodged lithely as Virgilius peered around, and escaped into the stove. After Virgilius, in despair, tottered upstairs to rejoin Johannes and drink ale spiked with powdered bats, Matog emerged and prowled restlessly about. "How long can this go on?" he demanded rhetorically.

Camilla clasped her hands. "Please, please, Matog. Don't keep me to my promise. I was sorry for you but I didn't realize how much it meant to Papa. The Baron may come tonight! It changes everything!"

Matog whirled to face her, tail bristling. "It changes nothing for *me!*" he said between what she assumed were his teeth. "It will be the same as always for *me*. FIRST, there will be panic. Then lofty questions Satan himself couldn't understand, much less answer. But it's DONE. It's the CUSTOM. How do they think them up? *Why?*"

"Just get it over with, Matog dear."

"I know what to expect from these meddling pedants," he cried. "They weave spells and concentrate darkly until they've materialized one of us, and then, and then . . ."

"What, Matog?"

"Then it's: 'BEGONE, INFAMOUS FIEND! TEMPT ME NOT!' " Matog paused and looked at Camilla with impersonal curiosity. "Do I tempt *you?*"

Camilla searched for a tactful reply. "I think you're very interesting," she said delicately. "And *unusual.*"

Matog suddenly shouted, waving his long thin arms and stamping his long prehensile feet. "I have NEVER, in my wildest dreams of infamy, thought of myself as tempting in ANY WAY WHATSOEVER! But 'Tempt me not!' they screech. Obviously set on being tempted in *some* odd way. And the *self-righteousness* of it! 'Begone, unclean Spirit, in the name of the Heavenly Powers!' . . . followed by a flood of abuse in Latin, abominably pronounced. 'Abominable'—that's another one. 'Abominable Fiend.' But if they cast the spell, we HAVE to come! We have to come—from home, and peace, and comfort. *And we can't leave until the spell wears off!*" His voice rose hysterically. "It's *MADDENING, I TELL YOU!*"

"Just this once, Matog."

"They can't wait," he fumed on, "to get a little bit of Hell within reach—they'll all but kill themselves to do it, evil-minded brutes—and then it's all *horror*" (he spoke mincingly) "and *indignation*. And exorcisms. With Bells. Tinkle-tinkle. Ugh."

Camilla said eagerly, "But *Papa* will be *glad* to see you!"

Matog turned on her again. "He'll try to strike a bargain for his soul, wait and see. I have done more asinine bargaining for the asses' souls of more bearded blockheads—not your father, of course, Camilla—than any demon save Mephistopheles. And Mephistopheles *enjoys* it. He's mainly a Human concept anyway, the poseur."

"Matog . . ."

"And never once was it my idea!" he bleated. "*And*, of course, very proper they feel about *cheating*. With Them, it's not how you cheat, it's *who* you cheat. And They talk about Hell. Why, we frighten our imps with tales of where *they* will go if they don't behave."

"Papa only wants to show you to the Baron," Camilla pleaded. "You only have to stand there and *pose*, for just a minute."

"There would be trouble, mark my words," retorted Matog. "Only the other day I had an ink bottle heaved at me by some reforming theologian. Just showed my face, and ZINGO!—No Camilla, I don't go out of my way for that sort of thing. It just isn't good enough. And Mynheer Virgilius has never been aught but a trial to me." He sat down, his rage exhausted. "No. I hold you to your promise. But you may tell me more about your anonymous lover, if that's any consolation."

"Oh," said Camilla, "that doesn't count any more."

Matog pricked up his ears—literally. "How so?"

"Having the feelings I did about him was very wrong. *Mistaken*, rather, because truly I didn't know."

"Know what?"

"I might as well tell you who he was, since of course it doesn't matter now. He was the Baron's steward, and is honorably wedded."

Matog's ears twitched uneasily. "Camilla," he said slowly, "I wish you hadn't told me all this. The situation you describe might, if you lived at the castle, lead to serious trouble. This places me under a Moral Obligation to get you there."

Camilla stared at him dumbfounded.

Suddenly there was an uproar: the sound of hooves, Lotte shouting that the inn looked like a pig-sty, the excited voices of Virgilius and Johannes as they all but tumbled into the cellar.

"You must have an apparition. Any apparition," Johannes jabbered. He saw Matog, and stood transfixed, finger pointing, jaws moving soundlessly.

"Camilla, my Robe," ordered Virgilius, struggling to keep his head and not noticing Matog until Camilla, running up with his seedy star-strewn Robe, took him by the shoulders and turned him to view her prize. "Look, Papa!"

Matog obediently struck a pose; very elegant, and still as a statue.

Virgilius gave a great cry and staggered backwards. Reaching out wildly, he seized a bronze ink-pot from the trestle and hurled it. It ricocheted off Matog's head, dousing him in ink.

"I knew it," whispered Matog. He began to shout. "I *knew* it! I *KNEW* IT!"

"Foul Fiend Avaunt!" cried Virgilius. "Exorciso te . . . oh merciful Heaven, I've forgotten the words."

"Papa! Don't be frightened! Matog has been here for days and days and . . ."

"My little daughter! At the mercy of a devil from Hell!"

"PAPA!" Camilla moaned.

Matog drew himself up with dignity, blotting ink with his tail. "You seem to be singularly ill-informed," he said with icy precision. "I am not a devil, I am a Fiend. Furthermore, I am not, as you seem to fear, the Demon of Lechery, Asmodeus. *MY* function," he added bitterly, "seems to be serving as target for the ink-pots of high-strung metaphysicians."

Unmoved by this reproach, Virgilius groaned. "In one instant I knew all of pain and grief. Remember, Johannes, last year, when six maidens in Pfaff were possessed by a devil? Poor unfortunate young creatures."

"Knowing as you do," said Matog cuttingly, "the intensity of concentration required to call up a devil, I marvel at your saying, 'Poor young creatures.' Poor *Asmodeus*."

Johannes exclaimed, "No no. I shall never forget how, after three days, a voice burst simultaneously from all six, beseeching the mercy of exorcism."

Matog glared at him. "That was *Asmodeus*. Six at a time is certainly absurd."

There was pounding at the door, voices at the top of the cellar stairs. Flustered, Johannes rushed over to Matog and began fluffing up his fur. He found a comb in his enormous apron. Reaching up, trembling violently, he feverishly applied it to Matog's mane. Matog obligingly held still, but said coldly, "You are gilding the lily."

It was Hans who descended first. He raised his eyebrows upon seeing Matog at his toilette, but remained superbly unshaken. He smiled covertly at Camilla. She could not meet his eyes, and her face felt rigid and heavy. Her mouth and throat were so parched she could not swallow.

Hans announced: "The Baron von Stellwiper von Vloy von Von."

The Baron was portly and florid, in his sixties, with a bristling blond mustache turning gray. He was sumptuously clad and carried a magnifying glass, being extremely short-sighted. Under the impression that the kneeling Johannes was a child, he patted him on the head and gave him a sweet. He gave Camilla a sweet. He investigated Virgilius' beard through his glass, and, satisfied by this identification, greeted him. "As you have doubtless surmised," he said, at the conclusion of formalities, "I have come to consider you as successor to poor Chimaerus. (I had Paracelsus in mind, but no matter.) Doubtless you have heard of the end of poor Chimaerus?" Virgilius opened his mouth, but the Baron continued. "I was approaching his quarters one fateful day, when I heard his triumphant shout of 'EUREKA!' Then there was an indignant cry, a shriek, and, just as I entered, a red flash up the chimney. I thought at once of you, good Virgilius. Poor Chimaerus lacked a certain je ne sais quoi . . ."

While talking, the Baron had wandered over to Matog. "And this is . . . ?" Then suspicion dawned. Matog wearily held his pose again while the Baron, aghast, went over him with his magnifying glass. When he realized who, or what, it was, he tottered backwards with a blood-curdling scream.

He flailed his arms.

He crashed through the glass and crystal of Virgilius' equipment.

He howled, "POWERS OF DARKNESS BEGONE."

He panted, "Exorciso te, spiritus imundus, Spiritus malefico . . ."

"No," said Matog with decision. "This is too much. The irony of it." He sprang, giving off blue sparks, and missed. He gnashed unsuspected fangs. The Baron's agility was phenomenal. He was out of the cellar in a trice, and so was Matog, in a comet of sulphurous smoke. Hans followed. There was a clap of thunder.

"I hope the Baron is pleased," Johannes said doubtfully. There seemed little else to say.

"Pray God you are right, Johannes," muttered Virgilius. "The old fellow is quick on his feet, what? I hope he hasn't joined Chimaerus."

That he had not, was thanks only to the spell's wearing off. Matog vanished in a clap of thunder, after chasing the Baron around the inn, playing cat and mouse with him. The Baron rushed into the kitchen and Lotte slammed the massive door behind him, shutting out a nice fireworks display but not the smell of sulphur. The Baron stumbled to the head of the cellar stairs, just as Johannes was saying, "After the Baron waited so long, just to *see* a devil would not have been enough. This was better."

"SPAWN OF HELL!" shouted the Baron down the stairs. "ASSASSINS! I banish you. You and your ill-starred little ones." He caught sight of Johannes, who was standing now. "That one has grown," he said, mystified. His voice again rose to a bellow. "Begone from this village ere the sun sets again, and never return to spread the contagion of superstition among the lower orders." He mopped his brow. "If I had not led a blameless life . . . but it is not to be thought of." Hans gently took his arm and led him away. He and Lotte persuaded the Baron to rest upstairs before attempting the ride back to the castle. Lotte exercised her seldom used but very considerable gifts of pleasing, and plyed him with strong ale and savoury meat.

Unaware of the pacific scene above their heads, the trio in the cellar contemplated the enormity of their misfortune.

Only Camilla, huddled by herself near the stove, could find consolation in knowing it to be all for the best.

"Banishment!" mourned Johannes. "And you tried so hard."

"We've nought before us but starvation or charity," said Virgilius. "To be sure, that is all we had before, but I had hoped."

"Ah Mynheer!" cried Johannes, with passion. "It is enough just to *know* Hope for a sweet instant, without holding her to account like a creditor."

Virgilius did not heed him. "Each day," he said, "is a Philosopher's Stone in reverse, changing, hour by hour, all our gold to lead."

They wept together. Hans returned.

"Revered Sir," he said breathlessly, "I took the liberty of returning while the Baron rests, since I have news which may relieve your mind. I argued your cause to the Baron while he sampled a most excellent roast. He withdraws the sentence of banishment."

"God be praised!" cried Johannes.

"And, while the Baron has renounced all that smacks of the Black Arts, he would still solicit your services . . ."

"Ha!" said Johannes proudly.

". . . as a veterinarian."

"Camilla!" Virgilius roared. "I TRUSTED YOU!"

"I reported to the Baron," Hans went on calmly, "upon your miraculous remedy which checked an epidemic of hog cholera."

Virgilius declaimed: "Days of affliction have taken hold upon me! They chase mine honor as the wind . . ."

Hans went on imperturbably. "You would, of course, reside in the castle—in the same tower as the laboratory. The Baron has sworn a solemn vow to never approach that tower again, but doubtless you can find it in yourself to be reconciled to that. The living quarters are quite luxurious, and you will of course dine with the Baron, and be shown all due honor. He has great reverence for learning and for the arts of healing, especially when applied to animals. They were his chief interest in life before the advent of the ill-fated Chimaerus. Here is gold in advance." He departed in a confused exchange of compliments.

"Master Virgilius," pleaded Johannes, with tears in his eyes. "Are you not happy?"

"I have fled this all my life, Johannes. Yet this ignoble destiny lay in wait for me even while I distilled the learning of the stars."

Johannes straightened up. His eyes were shining now. "But I, Meister," he said, "will go to my grave rejoicing that I knew one like unto the blessed St. Francis—one who distilled the learning of the stars, to heal the suffering beast; the wisest and humblest of philosophers, gentle Virgilius."

Johannes knew his friend well. Virgilius instantly responded. His face lit up, his shoulders straightened. "Certes," said Virgilius. "It is a great trust. Pray for me, Johannes, that I may not grow vainglorious."

As they climbed from the cellar, Camilla curled up on her pallet, feeling tired and strange to herself. Something was going to Happen. Tomorrow, life would begin.

Gahan Wilson

"I expect one seldom encounters the older, traditional hazards on your American courses."

SF writer and critic Alfred Bester once put together a composite All Star author out of the colleagues he admired most. One of the components was, of course, Isaac Asimov, cited by Bester for his "encyclopaedic enthusiasm." Enthusiasm which has thus far produced seventy-five books, science fiction and science fact; and probably four times that many short pieces. Dr. Asimov's latest fiction, *The Key,* was featured in the magazine's special Isaac Asimov issue and is a sample of another of his special talents—the ability to successfully blend the science-fiction and detective story.

THE KEY

by Isaac Asimov

I

Karl Jennings knew he was going to die. He had a matter of hours to live and much to do.

There was no reprieve from the death sentence, not here on the Moon, not with no communications in operation.

Even on Earth there were a few fugitive patches where, without radio handy, a man might die without the hand of his fellowman to help him, without the heart of his fellowman to pity him, without even the eye of his fellowman to discover the corpse— Here on the Moon, there were few spots that were otherwise.

Earthmen knew he was on the Moon, of course. He had been part of a geological expedition— No, selenological expedition! Odd, how his Earth-centered mind insisted on the "geo-."

Wearily, he drove himself to think, even as he worked.

Dying though he was, he still felt that artificially-imposed clarity of thought. Anxiously, he looked about. There was nothing to see. He was in the dark of the eternal shadow of the northern interior of the wall of the crater, a blackness relieved only by the intermittent blink of his flash. He kept that intermittent, partly because he dared not consume its power source before he was through and partly because he dared not take more than the minimum chance that it be seen.

On his left hand, toward the south along the nearby horizon of the Moon, was a crescent of bright white Sunlight. Beyond the horizon, and invisible, was the opposite lip of the crater. The Sun never peered high enough over the lip of his own edge of the crater to illuminate the floor immediately beneath his feet. He was safe from radiation—from that at least.

He dug carefully but clumsily, swathed as he was in his spacesuit. His side ached abominably.

The dust and broken rock did not take up the "fairy-castle" appearance characteristic of those portions of the Moon's surface exposed to the alteration of light and dark, heat and cold. Here, in eternal cold, the slow crumbling of the crater wall had simply piled fine rubble in a heterogeneous mass. It would not be easy to tell there had been digging going on.

He misjudged the unevenness of the dark surface for a moment and spilled a cupped handful of dusty fragments. The particles dropped with the slowness characteristic of the Moon and yet with the appearance of a blinding speed, for there was no air resistance to slow them further still and spread them out into a dusty haze.

Jennings' flash brightened for a moment, and he kicked a jagged rock out of the way.

He hadn't much time. He dug deeper into the dust.

A little deeper and he could push the Device into the depression and begin covering it. Strauss must not find it.

Strauss!

The other member of the team. Half-share in the discovery. Half-share in the renown.

If it were merely the whole share of the credit that Strauss had wanted, Jennings might have allowed it. The discovery was more important than any individual credit that might

go with it. But what Strauss wanted was something far
more; something Jennings would fight to prevent.

One of the few things Jennings was willing to die to prevent.

And he was dying.

They had found it together. Actually, Strauss had found
the ship; or better, the remains of the ship; or, better still,
what just conceivably might have been the remains of something analogous to a ship.

"Metal," said Strauss, as he picked up something ragged
and nearly amorphous. His eyes and face could just barely
be seen through the thick lead-glass of the visor, but his
rather harsh voice sounded clearly enough through the
suit-radio.

Jennings came drifting over from his own position half a
mile away. He said, "Odd! There is no free metal on the
Moon."

"There shouldn't be. But you know well enough they
haven't explored more than one percent of the Moon's surface. Who knows what can be found on it?"

Jennings grunted assent and reached out his gauntlet to
take the object.

It was true enough that almost anything might be found
on the Moon for all anyone really knew. Theirs was the
first privately-financed selenographic expedition ever to land
on the Moon. Till then, there had been only government-
conducted shot-gun affairs, with half a dozen ends in view.
It was a sign of the advancing space age that the Geological
Society could afford to send two men to the Moon for selenological studies only.

Strauss said, "It looks as though it once had a polished
surface."

"You're right," said Jennings. "Maybe there's more about."

They found three more pieces, two of trifling size and
one a jagged object that showed traces of a seam.

"Let's take them to the ship," said Strauss.

They took the small skim-boat back to the mother ship.
They shucked their suits once on board, something Jennings at least was always glad to do. He scratched vigorously at his ribs and rubbed his cheeks till his light skin reddened into welts.

Strauss eschewed such weakness and got to work. The

laser beam pock-marked the metal and the vapor recorded itself on the spectrograph. Titanium-steel, essentially, with a hint of cobalt and molybdenum.

"That's artificial, all right," said Strauss. His broad-boned face was as dour and as hard as ever. He showed no elation, although Jennings could feel his own heart begin to race.

It may have been the excitement that trapped Jennings into beginning, "This is a development against which we must steel ourselves—" with a faint stress on "steel" to indicate the play on words.

Strauss, however, looked at Jennings with an icy distaste, and the attempted set of puns was choked off.

Jennings sighed. He could never swing it, somehow. Never could! He remembered at the University— Well, never mind. The discovery they had made was worth a far better pun than any he could construct for all Strauss's calmness.

Jennings wondered if Strauss could possibly miss the significance.

He knew very little about Strauss, as a matter of fact, except by selenological reputation. That is, he had read Strauss's papers and he presumed Strauss had read his. Although their ships might well have passed by night in their University days, they had never happened to meet until after both had volunteered for this expedition and been accepted.

In the week's voyage, Jennings had grown uncomfortably aware of the other's stocky figure, his sandy hair and china-blue eyes, and the way the muscles over his prominent jaw-bones worked when he ate. Jennings, himself, much slighter in build, also blue-eyed, but with darker hair, tended to withdraw automatically from the heavy exudation of the other's power and drive.

Jennings said, "There's no record of any ship ever having landed on this part of the Moon. Certainly none has crashed."

"If it were part of a ship," said Strauss, "it should be smooth and polished. This is eroded, and without an atmosphere here, that means exposure to micrometeorite bombardment over many years."

Then he *did* see the significance. Jennings said, with an almost savage jubilation, "It's a nonhuman artifact. Creatures not of Earth once visited the Moon. Who knows how long ago?"

"Who knows?" agreed Strauss dryly.

"In the report—"

"Wait," said Strauss imperiously. "Time enough to report when we have something to report. If it was a ship, there will be more to it than what we now have."

But there was no point in looking further just then. They had been at it for hours, and the next meal and sleep were overdue. Better to tackle the whole job fresh and spend hours at it. They seemed to agree on that without speaking.

The Earth was low on the eastern horizon almost full in phase, bright and blue-streaked. Jennings looked at it while they ate and experienced, as he always did, a sharp homesickness.

"It looks peaceful enough," he said, "but there are six billion people busy on it."

Strauss looked up from some deep inner life of his own and said, "Six billion people ruining it!"

Jennings frowned. "You're not an Ultra, are you?"

Strauss said, "What the hell are you talking about?"

Jennings felt himself flush. A flush always showed against his fair skin, turning it pink at the slightest upset of the even tenor of his emotions. He found it intensely embarrassing.

He turned back to his food, without saying anything.

For a whole generation now, the Earth's population had held steady. No further increase could be afforded, everyone admitted that. There were those, in fact, who said that "no higher" wasn't enough; the population had to drop. Jennings himself sympathized with that point of view. The globe of Earth was being eaten alive by its heavy freight of humanity.

But *how* was the population to be made to drop; randomly, by encouraging the people to lower the birth rate still further, as and how they wished? Lately there had been the slow rise of a distant rumble which wanted not only a population drop but a selected drop—the survival of the fittest, with the self-declared fit choosing the criteria of fitness.

Jennings thought: I've insulted him, I suppose.

Later, when he was almost asleep, it suddenly occurred

to him that he knew virtually nothing of Strauss's character. What if it were his intention to go out now on a foraging expedition of his own so that he might get sole credit for—

He raised himself on his elbow in alarm, but Strauss was breathing heavily, and even as Jennings listened, the breathing grew into the characteristic burr of a snore.

They spent the next three days in a single-minded search for additional pieces. They found some. They found more than that. They found an area glowing with the tiny phosphorescence of Lunar bacteria. Such bacteria were common enough, but nowhere previously had their occurrence been reported in concentration so great as to cause a visible glow.

Strauss said, "An organic being, or his remains, may have been here once. He died, but the micro-organisms within him did not. In the end they consumed him."

"And spread perhaps," added Jennings. "That may be the source of Lunar bacteria generally. They may not be native at all but may be the result of contamination instead —eons ago."

"It works the other way, too," said Strauss. "Since the bacteria are completely different in very fundamental ways from any Earthly form of micro-organism, the creatures they parasitized—assuming this was their source—must have been fundamentally different, too. Another indication of extraterrestrial origin."

The trail ended in the wall of a small crater.

"It's a major digging job," said Jennings, his heart sinking. "We had better report this and get help."

"No," said Strauss, somberly. "There may be nothing to get help for. The crater might have formed a million years after the ship had crash-landed."

"And vaporized most of it, you mean, and left only what we've found?"

Strauss nodded.

Jennings said, "Let's try anyway. We can dig a bit. If we draw a line through the finds we've made so far and just keep on—"

Strauss was reluctant and worked half-heartedly, so that it was Jennings who made the real find. Surely that counted!

Even though Strauss had found the first piece of metal, Jennings had found the artifact itself.

It *was* an artifact—cradled three feet underground under the irregular shape of a boulder which had fallen in such a way that it left a hollow in its contact with the Moon's surface. In that hollow lay the artifact, protected from everything for a million years or more; protected from radiation, from micrometeors, from temperature change, so that it remained fresh and new forever.

Jennings labeled it at once the Device. It looked not remotely similar to any instrument either had ever seen, but then, as Jennings said, why should it?

"There are no rough edges that I can see," he said. "It may not be broken."

"There may be missing parts, though."

"Maybe," said Jennings, "but there seems to be nothing movable. It's all one piece and certainly oddly uneven." He noted his own play on words, then went on with a not-altogether-successful attempt at self-control. "*This* is what we need. A piece of worn metal or an area rich in bacteria is only material for deduction and dispute. But this is the real thing—a Device that is clearly of extraterrestrial manufacture."

It was on the table between them now, and both regarded it gravely.

Jennings said, "Let's put through a preliminary report, now."

"No!" said Strauss, in sharp and strenuous dissent. "Hell, no!"

"Why not?"

"Because if we do, it becomes a Society project. They'll swarm all over it and we won't be as much as a footnote when all is done. No!" Strauss looked almost sly. "Let's do all we can with it and get as much out of it as possible before the harpies descend."

Jennings thought about it. He couldn't deny that he, too, wanted to make certain that no credit was lost. But still—

He said, "I don't know that I like to take the chance, Strauss." For the first time he had an impulse to use the man's first name, but fought it off. "Look, Strauss," he said, "it's not right to wait. If this is of extraterrestrial origin, then it must be from some other planetary system. There

73

isn't a place in the Solar system, outside the Earth, that can possibly support an advanced life-form."

"Not proven, really," grunted Strauss, "but what if you're right?"

"Then it would mean that the creatures of the ship had interstellar travel and therefore had to be far in advance, technologically, of ourselves. Who knows what the Device can tell us about their advanced technology. It might be the key to—who knows what. It might be the clue to an unimaginable scientific revolution."

"That's romantic nonsense. If this is the product of a technology far advanced over ours, we'll learn nothing from it. Bring Einstein back to life and show him a microprotowarp and what would he make of it?"

"We can't be certain that we won't learn."

"So what, even so? What if there's a small delay? What if we assure credit for ourselves? What if we make sure that we ourselves go along with this, that we don't let go of it?"

"But Strauss," Jennings felt himself moved almost to tears in his anxiety to get across his sense of the importance of the Device, "what if we crash with it? What if we don't make it back to Earth? We can't risk this thing." He tapped it then, almost as though he were in love with it. "We should report it now and have them send ships out here to get it. It's too precious to—"

At the peak of his emotional intensity, the Device seemed to grow warm under his hand. A portion of its surface, half-hidden under a flap of metal, glowed phosphorescently.

Jennings jerked his hand away in a spasmodic gesture and the Device darkened. But it was enough; the moment had been infinitely revealing.

He said, almost choking. "It was like a window opening into your skull. I could see into your mind."

"I read yours," said Strauss, "or experienced it, or entered into it, or whatever you choose." He touched the Device in his cold, withdrawn way, but nothing happened.

"You're an Ultra," said Jennings angrily. "When I touched this," and he did so— "It's happening again. I see it. Are you a madman? Can you honestly believe it is humanly decent to condemn almost all the human race to extinction and destroy the versatility and variety of the species?"

74

His hand dropped away from the Device again, in repugnance at the glimpses revealed, and it grew dark again. Once more, Strauss touched it gingerly and again nothing happened.

Strauss said, "Let's not start a discussion, for God's sake— This thing is an aid to communication. A telepathic amplifier. Why not? The brain cells have each their electric potentials. Thought can be viewed as a wavering electromagnetic field of micro-intensities—"

Jennings turned away. He didn't want to speak to Strauss. He said, "We'll report it now. I don't give a damn about credit. Take it all. I just want it out of our hands."

For a moment Strauss remained in a brown study. Then he said, "It's more than a communicator. It responds to emotion and it amplifies emotion."

"What are you talking about?"

"Twice it started at your touch just now, although you'd been handling it all day with no effect. It still has no effect when I touch it."

"Well?"

"It reacted to you when you were in a state of high emotional tension. That's the requirement for activation, I suppose. And when you raved about the Ultras while you were holding it just now, I felt as you did, for just a moment."

"So you should."

"But, listen to me. Are you sure *you're* so right? There isn't a thinking man on Earth that doesn't know the planet would be better off with a population of one billion rather than six billion. If we used automation to the full—as now the hordes won't allow us to do—we could probably have a completely efficient and viable Earth with a population of no more than, say, five million— Listen to me, Jennings. Don't turn away, man."

The harshness in Strauss's voice almost vanished in his effort to be reasonably winning. "But we can't reduce the population democratically. You know that. It isn't the sex urge, because uterine inserts solved the birth control problem long ago; you know that. It's a matter of nationalism. Each ethnic group wants other groups to reduce themselves in population first, and I agree with them. I want my ethnic group, *our* ethnic group, to prevail. I want the Earth to be inherited by the elite, which means by men like ourselves. We're the true men, and the horde of half-apes who hold us down are destroying us all. They're doomed to death anyway; why not save ourselves?"

"No," said Jennings strenuously. "No one group has a monopoly on humanity. Your five million mirror-images, trapped in a humanity robbed of its variety and versatility, would die of boredom—and serve them right."

"Emotional nonsense, Jennings. You don't believe that. You've just been trained to believe it by our damn-fool equalitarians. Look, this Device is just what we need. Even if we can't build any others or understand how this one works, this one Device might do. If we could control or influence the minds of key men, then little by little, we can superimpose our views on the world. We already have an organization. You must know that if you've seen my mind. It's better motivated and better designed than any other organization on Earth. The brains of mankind flock to us daily. Why not you, too? This instrument is a key, as you see, but not just a key to a bit more knowledge. It is a key to the final solution of men's problems. Join us! Join us!" He had reached an earnestness that Jennings had never heard in him.

Strauss's hand fell on the Device, which flickered a second or two and went out.

Jennings smiled humorlessly. He saw the significance of that. Strauss had been deliberately trying to work himself into an emotional state intense enough to activate the Device and had failed.

"You can't work it," said Jennings, "you're too darned supermannishly self-controlled and can't break down, can you?" He took up the Device with hands that were trembling, and it phosphoresced at once.

"Then *you* work it. Get the credit for saving humanity."

"Not in a hundred million years," said Jennings, gasping and barely able to breathe in the intensity of his emotion. "I'm going to report this now."

"No," said Strauss. He picked up one of the table knives. "It's pointed enough, sharp enough."

"You needn't work so hard to make your point," said Jennings, even under the stress of the moment conscious of the pun. "I can see your plans. With the Device you can convince anyone that I never existed. You can bring about an Ultra victory."

Strauss nodded. "You read my mind perfectly."

"But you won't," gasped Jennings. "Not while I hold this." He was willing Strauss into immobility.

Strauss moved raggedly and subsided. He held the knife out stiffly and his arm trembled, but he did not advance.

Both were perspiring freely.

Strauss said between clenched teeth, "You can't keep it—up all—day."

The sensation was clear, but Jennings wasn't sure he had the words to describe it. It was, in physical terms, like holding a slippery animal of vast strength, one that wriggled incessantly. Jennings had to concentrate on the feeling of immobility.

He wasn't familiar with the Device. He didn't know how to use it skillfully. One might as well expect someone who had never seen a sword to pick one up and wield it with the grace of a musketeer.

"Exactly," said Strauss, following Jennings' train of thought. He took a fumbling step forward.

Jennings knew himself to be no match for Strauss's mad determination. They both knew that. But there was the skim-boat. Jennings had to get away. With the Device.

But Jennings had no secrets. Strauss saw his thought and tried to step between the other and the skim-boat.

Jennings redoubled his efforts. Not immobility, but unconsciousness. Sleep, Strauss, he thought desperately. Sleep!

Strauss slipped to his knees, heavy-lidded eyes closing.

Heart pounding, Jennings rushed forward. If he could strike him with something, snatch the knife—

But his thoughts had deviated from their all-important concentration on sleep, so that Strauss's hand was on his ankle, pulling downward with raw strength.

Strauss did not hesitate. As Jennings tumbled, the hand that held the knife rose and fell. Jennings felt the sharp pain and his mind reddened with fear and despair.

It was the very excess of emotion that raised the flicker of the Device to a blaze. Strauss's hold relaxed as Jennings silently and incoherently screamed fear and rage from his own mind to the other.

Strauss rolled over, face distorted.

Jennings rose unsteadily to his feet and backed away. He dared do nothing but concentrate on keeping the other unconscious. Any attempt at violent action would block out too much of his own mind-force, whatever it was; too much of his unskilled bumbling mind-force that could not lend itself to really effective use.

He backed toward the skim-boat. There would be a suit on board—bandages—

The skim-boat was not really meant for long-distance runs. Nor was Jennings, any longer. His right side was slick with blood despite the bandages. The interior of his suit was caked with it.

There was no sign of the ship itself on his tail, but surely it would come sooner or later. Its power was many times his own; it had detectors that would pick up the cloud of charge concentration left behind by his ion-drive reactors.

Desperately, Jennings had tried to reach Luna Station on his radio, but there was still no answer, and he stopped in despair. His signals would merely aid Strauss in pursuit.

He might reach Luna Station bodily, but he did not think he could make it. He would be picked off first. He would die and crash first. He wouldn't make it. He would have to hide the Device, put it away in a safe place, *then* make for Luna Station.

The Device—

He was not sure he was right. It might ruin the human race, but it was infinitely valuable. Should he destroy it altogether? It was the only remnant of non-human intelligent life. It held the secrets of an advanced technology; it was an instrument of an advanced science of the mind. Whatever the danger, consider the value— The potential value—

No, he must hide it so that it could be found again—but only by the enlightened Moderates of the government. Never by the Ultras—

The skim-boat flickered down along the northern inner rim of the crater. He knew which one it was, and the Device could be buried here. If he could not reach Luna Station thereafter, either in person or by radio, he would have to at least get away from the hiding spot; well away, so that his own person would not give it away. And he would have to leave *some* key to its location.

He was thinking with an unearthly clarity, it seemed to him. Was it the influence of the Device he was holding? Did it stimulate his thinking and guide him to the perfect message? Or was it the hallucination of the dying, and would none of it make any sense to anyone? He didn't know, but he had no choice. He had to try.

For Karl Jennings knew he was going to die. He had a matter of hours to live and much to do.

II

H. Seton Davenport of the American Division of the Terrestrial Bureau of Investigation rubbed the star-shaped scar on his left cheek absently. "I'm aware, sir, that the Ultras are dangerous."

The Division Head, M. T. Ashley, looked at Davenport narrowly. His gaunt cheeks were set in disapproving lines. Since he had sworn off smoking once again, he forced his groping fingers to close upon a stick of chewing gum, which he shelled, crumpled, and shoved into his mouth morosely. He was getting old, and bitter, too, and his short iron-gray mustache rasped when he rubbed his knuckles against it.

He said, "You don't know how dangerous. I wonder if anyone does. They are small in numbers, but strong among the powerful who, after all, are perfectly ready to consider themselves the elite. No one knows for certain who they are or how many."

"Not even the Bureau?"

"The Bureau is held back. We ourselves aren't free of the taint, for that matter. Are you?"

Davenport frowned. "I'm not an Ultra."

"I didn't say you were," said Ashley. "I asked if you were free of the taint? Have you considered what's been happening to the Earth in the last two centuries? Has it never occurred to you that a moderate decline in population would be a good thing? Have you never felt that it would be wonderful to get rid of the unintelligent, the incapable, the insensitive, and leave the rest. *I* have, damn it."

"I'm guilty of thinking that sometimes, yes. But considering something as a wish-fulfillment idea is one thing, but planning it as a practical scheme of action to be Hitlerized through is something else."

"The distance from wish to action isn't as great as you think. Convince yourself that the end is important enough, that the danger is great enough, and the means will grow increasingly less objectionable. Anyway, now that the Istanbul matter is taken care of, let me bring you up to date on this matter. Istanbul was of no importance in comparison— Do you know Agent Ferrant?"

"The one who's disappeared?— Not personally."

"Well, two months ago, a stranded ship was located on the Moon's surface. It had been conducting a privately-financed selenographic survey. The Russo-American Geological Society, which had sponsored the flight, reported the ship's failure to report. A routine search located it without much trouble within a reasonable distance of the site from which it made its last report.

"The ship was not damaged but its skim-boat was gone and with it one member of the crew. Name—Karl Jennings. The other man, James Strauss, was alive but in delirium. There was no sign of physical damage to Strauss, but he was quite insane. He still is, and that's important."

"Why?" put in Davenport.

"Because the medical team that investigated him reported neurochemical and neuroelectrical abnormalities of unprecedented nature. They'd never seen a case like it. Nothing human could have brought it about."

A flicker of a smile crossed Davenport's solemn face. "You suspect extraterrestrial invaders?"

"Maybe," said the other, with no smile at all. "But let me continue. A routine search in the neighborhood of the stranded ship revealed no signs of the skim-boat. Then Luna Station reported receipt of weak signals of uncertain origin. They had been tabbed as coming from the western rim of Mare Imbrium, but it was uncertain whether they were of human origin or not, and no vessel was believed to be in the vicinity. The signals had been ignored. With the skim-boat in mind, however, the search party headed out for Imbrium and located it. Jennings was aboard, dead. Knife-wound in one side; it's rather surprising he had lived as long as he did.

"Meanwhile the medicos were becoming increasingly disturbed at the nature of Strauss's babbling. They contacted the Bureau and our two men on the Moon—one of them happened to be Ferrant—arrived at the ship.

"Ferrant studied the tape-recordings of the babblings. There was no point in asking questions, for there was, and is, no way of reaching Strauss. There is a high wall between the universe and himself, probably a permanent one. However, the talk in delirium, although heavily repetitious and disjointed, can be made to make sense. Ferrant put it together like a jigsaw puzzle.

"Apparently, Strauss and Jennings had come across an object of some sort which they took to be of ancient and non-human manufacture, an artifact of some ship wrecked eons ago. Apparently, it could somehow be made to twist the human mind."

Davenport interrupted. "And it twisted Strauss's mind? Is that it?"

"That's exactly it. Strauss was an Ultra—we can say 'was' for he's only technically alive—and Jennings did not wish to surrender the object. Quite right, too. Strauss babbled of using it to bring about the self-liquidation, as he called it, of the undesirable. He wanted a final, ideal population of five million. There was a fight in which only Jennings, apparently, could handle the mind-thing, but in which Strauss had a knife. When Jennings left, he was knifed, but Strauss's mind had been destroyed."

"And where was the mind-thing?"

"Agent Ferrant acted decisively. He searched the ship and the surroundings again. There was no sign of anything that was neither a natural Lunar formation nor an obvious product of human technology. There was nothing that could be the mind-thing. He then searched the skim-boat and its surroundings. Again nothing."

"Could the first search team, the ones who suspected nothing— Could they have carried something off?"

"They swore they did not, and there is no reason to suspect them of lying. Then Ferrant's partner—"

"Who was he?"

"Gorbansky," said the District Head.

"I know him. We've worked together."

"I know you have. What do you think of him?"

"Capable and honest."

"All right. Gorbansky found something. Not an alien arti-fact, rather something most routinely human indeed. It was an ordinary white three-by-five card with writing on it, spindled, and in the middle finger of the right gauntlet. Presumably, Jennings had written it before his death and, also presumably, it represented the key to where he had hidden the object."

"What reason is there to think he had hidden it?"

"I said we had found it nowhere."

"I mean, what if he had destroyed it, as something too dangerous to leave intact."

"That's highly doubtful. If we accept the conversation as reconstructed from Strauss's ravings—and Ferrant built up what seems a tight word-for-word record of it—Jennings thought the mind-thing to be of key importance to humanity. He called it 'the clue to an unimaginable scientific revolu-tion.' He wouldn't destroy something like that. He would merely hide it from the Ultras and try to report its where-abouts to the government. Else why leave a clue to its where-abouts?"

Davenport shook his head, "You're arguing in a circle, chief. You say he left a clue because you think there is a hidden object, and you think there is a hidden object be-cause he left a clue."

"I admit that. Everything is dubious. Is Strauss's delirium meaningful? Is Ferrant's reconstruction valid? Is Jennings's clue really a clue? Is there a mind-thing, or a Device, as Jennings called it, or isn't there? There's no use asking such questions. Right now, we must act on the assumption that there is such a Device and that it must be found."

"Because Ferrant disappeared?"

"Exactly."

"Kidnapped by the Ultras?"

"Not at all. The card disappeared with him."

"Oh— I see."

"Ferrant has been under suspicion for a long time as a secret Ultra. He's not the only one in the Bureau under suspicion either. The evidence didn't warrant open action; we can't simply lay about on pure suspicion, you know, or we'll gut the Bureau from top to bottom. He was under surveillance."

"By whom?"

"By Gorbansky, of course. Fortunately, Gorbansky had filmed the card and sent the reproduction to the headquarters on Earth, but he admits he considered it as nothing more than a puzzling object and included it in the information sent to Earth only out of a desire to be routinely complete. Ferrant—the better mind of the two, I suppose —did see the significance and took action. He did so at great cost for he has given himself away and has destroyed his future usefulness to the Ultras, but there is a chance that there will be no need for the future usefulness. If the Ultras control the Device—"

"Perhaps Ferrant has the Device already."

"He was under surveillance, remember. Gorbansky swears the Device did not turn up anywhere."

"Gorbansky did not manage to stop Ferrant from leaving with the card. Perhaps he did not manage to stop him from obtaining the Device unnoticed, either."

Ashley tapped his fingers on the desk between them in an uneasy and uneven rhythm. He said at last, "I don't want to think that. If we find Ferrant, we may find out how much damage he's done. Till then, we must search for the Device. If Jennings hid it, he must have tried to get away from the hiding place. Else why leave a clue. It wouldn't be found in the vicinity."

"He might not have lived long enough to get away."

Again Ashley tapped, "The skim-boat showed signs of having engaged in a long, speedy flight and had all but crashed at the end. That is consistent with the view that Jennings was trying to place as much space as possible between himself and some hiding place."

"Can you tell from what direction he came?"

"Yes, but that's not likely to help. From the condition of the side vents, he had been deliberately tacking and veering."

Davenport sighed. "I suppose you have a copy of the card with you."

"I do. Here it is." He flipped a three-by-five replica toward Davenport. Davenport studied it for a few moments.

Davenport said, "I don't see any significance here."

"Neither did I, at first, nor did those I first consulted. But consider. Jennings must have thought that Strauss was in pursuit; he might not have known that Strauss had been put out of action, at least, not permanently. He was deadly afraid, then, that an Ultra would find him before a Moderate would. He dared not leave a clue too open. This," and the Division Head tapped the reproduction, "must represent a clue that is opaque on the surface but clear enough to anyone sufficiently ingenious."

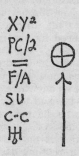

"Can we rely on that?" asked Davenport doubtfully. "After all, he was a dying, frightened man, who might have been subjected to this mind-altering object himself. He need not have been thinking clearly, or even humanly. For instance, why didn't he make an effort to reach Lunar Station? He ended half a circumference away almost. Was he too twisted to think clearly? Too paranoid to trust even the Station?— Yet he must have tried to reach them at first since they picked up signals. What I'm saying is that this card, which looks as though it is covered with gibberish, *is* covered with gibberish."

Ashley shook his head solemnly from side to side, like a tolling bell. "He was in panic, yes. And I suppose he lacked the presence of mind to try to reach Lunar Station. Only the need to run and escape possessed him. Even so this can't be gibberish. It hangs together too well. Every notation on the card can be made to make sense, and the whole can be made to hang together."

"Where's the sense, then?" asked Davenport.

"You'll notice that there are seven items on the left side

and two on the right. Consider the left-hand side first. The third one down looks like an equals sign. Does an equals sign mean anything to you, anything in particular?"

"An algebraic equation."

"That's general. Anything particular?"

"No."

"Suppose you consider it as a pair of parallel lines?"

"Euclid's fifth postulate?" suggested Davenport, groping.

"Good! There is a crater called Euclides on the Moon— the Greek name of the mathematician we call Euclid."

Davenport nodded. "I see your drift. As for F/A, that's force divided by acceleration, the definition of mass by Newton's second law of motion—"

"Yes, and there is a crater called Newton on the Moon also."

"Yes, but wait a while, the lowermost item is the astronomic symbol for the planet Uranus, and there is certainly no crater—or any other lunar object, so far as I know— that is named Uranus."

"You're right there. But Uranus was discovered by William Herschel, and the H that makes up part of the astronomic symbol is the initial of his name. As it happens there is a crater named Herschel on the Moon—three of them, in fact, since one is named for Caroline Herschel, his sister and another for John Herschel, his son."

Davenport thought a while, then said, "PC/2— Pressure times half the speed of light. I'm not familiar with that equation."

"Try craters. Try P for Ptolemaeus and C for Copernicus."

"And strike an average? Would that signify a spot exactly between Ptolemaeus and Copernicus?"

"I'm disappointed, Davenport," said Ashley sardonically. "I thought you knew your history of astronomy better than that. Ptolemy, or Ptolemaeus in Latin, presented a geocentric picture of the Solar system with the Earth at the center, while Copernicus presented a heliocentric one with the Sun at the center. One astronomer attempted a compromise, a picture halfway between that of Ptolemy and Copernicus—"

"Tycho Brahe!" said Davenport.

"Right. And the crater Tycho is the most conspicuous feature on the Moon's surface."

"All right. Let's take the rest. The C-C is a common way of writing a common type of chemical bond, and I think there is a crater named Bond."

"Yes, named for an American astronomer, W. C. Bond."

"The item on top, XY². Hmm. XYY. An X and two Y's. Wait! Alfonso X. He was the royal astronomer in medieval Spain who was called Alfonso the Wise. X the Wise. XYY. The crater Alphonsus."

"Very good. What's SU?"

"That stumps me, chief."

"I'll tell you one theory. It stands for Soviet Union, the old name for the Russian Region. It was the Soviet Union that first mapped the other side of the Moon, and maybe it's a crater there. Tsiolkovsky, for instance— You see, then, the symbols on the left can each be interpreted as standing for a crater: Alphonsus, Tycho, Euclides, Newton, Tsiolkovsky, Bond, Herschel."

"What about the symbols on the right-hand side?"

"That's perfectly transparent. The quartered circle is the astronomic symbol for the Earth. An arrow pointing to it indicates that the Earth must be directly overhead."

"Ah," said Davenport, "the Sinus Medii—the Middle Bay—over which the Earth is perpetually at Zenith. That's not a crater, so it's on the right-hand side, away from the other symbols."

"All right," said Ashley. "The notations all make sense, or they can be made to make sense, so there's at least a good chance that this isn't gibberish and that it is trying to tell us something. But what. So far we've got seven craters and a non-crater mentioned, and what does that mean. Presumably, the Device can only be in one place."

"Well," said Davenport heavily, "a crater can be a huge place to search. Even if we assume he hugged the shadow to avoid Solar radiation, there can be dozens of miles to examine in each case. Suppose the arrow pointing to the symbol for the Earth defines the crater where he hid the Device, the place from which the Earth can be seen nearest the zenith."

"That's been thought of, old man. It cuts out one place and leaves us with seven pin-pointed craters, the southernmost extremity of those north of the Lunar equator and the northernmost extremity of those south. But which of the seven?"

Davenport was frowning. So far, he hadn't thought of anything that hadn't already been thought of. "Search them all," he said brusquely.

Ashley crackled into brief laughter. "In the weeks since this has all come up, we've done exactly that."

"And what have you found?"

"Nothing. We haven't found a thing. We're still looking, though."

"Obviously one of the symbols isn't interpreted correctly."

"Obviously!"

"You said yourself there were three craters named Herschel. The symbol SU, if it means the Soviet Union and therefore the other side of the Moon, can stand for any crater on the other side: Lomonosov, Jules Verne, Joliot-Curie, any of them. For that matter the symbol of the Earth might stand for the crater Altas since he is pictured as supporting the Earth in some versions of the myth. The arrow might stand for the Straight Wall."

"There's no argument there, Davenport. But even if we get the right interpretation for the right symbol, how do we recognize it from among all the wrong interpretations, or from among the right interpretations of the wrong symbols? Somehow there's got to be something that leaps up at us from this card and gives us so clear a piece of information that we can tell it at once as the real thing from among all the red herrings. We've all failed and we need a fresh mind, Davenport. What do you see here?"

"I'll tell you one thing we could do," said Davenport reluctantly. "We can consult someone I— Oh, my God!" He half rose.

Ashley was all controlled excitement at once, "What do you see?"

Davenport could feel his hand trembling. He hoped his lips weren't. He said, "Tell me, have you checked on Jennings' past life?"

"Of course."

"Where did he go to college?"

"Eastern University."

A pang of joy shot through Davenport, but he held on.

87

That was not enough. "Did he take a course in extraterrology?"

"Of course, he did. That's routine for a geology major."

"All right, then, don't you know who teaches extraterrology at Eastern University?"

Ashley snapped his fingers. "That oddball, What's-his-name—Wendell Urth."

"Exactly, an oddball who is a brilliant man in his way. An oddball who's acted as a consultant for the Bureau on several occasions and given perfect satisfaction every time. An oddball I was going to suggest we consult this time and then noticed that this card was *telling* us to do so— An arrow pointing to the symbol for the Earth. A rebus that couldn't mean more clearly 'Go to Urth,' written by a man who was once a student of Urth and would know him."

Ashley stared at the card, "By God, it's possible— But what could Urth tell us about the card that we can't see for ourselves?"

Davenport said, with polite patience, "I suggest we ask him, sir."

III

Ashley looked about curiously, half wincing as he turned from one direction to another. He felt as though he had found himself in some arcane curiosity shop, darkened and dangerous, from which at any moment some demon might hurtle forth squealing.

The lighting was poor and the shadows many. The walls seemed distant, and dismally alive with book-films from floor to ceiling. There was a Galactic lens in soft three-dimensionality in one corner and behind it were star charts that could dimly be made out. A map of the Moon in another corner might, however, possibly be a map of Mars.

Only the desk in the center of the room was brilliantly lit by a tight-beamed lamp. It was littered with papers and opened printed books. A small viewer was threaded with film, and a clock with an old-fashioned round-faced dial hummed with subdued merriment.

Ashley found himself unable to recall that it was late afternoon outside and that the sun was quite definitely in the sky. Here, within, was a place of eternal night. There was no sign of any window, and the clear presence of circulating air did not spare him a claustrophobic sensation.

He found himself moving closer to Davenport, who seemed insensible to the unpleasantness of the situation.

Davenport said in a low voice, "He'll be here in a moment, sir."

"Is it always like this?" asked Ashley.

"Always. He never leaves this place, as far as I know, except to trot across the campus and attend his classes."

"Gentlemen! Gentlemen!" came a reedy, tenor voice. "I am so glad to see you. It is good of you to come."

A round figure of a man bustled in from another room, shedding shadow and emerging into the light.

He beamed at them, adjusting round, thick-lensed glasses upward so that he might look through them. As his fingers moved away, the glasses slipped downward at once to a precarious perch upon the round nubbin of his snub nose. "I am Wendell Urth," he said.

The scraggly gray Van Dyke on his pudgy, round chin did not in the least add to the dignity which the smiling face and the stubby ellipsoidal torso so noticeably lacked.

"Gentlemen! It is good of you to come," Urth repeated, as he jerked himself backward into a chair from which his legs dangled with the toes of his shoes a full inch above the floor. "Mr. Davenport remembers, perhaps, that it is a matter of—uh—some importance to me to remain here. I do not like to travel, except to walk, of course, and a walk across the campus is quite enough for me."

Ashley looked baffled as he remained standing, and Urth stared at him with a growing bafflement of his own. He pulled a handkerchief out and wiped his glasses, then replaced them, and said, "Oh, I see the difficulty. You want chairs. Yes. Well, just take some. If there are things on them, just push them off. Push them off. Sit down, please."

Davenport removed the books from one chair and placed them carefully on the floor. He pushed it toward Ashley, then took a human skull off a second chair and placed it even more carefully on Urth's desk. Its mandible, insecurely wired, unhinged as he transferred it, and it sat there with jaw askew.

"Never mind," said Urth, affably, "it will not hurt. Now tell me what is on your mind, gentlemen?"

Davenport waited a moment for Ashley to speak then, rather gladly, took over. "Dr. Urth, do you remember a student of yours named Jennings? Karl Jennings?"

Urth's smile vanished momentarily with the effort of recall. His somewhat protuberant eyes blinked. "No," he said at last. "Not at the moment."

"A geology major. He took your extraterrology course some years ago. I have his photograph here if that will help—"

Urth studied the photograph handed him with nearsighted concentration, but still looked doubtful.

Davenport drove on. "He left a cryptic message which is the key to a matter of great importance. We have so far failed to interpret it satisfactorily, but this much we see— it indicates we are to come to you."

"Indeed? How interesting! For what purpose are you to come to me?"

"Presumably for your advice on interpreting the message."

"May I see it?"

Silently, Ashley passed the slip of paper to Wendell Urth. The extraterrologist looked at it casually, turned it over and stared for a moment at the blank back. He said, "Where does it say to ask me?"

Ashley looked startled, but Davenport forestalled him by saying, "The arrow pointing to the symbol of the Earth. It seems clear."

"It is clearly an arrow pointing to the symbol for the planet Earth. I suppose it might literally mean 'go to the Earth' if this were found on some other world."

"It was found on the Moon, Dr. Urth, and it could, I suppose, mean that. However, the reference to you seemed clear once we realized that Jennings had been a student of yours."

"He took a course in extraterrology here at the University?"

"That's right."

"In what year, Mr. Davenport?"

"In '18."

"Ah. The puzzle is solved."

"You mean the significance of the message?" said Davenport.

"No, no. The message has no meaning to me. I mean the puzzle of why it is that I did not remember him, for I remember him now. He was a very quiet fellow, anxious, shy, self-effacing—not at all the sort of person anyone would remember. Without this," and he tapped the message, "I might never have remembered him."

"Why does the card change things?" asked Davenport.

"The reference to me is a play on words. Earth—Urth. Not very subtle, of course, but that is Jennings. His unattainable delight was the pun. My only clear memory of him is his occasional attempts to perpetrate puns. I enjoy puns, I adore puns, but Jennings—yes, I remember him well now—was atrocious at it. Either that, or distressingly obvious at it, as in this case. He lacked all talent for puns, yet craved them so much."

Ashley suddenly broke in. "This message consists entirely of a kind of word-play, Dr. Urth. At least, we believe so, and that fits in with what you say."

"Ah!" Urth adjusted his glasses and peered through them once more at the card and the symbols it carried. He pursed his plump lips then said cheerfully, "I make nothing of it."

"In that case—" began Ashley, his hands balling into fists.

"But if you tell me what it's all about," Urth went on, "then perhaps it might mean something."

Davenport said quickly, "May I, sir? I am confident that this man can be relied on—and it may help."

"Go ahead," muttered Ashley, "at this point, what can it hurt?"

Davenport condensed the tale, giving it in crisp, telegraphic sentences, while Urth listened carefully, moving his stubby fingers over the shining milk-white desk top as though he were sweeping up invisible cigar ashes. Toward the end of the recital, he hitched up his legs and sat with them crossed like an amiable Buddha.

When Davenport was done, Urth thought a moment, then

said, "Do you happen to have a transcript of the conversation reconstructed by Ferrant?"

"We do," said Davenport. "Would you like to see it?"

"Please."

Urth placed the strip of microfilm in a scanner and worked his way rapidly through it, his lips moving unintelligibly at some points. Then he tapped the reproduction of the cryptic message. "And this, you say, is the key to the entire matter? The crucial clue?"

"We think it is, Dr. Urth."

"But it is not the original. It is the reproduction."

"That is correct."

"The original has gone with this man, Ferrant, and you believe it to be in the hands of the Ultras."

"Quite possibly."

Urth shook his head and looked troubled. "Everyone knows my sympathies are not with the Ultras. I would fight them by all means, so I don't want to seem to be hanging back, but— What is there to say that this mind-affecting object exists at all? You have only the ravings of a psychotic and your dubious deductions from the reproduction of a mysterious set of marks that may mean nothing at all."

"Yes, Dr. Urth, but we can't take chances."

"How certain are you that this copy is accurate? What if the original has something on it that this lacks, something that makes the message quite clear, something without which the message must remain impenetrable."

"We are certain the copy is accurate."

"What about the reverse side? There is nothing on the back of this reproduction. What about the reverse of the original?"

"The agent who made the reproduction tells us that the back of the original was blank."

"Men can make mistakes."

"We have no reason to think he did, and we must work on the assumption that he didn't. At least until such time as the original is regained."

"Then you assure me," said Urth, "that any interpretation to be made of this message must be made on the basis of exactly what one sees here."

"We think so. We are virtually certain," said Davenport, with a sense of ebbing confidence.

Urth continued to look troubled. He said, "Why not leave the instrument where it is? If neither group finds it, so much the better. I disapprove of any tampering with minds and would not contribute to making it possible."

Davenport placed a restraining hand on Ashley's arm, sensing the other was about to speak. Davenport said, "Let me put it to you, Dr. Urth, that the mind-tampering aspect is not the whole of the Device. Suppose an Earth expedition to a distant primitive planet had dropped an old-fashioned radio there, and suppose the native population had discovered electric current but had not yet developed the vacuum tube.

"The population might discover that if the radio was hooked up to a current, certain glass objects within it would grow warm and would glow, but of course they would receive no intelligible sound, merely, at best, some buzzes and crackles. However, if they dropped the radio into a bathtub while it was plugged in, a person in that tub might be electrocuted. Should the people of this hypothetical planet therefore conclude that the device they were studying was designed solely for the purpose of killing people?"

"I see your analogy," said Urth. "You think that the mind-tampering property is merely an incidental function of the Device?"

"I'm sure of it," said Davenport earnestly. "If we can puzzle out its real purpose, earthly technology may leap ahead centuries."

"Then you agree with Jennings when he said—" Here Urth consulted the microfilm—" 'It might be the key to—who knows what? It might be the clue to an unimaginable scientific revolution.' "

"Exactly!"

"And yet the mind-tampering aspect is there and is infinitely dangerous. Whatever the radio's purpose, it *does* electrocute."

"Which is why we can't let the Ultras get it."

"Or the government either, perhaps?"

"But I must point out that there is a reasonable limit to caution. Consider that men have always held danger in their hands. The first flint knife in the old Stone Age, the first wooden club before that could kill. They could be used to bend weaker men to the will of stronger ones under threat of force and that, too, is a form of mind-tampering. What counts, Dr. Urth, is not the device itself, however dangerous it may be in the abstract, but the intentions of the men who make use of the Device. The Ultras have the declared intention of killing off more than 99.9 percent of humanity. The government, whatever the faults of the men composing it, would have no such intention."

"What *would* the government intend?"

"A scientific study of the Device. Even the mind-tampering aspect itself could yield infinite good. Put to enlightened use, it could educate us concerning the physical basis of mental function. We might learn to correct mental disorders or cure the Ultras. Mankind might learn to develop greater intelligence generally."

"How can I believe that such idealism will be put into practice?"

"*I* believe so. Consider that you face a possible turn to evil by the government if you help us, but you risk the certain and declared evil purpose of the Ultras if you don't."

Urth nodded thoughtfully. "Perhaps you're right. And yet I have a favor to ask of you. I have a niece who is, I believe, quite fond of me. She is constantly upset over the fact that I steadfastly refuse to indulge in the lunacy of travel. She states that she will not rest content until someday I accompany her to Europe or North Carolina or some other outlandish place—"

Ashley leaned forward earnestly, brushing Davenport's restraining gesture to one side. "Dr. Urth, if you help us find the Device and if it can be made to work, then I assure you that we will be glad to help you free yourself of your phobia against travel and make it possible for you to go with your niece anywhere you wish."

Urth's bulging eyes widened and he seemed to shrink within himself. For a moment, he looked wildly about as though he were already trapped. "*No!*" he gasped. "Not at all! Never!"

His voice dropped to an earnest, hoarse whisper. "Let me explain the nature of my fee. If I help you, if you retrieve the Device and learn its use, if the fact of my help becomes public, then my niece will be on the government like a fury. She is a terribly headstrong and shrill-voiced woman who will raise public subscriptions and organize demonstrations. She will stop at nothing. And yet you must not give in to her. You must *not!* You must resist all pressures. I wish to be left alone exactly as I am now. That is my absolute and minimum fee."

Ashley flushed. "Yes, of course, since that is your wish."

"I have your word?"

"You have my word."

"Please remember— I rely on you, too, Mr. Davenport."

"It will be as you wish," soothed Davenport. "And now, I presume, you can interpret the items?"

"The items?" asked Urth, seeming to focus his attention with difficulty on the card. "You mean these markings, XY^2 and so on?"

"Yes. What do they mean?"

"I don't know. Your interpretations are as good as any I suppose."

Ashley exploded. "Do you mean that all this talk about helping us is nonsense? What was this maundering about a fee, then?"

Wendell Urth looked confused and taken aback. "I would like to help you."

"But you don't know what these items mean."

"I—I don't. But I know what this message means."

"You do?" cried Davenport.

"Of course. Its meaning is transparent. I suspected it half way through your story. And I was sure of it once I read the reconstruction of the conversations between Strauss and Jennings. You would understand it yourself, gentlemen, if you would only stop to think."

"See here," said Ashley in exasperation. "You said you don't know what the items mean."

"I don't. I said I know what the *message* means."

"What is the message if it is not the items? Is it the paper, for Heaven's sake?"

"Yes, in a way."

"You mean invisible ink or something like that?"

"No! Why is it so hard for you to understand, when you yourself stand on the brink?"

Davenport leaned toward Ashley and said in a low voice, "Sir, if you'll let me handle it, please?"

Ashley snorted, then said in a stifled manner. "Go ahead."

ISAAC ASIMOV

"Dr. Urth," said Davenport, "will you give us your analysis?"

"Ah! Well, all right." The little extraterrologist settled back in his chair and mopped his damp forehead on his sleeve. "Let's consider the message. If you accept the quartered circle and the arrow as directing you to me, that leaves seven items. If these indeed refer to seven craters, six of them, at least, must be designed merely to distract, since the Device surely cannot be in more than one place. It contained no movable or detachable parts—it was all one piece.

"Then, too, none of the items are straightforward. SU might, by your interpretation, mean any place on the other side of the Moon, which is an area the size of South America. Again PC/2 can mean 'Tycho,' as Mr. Ashley says, or it can mean 'halfway between Ptolemaeus and Copernicus,' as Mr. Davenport thought, or for that matter 'halfway between Plato and Cassini.' To be sure, XY² could mean 'Alfonsus'—very ingenious interpretation, that—but it could refer to some coordinate system in which the Y-coordinate was the square of the X-coordinate. Similarly C-C would mean 'Bond' or it could mean 'halfway betweeen Cassini and Copernicus.' F/A could mean 'Newton' or it could mean 'between Fabricius and Archimedes.'

"In short, the items have so many meanings that they are meaningless. Even if one of them had meaning, it could not be selected from among the others so that it is only sensible to suppose that all the items are merely red herrings.

"It is necessary, then, to determine what about the message is completely unambiguous; what is perfectly clear. The answer to that can only be that it *is* a message; that it *is* a clue to a hiding place. That is the one thing we are certain about, isn't it?"

Davenport nodded, then said cautiously, "At least, we think we are certain of it."

"Well, you have referred to this message as the key to the whole matter. You have acted as though it were the crucial clue. Jennings himself referred to the device as a key or a clue. If we combine this serious view of the matter with Jennings' penchant for puns, a penchant which may have been heightened by the mind-tampering Device he was carrying— So let me tell you a story—

96

"In the last half of the sixteenth century, there lived a German Jesuit in Rome. He was a mathematician and astronomer of note and helped Pope Gregory XIII reform the calender in 1582, performing all the enormous calculations required. This astronomer admired Copernicus but he did not accept the heliocentric view of the Solar system. He clung to the older belief that the Earth was the center of the Universe.

"In 1650, nearly forty years after the death of this mathematician, the Moon was mapped by another Jesuit, the Italian astronomer, Giovanni Battista Riccioli. He named the craters after astronomers of the past and since he, too, rejected Copernicus, he selected the largest and most spectacular craters for those who placed the Earth at the center of the Universe—for Ptolemy, Hipparchus, Alfonso X, Tycho Brahe. The biggest crater Riccioli could find he reserved for his German Jesuit predecessor.

"This crater is actually only the second largest of the craters visible from Earth. The only larger crater is Bailly, which is right on the Moon's limb and is therefore very difficult to see from the Earth. Riccioli ignored it, and it was named for an astronomer who lived a century after his time and who was guillotined during the French Revolution."

Ashley was listening to all this restlessly. "But what has this to do with the message?"

"Why, everything," said Urth, with some surprise. "Did you not call this message the key to the whole business? Isn't it the crucial clue?"

"Yes, of course."

"Is there any doubt that we are dealing with something that is a clue or key to something else?"

"No, there isn't," said Ashley.

"Well, then— The name of the German Jesuit I have been speaking of is Christoph Klau—pronounced 'klow.' Don't you see the pun? Klau—clue?"

Ashley's entire body seemed to grow flabby with disappointment. "Far-fetched," he muttered.

Davenport said, anxiously, "Dr. Urth. There is no feature on the Moon named Klau as far as I know."

"Of course not," said Urth excitedly. "That is the whole point. At this period of history, the last half of the sixteenth century, European scholars were Latinizing their names. Klau did so. In place of the German 'u,' he made use of the equivalent letter, the Latin 'v.' He then added an 'ius' ending typical of Latin names and Christoph Klau became Christopher Clavius, and I suppose you are all aware of the giant crater we call Clavius."

"But—" began Davenport.

"Don't 'but' me," said Urth. "Just let me point out that the Latin word 'clavis' means 'key.' *Now* do you see the double and bilingual pun? Klau—clue, Clavius—clavis—key. In his whole life, Jennings could never have made a double, bilingual pun without the Device. Now he could, and I wonder if death might not have been almost triumphant under the circumstances. And he directed you to me because he knew I would remember his penchant for puns and because he knew I loved them too."

The two men of the Bureau were looking at him wide-eyed.

Urth said solemnly, "I would suggest you search the shaded rim of Clavius, at that point where the Earth is nearest the zenith."

Ashley rose. "Where is your videophone?"

"In the next room."

Ashley dashed. Davenport lingered behind. "Are you sure, Dr. Urth?"

"Quite sure. But even if I am wrong, I suspect it doesn't matter."

"What doesn't matter?"

"Whether you find it or not. For if the Ultras find the Device, they will probably be unable to use it."

"Why do you say that?"

"You asked me if Jennings had ever been a student of mine, but you never asked me about Strauss, who was also a geologist. He was a student of mine a year or so after Jennings. I remember him well."

"Oh?"

"An unpleasant man. Very cold. It is the hallmark of the Ultras, I think. They are all very cold, very rigid, very sure of themselves. They can't empathize, or they wouldn't speak of killing off billions of human beings. What emotions they possess are icy ones, self-absorbed ones, feelings incapable of spanning the distance between two human beings."

"I think I see."

"I'm sure you do. The conversation reconstructed from Strauss's ravings showed us he could not manipulate the Device. He lacked the emotional intensity, or the type of necessary emotion. I imagine all Ultras would. Jennings, who was not an Ultra, could manipulate it. Anyone who could use the Device would, I suspect, be incapable of deliberate cold-blooded cruelty. He might strike out of panic fear as Jennings struck at Strauss, but never out of calculation, as Strauss tried to strike at Jennings— In short, to put it tritely, I think the Device can be actuated by love, but never by hate, and the Ultras are nothing if not haters."

Davenport nodded. "I hope you're right. But then—why were you so suspicious of the government's motives, if you felt the wrong men could not manipulate the Device?"

Urth shrugged. "I wanted to make sure you could bluff and rationalize on your feet and make yourself convincingly persuasive at a moment's notice. After all, you may have to face my niece."

Mose Mallette is twenty-six, married, lives in Atlanta, attended MIT, University of Chattanooga, Georgia State College and was once a fallout shelter analyst for Civil Defense. He calls his dizzying view of the universe(s) " 'Galactic' humor because, whether limited to our galaxy or not, the action is always galloping through a stretch of space vaster than the solar system, and the unexpected bursts in through four or more dimensions." A good description and a good story.

THE SEVEN WONDERS OF THE UNIVERSE

by Mose Mallette

Early in the Centuries of Inanity, Professor D. K. G. Plockett announced, on the basis of his study of sacred chickens, in which he had deep knowledge, that the radius of the universe was 50 billion light-years. Newspapermen then had to spend thousands of words explaining that Dr. Plockett did not mean that a brick wall stopped you after traveling 50 billion light-years, but merely that the curvature of space could be represented by that figure. Shortly after this, the great cruiser, *Entropy At Last,* using the newly perfected Cherry-Pit Drive* to push back the frontiers of explored space, smashed bow foremost into what appeared to be a brick wall, of considerable extent, about 50 billion light-years from the Central Suns. Masons, rushed to the disaster scene, shook their heads sadly at the wall's obviously bad construction. Dr. Plockett retired into the Sacred Henhouse and refused to comment. Curiosity-seekers placed their ears against the wall's numerous cracks and claimed to hear

* *Trans. note.* This depends on viewing the universe as an infinite pit surrounded by a finite cherry.

sounds of a large party in progress on the other side. It was plain that our ideas about the "universe" were going to have to be revised. Cosmography got organized again after regular communication with the other universes was established, which followed quickly on the exchange, through one of the larger cracks, of a dry martini for the delightful beverage known as *swizz*.

Such was our introduction to that greatest arena of anxiety, the society of universes. After the customary six months of "initiation" war, designed to see if we could take care of ourselves in the usual border conflicts, we were accepted as a member in good standing. As civilization crawled back from the Stone Age on a million planets, an enlightened business leadership arose, looked about itself, and asked, "Where are the tourists?" Meaning, of course, the tourists we had fully expected from the other universes. But the tourists had come, had found Alligator Wrestling and Historic Birthplaces, had known horror, and had gone.

To entice them back, local businessmen decided to choose seven outstanding curiosities and promote them intensely—seven, because certain old legends spoke of an original Seven Wonders, such things as the Hanging Clotheslines of Brooklyn, the Whorehouse of Alexandria, the Mausoleum of the Empire State Building, and others yet more obscure. In the beginning some bad choices were made—the Thing That Grows never should have been exhibited, and hurt business a lot until messages stopped coming from that galaxy. And the Cosmic Drain and the Clusters of Madness both set off an unexpected amount of panic. But finally, after years of alternation between dullness and disaster, the present Seven emerged, the equals, we believe, of any wonders anywhere in the known plenum. The final line-up, as given in the authoritative *Dictionary for Dort-Worshipers* (Vertebrates' Edition) is as follows:

1. The University of Lesser Balak
2. The Copulation Pits of Venus (eastern section)
3. The Great Bearded Kumquat of Lagesh
4. The Copulation Pits of Venus (western section)
5. The Brass Nodes of the Universe
6. The Copulation Pits of Venus (middle section)
7. The Crystals of Lalande

(Some people have said that this choice of wonders places too much emphasis on sex. But in truth the emphasis is merely on copulation, which, as Herzenstube the Depraved has repeatedly testified*, is altogether different, and in any case admits of more variety.)

Probably the event that did more than any other to bring our Seven Wonders to plenum prominence was the epic series done on them by the magazine *Ylem*. Hours after the first issue hit the stands, travel bureaus, churches, and bars were besieged by an aroused public. Many were the attempts to explain those days of militant tourism on psychological and other grounds, but I think we need look no further than the Wonders themselves. Read now excerpts from the text of *Ylem's* classic articles†, and judge for yourself . . .

THE UNIVERSITY OF
LESSER BALAK

Lesser Balak is a bleak, smallish mass of dead rock revolving, from time to time, around Greater Balak, a bleak, smallish mass of dead rock, of, however, somewhat larger dimension than Lesser Balak. Or so it is believed. Landings on the two Balaks are recorded as early as the 14th Pelargonium, although it was not until three hundred years later that the system came to cosmos-wide prominence when Dr. Loup-Garou established his "health institute" there. Crust analysis by Moldewy shows the usual amounts of the lighter elements, anomalous concentrations of lutetium, erbium, and astatine, and a trace of that still unidentified substance that had such an unhappy effect on Moldewy. However, all this is quite irrelevant, since the University of Lesser Balak

* See, for example, Herzenstube vs. Metagalaxy, or his books, *Some Things Worth Doing* and *God Proposes, the Id Disposes.*

† Written by the greatest and most adventurous traveler in the continuum, the Immortal Pim. (It was Pim, you'll recall, who spent seven years in the Citadel of Terror disguised as a defective vacuum cleaner.) Unfortunately, the Immortal Pim met his end last year, when, returning to his home planet, he was shot as an undesirable alien.

is not located in the Balak system and never was. The title was chosen by one of the Founding Fathers of the University, after much study of the Kako-Gastric language, for the sake of euphony. Or so it is believed.

The Lesser Balak officials, when I finally discovered the whereabouts of their university, proved most cordial and cooperative. They gave me the run of the classrooms, arranged interviews with the faculty, and domiciled me in a small steel room, into which, on my first night there, concealed jets began to pour a mixture of phosphine, arsine and hydrogen cyanide. It seemed to me they were going to a lot of trouble to provide me with the atmosphere of my native planet. Then I realized—this was a manifestation of hostility. Quickly, I reviewed the relevant passages of Pentley's *Modes of Death.* I coughed, convulsed, rigidified, and slid agonizedly to the floor. Soon blowers cleared the room and a troop of men entered. I exhaled the breath I had been holding, whereupon the men coughed, convulsed, rigidified, and slid agonizedly to the floor. I made my escape, but necessarily had learned little about the University. However, I will reproduce my few notes for readers interested in an institution for which I can feel little fondness:

This is probably an example of the famed Balak lecture-demonstration method.

The instructor began dramatically, "Why did mighty Anukabet fall? How did it go, in a single instant apparently, from the thriving capital of the Ennius sector to a heap of shards and splinters? Azelfrage didn't know, Lisspun didn't know, not even Futtermassel knew. But today, thanks to the Noncebottle of Professor Sebub, we are going to find out. We are going to view Anukabet, from the safety of our seats, just minutes before the disaster is calculated to have occurred. Professor Sebub is shaking up the Noncebottle now, and in just a moment—ah, there it is, Anukabet in all its glory. What spires, what streets, what wise and gracious people! . . . You know, instead of just waiting and observing, I think I'll step into the Noncefield and speak to a few of the inhabitants. It would be interesting to know if they had any forebodings of the doom about to fall on them. So I'll just—"

"Professor . . ."

"Yes, Professor Sebub?"

"I don't think you undershtand vhat my Noncebottle does. There iss a mutual—"

"Oh, I can see what it does, Professor. Wonderful! Marvelous! Now if you'll just stand aside . . . There's a knowledgeable-looking gentleman walking along. Sir, sir, could you tell me—"

"Don't move!"

"What?"

"Don't move until you've seen Sally. I could tell, my good man, that you are a connoisseur of women. Sally is the girl for you. Long of leg, short of brain—and her motto is, 'Do Anything You Like and Like Anything You Do.' Sally! Here's one of your admirers!"

"But that's not—"

"Oh, a cheapskate, eh! Well, on your way, buddy, on your way."

"My goodness! I suppose a superior civilization does produce unusual tensions, but—? Well, here's someone else. Please, could you tell me—"

"Don't talk to *me!* I am a rantry-squeezer. A rantry-squeezer squeezes rantries. It is enough."

"How odd—he's running away! Frankly, students, I'm feeling a bit out of place here. I'm going to make one more attempt with this intense-looking fellow striding along toward me. Hey there, I was wondering—"

"Korec!? You dare to walk abroad! You eluded me once, but this time I, Mutagalla, will serve you well—"

"No-o! You've made a mistake! My name is William G. Frogpump, Professor of Enigmatic History at the University of—"

"Yes, Korec, you were ever one for devious mouthings. Don't look so frightened, Korec! I shall treat you honorably. I shall put your heart on my mantelpiece, where it will beat in sorrow beside that of your accursed brother. Ah, don't back away, my friend—it is too late. It was too late when you were born. Now, if you'll stand just so—yes, how very accommodating of you—"

"PROFESSOR SEBUB! ! HELP! !"

Professor Sebub rushed forward, tripped over the Noncebottle, and smashed it into shards and splinters . . .

Here are some sidelights on the only ULB faculty member I got to meet.

The students' favorite is of course colorful old Dr. Gallinule, who before coming to the University was better known as Marash the Feral, Torturer Extraordinary to the Unappeased Maw. In this latter capacity, Dr. Gallinule enjoyed a long career of public service, and the book he wrote upon his retirement, *Mind and Body—Their Weaknesses*, showed such sound scholarship and unexampled mastery of the subject that the University felt it could do no better than to have this great authority head the School of Medicine. It's hard to believe, after watching the old gentleman buckle on his galoshes, and totter leisurely across the Quad amid the bright hellos of his students, that this is the legendary figure who reduced Gron the Insensate to puling supplication, and who frustrated a germ-warfare attack by frightening away the enemy's germs. ("Fear is not a monopoly of the higher beings alone; appropriate stimuli will often rouse apprehension in the lowliest organisms," was the way Dr. Gallinule explained this latter feat.)

The ULB Library.

Undoubtedly the oddest thing about the ULB Library is that one does not consult the card catalog to find a desired book; one consults the books to find a desired catalog card. You see, what is spoken of as a "card" is actually, in most cases, an immense reference work, of much greater length and scope than the original item itself. This is because the ULB librarians do not consider a book properly catalogued until they have re-created its author's mind, noted the potentialities therein, and made an exhaustive commentary thereon. Naturally, this usually involves printing the complete text of every book which the author in question has written or will write—after which, of course, the author is apprised of his superfluity and told of the virtues of agriculture. Notwithstanding the generous land grants made available by the University, this policy has resulted in a certain amount of rancor.

Another odd thing about the ULB Library is that, unlike most university libraries, it is open to the public. However, the public never makes use of it. Nor, for that matter, do the University students. Nor the University faculty. This curious circumstance is accounted for by the fact that in the library lobby there is maintained a choice selection of time-tested pornography. Anyone is free to browse there and take any book he likes. In spite of this, no book has ever had to be replaced. "The really good books," the Director explains, "can take care of themselves." The only people who get past this psychological barrier (the others forget what they came for) are a few old scholars who never speak but occasionally exchange knowing glances. I asked the director, a man of mature but not immemorial years, how he had resisted the distraction of the pornography. "I wrote it," he said.

In view of this demonstrated broad-mindedness, I felt I could ask the Director to let me see some of the really racy items, the books that weren't displayed even in the lobby. "You'll be disappointed," he warned. "We only possess the catalog cards, and although they contain a work's total essence, and more besides, you will find them very different from what you expect." Nevertheless I persisted, and called for the card on Ho Tarkee's *How To Do with Those That Do Too*, that most degraded of all literary productions, for which Tarkee* was finally banished to the Null Class. The card was brought, and I was stunned to see that it was nothing but a little slip of white paper on which was written, "A sound mind in a sound body."

"Well, what did you expect?" the Director consoled me. "We are always interested in making a psychologically representative statement, and Tarkee was so healthy and guileless that there was nothing else to say. Now if you had called for the card on *Toby and Susie Learn about Growing Up*, you would have been brought a multi-volume treatise of such unrelieved depravity that the 300 scholars who collaborated on it voluntarily committed suicide, after their task was done, 'so that others might not be polluted,' as the epitaph has it. Frankly, though, for sheer old-fashioned smut you still can't beat Northcote's *Table of Elliptic Integrals*. But for a real tour de force of filth I recommend . . ."

THE GREAT BEARDED
KUMQUAT OF LAGESH

On the plain of Lagesh squats the Great Bearded Kum-

* Also the author of *Pleasures That Can Only Be Experienced Once.*

quat. ("Gah! Bearded! Disgusting!" was heard on all sides.)
The Great Bearded Kumquat answers any questions that
visitors are imprudent enough to put to it. Some fault has
been found with these answers, but the Great Bearded Kumquat never has found any fault with its visitors, whom it
pronounces "uniformly delicious."

THE BRASS NODES OF
THE UNIVERSE

The wonder about the Brass Nodes isn't the Nodes; it's
that anybody goes to see them. They're housed in a big
canvas tent, right between the All-Night Revival and the
Mad Caterpillar. Inside there's nothing but these two big
brass cylinders hanging in the air. People come up, and pat
them, and gawk at them, and then kind of sheepishly make
their way to the refreshment stand, as though they realized
they'd been taken, which of course they have been. Occasionally some old prophet will flop on his feet before them,
and confess his sins, or somebody else's, or swear eternal
obedience to the Nodes, and promise to preach their message through all the starways. But about this time it dawns
on the old geezer, what *is* their message, anyway? and he
ends up at the refreshment stand, looking more sheepish
than most.

THE CRYSTALS
OF LALANDE

The Crystals of Lalande seem to have been the outcome,
according to the histories that have survived from those
sunless days, of the encounter between the Ultimate Tor-
pidity and the Boundless Potency. The ensuing necrona
produced a number of grievous artifacts, among them the
Crystals. If skillfully tickled, the Crystals apparently have
the property of answering any question whatsoever, though
always with the greater or lesser derangement to the ques-
tioner's nervous system. If unskillfully tickled, they do their
will, and on this even the Nodar are silent. It is sufficient
to cite the case of Captain Weatherby, their discoverer, who,
mistaking them for the Crown Jewels of Szoloi, swept them
into his palm, clasped them avidly, fell back, screamed once

"The Others! The Others!" and immediately relapsed into that state which caused his remains to be committed to the Deeps.

THE COPULATION PITS
OF VENUS

The Pits are rectangular, square, hexagonal, spherical, hollow, solid, large, small, bright, dark, and, well—accounts differ, since those emerging from the Pits are not in an eminently coherent state. On the day I arrived, there was even more confusion than usual—a riot had broken out at the Altar to the Unknown Phallus, and a rumor was being spread that Suvallah the Chaste was due to be offered at the Eastern Pits in twenty minutes. I mingled with the crowd, refused several offers of obscure intent, and made my way to the hut of my old friend, Theodosius the Troglodyte, whose job it is to emerge every half hour, cry "Doom, Doom!" in an apocalyptic voice, and retreat into his hovel again. When I got there Theo threw down his copy of *Real Life Sex Stories* and greeted me warmly.

"Pim, how are you!"

"Oh, all right," I flapped back at him. "What's on the schedule for today?"

"Oh, the usual slack-season fillers. The All-Enfolding Node will sweep away the first lucky 900 into Pit 39, a new shipment of retired schoolteachers will be stripped, greased, and made to confront the Unmentionable, and those whose names begin with—let's see, what is it today . . . oh, yes, 'R'— will be declared Fair Game. And this evening Pilagor the Polyhedral Perverse is doing the Rape of Rome in the Arena of Lust, playing all the parts himself of course—you know how versatile Perry is."

Suvallah dropped in; she's a nice kid really, but what these slavering Terrans see in her I'll never know. Theo reminded her, "Sue, you're due to be offered up at the East Pits in a couple of minutes, better hot-foot it over there."

"Oh, damn," she groaned, "again? That's the third time today."

"Sue's getting a little snooty this season," Theo informed me after she had left. "It really went to her head when they built that 400-mile-high nude statue of her and the entire nation of Celibatia went mad from seeing it on their horizon."

"Yes," I mused, "these humanoids are frail vessels. What Arthur C. Clarke saw in them I'll never know. Thank the Pulsating Nexus that you and I were born *gnuteries,* and right-thinking *gnuteries* at that."

Since, after all, my assignment was to report on the Pits proper, I decided to stroll over that way and see as much as was safe. As I neared the entrance, that great motto, known to all space and time, glowed up over my head:

OH ! OH! OH!

Speculation on the significance of these syllables has long been rampant, but within my own lifetime Ma'avranui, keenest of all philosophers, finally thought through to their inmost meaning. I was with him at the time when, perched on the sprinkler pipe in his office, as was usual with him during deep thinking, he announced to his breathless secretary, "The motto is, obviously, a simple palilogetic formula used to indicate—" but then he lost his grip on the pipe and fell, head foremost onto his desk. After this unfortunate accident Ma'avranui showed no sign of his former near-infinite intelligence and had to take a job as slush-pusher in a slook mill. He has, I believe, made himself a modest reputation as a singer of Early Glornesian* Folk Songs, but I

* *Trans. note.* The Principate of Glornesia was discovered in the extensive stamp collection of Boyken R. Philpotts, when that famous explorer and philatelist lost his fortune and had to be put up for auction. Unfortunately Glornesia itself has never been located—Mr. Philpotts is being held incommunicado by his present owner—but the stamps themselves are so engrossing that a rich culture has sprung up around them. Not a year goes by without at least one aspiring author trying his hand at the Great Glornesian Novel, and Saviors of Glornesia declare themselves and are stoned with monotonous regularity. Illuminated volumes of Hackworth's massive *Rise and Fall of the Glornesian Principate* are to be seen in every cultivated home, and all the more patriotic history books contain a chapter on "Heroes
(footnote continued on next page)

fear that the university's Goodberry Chair will never again be so illustriously tenanted.

At the gate of the Middle Pit some sort of dispute was going on. A female humanoid was brandishing an umbrella and being told by the gatekeeper, "Lady, you can't take that thing inside"—but too late, the Handler had her, and she was pulled into the Mouth, leaving nothing behind but a long-drawn-out "Wa-alter-r-r-r," which probably has some erotic significance. But the real drama takes place at the Pits' debouchments, where a host of dazed and damaged life-forms can be found at any hour of the day. No one can pass through and be wholly unaffected. Today, picking my way carefully along the outskirts of this detritus, I sighted uncountable quivering humanoids curled into fetal balls, scores of Rhabdomanths with all hearts desynchronized, numerous Pandari showing the characteristic filigree of *wootlee*-starvation, several Hincnophores with dangerously distended norkles, and one poor Tegmite who had just turned bright blue, which means that his days of nitrogen-fixation are over. And, of course, the usual number of slumped bodies showing no response at all. What really happens to those poor creatures inside the Pits is an utter mystery. Some years ago the DVFC (Disabled Veterans of Foreign Copulation) agitated for an investigation of the subject, and government psychiatrists interviewed 42,318,204 speaking survivors of the Pits. The result was 42,318,203

(*footnote continued*)

of Old Glornesia." However, the discriminating reader will bear in mind, while enchanted by Hackworth's ponderous yet facile prose, and ravished by Finley's vaulting paeans in "Glornesia, My Glornesia"—that these and all similar works derive ultimately from but three genuine Glornesian stamps: the 1-*mufti* Rutabaga Yellow, the 2-*mufti* Peat Moss Green, and the many-*mufti* Bog Slime Gray. The last named, depicting an unidentified animal eating a mailsack, is most esteemed by philatelists, but your translator favors the 2-*mufti* green, which portrays what is assumed to be a Glornesian, naked on a couch, above a legend reading, "Tootsie —She Put Out." The insipid 1-*mufti*, illustrating as it does "A Real Cup of Coffee," can safely be left out of aesthetic consideration.

different stories. The lone correlation was elicited, not by the psychiatrists, but by Dr. Bascom Fishfoot, the great detective and sometime crime-czar, renowned for his incisive questioning of criminals and law officers. Dr. Fishfoot revealed this important and unique datum in Volume 406 of his masterwork, *Psychology of the Habitual Law-Abider*, but strange to say, Volume 406 has disappeared from all libraries, and Dr. Fishfoot was himself kidnapped some while back by a nebulous dark shape.

The spectacle I had just witnessed made me rather sick, and I was very glad to sit down for a few moments on a cool grassy bank beside the Fornication River. Lying there, watching the colorful slime floating by, I wondered what the great appeal of the Pits was. Even *gnuteries* have been tempted to give them a try. Fortunately, no *gnutery* has ever gone through with it—most of us have been devout dort-worshipers since earliest *gnewk*-hood, and accept the traditional view that this amusement is forbidden by the words in the Book of Dort that run, "A goblet, a goblet, yea, even a hoop, the eyes of time their seasons savor, and all things flow yet who can know, but such is life, business is business, and dort is not mocked, yea, yea." Still, there have been dissenters, and only last year Dyb, son of that warm-blooded cretin Gik, had the bad taste to stand up at the Council of Yar itself and suggest a rival interpretation. Of course he received the Three Frowns and retired in confusion, but the damage had been done, and now many of the newly hatched have departed from the path of right *mirgling*, right *ginz*-eating, and high *hysm*. The thought of this made me feel so low that I suddenly had a great need for Theo's cheerful conversation. But when I got back to his hut I found him absorbed in trying to come up with the day's Third Rumor. (Theo is required to spread at least three Disgusting Rumors every day.) This evening it just wouldn't come, and he finally decided to take a chance on consulting the Crystals of Lalande. Under Theo's skillful tickling they stirred ominously, and when I picked him off the floor he told me he had the answer. After wording it for maximum effect, he leaned out into the walkway and hissed, "Say, buddy." Immediately a large, skinny life-form detached itself from the crowd, ran over, and said, "So *you're* the one who sells filthy pictures! I've been looking all over for you. Well, here's what I like—"

"No, no, friend, you've got me wrong," Theo managed to interpose. "I was just about to let you in on my patented method for increasing—say, what do you want filthy pictures for, anyway? Have you seen the Temple of Total Release?"

"Yes."

"The Four-Day Orgasm of the Giant Fungus?"

"Yes."

"The Difficult Union of the Seven-Sexed Koor Creatures?"

"Yes."

"The Burying Alive of the Lost Tribes of Israel?"

"Yes."

"The Fertilization of Squalodon in the Averse Position?"

"Yes."

"The Talking Spermatozoa of the Over-Educated Yorb?"

"Yes."

"The Mating Chambers of the 90-ton Frog-Thing? The Indecent Pulsations of the Hrno Mass? The Engorged Ovipositors of the Anomalous Annelid?"

"Yes. Yes. Yes."

"Well, what do you want filthy pictures for, then?"

"Oh, they just make me go all squishy inside."

"Disgusting," Theo said and closed the door.

It was night now, and the howls from the Arena of Lust had begun, so, since Theo and I couldn't hear ourselves talk anymore, we got out our machiavelli sets and prepared for an evening's amusement. The origin of this game is lost in dim antiquity. It is played with 44,404 little living figures, partly controlled by the player to whom they belong, partly capable of thinking for themselves. Over a lifetime, a superior player can so educate his figures that they finally exceed his own ability; then he can retire and live on their winnings. This is the hope of every serious practitioner of the game. However, Theo and I had always played just for fun, and in consequence our little creatures knew nothing of those troubling innovations that so exercise our modern masters. We began the game in traditional fashion, with the Dubrovsky Gambit (Misunderstood), which consists in one side reading a proclamation, the other side reading a proclamation, each building a walled city, retiring into the walled city, holding a festival, and then each reading a proclamation again, in which the statements of the previous proclamation are denied in as sly a manner as possible. This is expected to sway the advantage one way or the other. But Theo and I had been through all this many times before, and through the succeeding stages too—debasing the currency, kidnapping the Sacred Ibis, hexing the royal beer, and unmasking the Mix-chievous Jongleurs. In the end, as usual, Theo's Purple Corybant seduced my Red Queen, who prevailed on the Playboy King to treat with the Decrepit War Minister, who was actually the Embittered Sophist in disguise, and this resulted in voluntary stalemate.

We got the pieces back in their boxes again with only the usual amount of resistance—they do so love to build walled cities—and went outside to look at the beautiful mile-high flames rising from sacked and pillaged Rome. "Very neat," Theo remarked. "Tomorrow there won't be a single trace of tonight's activities in the Arena, except for the corpses of the few thousand spectators who tried to get in the act. Perry worked for six years, and burned up half the planet, before he perfected the distension of his body into a controllable flame. But this is nothing. You should have seen the Thanaturian Games in 1212, when Perry's father, Ha'an the Unspeakable, hypnotized an audience of seven million into thinking that they were each individual cells of a *ruchbah* in heat, and it destroyed four suns looking for a mate."

We killed a couple more hours this way, exchanging reminiscences of the old days when great things were done, and quietly letting our pipes smoke us. Sue got in late, said, "Phew, they're sweaty in summer," and started leafing through Theo's *Real Life Sex Stories*, exclaiming "Gee!" every once in a while.

It was time for me to go. I surmised that I had collected enough material for my article, so I bid Theo and Sue goodbye—they were married last year you know (Sue said nothing but a *gnutery* or a stone would let her sleep at night) —and walked out into the dark midway. As I expected, several foot-pads descended on me, but I gave them one of the Lesser Frowns and they began to gibber pleasantly. The light in the Unmentionable's cage was still on, and I heard soft voices—probably he was conversing with his keeper on the Nature of the Good, a favorite topic of his for some years. When I reached the tubeway to the spaceport, I turned back to give the Pits and vicinity one last look. Far in the distance, the day's quota of lost children were being rounded up and herded into pens for next week's Amateur Night, but otherwise all was still.

Dog lovers may or may not be happy to know that a canine plays a substantial part in the delightful tale below, in which England's John Christopher lifts the veil to give us a glimpse into the world of the homosexual dog. (And you *still* wonder why they're not naming 'em Rover anymore?)

A FEW KINDRED SPIRITS

by John Christopher

In the animal creation, as in the human, there are spheres whose existence remain unsuspected until chance lifts a corner of the veil. One of these, as far as I was concerned, was the world of the homosexual dog. I only became aware of it when Shlobber came into my life.

Shlobber, of course, was a classic text-book case for deviation. Absentee father (admittedly a norm amongst dogs) and most decidedly possessive and domineering mother. She was black-and-white, terrier-type, with admixture of collie and spaniel and more elusive extras, and Shlobber was a child of her one and only litter. The intention was to get rid of all the pups to suitable homes, and this was, in fact, achieved. Shlobber, however, having proved over-boisterous for one of the children in the billet we found him, was brought back with apologies. Only as a transient, we thought, but somehow he stayed. Mother went away to be spayed, returned with joy to find her golden-haired son still on the scene, and launched into that career of aggressive, chivvying affection which determined and characterized their relationship. Hour after hour, day after day, she snapped and barked at him, and roughly bowled him over. And he, for his part, was, somewhat resentfully, devoted to her.

His perversity emerged later, and was first apparent when the bitch further up the lane came in season. She was, to

115

human view, an ugly mustard-coloured ill-kempt creature, but as far as dogs were concerned clearly of surpassing attraction. They came, it seemed, from the remotest corners of the island, stampeding through our garden on the way. Shlobber, larger at eighteen months than his mother, romped with her on the lawn, indifferent to all this. So I was not particularly surprised, a few weeks later, when I found him out on his own and making overtures to a male boxer.

After that the pattern set in firmly, but I still thought of him as exceptional. This remained the case until one day on the beach when he fell in with a roving pack of other dogs. There was a nervous-looking Labrador-cross, a thin white creature with a funny head and popping eyes, a paunchy spaniel, and a shaggy gray-brown beast at whose origins I could not begin to guess. Shlobber recognized these as soul-mates right away, and bounded off with them along the sands. I whistled him back, and he came slowly and reluctantly. In the afternoon he disappeared, and did not return until late at night.

He remained devoted to Mother when he was at home, but from that point, increasingly, he took to making excursions on his own. A couple of times I saw him on the beach with the same gang. They were at a distance, and I preferred to leave it that way. I did not care to know him when he was in that particular company, and I had the idea he felt the same way. There was no doubt that they were, in the specifically pejorative sense, a queer lot.

The further, and disturbing, insight came one day in early summer, when I had gone to the beach to think out an awkward problem in a story I was writing. My mind often works better on the horizontal, and so I lay on the sand and bent my mental energies to the task. But the characters who were giving trouble were both impossible and dull and, lulled by the sun and the soporific surf of transistor radios, I fell asleep. When I awoke, it was to the familiar bark of a dog—of Shlobber, in fact. Opening my eyes, I saw that he and the gang were not more than twenty yards away. I was about to close them again, in distaste, when something about the waddle of the paunchy spaniel caught my attention. I looked at him more closely, and thought of Birkinshaw.

As often happens, the donnée of the recognition sparked

off others. The thin white one—surely Andrew Stenner? The eyes, I saw now, were unmistakable. And the shaggy grey-brown thing with legs too short for his body. Peter Parsons! The Labrador-cross had the massive yet effeminate build that I remembered in James de Percy. Then who, I wondered, was Shlobber? And, for that matter, where?

Still half asleep, I glanced along the beach. He was there, all right, and so was a dog I had never seen before. A sort of whippet, spotted brown and white. He was smaller and frailer than Shlobber, but he was snapping at his heels with vicious and righteous anger. The anger of the betrayed, not only in friendship but in art. Jonathan Blumstein, to the life, or rather, I thought hazily, to the death.

My mind went back to the old days, to Fred Astaire and Ginger Rogers, to Munich, to Hutton's triple century at the Oval, to a girl called Gwen. Above all, to the gold and marble decor of the Buckingham. I knew who Shlobber was.

In 1938 I had an indulgent father, a habit of getting my own way, and high ambitions, particularly in relation to the arts. I was a day-boy at a well-known school in London and had decided that, instead of going up to Oxford in the autumn, I would become a writer. At an earlier stage I had written a few things for the school magazine, but all that trivia had now been abandoned. I proposed to write the definitive contemporary novel, which would be scathing and witty, yet profound and all-embracing. I felt that my experience and intuitive understanding went about ninety per cent of the way towards fitting me for this. The remaining ten per cent needed to be acquired. The Buckingham, I thought, famed throughout the world as a Mecca for literary men, was the best place to go to get started on it.

I looked old for my years, and had been brought up in an atmosphere where drinks and restaurants were taken for granted. It took some nerve, all the same, to walk through those wreaths of cigar smoke, to take my place at one of the marble-topped tables on which Whistler had been wont to sketch, to order a Pernod from a gnarled and ancient waiter who had very likely brought champagne to Oscar Wilde. Having got so far, my reserves were exhausted. I sat and clutched my glass and stared frozenly about me.

Everyone seemed old and rich and distinguished. And accompanied; only I sat alone.

Aware of my social failings, I took refuge in my art. I carried a small leather-bound notebook in which to jot down observations, descriptions, phrases which might otherwise be lost; and I brought this out and began, defensively, to write in it. My self-importance was restored. I sipped my Pernod and launched into a brief but scandalous imaginary biography of the fat woman with diamonds all over her on the other side of the room. Engrossed in this, I only looked up when a figure came between me and the light. I saw a thin man, pop-eyed, with a pale face but a warm smile. He nodded benignly.

"A chiel amang us, takin' notes."

I recognized him, not from his face but from the lilting accent of the Highlands. Andrew Stenner was a public personality in those pre-television days, a giant of radio. Additionally, a bon vivant and skilled water-colourist.

"Ye're a writer, I guess," he said. "Come over and meet Birkinshaw. He needs to be reminded of things—death and the younger generation."

He was a man who had many impulses and frequently acted on them. In this case the motivation was partly amiable, partly malicious. He was perceptive, and had seen, I think, my isolation and shyness, and pitied it. In addition, Birkinshaw, then at the height of his fame as a novelist, had a deeply rooted fear and envy of young writers, which it amused Stenner to exploit. He waved my mild demurrant aside, took my arm firmly, and led me to join the others.

They were all there, that first night. Birkinshaw, Parsons, de Percy, Blumstein and Redehead. Peter Parsons looking unkempt, his hair long and wild, his gaze curiously focussed on nothing, or on the memory of one of those cinema screens at which he spent so much time gazing, preparing his authoritative work on the Film. James de Percy, a stone engraver to be spoken of with Gill, his body huge, hands surprisingly delicate. Jonathan Blumstein, small and nervous, scrawny-necked behind his bow tie, talking, talking, talking. And David Redehead, who had been blonde and handsome and now had thinning hair and a look of failure, listening to all that Jonathan said.

Tongue-tied, I sat even quieter than he did. Under Birkinshaw's frowning stare I drank his champagne—his latest novel was both Literary Guild and Book Society Choice, and we were celebrating the fact—and to myself revelled in the consciousness of being in the company of artistic and distinguished men. In the morning there would be Latin Verse, which I had not prepared. But one lived for the moment, and in this moment one savoured Life.

More than twenty years later, sitting looking out to sea from an island in the Channel, I thought of those days. By the end of the evening, Birkinshaw had gleaned that I was raw and respectful, unpublished and unlikely to be published for some time to come. He thawed towards me and when, a few days later, I ventured back to the Buckingham, it was he who called me over. In the months that followed I became, if not an accepted member of the group, at least a kind of mascot, tolerated, encouraged, occasionally allowed to buy a drink. Meeting Peter Parsons at Birkinshaw's funeral, one dripping February day towards the end of the war, I made some remark about this, and he took his mind off composing artistic cinematic frames of the ceremony long enough to toss me an explanation.

"The same—as always." He spoke in clipped, oblique phrases. "You might have been—something—some day. To write about them. Boswell." He gurgled with bitter laughter. "To five moth-eaten Johnsons."

Presumably he excluded the sixth. The great work had never been completed, and the last time I had seen his name it had been on the cover of a badly printed booklet with a lot of fuzzy stills, many of them dealing with the female nude. A sad declension.

So much for my being accepted. The reverse of the coin puzzled me a little, too. Their conversation, apart from being intelligent, was untrammelled, and it did not take many evenings for me to realize that what I had heard rumoured of Birkinshaw and Blumstein was true of them all: they belonged to that freemasonry which comes after the Roman Catholics and neck and neck with Standard Oil. Expecting to be wooed, I had my maidenly refusals ready. But nothing of the sort happened. At the time I gave credit to my own inner purity. Later, though, I guessed the real reason. The qualities which, in their own sex, attracted them were beauty and intelligence. Looking back I sadly understood that I had failed to qualify in either respect.

Whatever had been the case in the past, there was, in fact, only one sexual link operating within the group. Blumstein and Redehead had been living together for a decade and a half in Blumstein's house in Cheyne Walk and their relationship had settled into something resembling a long established and moderately successful marriage. Blumstein had wealth and some talent; he had published three volumes of poetry which, although commercially unsuccessful, had gained him a reputation. Redehead came from a poor family and all he had to his credit were a score or so of little pieces published in little magazines. Belles lettres at their most precious. There had been one slim volume of them published, plainly at Blumstein's expense.

But fifteen years earlier, when they met, Redehead had had something else: physical beauty. It was this quality in him to which Blumstein, an ugly little man, had been devoted. And it did not last—by his early thirties, Redehead was growing coarse and fat, and beginning to lose his curly golden hair. The end, according to the cynics, was in sight. Blumstein would ease him out and install a younger, handsomer companion. It did not happen. Blumstein, perhaps, was less deferential, more condescending, than he had been; but he stayed true to his dilapidated sweetheart, and to the memory of his radiance. And Redehead, for his part, was both grateful and devoted. In public, no one could remember seeing them apart.

As if the past were not rampant enough already, the nearest transistor radio began playing "The Night is Young"; with electrified strings and a coal-heaver's voice, but recognizable. The dogs were in full pelt northwards along the beach, with the pudgy spaniel, Birkinshaw, waddling ten yards behind the rest. The song was Alice, who came after Gwen and more effectively. And Birkinshaw . . . That evening when I had gone late to the Buckingham, after an hour and a half of waiting for Alice to turn up for a date, and had found him deep in one of his more pompous perorations. Hurt and angry and cynical, I had taken my seat, and Blumstein had waved for the waiter, and Birkinshaw had gone on, and on, and on. He was talking about Time, which he gave the impression of having discovered even before Jack Priestley. It was at once the greatest illusion and the final reality. What had been, would be. All that we might be and love and suffer, we had been and loved and suffered in the past. We had walked the earth, and would walk it again.

"Kindred spirits find each other," he said. "We have sat at wine together under blue Attic skies, celebrating the news from Marathon. One day, perhaps, we shall sit on the moon, bathed in silver earthlight, drinking Martian champagne."

My gorge, disturbed already by the cruelty of Alice, rose. Not this spirit, I thought, and got up rudely while Birkinshaw was still tolling on, and left.

It was a temporary revulsion, provoked by my own heterosexual smart, and but for a couple of things I would probably have gone back the next week. The things were my sense of embarrassment over my abrupt and discourteous departure and, more important, a softening on the part of Alice. The whole of that winter I was her joyful and unhappy slave, with no time or energy to devote either to the Buckingham or literature. My reading was confined, feverishly, to scanning the lists for social events that would suit her voracious but fickle taste. I missed the announcement of Blumstein's death. I only accidentally saw the notice of his will when my eye, intent on the theatre advertisements in *The Star*, somehow slipped to the facing page. He had left a very tidy estate—upwards of fifty thousand after duty. There were some minor bequests, to servants and so on. These apart, everything was left to his old friend and companion, David Redehead. With youthful callousness, I mentally wished him well in his widowhood, and returned to the more important matter of finding a show to which I could persuade Alice to let me take her.

Alice's fancy turned with the spring, and this time decisively. She met a Commander R.N. and married him within a month. I think the speed of this, after her prolonged dabbling with me, was the biggest blow to my vanity. Certainly I took it badly. In my misery I went back to the Buckingham, and found them, except for the dead Blumstein, in their accustomed places. They received me with courtesy and amiability but I felt there was constraint—the constraint, perhaps, with which Shlobber's pack might have greeted a dog who had left them to follow a bitch on heat. I had made my difference, my exclusion from the company of kindred spirits, indelicately plain. I noted that Birkinshaw was wheezing more, that Parsons was developing a nervous twitch, and that Redehead, in the flush of wealth and bereavement, was looking ten times better and happier and more confident. I have seen the change in many widows since, but that was the first time. I thought of Alice as a widow, her Commander having gone down with his ship, of her delicate skin and fair silky hair against black satin, and was undone. Bored, and stinging with jealousy and desire, I made brief apologies and left.

It was over a year before I made my next visit, and then in uniform. I had been commissioned in the Royal Artillery in April, and in June was posted to the command of an anti-aircraft battery in, of all places, Hyde Park. I did not care much for what seemed to me the hysteric and self-consciously heroic attitude of London in the summer of Dunkirk, and I headed for the Buckingham as a repository of more permanent values. I found them all there and, as on that very first occasion, celebrating the success of a book. Not Birkinshaw's, though, but Redehead's.

It had been published two days earlier, on a Monday, and, it seemed, ecstatically reviewed the previous day in the two quality Sundays. (I had missed them, sleeping through the day in the aftermath of two night exercises and a Ministerial inspection in between.) And these reviews had been effective as well as laudatory. Redehead had lunched with his publisher that day at the Ivy and been told that sales were, for a book of this kind, superb. Belles lettres again, but successful belles lettres, belles lettres to which the cognoscenti took off their collective hat. Redehead was flushed with his triumph, but making an endearing effort to be modest about it. We drank '33 Krug, toasting his success with bibulous and, in my case at least, genuinely delighted good will. Even at that early age I had sufficient premonition of the future to find the Cinderella story of success after long years of failure one of my very favorite themes.

A couple of days later I bought the book, and on our next quiet night read it. It was, one might say, a forerunner of Cyril Connolly's "The Unquiet Grave," a series of loosely linked but roughly continuous pieces on Life, on the Human Condition, studded with maxims and epigrams and snatches of poetry. Like Connolly's bored and greedy despair at the war's end, this book, restless for change, optimistic in the face of the threatening gods, gallantly bogus, matched and re-echoed its time. Redhead, I saw, really had done it. He was, at long last, a lion.

I saw them occasionally thereafter, but time and mortality were breaking up the charmed circle. Stenner died of a coronary, a few minutes after ending an uplifting Post-Script to the nine o'clock News. In Italy, three years later, I heard of the death of Redhead, killed when a bomb destroyed the elegant Hampstead flat to which, after selling the Chelsea house, he had removed. Finally, back in London for the last ghastly winter of the war, there was Birkinshaw's death. I asked Parsons about de Percy, the only one of the group not accounted for. Multiple sclerosis, he told me, and not long to go. He went himself two years later, I think of frustration.

I have never been in the Buckingham since.

I thought of all this on my way back from the beach, and as I did so the initial fantasy seemed more and more ridiculous. By the time Shlobber returned, an hour later, I had it all disposed of as hallucination, an effect of sleep and sun. But I noticed that he was back earlier than usual and that, instead of belting ravenously into his supper as was his wont following an afternoon with the boys, he turned away from it. He had a nervous and harassed look, as though he expected the whippet to come yapping up behind him at any moment. When I went to read, he followed me. Seeking protection?

Putting down the book, I said:

"Redhead." His ears pricked, and slowly went down again. He stared miserably at my shoe. "I know it all," I told him. "Not only who you are, but what happened. We should have guessed, of course, but it was the belles lettres thing that fooled us. Blumstein taking over even the field of your own pitiful activity. Did you find out about it before he died? Or did you discover the manuscript among his effects? How did he die, Redhead?"

The head came up briefly, brown eyes looked into my

face from above the long muzzle, and then dropped. A very ordinary doggy action, one might say. Fortunately I had the house to myself.

"The point is that you found it and published it under your own name. That would have counted to Blumstein far more than a small thing like being murdered. You stole his great work, Redehead. And now that he's found you again, he is going to make you pay for it."

Shlobber got up and started to leave the room. He was a restless beast, not long happy in one spot, and normally I would have thought this characteristic. But I followed him to the kitchen, and stood over him.

"The biggest joke," I said, "is that it wasn't a good book after all. It was a silly pretentious footling book, and when people had got the we-stood-alone stars out of their eyes, they saw it for what it was. The most it can hope to achieve is a footnote in literary history, and a derisive one at that. Blumstein is still remembered as a good minor poet. Redehead goes down to posterity as the man who wrote the highbrow equivalent to 'We're Going to Hang Out our Washing on the Siegfried Line.'"

Shlobber went out—miserably, I thought, but he often looked miserable. He was missing for a day and then I was telephoned by the Animal Shelter. He had been brought in dead, after being run over by a car that failed to stop. I asked them if they would bury him, and they agreed.

Had he run under the wheels of the car deliberately, I wondered, in despair? Or been chivvied under them by the vengeful whippet-Blumstein? Suicide, or murder? Or accident? He had, after all, about as much road sense as a rhinoceros.

The years went by, a little faster all the time, and Shlobber and my theories about him were pushed back into the unvisited departments of my mind and there collected dust. I have children growing up, and the past is less interesting just now than the present. But recently one of my daughters decided she wanted another budgerigar, and I went with her to the Bird Farm to buy it.

There were several gigantic outdoor aviaries, and the proprietor had a net on the end of a long stick, to catch the bird she chose. He knew his budgerigars well, and was generous and helpful with advice. When she settled on a mauve bird, he said:

"Just as you like, young lady. But that's a cock."

She nodded. "I know—from the wattle."

"A hen's best, for a bird by itself."

"But it's not to be by itself. I've already got a hen. I want to breed from them."

"Well," he said, "I wouldn't pick that one. You go up along to the next cage. There's some good 'uns there."

When she had left he said:

"You know, it's a funny thing, you get some cocks that are useless for breeding. Not interested in hens at all. Spend their time with other cock birds." He grinned, shaking his head. "Queer, you might say."

I looked at the mauve bird. A kind of bulkiness to the set of the shoulders. De Percy? There were a group of them together up there in the corner of the aviary, amicably perched on a far-out twig of a barkless tree. A thin white one. Stenner? An emerald bird with a tatty ungroomed look, and a fat portentous creature in sage-green. Parsons? And Birkinshaw?

I looked for the two that were missing, but could not see them. Then there was a flash of colour across the aviary, a screeching of flight and pursuit—a small gray-blue pelting after a yellow with a bald patch on top.

"That's another thing," the proprietor said. "The way one bird can take against another, for no reason you can see. Those two, for instance. That blue one leads the yellow bird a dog's life."

At least they look prettier than they did.

Surely one of man's most difficult tasks is to learn to live with his memories. When, as for Douglas Quail, those include a dull job, a wilting marriage and little else, then something must be done. As, for instance, changing those memories.

WE CAN REMEMBER IT FOR YOU WHOLESALE

by Philip K. Dick

He awoke—and wanted Mars. The valleys, he thought. What would it be like to trudge among them? Great and greater yet: the dream grew as he became fully conscious, the dream and the yearning. He could almost feel the enveloping presence of the other world, which only Government agents and high officials had seen. A clerk like himself? Not likely.

"Are you getting up or not?" his wife Kirsten asked drowsily, with her usual hint of fierce crossness. "If you are, push the hot coffee button on the darn stove."

"Okay," Douglas Quail said, and made his way barefoot from the bedroom of their conapt to the kitchen. There, having dutifully pressed the hot coffee button, he seated himself at the kitchen table, brought out a yellow, small tin of fine Dean Swift snuff. He inhaled briskly, and the Beau Nash mixture stung his nose, burned the roof of his mouth. But still he inhaled it; it woke him up and allowed his dreams, his nocturnal desires and random wishes, to condense into a semblance of rationality.

I will go, he said to himself. Before I die I'll see Mars.

It was, of course, impossible, and he knew this even as he dreamed. But the daylight, the mundane noise of his wife now brushing her hair before the bedroom mirror—

everything conspired to remind him of what he was. A miserable little salaried employee, he said to himself with bitterness. Kirsten reminded him of this at least once a day and he did not blame her; it was a wife's job to bring her husband down to Earth. Down to Earth, he thought, and laughed. The figure of speech in this was literally apt.

"What are you sniggering about?" his wife asked as she swept into the kitchen, her long busy-pink robe wagging after her. "A dream, I bet. You're always full of them."

"Yes," he said, and gazed out the kitchen window at the hover-cars and traffic runnels, and all the little energetic people hurrying to work. In a little while he would be among them. As always.

"I'll bet it has to do with some woman," Kirsten said witheringly.

"No," he said. "A god. The god of war. He has wonderful craters with every kind of plant-life growing deep down in them."

"Listen." Kirsten crouched down beside him and spoke earnestly, the harsh quality momentarily gone from her voice. "The bottom of the ocean—*our* ocean is much more, an infinity of times more beautiful. You know that; everyone knows that. Rent an artificial gill-outfit for both of us, take a week off from work, and we can descend and live down there at one of those year-round aquatic resorts. And in addition—" She broke off. "You're not listening. You should be. Here is something a lot better than that compulsion, that obsession you have about Mars, and you don't even listen!" Her voice rose piercingly. "God in heaven, you're doomed, Doug! What's going to become of you?"

"I'm going to work," he said, rising to his feet, his breakfast forgotten. "That's what's going to become of me."

She eyed him. "You're getting worse. More fanatical every day. Where's it going to lead?"

"To Mars," he said, and opened the door to the closet to get down a fresh shirt to wear to work.

Having descended from the taxi Douglas Quail slowly walked across three densely-populated foot runnels and to the modern, attractively inviting doorway. There he halted, impeding mid-morning traffic, and with caution read the shifting-color neon sign. He had, in the past, scrutinized this sign before . . . but never had he come so close. This was very different; what he did now was something else. Something which sooner or later had to happen.

REKAL, INCORPORATED

Was this the answer? After all, an illusion, no matter how convincing, remained nothing more than an illusion. At least objectively. But subjectively—quite the opposite entirely.

And anyhow he had an appointment. Within the next five minutes.

Taking a deep breath of mildly smog-infested Chicago air, he walked through the dazzling poly-chromatic shimmer of the doorway and up to the receptionist's counter.

The nicely-articulated blonde at the counter, bare-bosomed and tidy, said pleasantly, "Good morning, Mr. Quail."

"Yes," he said. "I'm here to see about a Rekal course. As I guess you know."

"Not 'rekal' but *re*call," the receptionist corrected him. She picked up the receiver of the vid-phone by her smooth elbow and said into it, "Mr. Douglas Quail is here, Mr. McClane. May he come inside, now? Or is too soon?"

"Giz wetwa wum-wum wamp," the phone mumbled.

"Yes, Mr. Quail," she said. "You may go on in; Mr. Mc-Clane is expecting you." As he started off uncertainly she called after him, "Room D, Mr. Quail. To your right."

After a frustrating but brief moment of being lost he found the proper room. The door hung open and inside, at a big genuine walnut desk, sat a genial-looking man, middle-aged, wearing the latest Martian frog-pelt gray suit; his attire alone would have told Quail that he had come to the right person.

"Sit down, Douglas," McClane said, waving his plump hand toward a chair which faced the desk. "So you want to have gone to Mars. Very good."

Quail seated himself, feeling tense. "I'm not so sure this is worth the fee," he said. "It costs a lot and as far as I can see I really get nothing." Costs almost as much as going, he thought.

"You get tangible proof of your trip," McClane disagreed emphatically. "All the proof you'll need. Here; I'll show you." He dug within a drawer of his impressive desk.

"Ticket stub." Reaching into a manila folder he produced a small square of embossed cardboard. "It proves you went —and returned. Postcards." He laid out four franked picture 3-D full-color postcards in a neatly-arranged row on the desk for Quail to see. "Film. Shots you took of local sights on Mars with a rented movie camera." To Quail he displayed those, too. "Plus the names of people you met, two hundred poscreds worth of souvenirs, which will arrive— from Mars—within the following month. And passport, certificates listing the shots you received. And more." He glanced up keenly at Quail. "You'll know you went, all right," he said. "You won't remember us, won't remember me or ever having been here. It'll be a real trip in your mind; we guarantee that. A full two weeks of recall; every last piddling detail. Remember this: if at any time you doubt that you really took an extensive trip to Mars you can return here and get a full refund. You see?"

"But I didn't go," Quail said. "I won't have gone, no matter what proofs you provide me with." He took a deep, unsteady breath. "And I never was a secret agent with Interplan." It seemed impossible to him that Rekal, Incorporated's extra-factual memory implant would do its job—despite what he had heard people say.

"Mr. Quail," McClane said patiently. "As you explained in your letter to us, you have no chance, no possibility in the slightest, of ever actually getting to Mars; you can't afford it, and what is much more important, you could never qualify as an undercover agent for Interplan or anybody else. This is the only way you can achieve your, hem, lifelong dream; am I not correct, sir? You can't be this; you can't actually do this." He chuckled. "But you can *have been* and *have done*. We see to that. And our fee is reasonable; no hidden charges." He smiled encouragingly.

"Is an extra-factual memory that convincing?" Quail asked.

"More than the real thing, sir. Had you really gone to Mars as an Interplan agent, you would by now have forgotten a great deal; our analysis of true-mem systems— authentic recollections of major events in a person's life— shows that a variety of details are very quickly lost to the person. Forever. Part of the package we offer you is such deep implantation of recall that nothing is forgotten. The packet which is fed to you while you're comatose is the creation of trained experts, men who have spent years on Mars; in every case we verify details down to the last iota. And you've picked a rather easy extra-factual system; had you picked Pluto or wanted to be Emperor of the Inner Planet Alliance we'd have much more difficulty . . . and the charges would be considerably greater."

Reaching into his coat for his wallet, Quail said, "Okay. It's been my life-long ambition and I can see I'll never really do it. So I guess I'll have to settle for this."

"Don't think of it that way," McClane said severely. "You're not accepting second-best. The actual memory, with all its vagueness, omissions and ellipses, not to say distortions—that's second-best." He accepted the money and pressed a button on his desk. "All right, Mr. Quail," he said, as the door of his office opened and two burly men swiftly entered. "You're on your way to Mars as a secret agent." He rose, came over to shake Quail's nervous, moist hand. "Or rather, you have been on your way. This afternoon at four-thirty you will, um, arrive back here on Terra; a cab will leave you off at your conapt and as I say you will never remember seeing me or coming here; you won't, in fact, even remember having heard of our existence."

His mouth dry with nervousness, Quail followed the two technicians from the office; what happened next depended on them.

Will I actually believe I've been on Mars? he wondered. That I managed to fulfill my lifetime ambition? He had a strange, lingering intuition that something would go wrong. But just what—he did not know.

He would have to wait to find out.

The intercom on McClane's desk, which connected him with the work-area of the firm, buzzed and a voice said, "Mr. Quail is under sedation now, sir. Do you want to supervise this one, or shall we go ahead?"

"It's routine," McClane observed. "You may go ahead, Lowe; I don't think you'll run into any trouble." Programming an artificial memory of a trip to another planet—with or without the added fillip of being a secret agent—showed up on the firm's work-schedule with monotonous regularity. In one month, he calculated wryly, we must do twenty of these . . . ersatz interplanetary travel has become our bread and butter.

"Whatever you say, Mr. McClane," Lowe's voice came, and thereupon the intercom shut off.

Going to the vault section in the chamber behind his office, McClane searched about for a Three packet—trip to Mars—and a Sixty-two packet: secret Interplan spy. Finding the two packets, he returned with them to his desk, seated himself comfortably, poured out the contents—merchandise which would be planted in Quail's conapt while the lab technicians busied themselves installing the false memory.

A one-poscred sneaky-pete side arm, McClane reflected; that's the largest item. Sets us back financially the most. Then a pellet-sized transmitter, which could be swallowed if the agent were caught. Code book that astonishingly resembled the real thing . . . the firm's models were highly accurate: based, whenever possible, on actual U.S. military issue. Odd bits which made no intrinsic sense but which would be woven into the warp and woof of Quail's imaginary trip, would coincide with his memory: half an ancient silver fifty cent piece, several quotations from John Donne's sermons written incorrectly, each on a separate piece of transparent tissue-thin paper, several match folders from bars on Mars, a stainless steel spoon engraved PROPERTY OF DOME-MARS NATIONAL KIBBUZIM, a wire tapping coil which—

The intercom buzzed. "Mr. McClane, I'm sorry to bother you but something rather ominous has come up. Maybe it would be better if you were in here after all. Quail is already under sedation; he reacted well to the narkidrine; he's completely unconscious and receptive. But—"

"I'll be in." Sensing trouble, McClane left his office; a moment later he emerged in the work area.

On a hygienic bed lay Douglas Quail, breathing slowly and regularly, his eyes virtually shut; he seemed dimly— but only dimly—aware of the two technicians and now McClane himself.

"There's no space to insert false memory-patterns?" McClane felt irritation. "Merely drop out two work weeks; he's employed as a clerk at the West Coast Emigration Bureau, which is a government agency, so he undoubtedly has or had two weeks' vacation within the last year. That ought to do it." Petty details annoyed him. And always would.

"Our problem," Lowe said sharply, "is something quite different." He bent over the bed, said to Quail, "Tell Mr. McClane what you told us." To McClane he said, "Listen closely."

The gray-green eyes of the man lying supine in the bed focused on McClane's face. The eyes, he observed uneasily, had become hard; they had a polished, inorganic quality, like semi-precious tumbled stones. He was not sure that he liked what he saw; the brilliance was too cold. "What do you want now?" Quail said harshly. "You've broken my cover. Get out of here before I take you all apart." He studied McClane. "Especially you," he continued. "You're in charge of this counter-operation."

Lowe said, "How long were you on Mars?"

"One month," Quail said gratingly.

"And your purpose there?" Lowe demanded.

The meager lips twisted; Quail eyed him and did not speak. At last, drawling the words out so that they dripped with hostility, he said, "Agent for Interplan. As I already told you. Don't you record everything that's said? Play your vid-aud tape back for your boss and leave me alone." He shut his eyes, then; the hard brilliance ceased. McClane felt, instantly, a rushing splurge of relief.

Lowe said quietly, "This is a tough man, Mr. McClane."

"He won't be," McClane said, "after we arrange for him to lose his memory-chain again. He'll be as meek as before." To Quail he said, "So *this* is why you wanted to go to Mars so terribly badly."

Without opening his eyes Quail said, "I never wanted to go to Mars. I was assigned it—they handed it to me and there I was: stuck. Oh yeah, I admit I was curious about it; who wouldn't be?" Again he opened his eyes and surveyed the three of them, McClane in particular. "Quite a truth drug you've got here; it brought up things I had absolutely no memory of." He pondered. "I wonder about Kirsten," he said, half to himself. "Could she be in on it? An Interplan contact keeping an eye on me . . . to be certain I didn't regain my memory? No wonder she's been so derisive about my wanting to go there." Faintly, he smiled; the smile— one of understanding—disappeared almost at once.

McClane said, "Please believe me, Mr. Quail; we stumbled onto this entirely by accident. In the work we do—"

"I believe you," Quail said. He seemed tired, now; the drug was continuing to pull him under, deeper and deeper. "Where did I say I'd been?" he murmured. "Mars? Hard to remember—I know I'd like to see it; so would everybody. But me—" His voice trailed off. "Just a clerk, a nothing clerk."

Straightening up, Lowe said to his superior, "He wants a false memory implanted that corresponds to a trip he actually took. And a false reason which is the real reason. He's telling the truth; he's a long way down in the narkidrine. The trip is very vivid in his mind—at least under sedation. But apparently he doesn't recall it otherwise. Someone, probably at a government military-sciences lab, erased his conscious memories; all he knew was that going to Mars meant something special to him, and so did being a secret agent. They couldn't erase that; it's not a memory but a desire, undoubtedly the same one that motivated him to volunteer for the assignment in the first place."

The other technician, Keeler, said to McClane, "What do we do? Graft a false memory-pattern over the real memory? There's no telling what the results would be; he might remember some of the genuine trip, and the confusion might bring on a psychotic interlude. He'd have to hold two opposite premises in his mind simultaneously: that he went to Mars and that he didn't. That he's a genuine agent for Interplan and he's not, that it's spurious. I think we ought to revive him without any false memory implantation and send him out of here; this is hot."

"Agreed," McClane said. A thought came to him. "Can you predict what he'll remember when he comes out of sedation?"

"Impossible to tell," Lowe said. "He probably will have some dim, diffuse memory of his actual trip, now. And he'd probably be in grave doubt as to its validity; he'd probably decide our programming slipped a gear-tooth. And he'd remember coming here; that wouldn't be erased—unless you want it erased."

"The less we mess with this man," McClane said, "the better I like it. This is nothing for us to fool around with; we've been foolish enough to—or unlucky enough to—uncover a genuine Interplan spy who was a cover so perfect that up to now even he didn't know what he was—or rather is." The sooner they washed their hands of the man calling himself Douglas Quail the better.

"Are you going to plant packets Three and Sixty-two in his conapt?" Lowe said.

"No," McClane said. "And we're going to return half his fee."

" 'Half'! Why half?"

McClane said lamely, "It seems to be a good compromise."

As the cab carried him back to his conapt at the residential end of Chicago, Douglas Quail said to himself, It's sure good to be back on Terra.

Already the month-long period on Mars had begun to waver in his memory; he had only an image of profound gaping craters, an ever-present ancient erosion of hills, of vitality, of motion itself. A world of dust where little happened, where a good part of the day was spent checking and rechecking one's portable oxygen source. And then the life forms, the unassuming and modest gray-brown cacti and maw-worms.

As a matter of fact he had brought back several moribund examples of Martian fauna; he had smuggled them through customs. After all, they posed no menace; they couldn't survive in Earth's heavy atmosphere.

Reaching into his coat pocket he rummaged for the container of Martian maw-worms—

And found an envelope instead.

Lifting it out he discovered, to his perplexity, that it contained five hundred and seventy poscreds, in cred bills of low denomination.

Where'd I get this? he asked himself. Didn't I spend every 'cred I had on my trip?

With the money came a slip of paper marked: *one-half fee ret'd. By McClane.* And then the date. Today's date.

"Recall," he said aloud.

"Recall what, sir or madam?" the robot driver of the cab inquired respectfully.

"Do you have a phone book?" Quail demanded.

"Certainly, sir or madam." A slot opened; from it slid a microtape phone book for Cook County.

"It's spelled oddly," Quail said as he leafed through the

pages of the yellow section. He felt fear, then; abiding fear. "Here it is," he said. "Take me there, to Rekal, Incorporated. I've changed my mind; I don't want to go home."

"Yes sir, or madam, as the case may be," the driver said. A moment later the cab was zipping back in the opposite direction.

"May I make use of your phone?" he asked.

"Be my guest," the robot driver said. And presented a shiny new emperor 3-D color phone to him.

He dialed his own conapt. And after a pause found himself confronted by a miniature but chillingly realistic image of Kirsten on the small screen. "I've been to Mars," he said to her.

"You're drunk." Her lips writhed scornfully. "Or worse."

" 'S god's truth."

"When?" she demanded.

"I don't know." He felt confused. "A simulated trip, I think. By means of one of those artificial or extra-factual or whatever it is memory places. It didn't take."

Kirsten said witheringly, "You *are* drunk." And broke the connection at her end. He hung up, then, feeling his face flush. Always the same tone, he said hotly to himself. Always the retort, as if she knows everything and I know nothing. What a marriage. Keerist, he thought dismally.

A moment later the cab stopped at the curb before a modern, very attractive little pink building, over which a shifting, poly-chromatic neon sign read: REKAL, INCORPORATED.

The receptionist, chic and bare from the waist up, started in surprise, then gained masterful control of herself. "Oh hello Mr. Quail," she said nervously. "H-how are you? Did you forget something?"

"The rest of my fee back," he said.

More composed now the receptionist said, "Fee? I think you are mistaken, Mr. Quail. You were here discussing the feasibility of an extrafactual trip for you, but—" She shrugged her smooth pale shoulders. "As I understand it, no trip was taken."

Quail said, "I remember everything, miss. My letter to Rekal, Incorporated, which started this whole business off. I remember my arrival here, my visit with Mr. McClane. Then the two lab technicians taking me in tow and administering a drug to put me out." No wonder the firm had returned half his fee. The false memory of his "trip to Mars" hadn't taken—at least not entirely, not as he had been assured.

"Mr. Quail," the girl said, "although you are a minor clerk you are a good-looking man and it spoils your features to become angry. If it would make you feel any better, I might, ahem, let you take me out . . ."

He felt furious, then. "I remember you," he said savagely. "For instance the fact that your breasts are sprayed blue; that stuck in my mind. And I remember Mr. Mc-Clane's promise that if I remembered my visit to Rekal, Incorporated I'd receive my money back in full. Where is Mr. McClane?"

After a delay—probably as long as they could manage—he found himself once more seated facing the imposing walnut desk, exactly as he had been an hour or so earlier in the day.

"Some technique you have," Quail said sardonically. His disappointment—and resentment—were enormous, by now. "My so-called 'memory' of a trip to Mars as an undercover agent for Interplan is hazy and vague and shot full of contradictions. And I clearly remember my dealings here with you people. I ought to take this to the Better Business Bureau." He was burning angry, at this point; his sense of being cheated had overwhelmed him, had destroyed his customary aversion to participating in a public squabble.

Looking morose, as well as cautious, McClane said, "We capitulate, Quail. We'll refund the balance of your fee. I fully concede the fact that we did absolutely nothing for you." His tone was resigned.

Quail said accusingly, "You didn't even provide me with the various artifacts that you claimed would 'prove' to me I had been on Mars. All that song-and-dance you went into —it hasn't materialized into a damn thing. Not even a ticket stub. Nor postcards. Nor passport. Nor proof of immunization shots. Nor—"

"Listen, Quail," McClane said. "Suppose I told you—" He broke off. "Let it go." He pressed a button on his intercom. "Shirley, will you disburse five hundred and seventy more 'creds in the form of a cashier's check made out to

Douglas Quail? Thank you." He released the button, then glared at Quail.

Presently the check appeared; the receptionist placed it before McClane and once more vanished out of sight, leaving the two men alone, still facing each other across the surface of the massive walnut desk.

"Let me give you a word of advice," McClane said as he signed the check and passed it over. "Don't discuss your, ahem, recent trip to Mars with anyone."

"What trip?"

"Well, that's the thing." Doggedly, McClane said, "The trip you partially remember. Act as if you don't remember; pretend it never took place. Don't ask me why; just take my advice: it'll be better for all of us." He had begun to perspire. Freely. "Now, Mr. Quail, I have other business, other clients to see." He rose, showed Quail to the door.

Quail said, as he opened the door, "A firm that turns out such bad work shouldn't have any clients at all." He shut the door behind him.

On the way home in the cab Quail pondered the wording of his letter of complaint to the Better Business Bureau, Terra Division. As soon as he could get to his typewriter he'd get started; it was clearly his duty to warn other people away from Rekal, Incorporated.

When he got back to his conapt he seated himself before his Hermes Rocket portable, opened the drawers and rummaged for carbon paper—and noticed a small, familiar box. A box which he had carefully filled on Mars with Martian fauna and later smuggled through customs.

Opening the box he saw, to his disbelief, six dead mawworms and several varieties of the unicellular life on which the Martian worms fed. The protozoa were dried-up, dusty, but he recognized them; it had taken him an entire day picking among the vast dark alien boulders to find them. A wonderful illuminated journey of discovery.

But I didn't go to Mars, he realized.

Yet on the other hand—

Kirsten appeared at the doorway to the room, an armload of pale brown groceries gripped. "Why are you home in the middle of the day?" Her voice, in an eternity of sameness, was accusing.

"*Did I go to Mars?*" he asked her. "You would know."

"No, of course you didn't go to Mars, *you* would know that, I would think. Aren't you always bleating about going?"

He said, "By God, I think I went." After a pause he added, "And simultaneously I think I didn't go."

"Make up your mind."

"How can I?" He gestured. "I have both memory-tracts grafted inside my head; one is real and one isn't but I can't tell which is which. Why can't I rely on you? They haven't tinkered with you." She could do this much for him at least —even if she never did anything else.

Kirsten said in a level, controlled voice, "Doug, if you don't pull yourself together, we're through. I'm going to leave you."

"I'm in trouble." His voice came out husky and coarse. And shaking. "Probably I'm heading into a psychotic episode; I hope not, but—maybe that's it. It would explain everything, anyhow."

Setting down the bag of groceries, Kirsten stalked to the closet. "I was not kidding," she said to him quietly. She brought out a coat, got it on, walked back to the door of the conapt. "I'll phone you one of these days soon," she said tonelessly. "This is goodbye, Doug. I hope you pull out of this eventually; I really pray you do. For your sake."

"Wait," he said desperately. "Just tell me and make it absolute; I did go or I didn't—tell me which one." But they may have altered your memory-track also, he realized.

The door closed. His wife had left. Finally!

A voice behind him said, "Well, that's that. Now put up your hands, Quail. And also please turn around and face this way."

He turned, instinctively, without raising his hands.

The man who faced him wore the plum uniform of the Interplan Police Agency, and his gun appeared to be UN issue. And, for some odd reason, he seemed familiar to Quail; familiar in a blurred, distorted fashion which he could not pin down. So, jerkily, he raised his hands.

"You remember," the policeman said, "your trip to Mars. We know all your actions today and all your thoughts—in particular your very important thoughts on the trip home from Rekal, Incorporated." He explained, "We have a telep-

transmitter wired within your skull; it keeps us constantly informed."

A telepathic transmitter; use of a living plasma that had been discovered on Luna. He shuddered with self-aversion. The thing lived inside him, within his own brain, feeding, listening, feeding. But the Interplan police used them; that had come out even in the homeopapes. So this was probably true, dismal as it was.

"Why me?" Quail said huskily. What had he done—or thought? And what did this have to do with Rekal, Incorporated?

"Fundamentally," the Interplan cop said, "this has nothing to do with Rekal,; it's between you and us." He tapped his right ear. "I'm still picking up your mentational processes by way of your cephalic transmitter." In the man's ear Quail saw a small white-plastic plug. "So I have to warn you: anything you think may be held against you." He smiled. "Not that it matters now; you've already thought and spoken yourself into oblivion. What's annoying is the fact that under narkidrine at Rekal, Incorporated you told them, their technicians and the owner, Mr. McClane, about your trip; where you went, for whom, some of what you did. They're very frightened. They wish they had never laid eyes on you." He added reflectively, "They're right."

Quail said, "I never made any trip. It's a false memory-chain improperly planted in me by McClane's technicians." But then he thought of the box, in his desk drawer, containing the Martian life forms. And the trouble and hardship he had had gathering them. The memory seemed real. And the box of life forms; that certainly was real. Unless McClane had planted it. Perhaps this was one of the "proofs" which McClane had talked glibly about.

The memory of my trip to Mars, he thought, doesn't convince me—but unfortunately it has convinced the Interplan Police Agency. They think I really went to Mars and they think I at least partially realize it.

"We not only know you went to Mars," the Interplan cop agreed, in answer to his thoughts, "but we know that you now remember enough to be difficult for us. And there's no use expunging your conscious memory of all this, because if we do you'll simply show up at Rekal, Incorporated again and start over. And we can't do anything about Mc-

Clane and his operation because we have no jurisdiction over anyone except our own people. Anyhow, McClane hasn't committed any crime." He eyed Quail. "Nor, technically, have you. You didn't go to Rekal, Incorporated with the idea of regaining your memory; you went, as we realize, for the usual reason people go there—a love by plain, dull people for adventure." He added, "Unfortunately you're not plain, not dull, and you've already had too much excitement; the last thing in the universe you needed was a course from Rekal, Incorporated. Nothing could have been more lethal for you or for us. And, for that matter, for McClane."

Quail said, "Why is it 'difficult' for you if I remember my trip—my alleged trip—and what I did there?"

"Because," the Interplan harness bull said, "what you did is not in accord with our great white all-protecting father public image. You did, for us, what we never do. As you'll presently remember—thanks to narkidrine. That box of dead worms and algae has been sitting in your desk drawer for six months, ever since you got back. And at no time have you shown the slightest curiosity about it. We didn't even know you had it until you remembered it on your way home from Rekal; then we came here on the double to look for it." He added, unnecessarily, "Without any luck; there wasn't enough time."

A second Interplan cop joined the first one; the two briefly conferred. Meanwhile, Quail thought rapidly. He did remember more, now; the cop had been right about narkidrine. They—Interplan—probably used it themselves. Probably? He knew darn well they did; he had seen them putting a prisoner on it. Where would *that* be? Somewhere on Terra? More likely Luna, he decided, viewing the image rising from his highly defective—but rapidly less so—memory.

And he remembered something else. Their reason for sending him to Mars; the job he had done.

No wonder they had expunged his memory.

"Oh god," the first of the two Interplan cops said, breaking off his conversation with his companion. Obviously, he had picked up Quail's thoughts. "Well, this is a far worse problem, now; as bad as it can get." He walked toward

Quail, again covering him with his gun. "We've got to kill you," he said. "And right away."

Nervously, his fellow officer said, "Why right away? Can't we simply cart him off to Interplan New York and let them—"

"*He* knows why it has to be right away," the first cop said; he too looked nervous, now, but Quail realized that it was for an entirely different reason. His memory had been brought back almost entirely, now. And he fully understood the officer's tension.

"On Mars," Quail said hoarsely, "I killed a man. After getting past fifteen bodyguards. Some armed with sneaky-pete guns, the way you are." He had been trained, by Interplan, over a five year period to be an assassin. A professional killer. He knew ways to take out armed adversaries . . . such as these two officers; and the one with the ear-receiver knew it, too.

If he moved swiftly enough—

The gun fired. But he had already moved to one side, and at the same time he chopped down the gun-carrying officer. In an instant he had possession of the gun and was covering the other, confused, officer.

"Picked my thoughts up," Quail said, panting for breath. "He knew what I was going to do, but I did it anyhow."

Half sitting up, the injured officer grated, "He won't use that gun on you, Sam; I pick that up, too. He knows he's finished, and he knows we know it, too. Come on, Quail." Laboriously, grunting with pain, he got shakily to his feet. He held out his hand. "The gun," he said to Quail. "You can't use it, and if you turn it over to me I'll guarantee not to kill you; you'll be given a hearing, and someone higher up in Interplan will decide, not me. Maybe they can erase your memory once more; I don't know. But you know the thing I was going to kill you for; I couldn't keep you from remembering it. So my reason for wanting to kill you is in a sense past."

Quail, clutching the gun, bolted from the conapt, sprinted for the elevator. If you follow me, he thought, I'll kill you. So don't. He jabbed at the elevator button and, a moment later, the doors slid back.

The police hadn't followed him. Obviously they had

picked up his terse, tense thoughts and had decided not to take the chance.

With him inside the elevator descended. He had gotten away—for a time. But what next? Where could he go?

The elevator reached the ground floor; a moment later Quail had joined the mob of peds hurrying along the runnels. His head ached and he felt sick. But at least he had evaded death; they had come very close to shooting him on the spot, back in his own conapt.

And they probably will again, he decided. When they find me. And with this transmitter inside me, that won't take too long.

Ironically, he had gotten exactly what he had asked Rekal, Incorporated for. Adventure, peril, Interplan police at work, a secret and dangerous trip to Mars in which his life was at stake—everything he had wanted as a false memory.

The advantages of it being a memory—and nothing more —could now be appreciated.

On a park bench, alone, he sat dully watching a flock of perts: a semi-bird imported from Mars' two moons, capable of soaring flight, even against Earth's huge gravity.

Maybe I can find my way back to Mars, he pondered. But then what? It would be worse on Mars; the political organization whose leader he had assassinated would spot him the moment he stepped from the ship; he would have Interplan and *them* after him, there.

Can you hear me thinking? he wondered. Easy avenue to paranoia; sitting here alone he felt them tuning in on him, monitoring, recording, discussing . . . he shivered, rose to his feet, walked aimlessly, his hands deep in his pockets. No matter where I go, he realized. You'll always be with me. As long as I have this device inside my head.

I'll make a deal with you, he thought to himself—and to them. Can't you imprint a false-memory template on me again, as you did before, that I lived an average, routine life, never went to Mars? Never saw an Interplan uniform up close and never handled a gun?

A voice inside his brain answered, "As has been carefully explained to you: that would not be enough."

Astonished, he halted.

"We formerly communicated with you in this manner," the voice continued. "When you were operating in the field, on Mars. It's been months since we've done it; we assumed, in fact, that we'd never have to do so again. Where are you?"

"Walking," Quail said, "to my death." By your officers' guns, he added as an afterthought. "How can you be sure it wouldn't be enough?" he demanded. "Don't the Rekal techniques work?"

"As we said. If you're given a set of standard, average memories you get—restless. You'd inevitably seek out Rekal, or one of its competitors again. We can't go through this a second time."

"Suppose," Quail said, "once my authentic memories have been canceled, something more vital than standard memories are implanted. Something which would act to satisfy my craving," he said. "That's been proved; that's probably why you initially hired me. But you ought to be able to come up with something else—something equal. I was the richest man on Terra but I finally gave all my money to educational foundations. Or I was a famous deep-space explorer. Anything of that sort; wouldn't one of those do?"

Silence.

"Try it," he said desperately. "Get some of your top-notch military psychiatrists; explore my mind. Find out what my most expansive daydream is." He tried to think. "Women," he said. "Thousands of them, like Don Juan had. An interplanetary playboy—a mistress in every city on Earth, Luna and Mars. Only I gave that up, out of exhaustion. Please," he begged. "Try it."

"You'd voluntarily surrender, then?" the voice inside his head asked. "If we agreed to arrange such a solution? *If* it's possible?"

After an interval of hesitation he said, "Yes." I'll take the risk, he said to himself. That you don't simply kill me.

"You make the first move," the voice said presently. "Turn yourself over to us. And we'll investigate that line of possibility. If we can't do it, however, if your authentic memories begin to crop up again as they've done at this time, then—" There was silence and then the voice finished, "We'll have to destroy you. As you must understand. Well, Quail, you still want to try?"

"Yes," he said. Because the alternative was death now—
and for certain. At least this way he had a chance, slim as
it was.

"You present yourself at our main barracks in New York,"
the voice of the Interplan cop resumed. "At 580 Fifth Avenue,
floor twelve. Once you've surrendered yourself we'll have
our psychiatrists begin on you; we'll have personality-profile
tests made. We'll attempt to determine your absolute, ultimate fantasy wish—and then we'll bring you back to Rekal,
Incorporated, here; get them in on it, fulfilling that wish
in vicarious surrogate retrospection. And—good luck. We
do owe you something; you acted as a capable instrument
for us." The voice lacked malice; if anything, they—the organization—felt sympathy toward him.

"Thanks," Quail said. And began searching for a robot
cab.

"Mr. Quail," the stern-faced, elderly Interplan psychiatrist
said, "you possess a most interesting wish-fulfillment dream
fantsy. Probably nothing such as you consciously entertain or suppose. This is commonly the way; I hope it won't
upset you too much to hear about it."

The senior ranking Interplan officer present said briskly, "He better not be too much upset to hear about it, not
if he expects not to get shot."

"Unlike the fantasy of wanting to be an Interplan undercover agent," the psychiatrist continued, "which, being rela-
tively speaking a product of maturity, had a certain plausi-
bility to it, this production is a grotesque dream of your
childhood; it is no wonder you fail to recall it. Your fantasy
is this: you are nine years old, walking alone down a rustic
lane. An unfamiliar variety of space vessel from another
star system lands directly in front of you. No one on Earth
but you, Mr. Quail, sees it. The creatures within are very
small and helpless, somewhat on the order of field mice,
although they are attempting to invade Earth; tens of thousands of other such ships will soon be on their way, when
this advance party gives the go-ahead signal."

"And I suppose I stop them," Quail said, experiencing a
mixture of amusement and disgust. "Single-handed I wipe
them out. Probably by stepping on them with my foot."

"No," the psychiatrist said patiently. "You halt the in-

144

vasion, but not by destroying them. Instead, you show them kindness and mercy, even though by telepathy—their mode of communication—you know why they have come. They have never seen such humane traits exhibited by any sentient organism, and to show their appreciation they make a covenant with you."

Quail said, "They won't invade Earth as long as I'm alive."

"Exactly." To the Interplan officer the psychiatrist said, "You can see it does fit his personality, despite his feigned scorn."

"So by merely existing," Quail said, feeling a growing pleasure, "by simply being alive, I keep Earth safe from alien rule. I'm in effect, then, the most important person on Terra. Without lifting a finger."

"Yes indeed, sir," the psychiatrist said. "And this is bedrock in your psyche; this is a life-long childhood fantasy. Which, without depth and drug therapy, you never would have recalled. But it has always existed in you; it went underneath, but never ceased."

To McClane, who sat intently listening, the senior police official said, "Can you implant an extra-factual memory pattern that extreme in him?"

"We get handed every possible type of wish-fantasy there is," McClane said. "Frankly, I've heard a lot worse than this. Certainly we can handle it. Twenty-four hours from now he won't just *wish* he'd saved Earth; he'll devoutly believe it really happened."

The senior police official said, "You can start the job, then. In preparation we've already once again erased the memory in him of his trip to Mars."

Quail said, "What trip to Mars?"

No one answered him, so, reluctantly, he shelved the question. And anyhow a police vehicle had now put in its appearance; he, McClane and the senior police officer crowded into it, and presently they were on their way to Chicago and Rekal, Incorporated.

"You had better make no errors this time," the police officer said to heavy-set, nervous-looking McClane.

"I can't see what could go wrong," McClane mumbled, perspiring. "This has nothing to do with Mars or Interplan. Single-handedly stopping an invasion of Earth from another star-system." He shook his head at that. "Wow, what a kid dreams up. And by pious virtue, too; not by force. It's sort of quaint." He dabbed at his forehead with a large linen pocket handkerchief.

Nobody said anything.

"In fact," McClane said, "it's touching."

"But arrogant," the police official said starkly. "Inasmuch as when he dies the invasion will resume. No wonder he doesn't recall it; it's the most grandiose fantasy I ever ran across." He eyed Quail with disapproval. "And to think we put this man on our payroll."

When they reached Rekal, Incorporated the receptionist, Shirley, met them breathlessly in the outer office. "Welcome back, Mr. Quail," she fluttered, her melon-shaped breasts—today painted an incandescent orange—bobbing with agitation. "I'm sorry everything worked out so badly before; I'm sure this time it'll go better."

Still repeatedly dabbing at his shiny forehead with his neatly-folded Irish linen handkerchief, McClane said, "It better." Moving with rapidity he rounded up Lowe and Keeler, escorted them and Douglas Quail to the work area, and then, with Shirley and the senior police officer, returned to his familiar office. To wait.

"Do we have a packet made up for this, Mr. McClane?" Shirley asked, bumping against him in her agitation, then coloring modestly.

"I think we do." He tried to recall; then gave up and consulted the formal chart. "A combination," he decided aloud, "of packets Eighty-one, Twenty, and Six." From the vault section of the chamber behind his desk he fished out the appropriate packets, carried them to his desk for inspection. "From Eighty-one," he explained, "a magic healing rod given him—the client in question, this time Mr. Quail—by the race of beings from another system. A token of their gratitude."

"Does it work?" the police officer asked curiously.

"It did once," McClane explained. "But he, ahem, you see, used it up years ago, healing right and left. Now it's only a memento. But he remembers it working spectacularly." He chuckled, then opened packet Twenty. "Document from the UN Secretary General thanking him for saving Earth; this isn't precisely appropriate, because part of Quail's fantasy is that no one knows of the invasion except himself, but for the sake of verisimilitude we'll throw it in." He inspected packet Six, then. What came from this? He couldn't recall; frowning, he dug into the plastic bag as Shirley and the Interplan police officer watched intently.

"Writing," Shirley said. "In a funny language."

"This tells who they were," McClane said, "and where they came from. Including a detailed star map logging their flight here and the system of origin. Of course it's in *their* script, so he can't read it. But he remembers them reading it to him in his own tongue." He placed the three artifacts in the center of the desk. "These should be taken to Quail's conapt," he said to the police officer. "So that when he gets home he'll find them. And it'll confirm his fantasy. SOP— standard operating procedure." He chuckled apprehensively, wondering how matters were going with Lowe and Keeler.

The intercom buzzed. "Mr. McClane, I'm sorry to bother you." It was Lowe's voice; he froze as he recognized it, froze and became mute. "But something's come up. Maybe it would be better if you came in here and supervised. Like before, Quail reacted well to the narkidrine; he's unconscious, relaxed and receptive. But—"

McClane sprinted for the work area.

On a hygienic bed Douglas Quail lay breathing slowly and regularly, eyes half-shut, dimly conscious of those around him.

"We started interrogating him," Lowe said, white-faced. "To find out exactly when to place the fantasy-memory of him single-handedly having saved Earth. And strangely enough—"

"They told me not to tell," Douglas Quail mumbled in a dull drug-saturated voice. "That was the agreement. I wasn't even supposed to remember. But how could I forget an event like that?"

I guess it would be hard, McClane reflected. But you did—until now.

"They even gave me a scroll," Quail mumbled, "of gratitude. I have it hidden in my conapt; I'll show it to you."

To the Interplan officer who had followed after him, McClane said, "Well, I offer the suggestion that you better not kill him. If you do they'll return."

"They also gave me a magic invisible destroying rod,"

Quail mumbled, eyes totally shut, now. "That's how I killed that man on Mars you sent me to take out. It's in my drawer along with the box of Martian maw-worms and dried-up plant life."

Wordlessly, the Interplan officer turned and stalked from the work area.

I might as well put those packets of proof-artifacts away, McClane said to himself resignedly. He walked, step by step, back to his office. Including the citation from the UN Secretary General. After all—

The real one probably would not be long in coming.

Gahan Wilson

"It's just as I'd always hoped it would be."

John Shepley is a free-lance writer and translator whose short stories have appeared in *Paris Review, San Francisco Review* and *F&SF* and have been anthologized in *The Best American Short Stories of 1956* and *The Best from F&SF*. As is most good imaginative fiction, this story is concerned with the human condition, and for all its strangeness and power, it is not easy to isolate the "fantasy."

THREE FOR CARNIVAL

by John Shepley

It had been a dull place. But now all lovers of the arts, all lovers of tradition, all lovers, could rejoice that New York, after centuries of resistance, had officially adopted the custom of Carnival.

They had agreed to meet at the Battery at eight sharp to begin the last night, there where the fog is thick and the city looks out on the world, by the new ferry terminal. Mother Gimp was the first to arrive. She paced up and down in her skirts and shawls, glancing at her wrist-watch, the one token she had retained from another life. She carried a pail of water and a mop and from time to time admired herself in the mirror of a gum machine; in keeping with her disguise, she chuckled and mumbled aloud.

Now understand that Mother Gimp, for ordinary occasions, was mere Miss Barbara Rowe, blonde and hardly out of Iowa State, who worked as a publisher's reader on Madison Avenue, and took the subway every morning to get there. But here she was everybody's ugly old charwoman, she was something out of an expressionist play, she was a Mediterranean earth-goddess (crone phase). What's more, she had thought it all up herself. Life had so many overtones, as she had often mused, and now Carnival proved it! By the

150

way, who said "mere"? Mr. Cooperman didn't think her
mere, and neither perhaps did Lloyd. And the tiny gold
wrist-watch had been a graduation present from Daddy.

Mr. Cooperman came second. His parti-colored tights,
from Edel & Fitch, Costume Rentals, fitted him badly, the
mask on his face kept slipping askew, but Mother Gimp
would have recognized him anyway—he was Harlequin,
with a paint factory in Long Island City, a six-foot-two son
in the Army, and a wife in analysis. But he seemed a little
perplexed on seeing her. "Is it Barbara, lovely Barbara?" he
asked with a worried smile. Mother Gimp threw back her
head and laughed uproariously. Of course it was! Who else?

Meanwhile all this inconvenience because of Lloyd. If it
hadn't been for him and his ways, they could have started
in uptown somewhere, Barbara's apartment for instance,
where Mother Gimp would have brewed old-fashioneds. But
he lived on Staten Island with his parents, who ran a chicken
and vegetable farm; mornings he took the ferry to Man-
hattan, to his job in Davega's sporting goods store on lower
Broadway, then home in the evening; it had taken Carnival
to induce him to make the trip over twice in one day. Finally a hooting in the fog announced his arrival, and he stepped
ashore in his usual blue serge suit, starched collar and cheap
necktie, and with his tow-head and bumpkin smile, apologiz-
ing for being late. Lloyd, it seemed, was never anything but
Lloyd. (Imagine there being real farms in New York City!
—Barbara could never get over it.) "Just no imagination,
you!" shrieked Mother Gimp when she saw him.

Arm-in-arm, they set off uptown, Lloyd to left, Harlequin to right, Mother Gimp in the middle. She looked at her
watch—it was 8:27. What do you suppose Daddy was doing at this moment? He'd finished dinner, of course, long
ago, was probably sitting out on the screen-porch, listening
to the katydids and digesting his stock-market reports. To
punish Lloyd, she made him carry the pail and mop, but
at the corner of Broadway and Wall Street, she changed her
mind and made Harlequin carry them instead. Not much
going on in this part of town—the impact of Carnival had
fallen there earlier in the day. The shreds of banners flapped
from the lamp posts, the sidewalk in places was ankle-deep
with confetti, but there was little sign of what anyone,
whether Barbara or Mother Gimp, would have called life.

151

Lloyd pointed out Davega's windows, full of ice skates, foot-balls and crew-neck sweaters, which only he could make out in the darkness, and Harlequin patted him on the shoulder, praising him for the serious, hardworking young man that he so obviously was. At City Hall Park, two floats, flower-bedecked and capped by giant papier-mâché caricatures, had collided, and a night-squad was busily dismantling the wreckage. But were they Carnival Commission workers, or scavengers? It was impossible to tell. She looked at her watch—8:49. Going on Daddy's bedtime. She made them switch places, Harlequin to left, Lloyd to right, and took back her pail and mop. Why was she always to be the only one to enter into the spirit of things?

Ahead there were lights and noises. But why walk all the way? Now courtly Harlequin, out of his sleeve, produced a taxicab for the young folks, and on they went. Things were looking up! *"East Side, West Side . . ."* sang Mother Gimp, careening in the middle. Clickety-clickety went the meter, the driver sat hunched over the wheel, and she wanted to see his disguise. "Aw, Miss," he said tiredly, "can't ya stay *put* there in the back seat?" She settled back —people who couldn't *see* made her angry. *London Bridge is falling down . . .* "Oh, look!" she cried in wonder. For all of Canal Street was in flames.

From the big fires, children lit torches and ran to ignite their own little bonfires of egg crates, while Harlequin deplored the danger to life and property and Lloyd simply gawked. 9:17. Tipsy loiterers yelled greetings to them as they passed, and one threw a straw-covered wine bottle, but the driver dodged it skillfully and it bounced on the opposite sidewalk. Barbara suddenly opined that people who led significant everyday lives would have no need of Carnival, though she knew it was just her puritanical Iowa grandmother talking, not herself. (Daddy, trudging across the living room, would be giving a last sleepy look at the television.) They drove on, through canyons where only broken glass and trampled paper streamers testified to the day's passing glory. Mother Gimp called out to the driver to stop. She wanted to get out of the cab—she felt it her duty to mop up the streets. What was an old charwoman for? But Harlequin entreated her, and Lloyd looked so funny with his shocked expression, that she burst out laughing again

152

and urged the driver on. Ahead of them rose 14th Street
like an aurora borealis, a great barrier of light through which
they must pass.

A shattering screech of brakes, and the cab stopped in
Union Square. "This is as far as I go," growled the driver.
"Don't gimme no argument, you people." He leaned around,
and Mother Gimp looked at last into his sightless orbs. He
was Charon!—as she had suspected all along. She memorized
his number in case of further trouble. Harlequin was prof-
fering payment from his wallet, but she thrust herself forward, drowning out his protests. She took three coins out
of her mouth and paid the entire fare.

They strolled east along 14th Street, between twin lines
of lights, and she knew that Daddy was now safely upstairs in bed. Poor Lloyd looked so like a fish out of water
that she took his hand and tried to make him dance a step or
two with her. Harlequin played *cicerone*. Everything moved
him to a gentle, and sometimes ironic, nostalgia: a delicates-
sen (it wasn't there any more, but he evoked it so well that
you saw it) where you used to get the best pastrami sand-
wiches; a movie theater (still there) for which he once
couldn't afford even the fifteen cents for a seat in the balcony; an intellectuals' cafeteria, passed beyond recognition,
where he had argued with friends and pored over political
pamphlets (yes, he'd been quite a rebel in those days!); a
fire-trap loft calling itself a music academy where, a very
little lad, he had been sent to take violin lessons. As for
now, he had his paint business, went de luxe to Miami, and
to first nights on Broadway, but what could take the place
of youth? Barbara listened gravely, and from all the door-
ways, Carmens in crimson shawls, puffing cigarettes and
humming the *Habanera*, came out and listened too.

10:10. They took the Third Avenue El, a legendary struc-
ture which had almost lapsed beyond human memory, but
had been loving reconstructed, down to the last spittoon and
pot-bellied stove, for this last night of Carnival. The passengers wore paper hats, blew whistles and whirled noise-makers
—some were already ripping up the seats and filching the
signs to carry home as souvenirs. Mother Gimp, she wanted
to know all about Harlequin's wife. Was she pretty, or had
she been? Did she make him unhappy? Who, incidentally,

was her analyst, and how much did he charge? He corrected her philosophically. Harlequin (such were the joys of Carnival) had no wife—Mr. Cooperman (don't mention it!) did.

But what was Lloyd saying as, caught in a great throng, they tumbled down the stairs and poured themselves out onto 42nd Street? Something about (with a blush and stammer) people not needing one on a night like this. Not needing what?—a mask or an analyst? No, he meant a mask. People's usual one was enough, he said. Mother Gimp observed that Lloyd was in danger of becoming a wit, and she couldn't exactly say that the prospect pleased her, but Barbara giggled her agreement.

She went skipping ahead of them, singing and swinging her pail and mop. Let Lloyd sprint, and Harlequin puff, to catch up with her. Lexington, Park, Madison, a screaming of sirens, and an open truck with motorcycle police escort roared past transporting a bevy of can-can girls, most likely to the Coliseum. Two gossiping boys went by, identically disguised as Madame de Pompadour. Between Fifth Avenue and Times Square, the floats were still circulating, but willy-nilly. The effigies of world figures, presidents, prime ministers, scientists, stars of stage and screen, wrestlers, rolled their eyes and waggled papier-mâché arms, and more than one broke down with a snapped axle, while the assembled Pagliaccios, Fata Morganas, gypsies, pirates, cowboys and minstrels goggled and applauded. Oh, the tawdriness of the world's imagination! Mother Gimp didn't know whether to laugh or cry.

In the middle of Times Square, it seemed not a bad idea to make a choice. But Lloyd—what had he ever done? Mother Gimp, goddess of the waning moon, saw it all, keening merrily over the little life of man. Oh, sure, got born, the usual way. Got smacked on the backside. Mewled and puked, made pee-pee and po-po. Cry-baby, teacher's pet. Tops, model airplanes, stamp collection. Acne. Curtis High School on Staten Island, flunked geometry, almost flunked Latin. Stock-boy at Davega's, basement clerk, now rising assistant. Might someday become head clerk. Might marry, might father children. Would certainly someday (snip!) die.

And Harlequin, her mystic consort? Mother Gimp took a

deep breath. Had set kind limits and promoted virtue. Had charted the soul. Had been, and not been, the question. Had looked into a glass darkly, never face to face. Had loved not wisely but too well. Immortal melodies: the *Kol Nidre.* Immortal sayings: BRIGHTEN YOUR LIFE WITH COOPER-PAINTS!

They seemed to be on some side-street. Very grave creatures with phosphorescent eyes and stiffening fur came out to stare, but she scampered around them.

"I'll be Mrs. Irwin,
Plain little Mrs. Irwin . . ." she sang, and kicked up her legs.

Lloyd asked, "Who's the lucky Mr. Irwin?"

"I don't know." (Was it Barbara speaking?) "But there's always a Mr. Irwin for a girl like me."

She became for a moment, with longing, Mrs. Irwin J. Irwin, wife of a Newark accountant, of a car salesman in Scranton, of an economics teacher in Des Moines, of a Sensitive Young Man in Sacramento. She played a good bridge hand, took up watercolors, stood for human values, took *Time* and the Book of the Month, voted independent. On top of the television set sprawled two floppy rag dolls, Harlequin and Lloyd, keepsakes . . . No!—it was too ghastly. Back to Mother Gimp!

With a vengeance. Shrieking with hag-laughter, she sloshed the contents of her pail in the faces of the passers-by, and filthy and dripping, they roared back at her. She fixed an evil eye on them, and they broke out in boils and the Saint Vitus dance. She flung away her pail and mop—she flung away discretion, and Daddy's watch. Her skirts lifted high, she went pirouetting out over rooftops and abysses, dancing the *pas-de-trois,* the Carmagnole, the rigmarole, and dragging in her wake a remonstrating Harlequin, a Lloyd petrified with embarrassment. Oh, how she laughed at his expression! Marauding lions broke out of the Coliseum, and great Aztec altars smoldered with human sacrifice. And then they saw him—Mother Gimp saw him, Barbara saw him—it was *Daddy,* nobody else, wearing his Legion cap and with his fly unbuttoned, whooping it up among the can-can girls! They passed on and he was lost to sight.

Where were they now? The Bronx, by the look of it, or

some height above it. In a wilderness of tin cans and stray cats and little coupling dogs, Mother Gimp sat down and wept. No expressionist play was ever so hopeless as this, no earth-goddess's shrine ever so despoiled, no ugly old charwoman ever more unhappy. She drew her shawl over her head—and suddenly an anguished Harlequin was beside her, taking her in his arms, calling her his child, his angel, and promising her everything, a new wrist-watch, a trip to Miami, a divorce from his wife, anything, if only she'd be happy as she deserved to be, and not cry.

But what have we here? Who is this who rises up in wrath? Launcelot, Sir Galahad, Don Ferdinando?—no time to pick a name—quick—to the rescue! His steed was a gymnasium sidehorse, for armor he wore a baseball catcher's chest protector, with shoulder pads and hockey shin-guards, a fencing mask for visor, and a football helmet topped by a feather-duster plume—everything that the Davega branch store in East Fordham Road could hurriedly assemble at midnight the last night of Carnival to equip its chosen champion. But the sword in his hand was tempered and true, and the inscription on his shield (courtesy of Miss Eunice Jenks, teacher of Latin, now deceased, its last pale whisper through the corridors of Curtis High) read:

AMA ME FIDELITER
FIDEM MEAM NOTA

"*Miscreant! Coxcomb!*" cried this knight, and plunged his sword into Harlequin's breast.

And then there wasn't any Harlequin—only Mr. Saul Cooperman of Long Island City, in a gray business suit, standing there with his amiable smile and his hidden sorrows. He put out his hand. "Son," he said, "I thank you all the same. These disguises we put on get the better of us sometimes, don't they? Better to get out of them while we can— be ourselves, eh? I go now. If you would . . . would be so kind . . . as to convey to the young lady . . . my regrets . . . the delicacy of my feelings . . . my eternal respect . . ." He went away into the darkness, the sword still in his heart and its handle bobbing in the quiet of the night air.

Lloyd (he was just Lloyd now, astonished at what he had

done, and not a little abashed) watched him go. Then he turned. "Past midnight," he said. "Carnival is over. Look, they're already tearing down the El again. You're only Barbara and I'm only Lloyd."

Only? She stared back at him, her aged eyes and wrinkled face under the shawl now beyond all change or renewal. She had become her disguise.

A successful free-lance writer must be inventive and persistent. That these qualities also happen to be the mark of a successful collection man can sometimes be useful. Take Jose Silvera, for instance—a free lancer working on the biography of Hurford Shanks, a bird-headed tap-dancer turned politician. When Shanks reneges on the advance Silvera . . . well, for pure ingenuity and persistence Silvera can't be beat. But can he write?

EXPERIMENT IN AUTOBIOGRAPHY
by Ron Goulart

Through the silent fog Jose Silvera moved, leaving the gritty beach and dodging in among the sharp black rocks. Breathing for a moment through his mouth, he stopped in the gray dampness. Silvera spotted the old path that wound up the cliffside. He hunched one wide shoulder, flexed his left leg so that his blaster holster swung free and started upwards.

"Either cash or a certified money order," Silvera said to himself as he climbed. "No more checks."

At the cliff's top a great black and tan dog snarled and dived at him out of the thick mist. Silvera pivoted, stunned the animal with the flat of his hand and pitched it toward the unseen beach.

"Cash probably," he muttered. "They may not even have money orders here in the Azores."

The villa had the expected high stone wall, topped with a foot high death beam that sizzled faintly in the mist. Silvera felled a nearby tree, fashioned a pole and vaulted the wall clean.

He hit on his right thigh on top of a metallic patio table, toppled from that and almost skittered into the vapor topped swimming pool. He did a little balance retaining dance along the pool side and then zigzagged toward the big lemon-yellow house.

F. Tennyson Buchalter was jammed in a silver alloy chair evenly spreading quince jelly on an overtoasted English muffin when Silvera dived into the circular breakfast pavilion. "Yoicks," said the plump television producer.

"Two thousand dollars," said Silvera, his right hand a claw hovering over his blaster handle.

"Joe," said Buchalter, jelly on his thumb. "Miss Nolan sent you the check from Hollywood a month, a good month, maybe five weeks ago, Joe."

"Bounced," said Silvera, edging the check out of his tunic and tossing it.

The check spun, fluttered down into Buchalter's Lion Cross tea. "Insufficient funds," he read.

"Two thousand," said Silvera. "In cash. Now."

"Come on, Joe," said the producer. "Put the damn thing through again."

"We looked into it. There's no money in that particular account. Hasn't been since April 5 of 2094. Okay?"

Buchalter set aside his muffin, pointed at the tall Silvera with his jelly spreader. "Stories I've heard, a good many stories, about you, Joe. How you never let the Guild arbitrate for you."

Silvera spun out his pistol, said, "Pay me the money."

"You writers," said Buchalter. "I wish those mechanical brains had been able to write better dialogue. Then I wouldn't, really wouldn't at all, have to fool with temperamental guys like you."

"I get upset when people don't pay me."

"Okay, Joe, okay. But I could get you blacklisted." Buchalter pushed back from the table, grunted up out of the tight chair.

"Arnie Maxwell tried that," said Silvera.

The producer nodded. "I remember." He ticked his head twice at the doorway and a seven foot tall Negro stepped in, frowning at Silvera.

"The egress?" asked the Negro.

"No use," sighed Buchalter. "He, being a stubborn bastard, would just fight his way back in and unsettle my vacation even more. You wouldn't take a check on a Geneva bank, Joe?"

"Cash."

"Get Mr. Silvera 2000 in cash from the bedroom safe, Norman."

The Negro moved out of the room.

Buchalter scratched his kidneys and narrowed one eye. "We're thinking about doing a documentary on the swing music of the 20th century. Goodman, Shaw, Isham Jones. Pay five thousand."

"No," said Silvera. "You're on my blacklist for a while. Check with my agent in six months, though, if you come up with something else."

"If only you didn't write such good dialogue," said Buchalter as he took a handful of cash from the returned Norman.

Silvera's cruiser was not where he'd left it, beached in among a ring of freckled gray rock. As he stood, hands on hips, in the exact spot where he'd left the ship something banged his shoulder.

Silvera jerked aside, gun out.

Looked up. With his free hand he patted the pocket where the two thousand was.

"Jose," called a nasal voice up in the mist. "I've got your cruiser up here in the yacht. Climb aboard."

"Boy," said Silvera, catching the dangling ladder, "you'll travel a hell of a long way for ten percent."

At the entry way to the big cruiser yacht was Rilke Wheatstraw, a slender jumpy man with dark ringed eyes. "That's not the reason. Though you might as well give me the two hundred now, to keep the books straight. You did get the whole amount, didn't you?"

Silvera caught his agent's hand and came aboard. "Sure," he said. "I don't like guys who welch on what they owe freelance writers. One way or another, sooner or later, I like to collect." He gave Wheatstraw two hundred dollars.

His agent called out, "Start the ship for home, Cullen."

"You still have that fag for a pilot?"

"He's the best man I know for navigating in a fog. Let's go into the cocktail lounge. I've got a great new assignment for you."

Silvera sat in a black realeather chair and asked the automatic bar to wheel over a brandy. "So?"

Wheatstraw jiggled in his chair. "You're not against space travel, Jose. Right?"

"But not another deal like that industrial documentary on Jupiter."

"This," said his agent as their drinks rolled up on a burnished cart, "is a little different. This is a job to write a book."

"A book?" asked Silvera, sitting up. "I haven't done a book since those dime novels for the Mars frontier settlements."

"Not a novel this time," said Wheatstraw, wiping gin fizz foam from his pale lips. "An autobiography."

"Whose?"

"Well," said Wheatstraw, looking down. He raised his head and grinned. "I'd better mention that it pays 20,000."

"Fine," said Silvera. "What kind of an advance?"

"They'll pay travel expenses and hand over 5000 when you arrive."

"Travel expenses to where?"

"Well, this is a little way out, Jose. It's one of the planets in the Barnum system. It's a planet named Turmeric."

Silvera said, "Wait. Turmeric. That's where the people all have bird heads, isn't it?"

"Yes," said Wheatstraw. "This client wants you to ghost his autobiography. He's the Governor of Sector 2 up there. An important man, being considered for President."

"But he's got a bird head."

"As a matter of fact, he's got a head like a puffin."

"I don't know."

"The political situation," said Wheatstraw, "on Turmeric is a little tense. I have to send a writer who can handle himself, a good man with weapons or even bare hands. I could have got Reisberson but you know how he's been fainting lately."

"But a puffin head."

"20,000, Jose."

Silvera exhaled. "Okay. What's the guy's name?"

"Hurford Shanks."

"What can you tell me about him?"

"Well, before he went into politics," said Wheatstraw, "he was a tapdancer in the movies."

"Wonderful," said Silvera.

"This," said Hurford Shanks from the top of his desk, "is how we used to finish the act. Watch." He sailed off the pseudowood desk and landed in a splits on the floor. Two white feathers detached themselves from his puffin head.

"You always wear a straw hat in your office?" Silvera asked.

Shanks rubbed his big curving orange beak with his thumb. "Sure. Lots of the voters drop in here. Though I may be Governor, I'm not too busy to talk to the man from the marketplace and the crossroads. The highways and the byways. Don't you reporters take notes?"

"Freelance writer," said Silvera, lighting a cigarette. "No, I keep all the important stuff in my head. As long as we're asking questions, where's my money?"

"Money?"

"I've been at the Turmeric Crown Hotel for two days," Silvera told him. "Your people take care of my hotel bill and they gave me a punch card for a nearby cafeteria. But nobody's delivered the 5000 advance I was supposed to get on arrival."

"Really?" asked Shanks. He scissored his legs together and got up. "I instructed my secretary to send you a check. Well, well."

Silvera looked around the room, at the walls that were covered with autographed photos of bird headed actors and actresses and flags, then back at the Governor. "I'd like the money as soon as possible."

"There's a lot of pressure in the political game," said Shanks. He tossed his straw hat up, caught it on his elbow and cartwheeled it back on his feathery head. "I have many enemies. In particular a wild eyed agitator named St. John Moosabeck. A treason prone, radical, bearded fellow."

"He's got a beard?"

"It's a false one."

Silvera nodded. "We can get more into your show business career later. First maybe you ought to fill me in on your rise in politics."

Shanks snapped his beak and picked a framed photo off his desk. "It seems to me a man is more than just his politics, Silvera." He tossed him the picture.

It was some kind of ancient aircraft. Not a cruiser, not even an old-fashioned jet. "What is it?"

"My hobby," explained the Governor. "That's a Sopwith Camel. Back on your home planet they flew around in those things back in the 20th century. I have thirty-four of them. And teleporting them all the way to Turmeric from Earth has cost a pretty penny."

Silvera gave the photo back. "About your rise in the political sphere?"

Shanks picked up a memo pad and drew something on it. "I'll be at one of my concealed fields tomorrow in the morning, inspecting a batch of my planes. I find it's best not to let my rivals get wind of exactly where I pursue my hobbyhorse. At any rate, I'd like you to meet me at Field #1 tomorrow at ten. Give you an idea of what sort of a fellow I really am. See me among my little toys and so on."

A girl secretary with a ruffled grouse head shot into the room. "There's another food riot in the suburbs, Mr. Governor."

Shanks shook his head. "My political rivals, Silvera, have convinced some of the citizens that they're starving." To the girl he said, "I'll attend to it later, Mavis, and call out the militia or something. Right now." He crossed to an upright piano and flipped up the lid. "Right now I'm going to entertain Silvera with a medley of hits tunes from some of my famous movies."

Silvera hunched down in his chair and listened.

The android tapped on Silvera's hotel room door just as he was trying to get hot water to flow in the shower stall. Silvera, retying his robe, opened the door.

"You requested a stenographer?" asked the olive drab android.

"Right. Come in."

The andy was man headed, not quite as tall as Silvera, carrying a typewriter in its right hand. "I was originally programmed to be a gourmet chef," said the android. "But a temporary personnel gap here at the Turmeric Crown caused me to be rearranged." The machine sat down, crossed its legs and said, "I am ready to proceed."

"Why don't you," said Silvera, "wait till I get my pants on."

"As you wish."

Silvera moved to the bathroom area. He was pulling up his trousers when the android jumped him.

The whir of the surgical drill the andy had replaced its right hand with was loud in Silvera's ear as he bicycled them both back into the shower alcove.

"Death to the enemies of progress," cried the machine. "Death to the Earth hirelings of the corrupt government. Death to those who would glorify our lousy Governor."

The drill perforated Silvera's earlobe. He managed to shove the android's dangerous arm further away from his head. "You really feel that way about me?"

"No," said the android. "I say whatever they program."

Silvera ducked. "I see. Who hired you?"

"St. John Moosabeck of course."

"Oh, so." Silvera clutched at the android's head, managing to loosen a pair of screws. Shifting his shoulders, Silvera got the right position and, using the andy's arm as a lever, threw the machine across the room.

The android landed, as Silvera had calculated, with its loose-screwed head in the toilet installation. With a quick jump Silvera was at the flush button. The cascade of water made the android's head sizzle, blink and then short out.

Silvera jerked the ruined android out into the living room and dropped it behind a sofa. He dressed without showering, picked up his meal ticket and went out to the nearby cafeteria. The place was out of food.

The rioting awakened him early the next morning. A brick smashed through his window, something you didn't expect on the 13th floor.

Dressed and in the lobby, Silvera learned that St. John Moosabeck had started a series of vast riots, the ultimate object of which was the storming of the capital buildings. Silvera learned this from the lark-headed desk clerk, a loyalist, who was then interrupted by a bellboy who was pro-Moosabeck.

Silvera hustled through the confused lobby crowd and

out into the street. Buildings were burning, blasters were crackling. A police cruiser crashed into a fountain apexed by a statue of Shanks in a tap-dance attitude. A warbler-headed fat man trotted by with a deep-freeze on his shoulder. Three cartons of chicken parts fell in Silvera's path. He dodged and looked around for transportation. Shanks' office hadn't delivered the courtesy cruiser they'd promised.

Three woodpecker heads ran by waving torches. A parrot woman tried to throttle Silvera. Two teen-age orioles were stealing a bathtub from an antique shop next to the hotel. Further down the street, in front of the smashed in cafeteria, a crowd was wrestling with six assorted police officers. Silvera doubted he'd be able to get a taxi.

"But I'm going to get that 5000 advance before the country collapses," he thought. "Shanks might be at Airfield #1."

A cruiser buzzed the crowds, broadcasting pro-Moosabeck. Silvera made a running jump and caught the tail gate.

"What are you up to?" asked the big grackle-headed pilot as Silvera climbed in.

"I've always been interested in the broadcast media," said Silvera, stunning the man with the edge of his hand. He tied him in mike wires and, swinging into the control seat, caused the cruiser to climb up above the buildings. In fifteen minutes, following the Shanks-drawn map, he was at the Governor's hidden hobby field.

The small runway was flanked on each side by a half dozen antique airplanes. Silvera recognized one as a Ford Trimotor because it had been pictured on a stamp his grandfather'd once given him the summer he was interested in stamp collecting. Silvera dropped the cruiser down next to a ship with two sets of wings, jumped out and headed for the big curve-roof shed where people seemed to be gathered.

Two woodpecker heads were wheeling out a plane. When Silvera pulled up under the right wing Governor Shanks came running out of the shed with two suitcases.

"One of my passenger ships," said Shanks, nodding at the plane.

The men got the propellers spinning. "I wanted to talk about my money," said Silvera.

"The autobiography venture will have to be postponed, Silvera."

"5000, book or no book," said Silvera. "That's the agreement you signed with my agent."

"I'm sure an act of god, such as the imminent collapse of my regime," said Shanks, his orange bill flapping rapidly, "changes and cancels all agreements."

"Oh, no it doesn't," said Silvera. He swung his hand around to reach for his blaster. Somebody clamped his arms to his sides. Over his shoulder he saw the head of a fierce starling.

"You are in the grasp of Tully Spand," said the Governor. "Spand is prominent in our local underworld. Right now he's been trying to persuade me to pay me a small amount to tide him over until the fate of my government is determined."

"He's been holding back on the kickback dough," said Spand. "And the cemetery graft. Now that he's washed up I want to collect."

"Fix him," ordered Shanks, "and let's get on to the next money cache, Spand."

"Right," said Spand. He tightened his hold and someone else came up and slammed Silvera on the head with a length of pipe.

A couple of minutes after he fell he heard planes fly away.

"The money," said Silvera. He was inhaling something odd and it made him wake up and blink.

A rangy blonde girl in a tan jumpsuit was next to him on the runway, holding a white cylinder near his nose. "I didn't have any smelling salts but I hoped my perfume would maybe wake you up. I tried a nasal spray mist but you stayed out. My name is Anne Steiner. And you're Jose Silvera."

"You know me?" Silvera bent his neck and felt at his head.

"Don't poke that sore spot. Yes, I searched you when I found you. You're the writer, aren't you? I remember some of your credits back on Earth."

Silvera looked at her. She didn't have a bird head. She had a pretty, good-boned face. "You're who? And doing what here?"

"Anne Steiner," said the girl. "I'm with the Proven Worth Entertainment Corporation. Some pre-testing indicates that our clients on several planets would get a favorable audience reaction to a televised documentary on Governor Shanks' airplanes. It's one of the few collections anywhere, except for a man named MacQuarrie on Venus who won't play along with PWEC. Are you okay?"

"Sure," said Silvera as the girl helped him to his feet. "You see Shanks?"

"No. I was to meet him here today to talk over our project. I guess all the rioting has caused him to change his plans."

"Shanks is running," said Silvera. "Skipping with the government funds." He told the blonde what had happened. "You'd like to catch up with him probably."

"Yeah. I have this thing about collecting money that's owed me."

"Think he's likely to head for one of his other hidden fields?"

Silvera thought. "He had money stashed here. He might have it at the other places, too."

"I know where all the other fields are. Found out so we could do the documentary," said Anne. "Want to go look?"

He glanced toward the sound cruiser he'd flown out in. "It looks like they disabled my cruiser."

"And I came out on a bicycle," said the girl. "Hey, wait. They didn't wreck the airplanes."

"You can fly one?"

"Part of my research work. I learned to fly planes. Let's take the P-38." She pointed at the plane.

"Won't it be crowded?"

"We'll rip out some radio equipment and stuff," said Anne. "I've always wanted to try and fly one."

They found Shanks at the second field they tried. He and Tully Spand and a finch-headed man were throwing suitcases into a large transport plane as Anne circled the field.

"That's a DC-6," said the girl. "I'll land now. Okay?"

"Okay," said the crowded Silvera.

"I'm sorry about flying upside down over the mountains."

"You're doing fine."

Anne brought the P-38 in and taxied it to a stop in front of the DC-6. "Keep them from taking off."

Silvera squeezed out of the cockpit, dashed along the

wing. He jumped and caught one of the propellers of the DC-6 and swung up on its wing. He edged up to the ship, scrambled up on top of it.

Tully Spand shot at him from the other side.

Silvera shot back and then threw himself at the gangster. While they were tangling Shanks swung one of his suitcases at Silvera.

Someone shot the suitcase from the Governor's hands. The case flipped a somersault and bounced open. A packet of bills tumbled out.

"Earth money," said Silvera as he broke the thumb on Spand's gun hand.

"Easier to spend throughout the universe," said Governor Shanks, clamping the suitcase shut with his good hand.

"Step back," ordered Anne. She had a pistol pointed at the Governor and the finch hireling. "You, Spand. Let go the gun."

"It's a fight to the death," grunted Spand.

"Stop kidding," said Silvera. He slammed an elbow into Spand's beak, cracked it, knocked him out. Silvera rose, kicked open the fallen suitcase. "I'll take my 5000."

"To see you helping an obvious enemy of mine, Miss Steiner," said Governor Shanks, "saddens me."

Anne shrugged. To Silvera she said, "If we can refuel here we should be able to fly to the next territory. Be safe there."

Silvera was counting money but he paused to nod yes.

Kenneth Bulmer is a rather well-known SF writer in England, where he lives "in a tiny village in the blossom belt of Kent." His name may be unfamiliar to many readers in this country, a situation which we are delighted to improve by including this superior story. Its treatment is restrained, but its effect is uncommonly strong, and, we should add, grim.

THE ADJUSTED
by Kenneth Bulmer

On this morning as they went down to the pens the mild early sunlight gentled with soft radiance the broken brickwork and gaping concrete so that for a mocking moment the labyrinth assumed a semblance of normality. The two men walked delicately along the raised ramparts between the pens looking down through each transparent roof.

"The zoom they've designed on my new cine camera is fantastic—a recommended Best Buy." The elder of the two withdrew his foot sharply as he kicked a protruding stump of ferro-concrete. "What a frightful bore all this is, Rodney!" He spoke pettishly, like a man roused from an absorbing game to attend a broken fuse. "Every time I come here there are less people to care for."

"But we must care, Charles, surely?" The younger man tended to hang a half-body's distance in rear of his companion. "After all . . . Look at the poor darlings! One does try to remember they were human . . ."

Rain had fallen in the night although the morning sky smiled approvingly and oily puddles shimmered spectroscopically from depressions and worn patches in the concrete ramparts. Over the sheathing of the pens, fussily energetic cleaning robots swept and scrubbed and polished until the plastic kindled to invisibility, only vagrant gleams betraying its continued existence. The two men, Charles and Rodney, walked quickly with loud footfalls like men inspecting the tanks of an aquarium.

"But all these pens are empty, Charles!"

"Here, yes. We like to keep the survivors together. It makes caring for them easier and I think no one would begrudge us that."

"I should think not, Charles! Wendy bought me my new golf clubs yesterday and I can't wait to step on the greens. There's one thing about golf"—he pronounced it goff—"it keeps a fellow in shape."

"True. We shall be surfing next week. Randy Waller has this brand new fibre-glass motor cruiser—a fabulous boat—and we're having a tremendous time together down on the beach. Why don't you try to get away?"

"That's very civil of you, Charles. Very. Wendy would like that. I think even bridge and ponies are beginning to pall."

"Can't overdo a good thing, Rodney, you know what they say—"

A dozen aisles in from the perimeter the two men paused. A refuse robot, its capacious container shut tight, waddled past. Slime tricked from one corner. Rodney wrinkled up his nose and made a noise of disgust. Charles said: "You can never trust these robots to do a decent job. However clever they are and however much care and foresight we put into the programme for them, somehow they manage to foul something up." He made a note on his yellow report. "I'll have that attended to, pronto."

A few paces further on Charles stared down into the membrane spanning the pen roof. He sighed. "A whole family was quartered here the last time I was on duty. Now the pen is empty."

"Poor darlings," said Rodney. "But it was all for the best, even if they could never know that."

Before they reached the next pen, both men were once again in the ritual of discussing their latest possessions and plans. On the tail of: ". . . sweetest little hi-fi on the market with the stereo so bland you don't have to shut your eyes to see the orchestra . . ." they reached the first of the inhabited pens.

The hypno robot stood respectfully to one side, waiting. Charles checked his worksheet.

"The Robinsons. Ah, yes, I remember them. Grandfather was a skilled capstan man. He's dead now, luckily."

Rodney stared dow through the transparent covering that loving robot attention had burnished. "Just the father and mother, three children and the grandmother. I say, Charles!" Rodney stooped, hands on knees. "She looks—I rather think—I really do . . ."

The worksheets fluttered like a benediction as Charles slapped them under his arm decisively. "Quite right, Rodney. You've a quick eye. We'll have to see to her first."

As that train of attention smoothly wended its way to finality Rodney listened to the Robinsons' conversation through the microphone and loudspeaker hookups. Below him the pen showed four square concrete walls frilled here and there with the lace of condensation staining. No covering shielded the concrete floor. The six Robinsons sat on wooden boxes spaced about the area.

Mother Robinson sat with a silly, proud smile on her face. "Now hurry up, children. Your father has a big day ahead of him. It's our anniversary and we're all going on a picnic."

The three children—two boys and a girl—all shrilled into excited clamour like gulls pirouetting beyond a cliff edge. "Where are we going? Whose anniversary? When?"

"Now mind your tongues and eat your breakfasts." Mother Robinson rose from her splintered box and moved towards the sink and tap against the wall. "I've fixed you a special breakfast today—then you can watch tv until your father comes home from work."

"Won't be long, kids." Father Robinson pulled his single sack-like garment around him. "The foreman's a pal. I'm doing a half shift today, two hours."

Mother Robinson lifted the chipped enamel bowls from beside the sink. She held each one under the faucet and filled it with the porridge that spurted out as she turned the tap. "Now, Estelle and you boys—you mind your clothes! I don't want bacon and eggs giving me extra washing." She carried the bowls back on a tray and set one down to each member of the family. "I've put in an extra rasher, so think yourselves lucky."

The younger boy thrust in his spoon and began to slobber the porridge into his mouth. With his mouth full he said: "I only got one egg, Mum! I wannanuvver!"

"Greedy!" But the woman obediently rose and splashed more porridge into the bowl. "Here you are, Alfie. Now hush your tongue and eat up. Look at Bert!"

The older boy had the bowl inverted over his mouth and sucked with a siphoned mouth and loud noises. Porridge dropped to squash stickily onto his box and to add a fresh layer to the dried porridge laminating his garment.

"You can't do better than go to work on an egg," said Father Robinson. "And the bacon has 'Best Quality' stamped right through it. But I'd best be off. Don't want to be late today."

"Take a MidMunch, Dad. You can enjoy that without spoiling your appetite."

The man stood up and walked carefully towards a corner of the pen. He stood facing into the angle of the walls and his body and hands moved occasionally, the bedraggled hem of his clothing knuckling the floor.

"Grandma's quiet this morning, Mum." The remaining Robinsons continued sitting on their boxes, their gruel bowls empty on the harsh floor.

The mother hushed her eldest. "Now you leave your grandma alone, Estelle! She's just having a little nap. Go and watch the telly."

Obediently the three children turned as one to face a blank concrete wall. Mildew grew a roseate whorl. Their faces blanked, smooth and effortlessly becoming tuned receptors. The woman sat humped on her box. A dribble of porridge plopped to the floor.

"My now," she said tut-tuttingly. "Your father's left his Pools behind. The more you invest the better chance you stand. I wonder if I have time to go down to the supermarket? The bargains on the telly last night are worth having. M'mm." Her voice softened and she spoke reflectively to unresponsive ears. "It's going to be a lovely day today. Your dad's gone to a lot of trouble for this anniversary. I hope the weather keeps fine."

Above her head the roofing spanned clear and unbroken with the morning shadows of Charles and Rodney like bars across the plastic.

The eldest son Bert knuckled his eyes, the swollen joints straining their yellow flesh against his white wire-bristle eyebrows. "Gee! Lookit that rocket! They're gonna shmack right down on Mars if they don't figure out the drive toobes!" His thin body jerked on the raw box. "It's going! It's the commercials!"

"Hey, Mum!" said Estelle, the pendulous flesh of her neck sagging. "It's the commercials. Never mind, Alfie—it'll come back."

The mother glanced across at the mildewed concrete wall, the scrawny neck muscles distending her dessicated flesh, the blued hollows beneath jaw and ear concaving to blackness. The deep pitted lines of her face shifted their alignment as though to express pleasure. She passed one thin hand over the powdery refuse of her hair.

"I think I'll change my make up," she said in a dreamy voice. "I might even go blonde."

"What'd Dad say?"

"You 'tend to your telly, Estelle!"

Above them, Rodney glanced sharply at Charles. Charles nodded perfunctorily. A few aimless clouds yawed across the sky. "I think so, Rodney. I dislike this function of our duty, but at the least, it is a surcease of suffering for one more."

Under Charles' directions the hearse robot unzipped a corner of the roofing and descended. It touched the rhythmically moving figure of Father Robinson on its way towards Grandmother Robinson on her box. The man continued his sequence of movements, mitred into his corner.

"Robots!" exclaimed Charles. "The fool thing nearly knocked him over! And they were prattling about machines taking over from man! The good-for-nothing heaps of electronics!"

"If they weren't machines and therefore incapable of being so, I'd say robots were perverse." Rodney resumed his study of the Robinson family. "And as for that scare about taking over from us—" His smile held contempt.

The hearse robot extended its paps and with a sinewy economy of effort lifted Grandmother Robinson from her box to fold her efficiently into the coffin that had been readied ahead of time. Sunlight silvered along a metal arm. The low-key whirr of motors and a faint taste of oil on the air accompanied the routine procedures. The hearse robot back-tracked with Grandmother Robinson folded to its embrace.

"I've given up my Bingo for the anniversary," said Mother Robinson as the hearse robot sidled past her. "So I want you children to behave yourselves. No gallivanting off. If you want ice cream and lollipops you must do as you're told."

Alfie the younger son tugged impatiently at his porridge-stained garment and the dessicated material fluffed into a tear. "I wanna lollipop now!"

"Now look at you, you ungrateful imp!" Mother Robinson did not move from her box. "Tearing your best jacket? You wait 'til your father comes home!"

Alfie cringed back and the stiff hairs over the back of his head crushed down on the grey leathery flesh of his neck. His mother stirred herself reluctantly.

"I'd better get the dishes in the dishwasher." Mother Robinson creakingly collected the bowls and dropped them, one at a time, into the sink. "You tend to your tv."

On the concrete ramparts where now overnight water contracted its pools and haloed its evaporation, the hearse robot clicked past the two men. A shred of Grandma Robinson's coarse garment had caught in the lid of the coffin. Rodney took a step forward until Charles stayed him with a look.

"What difference does it make, Rodney?"

"You're right, of course, Charles. But—the poor dears—it's all they could have expected when their skills were overtaken. I'll feel so much lighter when they are all gone."

Charles beckoned the hypno robot. Multiple lenses probed impersonally downwards. The mocking sound of dynamos rose mincingly up the scale.

"Poor Grandma," said Estelle, her pendulous shape sagging the cassock clothing and planed by the severity of the box. "We do miss her so . . ."

"You hardly remember her, Estelle. She died when you and the boys were too small to understand such things."

Father Robinson jerked into motion exactly as though a gear train had meshed in his legs. One moment he was standing angled in his corner; the next he was turned about and shuffling wearily across to slough down on his box.

"You look tired, Dad."

"Two hours—half a shift—they make us work hard for our living. It's all these fancy new automations they're putting in. One day they won't want men to work at all, I shouldn't wonder."

"Oh, Dad! Don't spoil our anniversary."

"They seem happy," said Charles, wiping his face with a tissue. "The robot will dispose of the grandmother in the vats. Time we moved on."

Mother Robinson had returned to her box. The family of five now sat around the area, each on his box. Grandmother Robinson's box had at last fulfilled its function: it held her wizened body now for its last short journey, at once her conveyance and her coffin.

"Just let me check the vitamin and mineral content of the porridge, Charles." Rodney leaned over carefully towards the dials set in the angle where the Robinsons' food pipe branched from the main. "And a robot had better clean off their faucet. It's encrusted with dried porridge."

"Robots!" Charles said disgustedly. He made the necessary note.

The five figures clad in their stained vestments sat quiescently on their coffins in the square confinement of concrete walls. Occasionally they prattled on in lively fashion about the anniversary, their talk peppered with tv and comics and lollipops and bingo and the neighbours' back yard squalor.

Charles and Rodney walked more slowly now, each movement an effort beneath the midday sun, creeping circumspectly around the latticework ramparts.

"The average age stays around the same as the older ones die off and the younger ones age. The Robinsons, for instance, Rodney, must average out around forty-five to fifty."

Rodney halted to catch a breath, a hand pressed to his side. "It gives me the creeps to hear these ancients talking about lollipops and ice creams and buckets and spades. But we couldn't let them breed, the poor darlings, could we?"

The two paused with more frequency now as they pursued their tour of inspection. "You did check the hypno robot, Rodney?" Charles spoke with sharpness.

"Of course, Charles! What a question."

"If that robot fails us . . . I've seen pens filled with porridge and pens filled with—never mind. But one family broke the mesmerism when a robot malfunctioned. They acted—it was quite horrible—they acted like demented people. Running about and screaming—it was quite clear to me why that sort never adjusted."

"After all, they don't have our advantage of being adjusted logically. As soon as a rational regime was devised by the computers in statistical analysis of behaviour and the multivariate approach to psychology established our salvation, automation made the poor darlings redundant. But I always think of the essential dignity of the human being—"

"Why, naturally, Rodney! We couldn't have tolerated the mass killing of the redundants and equally we can't support them as they imagine themselves to be supported . . ."

"I'm sure they have a nice time, really—all things considered."

"What they experience has the same validity as though it was really happening."

"Restful, I always think, Charles."

"That's our burden, Rodney. Rest for them; but we have our responsibilities. But what a bore it is!"

"Yes. I shall be glad for my session with the analyst tomorrow. There is where you find true rest. And to think that ordinary men once used to pry into your own psychiatric makeup! They called themselves psychologists but they were really only psychic voyeurs. Now the machines can be perfectly dispassionate. So much more reassuring."

"They used to say conflict was everything; but here we have the conflict between reality and illusion—and, thankfully, it is quite clear that neither can win this insane contest."

"Quite, Charles," said Rodney primly.

The two men passed the last of the inhabited pens with the attendant robots like cranes perched watchfully on stalky legs above the shimmering-water surface of the transparent sheaths.

"Thank goodness that's over." Charles cautiously descended the slope towards the concrete road curving around the pen area. "However much I feel I am doing my duty to these people, I know I have put in a good day's work. Surfing for me! Relax in the sun! Soon we'll be in the company of the big boys of the world—that's living!"

"That feller we stopped at first—what was his name—Robinson—standing in a corner and twitching for work . . . We do a highly skilled—it makes you—I mean—"

"Now then, Rodney!" Charles hesitated at the road edge, turning his back carefully and tilting his head to look back at Rodney. "That's enough of that! We know our position." His face showed more animation. "I'm pleased with my new car . . . Triple carbs, aly heads, machine balanced, goes like a bomb—"

"She's a beauty, Charles." Rodney finished negotiating the gentle slope, puffing with exertion. "I'm pleased they've cut down on the chrome this year. More elegant—"

"Get in, Rodney. There's a big meal waiting with all the trimmings and my wine man recommended me a niersteiner that slides down like syrup and razor blades—I think you'll like it."

"You always could pick a fine wine, Charles."

Rodney stood beside Charles with an exaggerated motion of his legs. Charles held both hands out in front of him rounding on the empty air.

"I like the feel of the velvet steering ring," he said moving his hands smoothingly. "Adds a spot of class."

The two old men tottered gently away, their porridge textured garments wrapping them like shrouds, across the concrete to their own pens.

With a reckless laugh, Norman Spinrad here kicks aside the debris of misinformation surrounding Primitive Man, bores to the very roots of civilization, and gives us a brief and funny insight into the way it really was, and is, and will be.

THE AGE OF INVENTION

by Norman Spinrad

One morning, having nothing better to do, I went to visit my cousin Roach. Roach lived in one of those lizard-infested caves on the East Side of the mountain. Roach did not hunt bears. Roach did not grow grain. Roach spent his daylight hours throwing globs of bearfat, bison-chips and old rotten plants against the walls of his cave.

Roach said that he was an Artist. He said it with a capital "A." (Even though writing has not yet been invented.)

Unlikely as it may seem, Roach had a woman. She was, however, the ugliest female on the mountain. She spent her daylight hours lying on the dirty floor of Roach's cave and staring at the smears of old bearfat, moldy bison-chips and rotten plants on the wall.

She used to say that this was Roach's Soul. She would also say that Roach had a very big soul.

Very big and *very* smelly.

As I approached the mouth of Roach's cave, I smelt pungent smoke. In fact, the cave was filled with this smoke. In the middle of the cave sat Roach and his woman. They were burning a big pile of weeds and inhaling the smoke.

"What are you doing?" I asked.

"Turning on, baby," said Roach. "I've just invented it."

"What does 'turning on' mean?"

"Well, you get this weed, dig? You burn it, and then you honk the smoke."

I scratched my head, inadvertently killing several of my favorite fleas.

"Why do that?" I asked.

"It like gets you high."

"You don't seem any further off the ground than I am," I observed. "And you're still kinda runty."

Roach snorted in disgust. "Forget it, man," he said. "It's only for Artists, Philosophers and Metaphysicians, anyway. (Even though Philosophy and Metaphysics have not yet been invented.) Dig my latest!"

On the nearest wall of the cave, there was this big blob of bearfat. In the middle of it was this small piece of bison-chip. Red and green and brown plant stains surrounded this. It smelt as good as it looked.

"Uh . . . interesting. . . ." I said.

"Like a masterpiece, baby," Roach said proudly. "I call it 'The Soul of Man.' "

"Uh . . . 'The Sole of Man'? Er . . . it *does* sort of look like a foot."

"No, no, man! *Soul*, not *sole!*"

"But Roach, spelling hasn't been invented yet."

"Sorry. I forgot."

"Anyway," I said, trying to make him feel a little better, "it's very Artistic." (Whatever that meant.)

"Thanks, baby," Roach said sulkily.

"What's the matter, Roach?" I asked. He really looked awful.

"We haven't eaten in a week."

"Why don't you go out and kill a bear or something?" I suggested.

"I don't have the time to waste on hunting," Roach said indignantly. "I must live for Art!"

"It appears that you are dying for Art," I replied. "You can't do very much painting when you are dead."

"Well anyway," said Roach, in a very tiny voice, "I'm a pretty lousy hunter in the first place. I would probably starve even if I spent the whole day hunting. Or maybe a bear would kill *me*. This way, I'm at least like starving for a Reason."

I must admit it made a kind of sense. Roach is terribly nearsighted. Also amazingly scrawny. The original 90 pound weakling.

"Mmmmmmm. . . ." I observed.

"Mmmmmmm. . . . *what?*" asked Roach.

"Well, you know old Aardvark? He can't hunt either. So what he does is he makes spearheads and trades them for bears. Maybe you could . . . ?"

"Go into *business?*" Roach cried. "Become bourgeois? *Please!* I am an Artist. Besides," he added lamely, "I don't know how to make spearheads."

"Mmmmm. . . ."

"Mmmmm. . . ."

"I know!" I cried. "You could trade your paintings!"

"Cool, baby!" exclaimed Roach. "Er . . . only why would anyone want to trade food for a painting?"

"Why because . . . er . . . ah. . . ."

"I guess I'll just have to starve."

"Wait a minute," I said. "Er . . . if I can get someone to trade food for your paintings, will you give me some of the food, say . . . oh, one bear out of every ten?"

"Sure," said Roach. "What've I got to lose?"

"It's a deal then?"

"Deal, baby!"

I had just invented the Ten-Percenter.

So I went to see Peacock. Peacock lived in the weirdest cave on the mountain—all filled up with stuff like mooseskins dyed pink, stuffed armadillos, and walls covered with withered morning-glories. For some reason which I have not yet been able to fathom, the women of the more henpecked men on the mountain give Peacock bears to make the same kind of messes in their caves.

Peacock is pretty weird himself. He was dressed in a skintight sabertooth skin dyed bright violet.

"Hello sweets," Peacock said, as I entered his perfumed cave.

"Hello, Peacock," I said uneasily. "Heard about Roach?"

"Roach" shrilled Peacock. "That dirty, dirty man? That beatnik with the positively *unspeakable* cave?"

"That's him," I said. "Roach the Artist. Very good Artist, you know. After all, he invented it."

"Well what about that dreadful, dreadful creature?"

"Well you know your friend Cockatoo—?"

"Please, sweets!" shrieked Peacock. "Do not mention

that *thing* Cockatoo in my presence again! Cockatoo and I are on the outs. I don't know what I ever saw in him. He's gotten so unspeakably *butch*."

Cockatoo was this . . . uh . . . *friend* of Peacock's . . . or *was*. They . . . uh . . . invented something together. Nobody is quite sure what it was, but we've organized a Vice Squad, just in case.

"Yeah," I muttered. "Well anyway, Cockatoo is paying Roach twenty bears to do a painting in his cave. He says that having an Original Roach in his cave will make your cave look like . . . er . . . 'A *positive* sloth's den, bubby,' I think his words were."

"Oooooh!" shrieked Peacock. "Oooooh!" He began to jump around the cave, pounding his little fists against the walls. "That monster! That veritable *beast!* Oooh, it's *horrid,* that's what it is! What am I going to do, sweets, whatever am I going to do?"

"Well," I suggested, "Roach is my cousin, you know, and I do have some pull with him. I suppose I could convince him to do a painting in *your* cave instead of Cockatoo's. Especially if you paid *thirty* bears instead of twenty. . . ."

"Oh, *would you*, sweets? Would you really?"

"Well I don't know. I do kind of like you, Peacock, but on the other hand. . . ."

"Pretty, pretty, *pretty* please?"

I sighed heavily. "Okay, Peacock," I said. "You've talked me into it."

So Peacock got his Original Roach for thirty bears. Next week, I went to see Cockatoo, and I told him the story.

I got *him* to pay *forty* bears. Forty and thirty is seventy. Which gave me seven. Not bad for a couple hours' work. I better watch out, or someone'll invent income tax.

I saw Roach last week, the ingrate. He has moved to a bigger cave on the *West Side* of the mountain. He has a fine new leopard skin and *three* new women. He has even invented the Havana cigar, so he can have something expensive to smoke.

Unfortunately, he has discovered that he no longer needs me to make deals for him. His going price is eighty bears a painting. I, like a dope, neglected to invent the renewable exclusive agency contract. Can't invent 'em all, I suppose.

Roach has become truly insufferable, though. He now talks of "art" with a small "a" and "Bears" with a capital "B." He is the first Philistine.

He is going to get his.

How do you like my fine new leopard skin? Would you like one of my Havana cigars? Have you met this new woman yet? Have you seen my new cave?

I can buy and sell Roach now. I am the first tycoon. How did I do it? Well. . . .

Hog was the mountain bum. He never trimmed his beard. He didn't have a woman, not even an *ugly* one. He laid around his filthy cave all day, doing nothing but belching occasionally. A real slob.

But even a jerk like Hog can throw bearfat and bison-chips against a cave wall.

I made an Artist out of Hog. I did this by telling him he could make fifty bears a day just by throwing bearfat and bison-chips against the walls of other people's caves.

This appealed to Hog.

This time I did *not* neglect to invent the renewable exclusive agency contract. It was another ten percent deal.

Hog gets ten percent.

Then I went to Peacock's cave. I stared in dismay at Roach's painting. "What is *that?*" I sneered.

"That, sweets, is an Original Roach," Peacock crooned complacently. "Isn't it divine? Such sensitivity, such style, such grace, such—"

"*Roach?*" I snorted. "You *can't* be serious. Why that Neopseudoclassicalmodern stuff went out with the Brontosaurs. You're *miles* behind the times, Peacock," I said, thereby inventing the Art Critic. "*The* Artist today is of course the Great Hog."

"Hog?" whined Peacock. "Hog is beastly, beastly. A rude, stupid, smelly thing, a *positive* slob. Why his whole cave is a wretched mass of slop!"

"Exactly," I answered. "That's the source of his greatness. Hog is the mountain's foremost Slop Artist."

"Ooooh. . . . How much do the Great Hog's paintings cost?"

"One hundred bears apiece," I said smugly. "Cockatoo is already contracting to—"

"I told you never to mention that *creature* to me again!" Peacock shrieked. "He must not steal an Original Hog from me, do you hear? I simply couldn't *bear* it! But all this is getting so *expensive*. . . ."

I gave Peacock my best understanding smile. "Peacock, old man," I said, "I have a little business proposition for you. . . ."

Well, that's all there was to it. You guessed it, now when Peacock makes one of his messes in some henpecked caveman's cave, it always includes at least one Original Hog, or maybe a couple Original Treesloths—Treesloth being another jerk Artist I have under contract. I sell the painting to Peacock for a hundred bears, and he charges his suck—er, *client*, *two* hundred bears for the same mess of bearfat and bison-chips. Peacock calls this Interior Decorating.

I call it "Civilization." Maybe it'll last for a couple of months, if I'm lucky.

This story is about Walton Ulster, a musician and critic who is driven by a series of painful recollections to return to his home town. It is a story of time travel, but in a personal and psychological sense. Its scope is as broad, its intricacies as complex, as the mind of Ulster himself. Mr. Green's gripping narrative provides support for those who maintain that there are more mysteries between two human temples than there are in the farthest reaches of space.

APOLOGY TO INKY

by Robert M. Green, Jr.

Walton Ulster, between sleep and waking, heard a car horn go "ah-ooga," and thought: *that's a sound that's getting to be passé*. Even the boop-boop-a-doop horn, in spite of the teen-age sports with their roadsters, was getting to be passé, along with the biplane—

Walton snapped awake.

It was a wrenching, brain-battering awakening. He had not been deeply asleep, if he had been asleep at all, but he had been more than 30 years back, or down, in time, and to rocket in an instant from 1931 to 1965 was enough to give anyone a case of psychological bends.

Walton looked out the window of the bus and studied the highway traffic. There was not a car in sight older than 1950. Some humorist could have installed an "ah-ooga" horn from a junkyard Model T, but Walton wouldn't have heard it here in the back of the bus, with the wheels singing directly under his feet, and the cold air jet humming and burbling into his ear.

An "ah-ooga" horn would be charming really. Very much *in*. Like vintage cars. Walton weighed the idea of buying one and writing a concerto for it. It would have to be one

184

of those gimmicky, show-off pieces that struts its hour on the stage shouting, "Hey, look at me! What a brash, outrageous piece of effrontery am I!"

Walton remembered the time when he would have sneered at such blatant self-advertisement passing itself off as music, but that was when he was so full of music himself that it vibrated at his very fingertips, when he could say "to hell with the orchestration; let them play it on jew's-harps and frisco slide whistles and it will come out good; set it up for trained seals with bicycle horns; I don't care."

All right. But that was before the dreams—the waking dreams and sleeping dreams—and the shrill rising voices within him that cried out his guilt and left no room for music. His talent was barren now and he knew it, but a man who had been famous for his pride—arrogance, gall, conceit; what you will—could not turn humble all at once and bow meekly to denigrating truth.

If all he had left was a bag of tricks with which to titillate the novelty seekers, the tricks were good tricks—duet for garden hose and bagpipe, sonata for piano with tissue paper over the strings, "Borborygmy in Harmony" with taped sounds of authentic belches and belly rumbles, "Alley Cat Chorale" featuring tapes of honest-to-God alley cats yowling over a percussion base consisting of shoes being thrown against a sheet of galvanized steel—arresting though sterile manipulations of sound that enraged just about everybody and kept Walton's name in the newspapers.

That sort of thing would have to suffice for the present. Somehow someday, soon God willing, he would surely find a way to recharge his talent. Then he would go back to filling the air with glory, and he would damn well sue any conductor who presumed to perform even a part of any single smart-alec opus from this interlude of bleakness.

The talent-recharging trick, he was certain, was to put his finger on the specific moments of past time into which he seemed to be slipping in his waking dreams—the times which seemed to invoke at least the aura of the guilt for which as yet he could find no name—and then to find a link or common denominator for these fragments of time. The moments he was groping for, he was just about certain by now, were in the Spring of 1931 and the Winter of 1944.

Therefore, of course, Moira Hendricks had to be the common denominator. The more he thought about Moira these days—after 20 years of dogged effort not to think about her at all—the stronger became the pull of his dreams. He would hear a plane overhead and look up wondering whether it was a monoplane or a biplane, or, by a marvelous stroke of luck, a Ford Trimotor. He would find himself searching magazine racks for *Ballyhoo*, or *Judge*, or *College Humor*. He would twiddle the dial on the radio until his exasperated wife asked him what in the world he was looking for, and would realize with an embarrassed start that he was idly hoping to catch Ruth Etting singing "Shine on, Harvest Moon."

Those were the 1931 moments.

Then he would put his hand to his shirt collar and think, *oh my God, I've forgotten to put on my collar insignia!* He would automatically reach for non-existent crutches before getting up from his chair. He would hear—actually hear— Frank Sinatra singing "I'm gonna buy a paper doll that I can call my own." He would say to his wife, "Hey, you didn't throw away Dick Tracy, did you? How am I ever going to know whether Flat Top sizzled him with that flame thrower?" He would hear, from far-off juke boxes, the bossy right hand, saucy left hand and mocking voice of Fats Waller, and catch himself thinking, boozily, sentimentally, *See? See? He didn't die after all.*

Those were the 1944 moments.

But most significantly, the more he thought about Moira, the more he brooded about guilt, and the surer he became that whatever it was he was guilty of, she was the victim of it. If so, she was the one who could tell him. That was why he was making this trip. It wasn't going to be easy. He couldn't come out flatly and ask her if he had done anything to her about which he ought to feel guilty. Old friends, old loves could alter drastically in 20 years, but he doubted that Moira would ever lose her knack for puncturing tension with a gay little crack and making him feel like a self-dramatizing, rather pompous fake. Oddly, though he had had occasion to resent this knack of Moira's, it was part of her charm. It had kept him on his toes, and she had never punctured him except when he deserved puncturing. He had indeed lapsed on occasion into pomposity. It was still a bad habit of his, particularly with no Moira in his life to keep him in check, and he was going to have to guard against it when he met her.

It had been Walton's plan to take the bus clear down into Cincinnati; then pick up a Hamilton bus that would take him up to Glendale, some 14 miles north of the city. Now as he looked out the window and saw the gateway to Sharon Park, he realized that his bus was coming into Sharonville, which is also some 14 miles north of Cincinnati, but only about 3 miles east of Glendale. It struck him as ridiculous to ride 28 miles in a bus just to go 3 miles. It was an easy walk from Sharonville to Glendale. He had done it hundreds of times when he was a kid.

He got off the bus at Sharon Avenue, which leads to Glendale. A few other people were getting off at the same place; so he had time to change his mind and jump back aboard, back to the gentle, phony zephyrs of the air conditioner, as the 114-degree July heat slapped him in the face. But what the heck; he had no luggage; he'd walked farther than 3 miles on hotter days, back in the 1931 he was seeking to rediscover, and besides he could stand to lose a few pounds around the midriff.

First of all, he went into a drugstore telephone booth to call Moira at her mother's home.

"You didn't answer my letter," he said, "but I came anyway."

"Well, you told me you would if you didn't hear from me." The voice of the beloved as though 20 years had never been. It was as crisply cool as ever. No nonsense. Walton's hands were shaking. "I was expecting you, Walton."

"I wasn't sure my letter reached you."

"You might have known I'd still be in Mother's clutches."

"But when Aunt Jane told me you were Mrs. Moira Buntline, I sort of wondered—"

"Boy, you really are out of touch. I married Billy 17 years ago. I'm sure you were on the invitation list."

"Not if your mother had anything to do with it. Billy Buntline. I'll be damned. I never would have matched you two."

"Neither would Mother. After awhile Billy came to see it her way. It was as simple as that. No children. No settlement. He's married to Gladys Mallon now."

"That I can see."

187

"You wouldn't recognize her. She's fat and alcoholic."

"No! Well, look Moira, I'd better hang up. I've got a little walk ahead of me."

"Where are you calling from?"

"Sharonville. Nothing like a healthy hike—"

"Walton, you nut. In this heat?"

"I've done it a million times."

"You're not getting any younger. The miles are longer these days."

"I'm in pretty good shape, Moira."

"And the belts are shorter these days too. Your Aunt Jane tells me you're as fat as a pig. Look, don't come here. Mother is still Mother, only more so. Call me from Igler's when you get to Glendale, and I'll meet you there."

> *Her hair was long, her foot was light,*
> *And her eyes were wild.*

And her tongue was tart as ever. "Fat as a pig." As he hung up, Walton felt that sweet, long-forgotten throbbing ache within his rib cage that Tin Pan Alley still ascribed to the heart, though it was more likely an endocrine reaction. Moira forever. How liltingly she put you in your place. How he had ranted at it, how he had hoity-toitied at it, and how he had needed it. He had really brimmed over in those days—the days of Moira. He had brimmed over with music, with love, with inchoate philosophy, with hair-trigger perceptions. That was fine so long as it was on the level; Moira was with him, encouraging him, occasionally pruning the rank overgrowth. He was full of glory in those days, and Moira was involved in the glory. It was only when he was overweening and pretentious that she cut him down to size, but an arrogant young man with notions of being an artist can't always know when he is pretentious.

That was why 20 years ago he had fled from Moira and all his glory. But he was not so simple-minded as to think that he could flee back and recapture Moira and glory. There was more to it than that. Somehow he must also recapture himself—a scared kid with a dog—no, *two* dogs— an angry Army captain with crutches and shards of phonograph records. He didn't know how, or, really, why this was to be accomplished.

Walton wasn't wearing a summer suit. He didn't own one, to begin with, and wouldn't have worn one anyway, since it had been damp and windy in New York when he left there yesterday. He had forgotten about those southern Ohio summers.

He took off his suit coat, draped it over his arm, and began walking west on Sharon Avenue. Whether or not they really made the miles longer these days, they certainly did make the highways narrower. He remembered Sharon as a fine, wide road, with plenty of room on both sides for boys and dogs to ramble and for cars to park. Cars to park. Right up there on the left, just this side of the railroad tracks and in front of the locomotive round-house was where the Model A Ford was parked with a flat tire. The guilty Model A. The murderer of Inky. With a flat tire. Served it right.

No. There was no Model A there now. You couldn't even park a bicycle there without tying up traffic all the way to Glendale. Traffic was pretty nearly jammed up anyway. The road was wide enough for a comfortable flow of two-way traffic, but it didn't seem to be. Everything seemed hemmed in, squeezed together by some invisible pressure; Walton was bucking this pressure by sheer physical effort in order to stay out of the way of the laboring, monoxide-fuming cars. The heat pressed him down from above. Claustrophobia qualms fluttered through him, but he soothed himself with the assurance that he would soon be out of Sharonville and in wide open farm country. Maybe if he tried Boy Scout pace—50 steps walking, 50 running, he would be out of this unseen dungeon before the walls closed in and crushed him.

A silly notion. He was barely past the old Sharonville round-house, and already his shirt was drenched in sweat; his feet, as in a dream, seemed to be dragging through thick gelatin. It was still early in the afternoon, but the mixture of haze, heat waves, exhaust fumes, diesel smoke, and sweat-streaks on the lenses of his glasses distorted and darkened everything around him. Suddenly, above the sounds of automobile tires and motors, he heard the voice of a boy, across the street and behind him, calling:

"Here, Slimmy! Here, Slimmy!"

Walton looked over his shoulder. He couldn't have heard properly, over the highway noises. Possibly, without being fully aware of it, he had seen the liver-colored Chesapeake Bay retriever out of the corner of his eye, and the name "Slimmy" had merely leaped to his mind. The kid in the green sweater, kneeling by the absurdly right-angled high-bottomed Model A Ford, might have been calling "Here, Spot," or "Here, Rover." Besides, there was only one Slimmy, as Walton had found out after a number of experiences with other Chesapeake Bay retrievers.

Or possibly it was the setting, the background, because he had seen it in dream after dream. The old round-house was out of true, just as it was in the dreams, and might easily, as in some of the dreams, turn into a Rhenish castle which you entered to find everything upholstered in green and be waited upon by smiling servants dressed as Pullman porters.

The Model A Ford with the flat front tire was also out of the dreams. The boy in the green sweater, with Slimmy (Spot? Rover?) at his elbow, was squatting by the tire. He was doing something to it, but Walton couldn't see what. Spot-Rover was sniffing at the tire just as Slimmy sniffed it in the dreams, sniffing Inky's blood, still bright red and gleaming in the April sunlight, though Inky had been dead since St. Patrick's Day.

Whatever it was that the boy and dog were doing, it was damned dangerous. They were on the left side, the highway side of the car. With all that hemmed-in traffic.

Walton shouted a warning, then turned to cross the street in order to give the boy some avuncular advice. Just then, a parade of three monster diesel trucks blocked him and cut off his view of boy, dog, and Model A Ford.

Walton shrugged and resumed his walk. It would have been out of character for him to butt in. He was an inveterate minder of his own business; the kid undoubtedly would have suggested to him that he continue as such.

He noticed that he was weaving slightly. Damned carbon monoxide. Plus heat waves. Plus too vivid a recollection of a recurrent dream.

That was it! The dream! His motives had not been avuncular after all. He had simply wanted to see what crucial thing the boy was doing to that automobile tire, and the diesel trucks had forbidden him, just as blurring of focus or sudden awakening always forbade him in his dreams to see what was being done to the tire. Good Lord, had it come now to hallucinations in broad daylight?

He looked back toward the round-house. He knew the rule about hallucination. You merely had to utter, or even think "hallucination," and it would vanish. No. The boy and the dog and the Model A were still there. But from where he stood, the car looked too rounded and sloping to be a Model A, the boy's sweater looked more brown than green, and the dog looked more like a collie than a Chesapeake Bay. Damned glasses. Walton had nothing to wipe them with, except a dirty, sweat-sopping handkerchief.

He walked on.

Hallucination or not, the thing to do was to present it to Moira as such. He had been wondering how, in the face of her inevitable scorn, he was going to broach the subject of dreams. One of Moira's most engaging traits had been the trace of witch in her. Her crisp and merry practicality, her brusque impatience with emotional flatulence had been an acquired camouflage for an occult spirit sensitive to ghosts, bodiless voices in the dark, and nasty, vengeful pre-Olympian demigods. There had been madness in that big, creaky old house of the Hendricks. You saw it staring bleakly out of stiff ancestral portraits.

Walton supposed that she had inherited from her father—certainly not her savage vampire mother—the motherwit that gave her the arms and armor that had saved her and probably would always save her from being drawn wholly into her shadowy interior world—her witch world. She had succeeded in keeping everyone but Walton himself from seeing inside this armor. Maybe she had, through wishful thinking, seen some nonexistent quality in Walton, but inevitably he had failed her in the role of demon lover. He had gradually become enraptured with her voices in long unlit corridors, her deals with black powers. He had become, in fact, hooked.

> "I set her on my prancing steed,
> And nothing else saw all day long,
> For sidelong would she bend, and sing
> A faery's song."

But he could come only as far as the gates of her world.

No ghosts ever talked to him. He could only deal with her world in a poetic sense, and Moira's ghosts were not poetry; they were Tom, Dick and Harry. Poetry was dangerous to Walton; it led him to excesses, to the verge of utter sappiness. But only to the verge. At the crucial moment Moira's needle of matter-of-fact would pop the balloon. Damned witch.

Anyway, Inky wasn't in this handily contrived "hallucination," as he so often—implausibly—was, in the dreams. He wouldn't have to mention Inky, which was a blessing. Moira might be venomous about Inky.

No, that was unfair. It wasn't Moira, but Moira's mother who had destroyed Inky with the Model A Ford. Inky, pointless, clumsy black mongrel, always subordinate to Slimmy, had been a member of his inviolate boy's world, had been one of the components of love that glued that world together, and without Inky there had been nothing left for a boy to do but kick his way through the shatterable dome of someone else's world. Not to destroy. Just to get in there and perhaps to find new components of love. But the very entry into another world was and had to be an act of destruction. Moira's mother had been the shatterable dome, and he had shattered this dome by doing some secret thing to a punctured tire with bloodstains still on it. But Moira had been the component of love inside the dome, and he had found her. And what secret thing had he done to her? And why the fingers pointing at him?

Outside of Sharonville, where the open fields had been, Walton found himself more hemmed in than before—by factories and by concrete overpasses and underpasses for highways he remembered as bucolic lovers' lanes. One bridge, once reasonably broad, had now become too narrow to accommodate both foot and vehicular traffic. Maybe it didn't matter. Maybe no one walked any more—not out this way to be sure.

It seemed that the only way for a man on foot to cross this bridge was to wait for a hiatus in the traffic and then run like hell. As Walton was standing there in woozy befuddlement, a slow rattletrap truck approached the bridge, heading in the direction of Glendale. The tailgate was down, and Walton, forgetting the dignity fitting to his age and increasing portliness, leaped aboard. No doubt the driver would see him soon enough through his rear-view mirror, but he surely wouldn't stop on the bridge, and Walton had no intention of staying on the truck after the bridge was crossed. His conscience would be clear. He would still have walked from Sharonville to Glendale; no one would count a tiny ferry trip across an otherwise unfordable obstacle.

He was sitting on the tailgate, facing to the rear, when the cold came. Suddenly he was struggling to put on his suit jacket and huddle in it, whistling breathily over a shivering jaw. The tune he was whistling was "Mairzy Doats and Doazy Doats and Little Lamzy Divey; a Kiddly Divey too; wouldn't you?" That was a tune he hadn't heard for 20 years or so. He wouldn't have remembered all the words yesterday, but he did at this moment.

Walton knew it wasn't as cold as it seemed to be. These broiling humid days could trick you sometimes. A change of wind, a sudden downdraft of high cool air might lower the temperature no more than five degrees and yet feel positively wintry against your sweat-soaked body.

Right behind the truck was a big black old car. Walton was no good at guessing makes or vintages of cars, but he guessed that this was a pre-World War II model—1939 or 40—and a Packard. In truth, Walton could barely tell a Packard from a jeep. Moreover his eyes, unpampered by spectacles, watered and blurred in the sudden drop of temperature.

But in the dream—the other dream—it was always a Packard, only he was *inside* it. The car behind him then was no hallucination, but the Packardness of it surely was, and for the first time Walton began to wonder if his coming back here for the first time after so many years to the scene of his crimes (?) was not going to make things worse instead of better.

Walton could see clearly the flashing black eyes and tight angry lips of the young woman who was driving; he could see her blue-black hair, set in a long, barbaric version of a page-boy bob and spreading out onto her shoulders from under a pale blue babushka to lend splendor to a pathetic old dyed squirrel coat. Next to her he could see the gesticulating Army captain, bundled up in his greatcoat, his crutches propped up beside him against the back of the seat.

Once again the dream was taking the place of objective vision. Walton proved it. He closed his eyes and still saw the Packard, the young woman and the gesticulating captain. He would palm this one off on Moira too as a hallucination. She would take it seriously and perhaps revel in it, but Walton didn't dare take it seriously, and far from reveling in it he steeled himself to fight it. This sort of thing was nothing to him but a cold gray warning—an intimation of creeping psychosis.

He blinked several times and pounded his forehead with the heel of his hand; his objective eyesight gradually got the better of his psychic eyesight, and what he saw in the car back there was the figures of two people only vaguely discernible through the blur of his drenched eyes and the glint of afternoon sunlight on the car's windshield. The person driving appeared to be a woman all right, but surely not in babushka and dyed squirrel coat at this time of year, despite the sudden illusion of chill. The man might or might not be a soldier. He seemed to be wearing some kind of visored hat (did they wear those in today's Army?), but it could be a sport's cap or boating cap.

The man was indeed gesticulating. Goddamn it, he was breaking phonograph records. Goddamn it, he was nothing of the sort. That was the goddamn dream again. The hell it was. You could see the labels clearly. Harry James, Bunny Berigan, Benny Goodman, Artie Shaw, Count Basie, Jimmy Lunceford, Duke Ellington. That, of course, proved it was all a crock, because even without blur or glint, even with good glasses or 20-20 vision, you couldn't read those labels from this distance and under the present circumstances, Walton couldn't even have made out the silhouette of an uplifted phonograph record.

The records weren't all that important. Except for some of the Basies and Ellingtons, they weren't records he would spend money on today, but there was a time when they had been to him what Chapman's Homer had been to Keats.

It hadn't been only the music. Those records had been a bond between him and Moira. They were a background for long summer evenings of chaste necking on moonlit lawns, of spinning moonlit plans for a—then conceivable—wildly romantic and interminable future. Therefore at a certain insane yet perfectly lucid moment in a frosty-windowed

Packard which was burning up its OPA gas coupons for a week, it had become necessary for a flaming Army captain to smash some records he had loved in order to break a bond he had loved. But no Waller records. Fats was scarcely cold in his grave. And this was the reason for the grab of an out-of-focus dream that now no longer needed to wait on sleep.

Suddenly the man (?) in the car made some sort of violent gesture. There seemed to be some movement of the crutches, if they were crutches, which they damn well had better not be or ding, ding, here comes the wagon. The big car went into a skid and hit the side of the bridge, not hard enough to do more than crumple a fender, but hard enough to stop the car. Since he was now across the bridge, he jumped off the tailgate of the truck and started back to see if anyone was hurt.

The car suddenly backed away from the guard rail and shot ahead so quickly that Walton had to straddle the rail to keep from being grazed. As it passed him he had a quick glimpse of the fortyish woman at the wheel. She was wearing a sleeveless lavender summer dress. The car had tail fins. It was probably a Cadillac of mid-50s' vintage; certainly not a pre-World War II Packard. The surprise zephyr had passed, and heat waves thrummed again on Walton's temples.

He took his coat off again and tied the sleeves loosely around his waist. Forward march. Hut-two. That was the ticket. Head up, shoulders back, chest out, belly in. Hut-hoo-hreep-hope. My head is bloody but unbowed.

He could still feel the rage of the Army captain who wasn't there. He always woke up still trembling with it after the dream. But what was it all about?

Walton remember his days of brooding at the Army hospital, while he was waiting for the retirement board to meet and turn him loose.

Before the war he had somehow acquired a Macedonian bagpipe, softer and more sweetly plaintive in tone than the Scottish Highland pipe, and he had seized on the idea of using it as instrumental accompaniment for a choral setting of Keats' "Grecian Urn." *Therefore, ye soft pipes, play on.* He had worked out a simple ground melody for the bagpipe, but Army life had swallowed him up before he could put down the bagpipe variations or any of the voice parts. In North Africa, a shell fragment in the knee-cap set him free again.

For three months after his first hospitalization he was able to do nothing but torture his original ground melody into labored, wooden variations, and drudge away at the architecture of chord progressions. Finally, in October, when he was about to be retired from an Army general hospital in Texas, the muse began to take grudging pity on him; little by little the melodies started to come back.

Clumping around the hospital ward on his crutches, he pieced together a jig-saw picture of the future that would be thrust upon him if he went with the drift of things. In a few days he would be out of the Army. In a few months he would be free of his crutches, limping up and down the city streets looking for a job. In a year or so he would be married to Moira, and within five years he would have children, pediatricians, mortgages, commutation tickets, crab grass——and no melodies, ever again.

This was unthinkable; this was suicide. The only alternative was to stand up to the dismay and anger of his mother and father and uncles and aunts, and renounce the world for his melodies. Renouncing the world might mean the renunciation of Moira, but this was not up to him; it was up to Moira. He would live in the modern equivalent of a city garret, and he would earn rent and grocery money by teaching harmony and counterpoint or by playing piano in a cocktail lounge. If Moira loved him enough to live this life with him, wholly *with* him, undeviatingly on his side, his renunciation would be sweet. If not, it would be agony, at least at first, but a necessary agony.

Moira had gotten out the old puncturing needle just once too often. She had made him look and feel like an overdramatic egotist. She had laughed gaily at his garret. It was a bright and lilting laugh, that pretended not to be what it really was—a sneer at the melodies that spangled the dome of his world—a sneer, somehow, at Inky.

The shards of the phonograph records were Inky's broken body. He had picked up a whole disk—Artie Shaw's "Begin the Beguine," Moira's favorite—and seen blood on it, on hub and spokes and tire.

But if this was the way it had really happened, then he,

Walton, was in the right, and Moira in the wrong. Why then, the voices and pointing fingers in the dark?

Walton marched bravely up a gradual hill where, at this time of year, fields of corn and wheat once purred with joy in green and gold under the heat, and cottonwood fringes blinked from green to silver at the hint of a breeze. Now, on both sides of Sharon Avenue, there were rows of small homes and desperate lawns clinging to bare survival through the mercy of whirling sprinklers.

At the edge of Glendale, completely obliterating a monstrous field through which he, Caesar, and Inky, Labienus, had once pursued Slimmy, the noble Vercingetorix, in a forest of weeds, was a vast, functional high school.

Ahead of Walton, the land sloped gradually down to Albion Creek, which ran perpendicular to Sharon Avenue, then gradually up. Most of Glendale, including the village center, was on the far slope, though from where Walton stood it looked more like a woods than a village. Home was more than home; it was an oasis, and thank God the skyline was unchanged. Farthest to the left was the pointed spire of the Presbyterian church; next, looking taller because it was at the top of the slope, was the flat-topped, English Gothic steeple of the Episcopal church; then, looming like a mystic druid stronghold, the cone-topped cylinder of the old stone and concrete water tower, all covered with ivy.

Covered with ivy! How in hell could he see, with or without his glasses, ivy more than a mile away? How, for that matter, could he see a water tower that had been torn down more than 30 years ago.

He blinked his eyes and punched his temple, and the tower, properly, vanished. Got to keep making these little corrections. Got to ward off the little guys in the white suits.

Up ahead of him to the right, on this side of Albion Creek, was the new (new in 1930) water tower, functional and ivyless: a giant kettle perched on daddy-long-legs. He saw a boy with a green sweater turn off the highway and stroll toward the tower, through the trees. The boy was followed by a liver-colored dog. Possibly a Chesapeake Bay retriever. Slimmy. And a black, ungainly, huge-pawed— Oh no, Oh no. Pound the old temple. Blink the old eyes. Correct every last little detail.

Walton wondered if there was anything nowadays to at-

tract a kid and a dog to the water tower. There used to be
a lovely dump, with rusted old auto bodies to climb into
and bottles and jugs to throw at rats and sometimes a treas-
ure to take home—a chair, for example, with only one leg
broken, which would help furnish that always projected but
somehow never built secret clubhouse.

Walton knew that if he followed the boy he would come
to no dump at all but to trim lawns, and probably to neat
walks, or drives, with, no doubt, flowers planted along the
borders. He hadn't been near the new water tower in over
thirty years, and he had no intention of going near it now,
but there were respectable, landscaped, tree-shadowed
homes with two-car garages along this part of Sharon Avenue
today, possibly inhabited by some of the same guys with
whom he had bottled rats to death in the old days, and it
stood to reason that the presence of a lovely dump would
be intolerable.

He wondered if anyone was looking out a window at him,
saying: "Why that looks like little Walton Ulster." It was
more likely, since he had not been able to shave today and
since dust had glued itself to his sweat-drenched shirt, that
anyone seeing him out here on the highway would say,
"Who is that fat bum waddling along out there?"

Knotty skirted the dump, trying not to make himself conspicuous. Maybe there would be some kids with 22s, shooting at tin cans, or, with luck, rats, and if they didn't see
him they might shoot in his direction. He knew he would
be too yellow to stand up in front of the firing squad, but it
would be kind of nice to be hit by a stray bullet if you
didn't really expect it but just sort of idly hoped for it.

There just wasn't any other way out of the mess he was
in, except maybe a disease like tuberculosis which would
get him off to a sanitarium somewhere so he could start all
over again. People would be sorry for him, and they would
forgive him for some of the things they were bound to find
out about pretty soon. They would never find out the whole
thing about Mrs. Hendricks. Maybe she wouldn't be killed
instantly. Maybe she would live long enough to talk, and
Moira Hendricks would rat and tell somebody everything
she knew, but everybody knew there was insanity in the

Hendricks family, and it would be Moira's word against the word of a poor sick kid wasting away in a sanitarium.

There was a guy he knew in High School in Cincinnati who had TB. His family was too poor to send him to a sanitarium, and he was probably at home or in the General Hospital. Knotty's freshman class at Walnut Hills, or anyway the kids in Knotty's home room, had all chipped in to help pay for the guy's doctor's bills or medicine or something like that. His sister was a senior, and maybe Knotty could get her to take him to visit her brother. It would look very sweet and thoughtful, and Knotty could make some kind of deal with the guy. Suppose, say, the guy had a bowl by his bed to spit in, and Knotty could take it home and rub the glop all over a lot of needle prickles on the back of his hand. Or he could—ik—drink it.

Aw, but heck, you couldn't get tuberculosis in two weeks. Or maybe you could get the germ, but you couldn't get anything that showed enough on the outside so you could get your mother to take you to a doctor for an examination. In two weeks the jig would be up. The April report card would be out, and it wouldn't be a good idea to forge his father's signature again. He had done an expert job on the March report card and his father had been too busy to notice what time of month it was, but just the other day he had said, "Isn't it a pretty long time between marking periods? It seems to me there was snow on the ground the last time I signed one of yours." Knotty had squeaked through that one by reminding his father of a freak snow storm that had come a few days after St. Patrick's Day. Naturally, his father hadn't marked it on his calendar, and it could just as easily have occurred March 31 as March 19 or 20, but he had frowned and shrugged and said, "Well, time can fool you. Particularly when you're on the road a lot. I'll have to write something on my memo pad for April 30th."

Boy, that was really going to be a report card. Knotty was going to have to go some to explain the "incomplete" in Math and Latin. He just couldn't tell the truth: that he had been cutting those classes for two solid months.

A guy could get into one of these things without meaning any harm, but it was just about impossible to get out. He only meant to cut that one class in Math the day he was supposed to bring in three homework make-up assignments or get sent to the principal's office. He didn't know why he was still afraid to be sent to the principal's office, but he was. Well, it was a simple enough matter to go to the nurse just before class and groan a little. His sinuses were always pretty badly congested at this time of year anyway, and if he didn't really have a headache, he had a perfect right to one; it wasn't hard to persuade the nurse to give him some aspirin and make him lie down for an hour or so. The only trouble was that he had met another guy in the nurse's office—a sophomore Knotty knew in the orchestra— who had a pretty good idea for a hit tune, but just couldn't get anywhere with the verse or the release; so by the time he and Knotty had something worked out that really sounded smoo-oo-ooth, two hours had gone by, and Knotty had cut Latin class too. The Math teacher was a sour-faced fat woman, all covered with chalk dust. She just looked down her nose at the guys like Knotty who couldn't get Math. But the Latin was a nice old maidy auntie sort of lady who was always being *disappointed* in Knotty, which was worse than having someone look down her nose at him. Well, naturally, Knotty had planned to catch up on his Latin and Math that night, but, naturally, he had some more work to do on this song, and—well—by the third or fourth day of this sort of thing he was just plain scared to go face his Latin and Math teachers. What's more, the homework kept piling up until there was more than he could make up in a hundred years. About the middle of March he had thought maybe if he went up to somebody and made a clean breast of everything, he would get yelled at a little and then things would get worked out some way, but he kept putting it off and putting it off, and when he finally forged his father's signature to the report card he was too deep in crime to figure a way out.

Well, there weren't going to be any stray bullets for Knotty today, because there was nobody out shooting in the dump. Knotty picked up an armload of bottles of different sizes: tough blue milk-of-magnesia bottles, elegant green mineral water bottles, brown cod-liver-oil bottles, pop bottles, castor oil bottles. With Slimmy cavorting wildly around him, tail flagrantly up and thrashing, Knott walked through the line of trees that fringed Albion Creek, into a foliage-vaulted otherworld. He lined up his bottles beside the creek. This time of year there was plenty of water in the creek, and the stink of sewage was not as bad as it would be by July or August. He sat down and began experimenting with various levels of water in his bottles, blowing across the mouths of the bottles, pouring out or adding a little water, then blowing again, until he had, for each bottle, the precise tone he wanted. Slimmy sat down beside him and whined each time he produced a tone. It was probably true that the musical notes bothered the dog's ears, but they didn't drive him away.

When he was satisfied with the tone of each bottle, Knotty placed them in a row in front of him, the deepest-toned bottle farthest to the left, the next deepest-toned beside it, and so on up, from left to right, to the little shrill medicine bottles.

"Okay, Slimmy," he said. "This is gonna be an ode for Inky."

Slim pricked up his ears at the sound of the familiar name.

"That's right, Slimmer. You were the best, but we always loved old Inker, didn't we? We used to make fun of him because he was clumsy and couldn't do half the things you did, but we loved old Inker. Didn't we, Slimmy boy? This is gonna be an ode to tell old Inker we're sorry for all the times we teased him, 'cause we never had a chance to tell him when he was alive. Did we, Slimmy boy?"

Slim whimpered and bathed Knotty's face with his tongue.

The "ode" was in reality a dirge. For mechanical reasons it had to be. In order to go from one note to another, you had to put a different bottle to your lips at the same time you put down the last bottle you had blown and groped for the next one you would need. Knotty was dexterous, but not dexterous enough to produce a trill or a grace note or a liquid arpeggio; however, by over-blowing the deep-toned bottles, he could produce a sudden jump from a solemn moan to a wild shrill wail. All in all, the music he forced from his bottles was majestic, and fitting to the greenwillow, bird-twittering cathedral in which it was played. Assuredly Inky got the message.

After a few minutes the constant blowing made Knotty dizzy, and he stopped for a rest. Once more he went back in his mind to his unsolvable problems, and found himself, to his surprise, chuckling. People were always saying, "Some day you'll look back on this and laugh," and now, unaccountably, it *was* "someday" and he *was* looking back and laughing, with some scorn, at the pathetic molehills a damnfool 13-year-old kid seemed to think were mountains.

Well, what he was doing to Mrs. Hendricks' flat tire wasn't any molehill, but the grown-ups who were watching him do it as they drove by in their cars, they didn't know what he was doing, and they never would. Some things were all right if they were necessary and you didn't get caught.

He knew what all those grown-ups were thinking. "Golly, what I wouldn't give to be a boy again and wander along the highway with a good old dog like that."

And what he, Knotty, was thinking about the grown-ups, here and now in his greenwillow April cathedral, was "I've got something you haven't got." This was true, for all of a sudden he knew exactly what new turn of melody to blow on his bottles in memory of Inky.

That was the trick. You had to know exactly what the next note *had* to be. If you had to force it or puzzle it out, it was no good, and you might as well quit playing till it came to you. It was like the chicken laying the egg; the chicken didn't plan on it or work at it; when the egg was there to be laid, what else could the chicken do with it but lay it.

Knotty blew a long-drawn-out steamboat whistle hoot on his biggest bottle, a half-gallon jug that had contained something vile-smelling. He wished he had a *gallon* jug; his melody line was sweetening now, and he felt it needed the seasoning of a really full-bellied bass. But unbroken gallon jugs were almost impossible to find in this dump. They were too tempting as targets for boys with rocks, air rifles or 22s.

After finishing the tune, he smashed each bottle, one at a time, starting with the littlest bottle, going from right to left. He didn't know why he did this, but it seemed to be a necessary part of the ritual.

He stood up and turned to leave his arcade. Sitting on the stump of a lightning-struck willow tree was an old man, maybe 80 or even 90—a jowly old man, almost bald, with a writing pad in his lap and a funny-looking pencil in his hand.

APOLOGY TO INKY

"I believe I've got every note," said the old man. "Thank you very much."

"Golly," said Knotty. "You mean you were writing down that stuff I was playing?"

"From start to finish. Let's see. Your title for the tune is —uh—"

"Ode to Inky," said Knotty.

"Oh yes. Good old Inky. Tell me: does it invoke Inky? I mean, does it bring him back? Do you see him?"

"Oh, *heck* no. It's just sort of a memory—well—like an apology to Inky. I mean—well—Slimmy and me—that is, when Inky was alive, we never—"

"I know, I know. Nobody ever does. That's the guilt that makes the world go round. Don't wallow in it though. Guilt is really another form of pride, but you won't understand this until you're a great deal older, and I won't try to explain it to you. 'Apology to Inky.' Don't you think that's a better title than 'Ode'?"

"Well, golly, I never— Well, sure, I guess so. I just never thought about it as a real composition—like written down and all that."

" 'Apology to Inky' is the title then. 'Apology to Inky' by —uh—"

"Retslu Notlaw. That's my nom de plume, sort of. We used to have a gang a couple of years ago, and all the guys did their names that way. Mine was the only one that stuck." Knotty looked over the old man's shoulder as he wrote in this pad. "Say, gee, what kind of an Eversharp is that you got there? The writing looks like ink."

"It's called a ball-point pen," said the old man, quickly pocketing it. "I don't think I ought to show it to you. You're getting too far ahead of yourself."

"I don't get it," said Knotty. "Say, how come you found this place? How come Slimmy didn't let me know you were here?"

"Slimmy knows me," said the old man. "I think. I would have liked it if he had jumped up and licked my face."

"Huh?"

"In any event, this place is no stranger to me. I can almost see the trees that used to be here. The alameda of willows. The glorious tin cans and rusty axles. And the rats."

"I don't get it."

"For your sake, I hope not. Forgive a moderately insane old man. And accept my humble gratitude for 'Apology to Inky.' "

"Gee, I wish you could stick around. You've got me all mixed up."

"You were worse mixed up before you saw me. Remember that. Now, I really can't stay. I have an engagement with my hair shirt."

"Wait a sec, please. What are you going to do with the music you wrote down?"

The old man had already stepped out of sight through the fringe of willows. Knotty ran after him, out into the open dump, but could see no sign of anyone.

"Oh, shoot," he said. "I did the Inky tune better than ever. I wish I could see it the way he wrote it down. I never told him I just make it up as I go along, and it won't be anywhere's near as good tomorrow."

Walton Ulster gasped with pleasure as the cool air of Igler's Drug Store embraced him and caressed his sopping shirt. He looked around, wondering if he would see a familiar face behind one of the counters, when he heard her voice.

"Walton Ulster: I'd hardly recognize you."

There she was, sitting at one of the tables, sipping Coke through a straw. Beware! Beware! Her flashing eyes, her floating hair! Impossible that she should have aged not a single day in 20 years. It must be a miracle of make-up, he thought, but it was certainly invisible to the naked eye. Witchcraft?

He strode toward her, with both hands outstretched, and she looked up at him with startled hostility.

"Walton! It *is* you, isn't it?"

The voice came from *behind* him.

He spun around. She was sitting at the counter, sipping hot black coffee. She had aged some, but not much. There were little lines at the corners of her eyes and on her neck, her lips were a trifle thinner than they had been, and her hair, still long but not barbarian, was salted attractively with gray. She had made no attempt to hide behind heavy make-up, lipstick or dye. Her figure was youthful, and Walton would have bet she wasn't wearing a girdle.

"My God, Moira, you're a damned handsome woman. If

I didn't know better I wouldn't believe you were over 30."

"I wish I could say the same for you. Aunt Jane is right. You're fat as a pig."

"I guess I could lose a few pounds. The doctor says I'm not dangerously overweight."

"Oh, shut up, Walton, you sensitive plant. Give me a kiss."

He put his lips to hers, intending nothing more serious than a kissing-cousin's peck, but the surprisingly soft responsiveness of her lips, enhanced by a sudden, rather embarrassing vision of the girl with the wild black hair drinking Coke at the table just behind him, made him, momentarily, drunk. He pressed Moira to him.

She threw her head back, laughing gently.

"Decorum's the word, old boy. Here in Igler's anyway."

"I don't understand myself," he said. "The years just seemed to blow away."

"You'd better watch it. You'll get picked up as a dirty old man. What's with the hot number at the table back there?"

"You won't believe it, Moira. She was the first person I saw when I came in here, and I thought she was you. Do you have a dry handkerchief I can clean my glasses with?"

"It's a good thing you didn't accost her. She's jumpy about something. I saw her pour something out of a flask into her Coke. Here, will a Kleenex do?"

Walton began to polish his glasses.

"Join me in a cup of coffee," said Moira.

"I couldn't. I'm parboiled. Oh, for a glass of ice cold beer."

"Mercy. In Igler's?"

"Let's go over to Bob Heine's. I can unbutton a few more buttons on my shirt and put my feet on the table. Or is that too disreputable for you?"

"It isn't Heine's any more. It's very reputable now. Very in. Lots of decor, fine cuisine, waiters with uniforms, early American hitching posts, steel engravings. . . ."

"Beer on tap?"

"The best. It's called the Iron Horse, if that gives you any kind of a picture."

"I have a picture of beer."

"Oh, I don't know, Walton. I suppose they'd be too nice to refuse to serve you, but I won't go there with you. Not until you've had a shower and put on a clean shirt with a tie."

"Can Glendale support a place like that?"

"Progress, old boy. Oh, the village itself hasn't changed much. Same old winding roads and trees and lawns. But we're surrounded by industry now, and that means bright young executives putting the best foot forward. If you were a bright young executive, would you take a customer to lunch in a place like Heine's?"

"We had lovely afternoons there. I wish they'd suspend progress long enough for people like me to catch up with ourselves." He put on his glasses and turned to look at the girl at the table.

"She does look remarkably like you, Moira."

"I had a squirrel coat like that once, but I wouldn't have dreamed of wearing it out on the hottest day of summer."

Being a normal male, Walton had not noticed what Moira was wearing until just this moment. Her sleeveless lavender summer dress was just right for her and just right for the weather.

"What kind of a car do you drive, Moira?"

"A '54 Cadillac. It's a souvenir of my pointless liaison with the Buntline money. Billy let me have it after the divorce, which was unnecessary, but sweet."

"That's a picture of Billy Buntline. Unnecessary but sweet."

"I didn't know you had claws under those darling pink paddies of yours, Walton. It really *was* sweet. I couldn't afford another car, and I can get another five years out of this one with judicious replacement of withering parts here and there."

"What were you doing out on Sharon Avenue this afternoon?"

"Looking for you, you vaunting ass. When you told me you were going to walk all the way from Sharonville in this heat —and at your age too—my first thought was 'let him learn the hard way.' Then I had a picture of you lying lobster-red by the highway; so I told Mother some cock-and-bull story and came out to find you."

"You drove right by me."

"I drove by a portly, sweaty hobo lurching along in the curb. I saw no connection between him and Walton Ulster, distinguished New York music critic and enfant terrible of the concert hall. For heaven's sake, join me in something. Cherry Coke?"

"My favorite used to be vanilla phosphate. On second thought, I think I'll have a lime Coke. Do you suppose that girl would let us look at her flask for a few rapturous seconds."

The boy in the green sweater came in. The liver-colored dog sat patiently on the sidewalk just outside the door.

"Good heavens, Walton," Moira whispered. "That boy looks just like you when you were 13 or 14."

"I was never that skinny," said Walton.

The boy came up to the counter and ordered a vanilla phosphate. Walton ordered his lime Coke. It suddenly occurred to him that the people behind the counters astonishingly resembled the people of 1931. He knew that if they were still alive, Mr. Igler and Miss Katie would be over 100 now, Miss Tillie and Miss Frances would be in their sixties or seventies, and Wilbur at least in his late fifties. *I'm not hallucinating*, he thought. *I'm only seeing imaginary resemblances my subconscious wants to see.* Be Nonchalant. Light a Murad. Were there Murads any more? Just for fun he asked the one who looked like Wilbur to bring him a Murad, and Wilbur did. He took one out and lit it—nonchalantly. It was too strong for a taste long since cravenly conditioned to filter cigarettes.

Moira said, "I'll be darned. The things they can come up with."

"It's stale. Probably been sitting here for 30 years."

Some other boys came in and joined the kid with the green sweater. They ordered phosphates of various flavors and sat down by the window to flip through the movie magazines. There had been a time when Mr. Igler endured this sort of imposition.

"Hey. Here's a picture of Joan Crawford. She's my dream queen."

"Mine's Janet Gaynor. She's like a real kind of a girl."

"Hey. It says maybe Doug Fairbanks is quitting the movies."

"That's a heck of a note. Hey. Did you know Edward G. Robinson is really a nice guy in real life?"

Moira said, "Why so dreamy?"

"I was just listening to the kids."

"You must have super-ears. I can't hear a word from here. Look, Walton, I really do love seeing you, but I have a tyrannical invalid for a mother, and she expects me home. What is it you wanted to talk to me about?"

"Well, for one thing, your mother. After all these years you had to tell her a cock-and-bull story just to meet me for a few minutes in Igler's?"

"You know she hasn't been rational since the accident. She has always held you to blame. You and that black mutt."

"Moira, I ought to tell you; after more than 30 years, my temples still throb at the sound of the word 'mutt.' "

"I apologize, Walton. We don't need to drag that business out into the light of day again."

"Yes we do. That's just it. I'm fouled up, Moira, and I'm trying to grope my way into the past to find some answers that might help. You're the key, Moira. What happened to us?"

"What could be simpler. 'Us' was lovely, but 'us' was out of the question. You were a pretty far-out boy. You were dedicated, determined on poverty, and all in all, a lovable— God, how lovable—sap. I was a bird-brained debutante dreaming of an escape from my mother, a Cadillac, and a rich husband—in that order. Well, I got the Cadillac and the rich husband, and I still have the Cadillac. Next question."

Walton frowned. Was Moira making this up to save face?

"That's not the way it was at all," he said. "I was an arrogant, pompous cad. I treated you like dirt. Why? How?"

"You were all of that when you wanted to be. I didn't mind much. You always got over it pretty quickly. So. Now. You've had a successful career. You have a charming wife and lovely children. Aunt Jane keeps me posted. But you say you're fouled up."

"Please don't rush me, Moira. Let me collect my thoughts."

Four girls in their early teens came in, wearing the green and white uniforms of Hillsdale School for young ladies. They walked haughtily past the boys, hiding their secret smiles, and went to the corner where, Walton knew, the Hit-of-the-Week records were on display. The boys ambled over to join them, some swaggering, some slouching, all projecting huge indifference.

Girl: "The one I liked best was 'The moon and you appear to be/so near and yet so far from me.' "

Another girl: " 'I'm through with love; I'll never fall again/say adieu to love; don't ever call again.' That's my theme song."

Another girl: " 'I am just a lonesome lover.' That's mine."

Boy: "Nerts on Rudy Vallee. He sings like a girl."

Another boy: "Bing Crosby sings okay."

Girl: "Oh, he's divine."

Boy: "What about Maurice Chevalier? He makes me sick."

Girl: "My mother thinks he's divine."

Boy in green sweater: "Oooooogh! So does mine. You wanta know who my favorite is? My favorite is Elmer Zilch."

(Laughter.)

Walton tensed, waiting for the phone of doom to ring. He was almost relieved when it did. The one who looked like Mr. Igler answered it and went to the teen-age girl with the wildest, longest, blackest hair of all to tell her the call was for her.

Just then, an Army captain, his greatcoat buttoned to his throat, came in on crutches, looked around almost timidly, then walked over to the young lady with the dyed squirrel fur coat. She glowered at her empty Coke glass, refusing to look at him, but he sat down anyway.

The young lady spoke through her teeth, still refusing to look at him. "Did you have a good time at Bob Heine's? Did you search your soul, or did you get loaded?"

"I just had a couple of slow, slo-o-ow beers. Give me a break, Mo. To err is human; to forgive, divine."

Teen-age girl (in background): "I have a divine idea. Let's go to my place and play Truth'n'Consequences."

Another girl: "Divine!"

Boy in green sweater: "Swell. Wait till Moira gets off the phone and we'll all go."

First girl: "Divine."

The young lady with the dyed squirrel fur coat deigned now to look at the captain. "I'm not divine," she said. "I'm not the one to do the forgiving anyway. You behaved like a brat, but I might have known you would when the message seeped through the rock wall of your ego. You simply can't take a hint unless it's delivered with a baseball bat."

"Hint? What are you talking about?"

"How can an intelligent man be so dense? Even before you went into the Army, I tried to tell you in as nice a way as possible. What did you do with the letters I sent you? Just glance at them and throw them away? Didn't you ever try to read between the lines? I didn't want to hurt you but you've been making it difficult for both of us. You have your plans; fine! Well, I have mine too, and they don't include you. I can't make it any blunter than that. I'm sorry, Wall. I'm really very fond of you."

Walton wished he could stop up his ears without making a spectacle of himself. He hated overhearing this conversation. It was all wrong—cockeyed—out of true. The man should be the one to strike; not the girl.

The captain said, almost whining, "Oh, Mo. Mo. It can't be like this. I swear to God, I've really got it inside of me now. We could be great together. I've got it."

Walton took another sip of his lime Coke. "The truth is, Moira," he said, "I just haven't got it. I haven't had it for I don't know how many years. I make a fair living teaching and writing reviews, and I attract attention with my outrageous bag of instrumental tricks, but tap me with a rubber mallet and all you'll get is a hollow boing."

"What about your wife?"

"That's all over, Moira. It's been over for a long time, but now that the kids are in college we're ready to make it legal. Everything will be civilized. I haven't any right to be bitter. My God, it wasn't her fault she was loaded with dough. It wasn't her fault I turned out to be a hollow man, and a damned resentful, boorish hollow man at that. She's been more than patient."

"You don't have to tell me," said Moira. "I know the combination. So you married money too?"

"More than that. She was—still is—a very sexy broad. She believed in me. We had our moments of romance. But you're right. It was a lousy combination. We should have known it at the start."

"Did you smash phonograph records?"

"Worse."

"Whose side are the children on?"

"It hasn't come to that. I suppose if it does, they'll stand up for their mother. But they're good, level-headed kids. They won't be estranged from either of us. Fact, they'll probably be relieved. Divorce solves a lot of unacknowledged problems. Not that it will really solve mine."

"What *will?*"

"I told you, Moira. I've got to catch up with myself, recapture my past. I have the feeling I once did something dreadful, too dreadful to be carried in my memory—something having to do with you and me. I've got to work my way back to it. With your help. I've got to find a name for it, and, please God, purge myself of it."

"All right, Walton, I want you to listen to me, and, damn it, take me seriously, or I'll bounce something off your head. To begin with, forget all that jazz about Hell having no fury like a woman scorned. I've had plenty of experience in swallowing my pride. I've even come to find it rather nutritious. For Pete's sake, Walton Ulster, why don't we un-do all this silly damn nonsense and get married to each other?"

Walton looked at her in amazement. "You know, it's the funniest darn thing, but I was just about to say the same thing. It hadn't occurred to me till just now. But—hadn't there ought to be a courtship? Flowers? Candy? Serenades?"

There was a commotion among the teen-agers. The girl with the long black hair was weeping and ranting.

"It's all your fault, Knotty. You killed her. You and that —that *damn* mutt of yours."

"Inky didn't have anything to do with it," said the boy in the green sweater.

"Don't you dare talk to me, you *murderer*. Don't ever talk to me again."

She fled from the store.

"Golly, Knotty," said a boy. "What did *you* have to do with it?"

Girl: "She isn't really *dead*, is she?"

Walton strode over to the group of youngsters. He gripped the green-sweatered boy by the upper arms and said through his teeth, "What *did* you have to do with it?"

"Ow," said the boy with the green sweater.

"You fixed the wheel, didn't you?"

"You can't prove anything," said Knotty.

"Mr. Igler" came up, tapped Walton on the shoulder and beckoned him to a private corner of the store.

"I don't know why you're making this your business,

mister, but I'd better set you straight. Something very serious has—"

"I know. Mrs. Hendricks has been in an auto accident. She's not dead."

"How in the deuce could *you* know *that?*"

Play it cool.

"I overheard the kids," Walton lied.

"Well, you're right. She's not dead, and Doc Allen thinks she'll probably pull through. The shame of it is, her brain will probably be affected some, and—do you know Mrs. Hendricks?"

"Quite well."

"A handsome woman. But her head went through the windshield."

"God, her face!" said Walton. "That's terrible."

"But it doesn't have a blessed thing to do with Knotty over there. I don't know what little Moira was fussing about. Upset, I guess. Well, it's only natural. But Knotty didn't do anything."

"How in the world could *you* know *that?*"

"Well, plenty of people saw the accident. She was in her old Model T, and her brother was driving."

"Ducky Cook?"

"That's right. The soft-headed one. If they had drivers' licenses in Ohio, he wouldn't be allowed to drive. Well, what's done—"

"Wait. You said the Model T. You mean the Model A, don't you?"

"Nope. The tin lizzie. The *new* Ford had a flat tire out on Sharon Avenue. She came in here and phoned for Ducky to come pick her up in the *old* Ford and drive out to change the tire. They weren't far from here when it happened. A big black dog ran out in the road and Mrs. Hendricks grabbed the steering wheel to swerve the car away from it. Smashed right into an iron street-light pole. Ducky was killed right away. In some ways, I guess *that's* a blessing."

Knotty's voice became shrill.

"All right, all right," he shouted. "I fixed the wheel!"

Mr. Igler and Walton hurried over to the cluster of youngsters. Mr. Igler was scolding, "That's enough of that, young man. This is nothing to joke about."

"I'm not joking. I fixed the wheel."

"Aw, go on," said one of the boys. "You wouldn't even know *how* to fix a wheel. What did you do?"

"All right, I'll tell you," said Knotty. "I don't care. I wrote the Lord's Prayer backwards all around the tire. All of it."

Everyone but Walton roared with laughter.

"All right," said Knotty, his voice trembling. "You wouldn't like it if I wrote the Lord's Prayer backwards on something of yours. It's not funny. 'Nema. Rever dna reverof, yrolg eht—' "

"Oh boy. Oh wow. You're nertzy."

"You oughta be in a padded cell in Longview."

Knotty turned red. Tears came to his eyes, and he ran out of the store.

Walton wondered if he ought to run after the boy and tell him about the Model T. He couldn't ask Moira for advice.

He decided against it. *Ding, ding; here comes the wagon.*

"What was that rumpus about?" asked Moira.

"Automobile accident. Little girl's mother was badly hurt."

"The poor dear. What was the little boy so excited about?"

"Oh, kid stuff. You never can tell."

"I swear, he looked just like you as a little boy. What moved you to horn in?"

"Kid's probably one of my second cousins. I had an impulse to go over and introduce myself and find out what he was mixed up in. I'm glad I didn't, now that I think of it. I love my relatives, but I don't dare let any one of them know I'm in town. I'd be stuck for the next two days paying duty calls on uncles and aunts and cousins and friends, and I've got a deadline to meet in New York."

"Not much time for all that courtship you were talking about."

"Come to New York with me. We'll do the town. Please, Moira."

"I'd love it, Walton, but there's always Mother. Damn! For one wild, delirious moment there I actually forgot Mother. *We* can't get married, Walton. We can't even have an affair."

"Moira, look. One of the reasons I married Nancy was that I wasn't cut out to be a monk. I took the soft, fat way out, and if I wasn't hollow to begin with, *that* did the job. I need a hair shirt, Moira—something to beat me down from time to time, to force humility on me. Come to New York *with* your mother, Moira. All *three* of us will do the town."

"Isn't it wonderful, Walton, that we can sit here like this without a drop of Dutch courage between us and be honest with each other. It's a new kick for me. God, how I've needed it."

"This isn't a build-up to one of those histrionic abnegation scenes? Wringing of the hands. 'No, Walton; I must bear alone the burden of my mother. I cannot allow you to make this sacrifice.'"

"All right, Walton. You needn't pitch so hard. I've had my own share of sacrifice until it's coming out my ears; so maybe it *is* your turn. Marriage is still an open question then. But not New York. That's *out* of the question. Mother can't leave the house, and I can't leave her alone in it for very long. Oh, she's not so far gone that she doesn't know who she is and where she is— And, by the way, that's the answer to your next question: Why don't I put her in an institution?"

"That wasn't going to be my next question. I don't condone torture. I'll accept your mother as she is. I'll turn the other cheek a hundred times a day. I know it won't be idyllic, but I'm old enough not to believe in idylls, and maybe someday she'll come to accept *me*, if not as a member of the family, at least as a useful and familiar accessory around the house."

There was a crash behind them. The captain was on his feet, his chair lying on the floor behind him, shouting:

"You don't fool me for a minute. Your damn mother has poisoned your mind against me. You want to know what I think? She's just putting on an act. She was a run-of-the-mill neurotic until she killed my dog, and ever since then she's been hiding behind this phony brain injury. She's been loading all her guilt onto me! She's got you right where she wants you."

The young lady stiffened. "Well! The very idea!"

"Don't get on your high horse. If she's really as nutty as everyone says she is, why don't you have her put away?"

"Well, if you're going to have another tantrum, I'm leaving."

"I'll beat you to it. I'm going over to Bob Heine's and really tie one on this time. See you around one of these years."

He marched out, turning up the collar of his greatcoat as the door closed behind him.

"Was that it?" Walton asked.

"Was what it?"

"Now, don't tell me you didn't hear that little interchange."

"I didn't hear the words. I heard an angry voice; that's all. My God, Walton, you've got sharp ears. Does that go with having perfect pitch?"

"It goes with being hollow. Like a little pitcher. Look, Moira, a little while ago I heard the little girl who was over in the corner telling the little boy in the green sweater it was all his fault that her mother was in an accident. Just now, I heard our stiff-necked friend, the captain, telling his lady friend that her mother was unloading her own guilt on him. Do you want to marry a man who hallucinates in broad daylight?"

"Don't be silly, Walton. You're in some kind of a crisis, and you're reading your own memories into everything you hear. Your little dramas aren't unique. Neither are mine."

"Did your mother really feel guilty about Inky?"

"That was your black mongrel, wasn't it. You don't think Mother ran over it on purpose?"

"Of course not."

"I wish you could make her realize that, but of course it's too late. She's not very—uh—reachable. I never knew myself what you really thought, and I didn't dare ask. You were too young to know what you were doing, and I was too young to understand what the death of one mongrel dog can mean to a little boy. I did forgive you though for standing there that horrible day shouting 'murderer' at Mother. I even stopped having dreams about it. But Mother didn't."

"But Moira, I never did that."

"You were beside yourself, Walton. You were standing there looking at the dead dog in the street, and Mother and I were in the car, both of us trying to think of something kind to say. I didn't realize it then, but Mother had been—well—eccentric ever since Daddy died. She couldn't stand to be upset. I know she *meant* to be kind, but any kind of emotional crisis just brought out the poison in her. What she said was true enough, but—"

"She said Inky was a mutt. She said I ought to be grateful I still had a fine thoroughbred like Slimmy, and she hoped I wouldn't waste time grieving over a no-good mutt."

"I know. It was terrible. She was beside herself too, and she had no control over her words. She could see how unhappy you were, and it tore her to pieces. All she was trying to say was 'damn you, child, don't stand there being unhappy in front of me and making me unhappy. I've got enough to be unhappy about.'"

"I know, I know. So I called her a murderer. I didn't remember that. I do remember thinking it."

"You have a handy forgettory. I wish Mother did."

"Why is it that when we're old enough not to be able to hurt anyone very much, we finally learn how to refrain?"

The young lady behind them stood up and put on her dyed squirrel fur coat. She said to Miss Frances, "Charge it to me," and walked out. An old man, jowly and almost bald, bowed to her outside on the sidewalk.

"Are you up to facing Mother today, Walton?" asked Moira.

"Might as well be today. I ought to buy a clean shirt somewhere first. Can you sneak me in the back door to shave and change before the ordeal?"

"We'll work something out. Then afterwards it's drinks and duck a l'orange at the Iron Horse. Deal?"

"Deal. If you can get away from Mother that long."

Outside, the young lady was saying to the jowly old man, "Well, the windshield was frosted, and when I saw you there on the side of the bridge I had an illusion that there was an extra traffic lane on the right side of the bridge. It's the funniest thing, I had this idea you were someone I knew, someone who had something to tell me. Something important. I pulled over to the right, and then—bang!"

"Did the captain see me too?"

"Maybe. I don't know. I can't imagine what I thought you had to tell me."

The old man chuckled. "I can't either. A man my age gives out a lot of advice, but it's hardly ever solicited and it never does any good. Well, it's been a pleasure, ma'am."

As the young lady was getting into the car, Walton said

to the old man, "I know a piece of advice you could have
given her. You could have told her to march right over to
Bob Heine's and join a certain captain in about 20 salubrious
belts of bourbon."

"Good Lord, Walton. *Bob Heine's?*" said Moira. "And
what an old buttinsky you've turned into."

"Perfectly all right, ma'am," said the old man. "Mr. Ulster
and I are acquainted."

Walton peered at the old man.

"Why, yes. Yes," he said. "The freemasonry of the mad."
Ding, ding!

The old man looked reflectively in the direction of the
Iron Horse, cat-cornered across the village square.

"Bob Heine's," he said. "Oh yes, of course. You'd hardly
recognize the village now."

"Oh, I don't know," said Walton. "The outskirts have
changed a lot, but once you're in the village everything looks
pretty much the same. A little remodeling here and there,
but—"

"Of course. I wasn't thinking. It wasn't till 1983 they
tore down the—"

"Easy does it," Walton hissed. "Ding, ding."

"That's right," said the old man. "Pardon the senility of
an octogenarian. 'Play it cool.' That's the expression, isn't
it?"

"Not too easy in weather like this," said Walton, wiping
his forehead with the sleeve of his shirt.

"As for the advice you were talking about," said the old
man. "It would be an act of cruelty. Those young people
would destroy each other in about two years."

Walton glanced nervously at Moira.

"Oh, not you two. Not you two," said the old man.
"You've both been through the purifier's flame. If benedic-
tions are in order, please accept mine."

A gun-metal blue sports car that looked like a water bug
pulled up to the curb and a hollow-cheeked, deep-eyed,
but still strangely beautiful old lady put her head out the
window.

"I've been looking all over for you, Wally. Mother is
worried about you. Where on earth have you been?"

"Oh, alone and palely loitering," said the old man. "The
sedge is withered from the lake, and no birds sing."

The old lady laughed.

"Don't mind him," she said. "He would like me to be the Belle Dame Sans Merci. There's a bit of witch in me, but I'm not that."

"Okay, okay," said the old man, opening the car door on her side. "Take me to your elfin grot."

"You're a dirty old man," said the old lady.

"Move over," said the old man. "You're too decrepit to drive."

The old man climbed in the bug car beside his wife, and took her hand.

"Can you imagine?" he said to Walton. "Here I am 85 years old and ought to be lounging in slippered ease, but I've got a mother-in-law 105 years old and I spend my days pushing her around in the wheel chair like a dutiful son."

"Oh, you *know* you and Mother get along *beautifully*."

"Of course," said the old man, winking at Walton. "It's the freemasonry of the mad. She fusses at me and pampers me and depends upon me. I fuss at her and pamper her and depend upon her. We're both of us making something up to each other, something that happened so long ago we ought to have made it up by now. But you see, every day is yesterday all over again. By the way, you didn't happen to see a boy in a green sweater trailed by a liver-colored dog?"

"He was in Igler's a little while ago, but he's not there now."

"Oh well," said the old man, "I know where he lives. Maybe I can catch him before he reaches home."

"You and that boy," said the old lady. "One of these days I'm going to turn you in for child molestation. That is, if you ever find him."

"Oh, I found him. This afternoon." The old man laughed, put the palm of his hand on the old lady's face and gave it a gentle shove.

"Wife beater," she said.

"Be happy, you two," the old man called to Walton and Moira. "Be patient. You'll find it. You'll find it."

He drove away.

"Good Lord, what was that all about?" asked Moira.

Knotty dragged his feet along the sidewalk leading to home. He started to worry a little stone with his foot, intending half-heartedly to see if he could kick it all the way home, but he lost interest after the fourth kick. Well, he knew what Mom was going to say. "Where have you been and what did you do, darling?" "Well, Mom, I just happened to hike to Sharonville and I just happened to see Mrs. Hendricks' car by the side of the road with a flat tire and I just happened to—"

Oboyoboyoboy.

Aw, to heck with everybody.

This screwy little car that looked just like a water bug came to a stop beside him, and there was this same old old man he had seen earlier by the dump. There was an old old woman with him.

"Oh, hi," he said listlessly.

"Look, Knotty," said the old man. "I've done a lot of thinking about this score. Does the instrumentation really matter? I mean, does it have to be bottles?"

"Well, it doesn't *haf* to, I guess, but you'd have to make it different if you played it on an accordion or a piano, say. I mean, you'd want to put in some fast notes and stuff. And on a harmonica, you'd want to blow in some chords."

"I'm glad you called my attention to that," said the old man. "Stupid of me not to have thought of it myself. All right. Bottles it is. I did think though that some kind of bass harmony—"

"Yeh, yeah," said Knotty, enthusiastic now. "Cellos would be swell, don't you think? Just a bunch of cellos."

"Cellos *would* be swell," said the old old man.

"Will I get to hear it?"

"You'll get to hear it, Knotty. Be patient. Don't hold your breath. And, say, Knotty—"

"Yeah?"

"I kind of think Inky will like it."

"Shucks. Dogs don't like music. It hurts their ears."

Roger Zelazny was the recipient of two of the five awards presented at the first Science Fiction Writers of America banquet: THE DOORS OF HIS FACE, THE LAMPS OF HIS MOUTH for best novelet and HE WHO SHAPES for best novella. The dinner was notable for its lack of panegyrical comment, but we will be holding no one from their fruit cup if we say here that we feel the awards well deserved—because Mr. Zelazny writes with style and feeling, because he fashions inventive situations and real characters, because his stories are highly individual without being repetitious, and finally because he has given us the opportunity to publish such fine pieces as A ROSE FOR ECCLESIASTES; THE DOORS OF HIS FACE, THE LAMPS OF HIS MOUTH; AND CALL ME CONRAD; and, here THIS MOMENT OF THE STORM.

THIS MOMENT OF THE STORM

by Roger Zelazny

Back on Earth, my old philosophy prof—possibly because he'd misplaced his lecture notes—came into the classroom one day and scrutinized his sixteen victims for the space of half a minute. Satisfied then, that a sufficiently profound note had been established, he asked:

"What is a man?"

He had known exactly what he was doing. He'd had an hour and a half to kill, and eleven of the sixteen were coeds (nine of them in liberal arts, and the other two stuck with an Area Requirement).

One of the other two, who was in the pre-med program, proceeded to provide a strict biological classification.

The prof (McNitt was his name, I suddenly recall) nodded then, and asked:

"Is that all?"

And there was his hour and a half.

I learned that Man is the Reasoning Animal, Man is the One Who Laughs, Man is greater than beasts but less than angels, Man is the one who watches himself watch himself doing things he knows are absurd (this from a Comparative Lit gal), Man is the culture-transmitting animal, Man is the spirit which aspires, affirms, loves, the one who uses tools, buries his dead, devises religions, and the one who tries to define hmself. (That last from Paul Schwartz, my room-mate—which I thought pretty good, on the spur of the moment. Wonder whatever became of Paul?)

Anyhow, to most of these I say "perhaps" or "partly, but—" or just plain "crap!" I still think mine was the best, because I had a chance to try it out, on Tierra del Cygnus, Land of the Swan . . .

I'd said, "Man is the sum total of everything he has done, wishes to do or not to do, and wishes he had done, or hadn't."

Stop and think about it for a minute. It's purposely as general as the others, but it's got room in it for the biology and the laughing and the aspiring, as well as the culture-transmitting, the love, and the room full of mirrors, and the defining. I even left the door open for religion, you'll note. But it's limiting, too. Ever met an oyster to whom the final phrases apply?

Tierra del Cygnus, Land of the Swan—delightful name. Delightful place too, for quite awhile . . .

It was there that I saw Man's definitions, one by one, wiped from off the big blackboard, until only mine was left. . . . My radio had been playing more static than usual. That's all.

For several hours there was no other indication of what was to come.

My hundred-thirty eyes had watched Betty all morning, on that clear, cool spring day with the sun pouring down its honey and lightning upon the amber fields, flowing through the streets, invading western store-fronts, drying curbstones, and washing the olive and umber buds that speared the skin of the trees there by the roadway; and the light that wrung the blue from the flag before Town Hall made orange mirrors out of windows, chased purple and violet patches across the shoulders of Saint Stephen's Range, some thirty

miles distant, and came down upon the forest at its feet
like some supernatural madman with a million buckets of
paint—each of a different shade of green, yellow, orange,
blue and red—to daub with miles-wide brushes at its heav-
ing sea of growth.

Mornings the sky is cobalt, midday is turquoise, and sun-
set is emeralds and rubies, hard and flashing. It was halfway between cobalt and seamist at 1100 hours, when I
watched Betty with my hundred-thirty eyes and saw nothing to indicate what was about to be. There was only that
persistent piece of static, accompanying the piano and
strings within my portable.

It's funny how the mind personifies, engenders. Ships
are always women: You say, "She's a good old tub," or,
"She's a fast, tough number, this one," slapping a bulwark
and feeling the aura of femininity that clings to the vessel's curves; or conversely, "He's a bastard to start, that little Sam!" as you kick the auxiliary engine in an inland transport-vehicle; and hurricanes are always women, and moons,
and seas. Cities, though, are different. Generally, they're
neuter. Nobody calls New York or San Francisco "he" or
"she." Usually, cities are just "it."

Sometimes, however, they do come to take on the at-
tributes of sex. Usually, this is in the case of small cities
near to the Mediterranean, back on Earth. Perhaps this is
because of the sex-ridden nouns of the languages which prevail in that vicinity, in which case it tells us more about the
inhabitants than it does about the habitations. But I feel that
it goes deeper than that.

Betty was Beta Station for less than ten years. After two
decades she was Betty officially, by act of Town Council.
Why? Well, I felt at the time (ninety-some years ago), and
still feel, that it was because she was what she was—a place
of rest and repair, of surface-cooked meals and of new
voices, new faces, of landscapes, weather, and natural light
again, after that long haul through the big night, with its
casting away of so much. She is not home, she is seldom
destination, but she is like unto both. When you come upon
light and warmth and music after darkness and cold and
silence, it is Woman. The oldtime Mediterranean sailor must
have felt it when he first spied port at the end of a voyage.

222

I felt it when I first saw Beta Station—Betty—and the second time I saw her, also.

I am her Hell Cop.

. . . When six or seven of my hundred-thirty eyes flickered, then saw again, and the music was suddenly washed away by a wave of static, it was then that I began to feel uneasy.

I called Weather Central for a report, and the recorded girlvoice told me that seasonal rains were expected in the afternoon or early evening. I hung up and switched an eye from ventral to dorsal-vision.

Not a cloud. Not a ripple. Only a formation of green-winged sky-toads, heading north, crossed the field of lens.

I switched it back, and I watched the traffic flow, slowly, and without congestion, along Betty's prim, well-tended streets. Three men were leaving the bank and two more were entering. I recognized the three who were leaving, and in my mind I waved as I passed by. All was still at the post office, and patterns of normal activity, lay upon the steel mills, the stockyard, the plast-synth plants, the airport, the spacer pads, and the surfaces of all the shopping complexes; vehicles came and went at the Inland Transport-Vehicle garages, crawling from the rainbow forest and the mountains beyond like dark slugs, leaving tread-trails to mark their comings and goings through wilderness; and the fields of the countryside were still yellow and brown, with occasional patches of green and pink; the country houses, mainly simple A-frame affairs, were chisel blade, spike-tooth, spire and steeple, each with a big lightning rod, and dipped in many colors and scooped up in the cups of my seeing and dumped out again, as I sent my eyes on their rounds and tended my gallery of one hundred-thirty changing pictures, on the big wall of the Trouble Center, there atop the Watch Tower of Town Hall.

The static came and went until I had to shut off the radio. Fragments of music are worse than no music at all.

My eyes, coasting weightless along magnetic lines, began to blink.

I knew then that we were in for something.

I sent an eye scurrying off toward Saint Stephen's at full speed, which meant a wait of about twenty minutes until it topped the range. Another, I sent straight up, skywards, which meant perhaps ten minutes for a long shot of the same scene. Then I put the auto-scan in full charge of operations and went downstairs for a cup of coffee.

I entered the Mayor's outer office, winked at Lottie, the receptionist, and glanced at the inner door.

"Mayor in?" I asked.

I got an occasional smile from Lottie, a slightly heavy, but well-rounded girl of indeterminate age and intermittent acne, but this wasn't one of the occasions.

"Yes," she said, returning to the papers on her desk.

"Alone?"

She nodded, and her earrings danced. Dark eyes and dark complexion, she could have been kind of sharp, if only she'd fix her hair and use more makeup. Well . . .

I crossed to the door and knocked.

"Who?" asked the Mayor.

"Me," I said, opening it, "Godfrey Justin Holmes—'God' for short. I want someone to drink coffee with, and you're elected."

She turned in her swivel chair, away from the window she had been studying, and her blonde-hair-white-hair-fused, short and parted in the middle, gave a little stir as she turned—like a sunshot snowdrift struck by sudden winds.

She smiled and said, "I'm busy."

"Eyes green, chin small, cute little ears—I love them all" —from an anonymous Valentine I'd sent her two months previous, and true.

". . . But not too busy to have coffee with God," she stated. "Have a throne, and I'll make us some instant."

I did, and she did.

While she was doing it, I leaned back, lit a cigarette I'd borrowed from her canister, and remarked, "Looks like rain."

"Uh-huh," she said.

"Not just making conversation," I told her. "There's a bad storm brewing somewhere—over Saint Stephen's, I think. I'll know real soon."

"Yes, grandfather," she said, bringing me my coffee. "You old timers with all your aches and pains are often better than Weather Central, it's an established fact. I won't argue."

She smiled, frowned, then smiled again.

I set my cup on the edge of her desk.

"Just wait and see," I said. "If it makes it over the mountains, it'll be a nasty high-voltage job. It's already jazzing up reception."

Big-bowed white blouse, and black skirt around a well-kept figure. She'd be forty in the fall, but she'd never completely tamed her facial reflexes—which was most engaging, so far as I was concerned. Spontaneity of expression so often vanishes so soon. I could see the sort of child she'd been by looking at her, listening to her now. The thought of being forty was bothering her again, too, I could tell. She always kids me about age when age is bothering her.

See, I'm around thirty-five, actually, which makes me her junior by a bit, but she'd heard her grandfather speak of me when she was a kid, before I came back again this last time. I'd filled out the balance of his two-year term, back when Betty-Beta's first mayor, Wyeth, had died after two months in office. I was born five hundred ninety-seven years ago, on Earth, but I spent about five hundred sixty-two of those years sleeping, during my long jaunts between the stars. I've made a few more trips than a few others; consequently, I am an anachronism. I am really, of course, only as old as I look—but still, people always seem to feel that I've cheated somehow, especially women in their middle years. Sometimes it is most disconcerting . . .

"Eleanor," said I, "your term will be up in November. Are you still thinking of running again?"

She took off her narrow, elegantly-trimmed glasses and brushed her eyelids with thumb and forefinger. Then she took a sip of coffee.

"I haven't made up my mind."

"I ask not for press-release purposes," I said, "but for my own."

"Really, I haven't decided," she told me. "I don't know . . ."

"Okay, just checking. Let me know if you do."

I drank some coffee.

After a time, she said, "Dinner Saturday? As usual?"

"Yes, good."

"I'll tell you then."

"Fine—capital."

As she looked down into her coffee, I saw a little girl staring into a pool, waiting for it to clear, to see her reflection or to see the bottom of the pool, or perhaps both.

She smiled at whatever it was she finally saw.

"A bad storm?" she asked me.

"Yep. Feel it in my bones."

"Tell it to go away?"

"Tried. Don't think it will, though."

"Better batten some hatches, then."

"It wouldn't hurt and it might help."

"The weather satellite will be overhead in another half hour. You'll have something sooner?"

"Think so. Probably any minute."

I finished my coffee, washed out the cup.

"Let me know right away what it is."

"Check. Thanks for the coffee."

Lottie was still working and did not look up as I passed.

Upstairs again, my highest eye was now high enough. I stood it on its tail and collected a view of the distance: Fleecy mobs of clouds boiled and frothed on the other side of Saint Stephen's. The mountain range seemed a break-wall, a dam, a rocky shoreline. Beyond it, the waters were troubled.

My other eye was almost in position. I waited the space of half a cigarette, then it delivered me a sight:

Gray, and wet and impenetrable, a curtain across the countryside, that's what I saw.

. . . And advancing.

I called Eleanor.

"It's gonna rain, chillun," I said.

"Worth some sandbags?"

"Possibly."

"Better be ready then. Okay. Thanks."

I returned to my watching.

Tierra del Cygnus, Land of the Swan—delightful name. It refers to both the planet and its sole continent.

How to describe the world, like quick? Well, roughly Earth-size; actually a bit smaller, and more watery. —As for the main landmass, first hold a mirror up to South America, to get the big bump from the right side over to the left, then rotate it ninety degrees in a counter-clockwise direction and push it up into the northern hemisphere. Got that? Good. Now grab it by the tail and pull. Stretch it another six or seven hundred miles, slimming down the middle as you do, and let the last five or six hundred fall across the equator. There you have Cygnus, its big gulf partly in the tropics, partly not. Just for the sake of thoroughness, while you're about it, break Australia into eight pieces and drop them about at random down in the southern hemisphere, calling them after the first eight letters in the Greek alphabet. Put a big scoop of vanilla at each pole, and don't forget to tilt the globe about eighteen degrees before you leave. Thanks.

I recalled my wandering eyes, and I kept a few of the others turned toward Saint Stephen's until the cloudbanks breasted the range about an hour later. By then, though, the weather satellite had passed over and picked the thing up also. It reported quite an extensive cloud cover on the other side. The storm had sprung up quickly, as they often do here on Cygnus. Often, too, they disperse just as quickly, after an hour or so of heaven's artillery. But then there are the bad ones—sometimes lingering and lingering, and bearing more thunderbolts in their quivers than any Earth storm.

Betty's position, too, is occasionally precarious, though its advantages, in general, offset its liabilities. We are located on the gulf, about twenty miles inland, and are approximately three miles removed (in the main) from a major river, the Noble; part of Betty does extend down to its banks, but this is a smaller part. We are almost a strip city, falling mainly into an area some seven miles in length and two miles wide, stretching inland, east from the river, and running roughly parallel to the distant seacoast. Around eight percent of the 100,000 population is concentrated about the business district, five miles in from the river.

We are not the lowest land about, but we are far from being the highest. We are certainly the most level in the area. This latter feature, as well as our nearness to the equator, was a deciding factor in the establishment of Beta Station. Some other things were our proximity both to the ocean and to a large river. There are nine other cities on the continent, all of them younger and smaller, and three of them located upriver from us. We are the potential capital of a potential country.

We're a good, smooth, easy landing site for drop-boats from orbiting interstellar vehicles, and we have major assets for future growth and coordination when it comes to expanding across the continent. Our original *raison d'etre*, though, was Stopover, repair-point, supply depot, and refreshment stand, physical and psychological, on the way out to other, more settled worlds, further along the line. Cyg was discovered later than many others—it just happened that way—and the others got off to earlier starts. Hence, the others generally attract more colonists. We are still quite primitive. Self-sufficiency, in order to work on our population: land scale, demanded a society on the order of that of the mid-nineteenth century in the American southwest—at least for purposes of getting started. Even now, Cyg is still partly on a natural economy system, although Earth Central technically determines the coin of the realm.

Why Stopover, if you sleep most of the time between the stars?

Think about it awhile, and I'll tell you later if you're right.

The thunderheads rose in the east, sending billows and streamers this way and that, until it seemed from the formations that Saint Stephen's was a balcony full of monsters, leaning and craning their necks over the rail in the direction of the stage, us. Cloud piled upon slate-colored cloud, and then the wall slowly began to topple.

I heard the first rumbles of thunder almost half an hour after lunch, so I knew it wasn't my stomach.

Despite all my eyes, I moved to a window to watch. It was like a big, gray, aerial glacier plowing the sky.

There was a wind now, for I saw the trees suddenly quiver and bow down. This would be our first storm of the season. The turquoise fell back before it, and finally it smothered the sun itself. Then there were drops upon the windowpane, then rivulets.

Flint-like, the highest peaks of Saint Stephen's scraped its belly and were showered with sparks. After a moment it bumped into something with a terrible crash, and the rivulets on the quartz panes turned into rivers.

I went back to my gallery, to smile at dozens of views of people scurrying for shelter. A smart few had umbrellas and raincoats. The rest ran like blazes. People never pay attention to weather reports; this, I believe, is a constant factor in man's psychological makeup, stemming probably from an ancient tribal distrust of the shaman. You want them to be wrong. If they're right, then they're somehow superior, and this is even more uncomfortable than getting wet.

I remembered then that I had forgotten my raincoat, umbrella and rubbers. But it *had* been a beautiful morning, and W.C. *could* have been wrong . . .

Well, I had another cigarette and leaned back in my big chair. No storm in the world could knock my eyes out of the sky.

I switched on the filters and sat and watched the rain pour past.

Five hours later it was still raining, and rumbling and dark.

I'd had hopes that it would let up by quitting time, but when Chuck Fuller came around the picture still hadn't changed any. Chuck was my relief that night, the evening Hell Cop.

He seated himself beside my desk.

"You're early," I said. "They don't start paying you for another hour."

"Too wet to do anything but sit. Rather sit here than at home."

"Leaky roof?"

He shook his head.

"Mother-in-law. Visiting again."

I nodded.

One of the disadvantages of a small world.

He clasped his hands behind his neck and leaned back in the chair, staring off in the direction of the window. I could feel one of his outbursts coming.

"You know how old I am?" he asked, after awhile.

"No," I said, which was a lie. He was twenty-nine.

"Twenty-seven," he told me, "and going to be twenty-eight soon. Know where I've been?"

"No."

"No place, that's where! I was born and raised on this crummy world! And I married and I settled down here—and I've never been off it. Never could afford it when I was younger. Now I've got a family . . ."

He leaned forward again, rested his elbows on his knees, like a kid. Chuck would look like a kid when he was fifty.
—Blond hair, close-cropped, pug nose, kind of scrawny,

takes a suntan quickly, and well. Maybe he'd act like a kid at fifty, too. I'll never know.

I didn't say anything because I didn't have anything to say.

He was quiet for a long while again.

Then he said, "*You*'ve been around."

After a minute, he went on:

"You were born on Earth. Earth! And you visited lots of other worlds too, before I was even born. Earth is only a name to me. And pictures. And all the others—they're the same! Pictures. Names . . ."

I waited, then after I grew tired of waiting I said, " 'Miniver Cheevy, child of scorn . . .' "

"What does that mean?"

"It's the beginning to an ancient poem. It's an ancient poem now, but it wasn't really ancient when I was a boy. Just old. *I* had friends, relatives, even in-laws, once myself. They are not just bones now. They are dust. Real dust, not metaphorical dust. The past fifteen years seem fifteen years to me, the same as to you, but they're not. They are already many chapters back in the history books. Whenever you travel between the stars you automatically bury the past. The world you leave will be filled with strangers if you ever return—or caricatures of your friends, your relatives, even yourself. It's no great trick to be a grandfather at sixty, a great-grandfather at seventy-five or eighty—but go away for three hundred years, and then come back and meet your great-great-great-great-great-great-great-great-great-great-great-great-grandson, who happens to be fifty-five years old, and puzzled, when you look him up. It shows you just how alone you really are. You are not simply a man without a country or without a world. You are a man without a time. You and the centuries do not belong to each other. You are like the rubbish that drifts between the stars."

"It would be worth it," he said.

I laughed. I'd had to listen to his gripes every month or two for over a year and a half. It had never bothered me much before, so I guess it was a cumulative effect that day—the rain, and Saturday night next, and my recent library visits, *and* his complaining, that had set me off.

His last comment had been too much. "It would be worth it." What could I say to that?

I laughed.

He turned bright red.

"You're laughing at me!"

He stood up and glared down.

"No I'm not," I said, "I'm laughing at me. I shouldn't have been bothered by what you said, but *I* was. That tells me something funny about me."

"What?"

"I'm getting sentimental in my old age, and that's funny."

"Oh." He turned his back on me and walked over to the window and stared out. Then he jammed his hands into his pockets and turned around and looked at me.

"Aren't you happy?" he asked. "Really, I mean? You've got money, and no strings on you. You could pick up and leave on the next I-V that passes, if you wanted to."

"Sure I'm happy," I told him. "My coffee was cold. Forget it."

"Oh," again. He turned back to the window in time to catch a bright flash full in the face, and to have to compete with thunder to get his next words out. "I'm sorry," I heard him say, as in the distance. "It just seems to me that you should be one of the happiest guys around . . ."

"I am. It's the weather today. It's got everybody down in the mouth, yourself included."

"Yeah, you're right," he said. "Look at it rain, will you? Haven't seen any rain in months . . ."

"They've been saving it all up for today."

He chuckled.

"I'm going down for a cup of coffee and a sandwich before I sign on. Can I bring you anything?"

"No, thanks."

"Okay. See you in a little while."

He walked out whistling. He never stays depressed. Like a kid's moods, his moods, up and down, up and down . . . And he's a Hell Cop. Probably the worst possible job for him, having to keep his attention in one place for so long. They say the job title comes from the name of an antique flying vehicle—a hellcopter, I think. We send our eyes on their appointed rounds, and they can hover or soar or back up, just like those old machines could. We patrol the

231

city and the adjacent countryside. Law enforcement isn't much of a problem on Cyg. We never peek in windows or send an eye into a building without an invitation. Our testimony is admissible in court—or, if we're fast enough to press a couple buttons, the tape that we make does an even better job—and we can dispatch live or robot cops in a hurry, depending on which will do a better job.

There isn't much crime on Cyg, though, despite the fact that everybody carries a sidearm of some kind, even little kids. Everybody knows pretty much what their neighbors are up to, and there aren't too many places for a fugitive to run. We're mainly aerial traffic cops, with an eye out for local wildlife (which is the reason for all the sidearms).

S.P.C.U. is what we call the latter function—Society for the Prevention of Cruelty to Us—which is the reason each of my hundred-thirty eyes has six forty-five caliber eye-lashes.

There are things like the cute little panda-puppy—oh, about three feet high at the shoulder when it sits down on its rear like a teddy bear, and with big, square, silky ears, a curly pinto coat, large, limpid, brown eyes, pink tongue, button nose, powder puff tail, sharp little white teeth more poisonous than a Quemeda island viper's, and possessed of a way with mammal entrails like unto the way of an imaginative cat with a rope of catnip.

Then there's a *snapper*, which *looks* as mean as it sounds: a feathered reptile, with three horns on its armored head—one beneath each eye, like a tusk, and one curving skyward from the top of its nose—legs about eighteen inches long, and a four-foot tail which it raises straight into the air whenever it jogs along at greyhound speed, and which it swings like a sandbag—and a mouth full of long, sharp teeth.

Also, there are amphibious things which come from the ocean by way of the river on occasion. I'd rather not speak of them. They're kind of ugly and vicious.

Anyway, those are some of the reasons why there are Hell Cops—not just on Cyg, but on many, many frontier worlds. I've been employed in that capacity on several of them, and I've found that an experienced H.C. can always find a job Out Here. It's like being a professional clerk back home.

Chuck took longer than I thought he would, came back

after I was technically off duty, looked happy though, so I
didn't say anything. There was some pale lipstick on his collar and a grin on his face, so I bade him good morrow,
picked up my cane, and departed in the direction of the
big washing machine.

It was coming down too hard for me to go the two blocks
to my car on foot.

I called a cab and waited another fifteen minutes. Eleanor
had decided to keep Mayor's Hours, and she'd departed
shortly after lunch; and almost the entire staff had been released an hour early because of the weather. Consequently,
Town Hall was full of dark offices and echoes. I waited in
the hallway behind the main door, listening to the purr of
the rain as it fell, and hearing its gurgle as it found its way
into the gutters. It beat the street and shook the window-
panes and made the windows cold to touch.

I'd planned on spending the evening at the library, but
I changed my plans as I watched the weather happen. —Tomorrow, or the next day, I decided. It was an evening for
a good meal, a hot bath, my own books and brandy, and
early to bed. It was good sleeping weather, if nothing else.
A cab pulled up in front of the Hall and blew its horn.

I ran.

The next day the rain let up for perhaps an hour in the
morning. Then a slow drizzle began; and it did not stop
again.

It went on to become a steady downpour by afternoon.

The following day was Friday, which I always have off,
and I was glad that it was.

Put dittos under Thursday's weather report. That's Friday.

But I decided to do something anyway.

I lived down in that section of town near the river. The
Noble was swollen, and the rains kept adding to it. Sewers
had begun to clog and back up; water ran in the streets.
The rain kept coming down and widening the puddles and
lakelets, and it was accompanied by drum solos in the sky
and the falling of bright forks and saw-blades. Dead sky-
toads were washed along the gutters, like burnt-out fireworks. Ball lightning drifted across Town Square; Saint

Elmo's Fire clung to the flag pole, the Watch Tower, and the big statue of Wyeth trying to look heroic.

I headed uptown to the library, pushing my car slowly through the countless beaded curtains. The big furniture movers in the sky were obviously non-union, because they weren't taking any coffee breaks. Finally, I found a parking place and I umbrellaed my way to the library and entered. I have become something of a bibliophile in recent years. It is not so much that I hunger and thirst after knowledge, but that I am news-starved.

It all goes back to my position in the big mixmaster. Admitted, there are *some* things faster than light, like the phase velocities of radio waves in ion plasma, or the tips of the ion-modulated light-beams of Duckbill, the comm-setup back in Sol System, whenever the hinges of the beak snap shut on Earth—but these are highly restricted instances, with no application whatsoever to the passage of shiploads of people and objects between the stars. You can't exceed light-speed when it comes to the movement of matter. You can edge up pretty close, but that's about it.

Life can be suspended though, that's easy—it can be switched off and switched back on again with no trouble at all. This is why *I* have lasted so long. If we can't speed up the ships, we *can* slow down the people—slow them until they stop—and *let* the vessel, moving at near-lightspeed, take half a century, or more if it needs it, to convey its passengers to where they are going. This is why I am very alone. Each little death means resurrection into both another land and another time. I have had several, and *this* is why I have become a bibliophile: news travels slowly, as slowly as the ships and the people. Buy a newspaper before you hop aboard ship and it will still be a newspaper when you reach your destination—but back where you bought it, it would be considered a historical document. Send a letter back to Earth and your correspondent's grandson may be able to get an answer back to your great-grandson, if the message makes real good connections and both kids live long enough.

All the little libraries Out Here are full of rare books—first editions of best sellers which people pick up before they leave Someplace Else, and which they often donate after they've finished. We assume that these books have entered the public domain by the time they reach here, and we reproduce them and circulate our own editions. No author has ever sued, and no reproducer has ever been around to be sued by representatives, designates, or assigns.

We are completely autonomous and are always behind the times, because there is a transit-lag which cannot be overcome. Earth Central, therefore, exercises about as much control over us as a boy jiggling a broken string while looking up at his kite.

Perhaps Yeats had something like this in mind when he wrote that fine line, "Things fall apart; the center cannot hold." I doubt it, but I still have to go to the library to read the news.

The day melted around me.

The words flowed across the screen in my booth as I read newspapers and magazines, untouched by human hands, and the waters flowed across Betty's acres, pouring down from the mountains now, washing the floors of the forest, churning our fields to peanut-butter, flooding basements, soaking its way through everything, and tracking our streets with mud.

I hit the library cafeteria for lunch, where I learned from a girl in a green apron and yellow skirts (which swished pleasantly) that the sandbag crews were now hard at work and that there was no eastbound traffic past Town Square.

After lunch I put on my slicker and boots and walked up that way.

Sure enough, the sandbag wall was already waist high across Main Street; but then, the water *was* swirling around at ankle level, and more of it falling every minute.

I looked up at old Wyeth's statue. His halo had gone away now, which was sort of to be expected. It had made an honest mistake and realized it after a short time.

He was holding a pair of glasses in his left hand and sort of glancing down at me, as though a bit apprehensive, wondering perhaps, there inside all that bronze, if I would tell on him now and ruin his hard, wet, greenish splendor. Tell . . . ? I guess I was the only one left around who really remembered the man. He had wanted to be the father of this great new country, literally, and he'd tried awfully hard. Three months in office and I'd had to fill out the rest of the two-year term. The death certificate gave the cause as "heart stoppage," but it didn't mention the piece of lead which had helped slow things down a bit. Everyone involved is gone now: the irate husband, the frightened wife, the coroner. All but me. And I won't tell anybody if Wyeth's statue won't, because he's a hero now, and we need heroes' statues Out Here even more than we do heroes. He *did* engineer a nice piece of relief work during the Butler Township floods, and he may as well be remembered for that.

I winked at my old boss, and the rain dripped from his nose and fell into the puddle at my feet.

I walked back to the library through loud sounds and bright flashes, hearing the splashing and the curses of the work crew as the men began to block off another street. Black, overhead, an eye drifted past. I waved, and the filter snapped up and back down again. I think H.C. John Keams was tending shop that afternoon, but I'm not sure.

Suddenly the heavens opened up and it was like standing under a waterfall.

I reached for a wall and there wasn't one, slipped then, and managed to catch myself with my cane before I flopped. I found a doorway and huddled.

Ten minutes of lightning and thunder followed. Then, after the blindness and the deafness passed away and the rains had eased a bit, I saw that the street (Second Avenue) had become a river. Bearing all sorts of garbage, papers, hats, sticks, mud, it sloshed past my niche, gurgling nastily. It looked to be over my boot tops, so I waited for it to subside.

It didn't.

It got right up there with me and started to play footsie. So, then seemed as good a time as any. Things certainly weren't getting any better.

I tried to run, but with filled boots the best you can manage is a fast wade, and my boots were filled after three steps.

That shot the afternoon. How can you concentrate on anything with wet feet? I made it back to the parking lot, then churned my way homeward, feeling like a riverboat captain who really wanted to be a camel driver.

It seemed more like evening than afternoon when I pulled

up into my damp but unflooded garage. It seemed more like night than evening in the alley I cut through on the way to my apartment's back entrance. I hadn't seen the sun for several days, and it's funny how much you can miss it when it takes a vacation. The sky was a sable dome, and the high brick walls of the alley were cleaner than I'd ever seen them, despite the shadows.

I stayed close to the lefthand wall, in order to miss some of the rain. As I had driven along the river I'd noticed that it was already reaching after the high water marks on the sides of the piers. The Noble was a big, spoiled, blood sausage, ready to burst its skin. A lightning flash showed me the whole alley, and I slowed in order to avoid puddles.

I moved ahead, thinking of dry socks and dry martinis, turned a corner to the right, and it struck at me: an org.

Half of its segmented body was reared at a forty-five degree angle above the pavement, which placed its wide head with the traffic-signal eyes saying "Stop," about three and a half feet off the ground, as it rolled toward me on all its pale little legs, with its mouthful of death aimed at my middle.

I pause now in my narrative for a long digression concerning my childhood, which, if you will but consider the circumstances, I was obviously quite fresh on in an instant:

Born, raised, educated on Earth, I had worked two summers in a stockyard while going to college. I still remember the smells and the noises of the cattle; I used to prod them out of the pens and on their way up the last mile. And I remember the smells and noises of the university: the formaldehyde in the Bio labs, the sounds of Freshmen slaughtering French verbs, the overpowering aroma of coffee mixed with cigarette smoke in the Student Union, the splash of the newly-pinned frat man as his brothers tossed him into the lagoon down in front of the Art Museum, the sounds of ignored chapel bells and class bells, the smell of the lawn after the year's first mowing (with big, black Andy perched on his grass-chewing monster, baseball cap down to his eyebrows, cigarette somehow not burning his left cheek), and always, the *tick-tick-snick-stamp!* as I moved up or down the strip. I had not wanted to take General Physical Education, but four semesters of it were required. The only out was to take a class in a special sport. I picked fencing because tennis, basketball, boxing, wrestling, handball, judo, all sounded too strenuous, and I couldn't afford a set of golf clubs. Little did I suspect what would follow this choice. It was as strenuous as any of the others, and more than several. But I liked it. So I tried out for the team in my Sophomore year, made it on the épée squad, and picked up three varsity letters, because I stuck with it through my Senior year. Which all goes to show: Cattle who persevere in looking for an easy out still wind up in the abattoir, but they may enjoy the trip a little more.

When I came out here on the raw frontier where people all carry weapons, I had my cane made. It combines the better features of the épée and the cattle prod. Only, it is the kind of prod which, if you were to prod cattle with, they would never move again.

Over eight hundred volts, max, when the tip touches, if the stud in the handle is depressed properly . . .

My arm shot out and up and my fingers depressed the stud properly as it moved.

That was it for the org.

A noise came from between the rows of razor blades in its mouth as I scored a touch on its soft underbelly and whipped my arm away to the side—a noise halfway between an exhalation and "peep"—and that was it for the org (short for "organism-with-a-long-name-which-I-can't-remember").

I switched off my cane and walked around it. It was one of those things which sometimes come out of the river. I remember that I looked back at it three times, then I switched the cane on again at max and kept it that way till I was inside my apartment with the door locked behind me and all the lights burning.

Then I permitted myself to tremble, and after awhile I changed my socks and mixed my drink.

May your alleys be safe from orgs.

Saturday.

More rain.

Wetness was all.

The entire east side had been shored with sandbags. In some places they served only to create sandy waterfalls, where otherwise the streams would have flowed more evenly and perhaps a trifle more clearly. In other places they held it all back, for a while.

By then, there were six deaths as a direct result of the rains.

By then, there had been fires caused by the lightning, accidents by the water, sicknesses by the dampness, the cold.

By then, property damages were beginning to mount pretty high.

Everyone was tired and angry and miserable and wet, by then. This included me.

Though Saturday was Saturday, I went to work. I worked in Eleanor's office, with her. We had the big relief map spread on a table, and six mobile eyescreens were lined against one wall. Six eyes hovered above the half-dozen emergency points and kept us abreast of the actions taken upon them. Several new telephones and a big radio set stood on the desk. Five ashtrays looked as if they wanted to be empty, and the coffee pot chuckled cynically at human activity.

The Noble had almost reached its high water mark. We were not an isolated storm center by any means. Up river, Butler Township was hurting, Swan's Nest was adrip, Laurie was weeping into the river, and the wilderness in between was shaking and streaming.

Even though we were in direct contact we went into the field on three occasions that morning—once, when the north-south bridge over the Lance River collapsed and was washed down toward the Noble as far as the bend by the Mack steel mill; again, when the Wildwood Cemetery, set up on a storm-gouged hill to the east, was plowed deeply, graves opened, and several coffins set awash; and finally, when three houses full of people toppled, far to the east. Eleanor's small flyer was buffeted by the winds as we fought our way through to these sites for on-the-spot supervision; I navigated almost completely by instruments. Downtown proper was accommodating evacuees left and right by then. I took three showers that morning and changed clothes twice.

Things slowed down a bit in the afternoon, including the rain. The cloud cover didn't break, but a drizzle-point was reached which permitted us to gain a little on the waters.

Retaining walls were reinforced, evacuees were fed and dried, some of the rubbish was cleaned up. Four of the six eyes were returned to their patrols, because four of the emergency points were no longer emergency points.

. . . And we wanted all of the eyes for the org patrol.

Inhabitants of the drenched forest were also on the move. Seven *snappers* and a horde of panda-puppies were shot that day, as well as a few crawly things from the troubled waters of the Noble—not to mention assorted branch-snakes, stingbats, borers, and land-eels.

By 1900 hours it seemed that a stalemate had been achieved. Eleanor and I climbed into her flyer and drifted skyward.

We kept rising. Finally, there was a hiss as the cabin began to pressurize itself. The night was all around us. Eleanor's face, in the light from the instrument panel, was a mask of weariness. She raised her hands to her temples as if to remove it, and then when I looked back again it appeared that she had. A faint smile lay across her lips now and her eyes sparkled. A stray strand of hair shadowed her brow.

"Where are you taking me?" she asked.

"Up, high," said I, "above the storm."

"Why?"

"It's been many days," I said, "since we have seen an uncluttered sky."

"True," she agreed, and as she leaned forward to light a cigarette I noticed that the part in her hair had gone all askew. I wanted to reach out and straighten it for her, but I didn't.

We plunged into the sea of clouds.

Dark was the sky, moonless. The stars shone like broken diamonds. The clouds were a floor of lava.

We drifted. We stared up into the heavens. I "anchored" the flyer, like an eye set to hover, and lit a cigarette myself.

"You are older than I am," she finally said, "really. You know?"

"No."

"There is a certain wisdom, a certain strength, something like the essence of the time that passes—that seeps into a man as he sleeps between the stars. I know, because I can feel it when I'm around you."

"No," I said.

"Then maybe it's people expecting you to have the strength of centuries that gives you something like it. It was probably there to begin with."

"No."

She chuckled.

"It isn't exactly a positive sort of thing either."

I laughed.

"You asked me if I was going to run for office again this fall. The answer is 'no.' I'm planning on retiring. I want to settle down."

"With anyone special?"

"Yes, very special, Juss," she said, and she smiled at me and I kissed her, but not too long, because the ash was about to fall off her cigarette and down the back of my neck.

So we put both cigarettes out and drifted above the invisible city, beneath a sky without a moon.

I mentioned earlier that I would tell you about Stopovers. If you are going a distance of a hundred forty-five light years and are taking maybe a hundred-fifty actual years to do it, why stop and stretch your legs?

Well, first of all and mainly, almost nobody sleeps out the whole jaunt. There are lots of little gadgets which require human monitoring at all times. No one is going to sit there for a hundred-fifty years and watch them, all by himself. So everyone takes a turn or two, passengers included. They are all briefed on what to do till the doctor comes, and who to awaken and how to go about it, should troubles crop up. Then everyone takes a turn at guard mount for a month or so, along with a few companions. There are always hundreds of people aboard, and after you've worked down through the role you take it again from the top. All sorts of mechanical agents are backing them up, many of which they are unaware of (to protect *against* them, as well as *with* them—in the improbable instance of several oddballs getting together and deciding to open a window, change course, murder passengers, or things like that), and the people are well-screened and carefully matched up, so as to check and balance each other as well as the machinery. All of this because gadgets and people both bear watching.

After several turns at ship's guard, interspersed with periods of cold sleep, you tend to grow claustrophobic and somewhat depressed. Hence, when there is an available Stopover, it is utilized, to restore mental equilibrium and to rearouse flagging animal spirits. This also serves the purpose of enriching the life and economy of the Stopover world, by whatever information and activities you may have in you.

Stopover, therefore, has become a traditional holiday on many worlds, characterized by festivals and celebrations on some of the smaller ones, and often by parades and world-wide broadcast interviews and press conferences on those with greater populations. I understand that it is now pretty much the same on Earth, too, whenever colonial visitors stop by. In fact, one fairly unsuccessful young starlet, Marilyn Austin, made a long voyage Out, stayed a few months, and returned on the next vessel headed back. After appearing on tri-dee a couple times, sounding off about interstellar culture, and flashing her white, white teeth, she picked up a flush contract, a third husband, and her first big part in tapes. All of which goes to show the value of Stopovers.

I landed us atop Helix, Betty's largest apartment-complex, wherein Eleanor had her double-balconied corner suite, affording views both of the distant Noble and of the lights of Posh Valley, Betty's residential section.

Eleanor prepared steaks, with baked potato, cooked corn, beer—everything I liked. I was happy and sated and such, and I stayed till around midnight, making plans for our future. Then I took a cab back to Town Square, where I was parked.

When I arrived, I thought I'd check with the Trouble Center just to see how things were going. So I entered the Hall, stamped my feet, brushed off excess waters, hung my coat, and proceeded up the empty hallway to the elevator.

The elevator was too quiet. They're supposed to rattle, you know? They shouldn't sigh softly and have doors that open and close without a sound. So I walked around an embarrassing corner on my way to the Trouble Center.

It was a pose Rodin might have enjoyed working with. All I can say is that it's a good thing I stopped by when I did, rather than five or ten minutes later.

Chuck Fuller and Lottie, Eleanor's secretary, were practicing mouth to mouth resuscitation and keeping the victim warm techniques, there on the couch in the little alcove off to the side of the big door to T.C.

Chuck's back was to me, but Lottie spotted me over his shoulder, and her eyes widened and she pushed him away. He turned his head quickly.

"Juss . . ." he said.

I nodded.

"Just passing by," I told him. "Thought I'd stop in to say hello and take a look at the eyes."

"Uh—everything's going real well," he said, stepping back into the hallway. "It's on auto right now, and I'm on my —uh, coffee break. Lottie is on night duty, and she came by to—to see if we had any reports we needed typed. She had a dizzy spell, so we came out here where the couch . . ."

"Yeah, she looks a little—peaked," I said. "There are smelling salts and aspirins in the medicine chest."

I walked on by into the Center, feeling awkward.

Chuck followed me after a couple minutes. I was watching the screens when he came up beside me. Things appeared to be somewhat in hand, though the rains were still moistening the one hundred thirty views of Betty.

"Uh, Juss," he said, "I didn't know you were coming by . . ."

"Obviously."

"What I'm getting at is—you won't report me, will you?"

"No, I won't report you."

". . . And you wouldn't mention it to Cynthia, would you?"

"Your extracurricular activities," I said, "are your own business. As a friend, I suggest you do them on your own time and in a more propitious location. But it's already beginning to slip my mind. I'm sure I'll forget the whole thing in another minute."

"Thanks, Juss," he said.

I nodded.

"What's Weather Central have to say these days?" I asked, raising the phone.

He shook his head, so I dialed and listened.

"Bad," I said, hanging up. "More wet to come."

"Damn," he announced and lit a cigarette, his hands shaking. "This weather's getting me down."

"Me too," said I. "I'm going to run now, because I want to get home before it starts in bad again. I'll probably be around tomorrow. See you."

"Night."

I elevated back down, fetched my coat, and left. I didn't see Lottie anywhere about, but she probably was, waiting for me to go.

I got to my car and was halfway home before the faucets came on full again. The sky was torn open with lightnings, and a sizzlecloud stalked the city like a long-legged arachnid, forking down bright limbs and leaving tracks of fire where it went. I made it home in another fifteen minutes, and the phenomenon was still in progress as I entered the garage. As I walked up the alley (cane switched on) I could hear the distant sizzle and the rumble, and a steady half-light filled the spaces between the buildings, from its *flash-burn-flash-burn* striding.

Inside, I listened to the thunder and the rain, and I watched the apocalypse off in the distance.

Delirium of city under storm—

The buildings across the way were quite clear in the pulsing light of the thing. The lamps were turned off in my apartment so that I could better appreciate the vision. All of the shadows seemed incredibly black and inky, lying right beside glowing stairways, pediments, windowsills, balconies; and all of that which was illuminated seemed to burn as though with an internal light. Overhead, the living/not living insect-thing of fire stalked, and an eye wearing a blue halo was moving across the tops of nearby buildings. The fires pulsed and the clouds burnt like the hills of Gehenna; the thunders burbled and banged; and the white rain drilled into the roadway which had erupted into a steaming lather. Then a *snapper*, tri-horned, wet-feathered, demon-faced, sword-tailed, and green, raced from around a corner, a moment after I'd heard a sound which I had thought to be a part of the thunder. The creature ran, at an incredible speed, along the smoky pavement. The eye swooped after it, adding a hail of lead to the falling rain-drops. Both vanished up another street. It had taken but an instant, but in that instant it had resolved a question in my mind as to who should do the painting. Not El Greco, not Blake; no: Bosch. Without any question, Bosch—with his nightmare visions of the streets of Hell. He would be the one to do justice to this moment of the storm.

I watched until the sizzlecloud drew its legs up into itself, hung like a burning cocoon, then died like an ember retreating into ash. Suddenly, it was very dark and there was only the rain.

Sunday was the day of chaos.

Candles burned, churches burned, people drowned, beasts ran wild in the streets (or swam there), houses were torn up by the roots and bounced like paper boats along the waterways, the great wind came down upon us, and after that the madness.

I was not able to drive to Town Hall, so Eleanor sent her flyer after me.

The basement was filled with water, and the ground floor was like Neptune's waiting room. All previous high water marks had been passed.

We were in the middle of the worst storm in Betty's history.

Operations had been transferred up onto the third floor. There was no way to stop things now. It was just a matter of riding it out and giving what relief we could. I sat before my gallery and watched.

It rained buckets, it rained vats; it rained swimming pools and lakes and rivers. For a while it seemed that it rained oceans upon us. This was partly because of the wind which came in from the gulf and suddenly made it seem to rain sideways with the force of its blasts. It began at about noon and was gone in a few hours, but when it left our town was broken and bleeding. Wyeth lay on his bronze side, the flagpole was gone, there was no building without broken windows and water inside. We were suddenly suffering lapses of electrical power, and one of my eyes showed three pandapuppies devouring a dead child. Cursing, I killed them across the rain and distance. Eleanor wept at my side. There was a report later of a pregnant woman who could only deliver by Caesarean section, trapped on a hilltop with her family, and in labor. We were still trying to get through to her with a flyer, but the winds . . . I saw burning buildings and the corpses of people and animals. I saw half-buried cars and splintered homes. I saw waterfalls where there had been no waterfalls before. I fired many rounds that day, and not just at beasts from the forest. Sixteen of my eyes had been shot out by looters. I hope that I never again see some of the films I made that day.

When the worst Sunday night in my life began, and the rains did not cease, I knew the meaning of despair for the third time in my life.

Eleanor and I were in the Trouble Center. The lights had just gone out for the eighth time. The rest of the staff was down on the third floor. We sat there in the dark without moving, without being able to do a single thing to halt the course of chaos. We couldn't even watch it until the power came back on.

So we talked.

Whether it was for five minutes or an hour, I don't really know. I remember telling her, though, about the girl buried on another world, whose death had set me to running. Two trips to two worlds and I had broken my bond with the times. But a hundred years of travel do not bring a century of forgetfulness—not when you cheat time with the *petite mort* of the cold sleep. Time's vengeance is memory, and though for an age you plunder the eye of seeing and empty the ear of sound, when you awaken your past is still with you. The worst thing to do then is to return to visit your wife's nameless grave in a changed land, to come back as a stranger to the place you had made your home. You run again then, and after a time you *do* forget, some, because a certain amount of actual time must pass for you also. But by then you are alone, all by yourself: completely alone. That was the *first* time in my life that I knew the meaning of despair. I read, I worked, I drank, I whored, but came the morning after and I was always me, by myself. I jumped from world to world, hoping things would be different, but with each change I was further away from all the things I had known.

Then another feeling gradually came upon me, and a really terrible feeling it was: There *must* be a time and a place best suited for each person who has ever lived. After the worst of my grief had left me and I had come to terms with the vanished past, I wondered about a man's place in time and in space. Where, and *when* in the cosmos would I most like to live out the balance of my days? —To live at my fullest potential? The past *was* dead, but perhaps a better time waited on some as yet undiscovered world, waited at one yet-to-be recorded moment in its history. How could I *ever* know? How could I ever be sure that my Golden Age did not lay but one more world away, and that I might be struggling in a Dark Era while the Renaissance of my days was but a ticket, a visa and a diary-page removed? That was my *second* despair. I did not know the answer until I came to the Land of the Swan. I do not know why I loved you, Eleanor, but I did, and that was my answer. Then the rains came.

When the lights returned we sat there and smoked. She had told me of her husband, who had died a hero's death in time to save him from the delirium tremors which would have ended his days. Died as the bravest die—not knowing why—because of a reflex, which after all had been a part of him, a reflex which had made him cast himself into the path of a pack of wolf-like creatures attacking the exploring party he was with—off in that forest at the foot of Saint Stephen's—to fight them with a machete and to be torn apart by them while his companions fled to the camp, where they made a stand and saved themselves. Such is the essence of valor: an unthinking moment, a spark along the spinal nerves, predetermined by the sum total of everything you have ever done, wished to do or not to do, and wish you had done, or hadn't, and then comes the pain.

We watched the gallery on the wall. Man is the reasoning animal? Greater than beasts but less than angels? Not the murderer I shot that night. He wasn't even the one who uses tools or buries his dead. —Laughs, aspires, affirms? I didn't see any of those going on. —Watches himself watch himself doing what he knows is absurd? Too sophisticated. He just did the absurd without watching. Like running back into a burning house after his favorite pipe and a can of tobacco. —Devises religions? I saw people praying, but they weren't devising. They were making last-ditch efforts at saving themselves, after they'd exhausted everything else they knew to do. Reflex.

The creature who loves?

That's the only one I might not be able to gainsay.

I saw a mother holding her daughter up on her shoulders while the water swirled above her armpits, and the little girl was holding her doll up above *her* shoulders, in the same way. But isn't that—the love—a part of the total? Of everything you have ever done, or wished? Positive or neg? I know that it is what made me leave my post, running, and what made me climb into Eleanor's flyer and what made me fight my way through the storm and out to that particular scene.

I didn't get there in time.

I shall never forget how glad I was that someone else did. Johnny Keams blinked his lights above me as he rose, and he radioed down:

"It's all right. They're okay. Even the doll."

"Good," I said, and headed back.

As I set the ship down on its balcony landing, one figure came toward me. As I stepped down, a gun appeared in Chuck's hand.

"I wouldn't kill you, Juss," he began, "but I'd wound you. Face that wall. I'm taking the flyer."

"Are you crazy?" I asked him.

"I know what I'm doing. I need it, Juss."

"Well, if you need it, there it is. You don't have to point a gun at me. I just got through needing it myself. Take it."

"Lottie and I both need it," he said. "Turn around!"

I turned toward the wall.

"What do you mean?" I asked.

"We're going away, together—now!"

"You *are* crazy," I said. "This is no time . . ."

"C'mon, Lottie," he called, and there was a rush of feet behind me and I heard the flyer's door open.

"Chuck!" I said. "We need you now! You can settle this thing peacefully, in a week, in a month, after some order has been restored. There *are* such things as divorces, you know."

"That won't get me off this world, Juss."

"So how is *this* going to?"

I turned, and I saw that he had picked up a large canvas bag from somewhere and had it slung over his left shoulder, like Santa Claus.

"Turn back around! I don't want to shoot you," he warned.

248

The suspicion came, grew stronger.

"Chuck, have you been looting?" I asked him.

"Turn around!"

"All right, I'll turn around. How far do you think you'll get?"

"Far enough," he said. "Far enough so that no one will find us—and when the time comes, we'll leave this world."

"No," I said. "I don't think you will, because I know you."

"We'll see." His voice was further away then.

I heard three rapid footsteps and the slamming of a door. I turned then, in time to see the flyer rising from the balcony.

I watched it go. I never saw either of them again.

Inside, two men were unconscious on the floor. It turned out that they were not seriously hurt. After I saw them cared for, I rejoined Eleanor in the Tower.

All that night did we wait, emptied, for morning.

Somehow, it came.

We sat and watched the light flow through the rain. So much had happened so quickly. So many things had occurred during the past week that we were unprepared for morning.

It brought an end to the rains.

A good wind came from out of the north and fought with the clouds, like En-ki with the serpent Tiamat. Suddenly, there was a canyon of cobalt.

A cloudquake shook the heavens and chasms of light opened across its dark landscape.

It was coming apart as we watched.

I heard a cheer, and I croaked in unison with it as the sun appeared.

The good, warm, drying, beneficent sun drew the highest peak of Saint Stephen's to its face and kissed both its cheeks.

There was a crowd before each window. I joined one and stared, perhaps for ten minutes.

When you awaken from a nightmare you do not normally find its ruins lying about your bedroom. This is one way of telling whether or not something was only a bad dream, or whether or not you are really awake.

We walked the streets in great boots. Mud was everywhere. It was in basements and in machinery and in sewers and in living room clothes closets. It was on buildings and on cars and on people and on the branches of trees. It was broken brown blisters drying and waiting to be peeled off from clean tissue. Swarms of skytoads rose into the air when we approached, hovered like dragon-flies, returned to spoiling food stores after we had passed. Insects were having a hey-day, too. Betty would have to be deloused. So many things were overturned or fallen down, and half-buried in the brown Sargassos of the streets. The dead had not yet been numbered. The water still ran by, but sluggish and foul. A stench was beginning to rise across the city. There were smashed-in store fronts and there was glass everywhere, and bridges fallen down and holes in the streets . . . But why go on? If you don't get the picture by now, you never will. It was the big morning after, following a drunken party by the gods. It is the lot of mortal man always to clean up their leavings or to be buried beneath them.

So clean we did, but by noon Eleanor could no longer stand. So I took her home with me, because we were working down near the harbor section and my place was nearer.

That's almost the whole story—light to darkness to light —except for the end, which I don't really know. I'll tell you of its beginning, though . . .

I dropped her off at the head of the alleyway, and she went on toward my apartment while I parked the car. Why didn't I keep her with me? I don't know. Unless it was because the morning sun made the world seem at peace, despite its filth. Unless it was because I was in love and the darkness was over, and the spirit of the night had surely departed.

I parked the car and started up the alley. I was halfway before the corner where I had met the org when I heard her cry out.

I ran. Fear gave me speed and strength and I ran to the corner and turned it.

The man had a bag, not unlike the one Chuck had carried away with him, lying beside the puddle in which he stood. He was going through Eleanor's purse, and she lay on the ground—so still!—with blood on the side of her head.

I cursed him and ran toward him, switching on my cane

250

as I went. He turned, dropped her purse, and reached for the gun in his belt.

We were about thirty feet apart, so I threw my cane. He drew his gun, pointed it at me, and my cane fell into the puddle in which he stood.

Flights of angels sang him to his rest, perhaps.

She was breathing, so I got her inside and got hold of a doctor—I don't remember how, not too clearly, anyway—and I waited and waited.

She lived for another twelve hours and then she died. She recovered consciousness twice before they operated on her, and not again after. She didn't say anything. She smiled at me once, and went to sleep again.

I don't know.

Anything, really.

It happened again that I became Betty's mayor, to fill in until November, to oversee the rebuilding. I worked, I worked my head off, and I left her bright and shiny, as I had found her. I think I could have won if I had run for the job that fall, but I did not want it.

The Town Council overrode my objections and voted to erect a statue of Godfrey Justin Holmes beside the statue of Eleanor Schirrer which was to stand in the Square across from cleaned-up Wyeth. I guess it's out there now.

I said that I would never return, but who knows? In a couple years, after some more history has passed, I may revisit a Betty full of strangers, if only to place a wreath at the foot of the one statue. Who knows but that the entire continent may be steaming and clanking and whirring with automation by then, and filled with people from shore to shining shore?

There was a Stopover at the end of the year and I waved good-bye and climbed aboard and went away, anywhere.

I went aboard and went away, to sleep again the cold sleep.

Delirium of ship among stars—

Years have passed, I suppose. I'm not really counting them any more. But I think of this thing often: Perhaps there is a Golden Age someplace, a Renaissance for me sometime, a special time somewhere, somewhere but a ticket, a visa, a diary-page away. I don't know where or when. Who does? Where are all the rains of yesterday?

In the invisible city?

Inside me?

It is cold and quiet outside and the horizon is infinity. There is no sense of movement.

There is no moon, and the stars are very bright, like broken diamonds, all.

Award Winning
Science Fiction Specials

ACE SCIENCE FICTION DOUBLES
Two books back-to-back for just 75c

05595 **Beyond Capella** Rackham
The Electric Sword-Swallowers Bulmer

11182 **Clockwork's Pirate**
Ghost Breaker Goulart

11560 **The Communipaths** Elgin
The Noblest Experiment in the Galaxy
Trimble

13783 **The Dark Dimensions**
Alternate Orbits Chandler

13793 **Dark of the Woods**
Soft Come the Dragons Koontz

13805 **Dark Planet** Rackham
The Herod Men Kamin

51375 **The Mad Goblin**
Lord of the Trees Farmer

58880 **Alice's World**
No Time for Heroes Lundwall

71802 **Recoil** Nunes
Lallia Tubb

76096 **The Ships of Durostorum** Bulmer
Alton's Unguessable Sutton

78400 **The Star Virus** Bayley
Mask of Chaos Jakes

81610 **To Venus! To Venus!** Grinnell
The Wagered World Janifer and Treibich